Joss Wood loves books and traveling—especially to the wild places of Southern Africa. She has the domestic skills of a potted plant and drinks far too much coffee.

Joss has written for Mills & Boon Modern Romance and, most recently, the Mills & Boon Desire line. After a career in business, she now writes full-time. Joss is a member of the Romance Writers of America and Romance Writers of South Africa.

HelenKay Dimon is a divorce lawyer turned full-time author. Her bestselling and award-winning books have been showcased in numerous venues, including the *Washington Post* and *Cosmopolitan*. She is an RT Reviewers' Choice Best Book Award winner and has been a finalist for the Romance Writers of America's RITA® Award multiple times.

Also by Joss Wood

Convenient Cinderella Bride
His Ex's Well-Kept Secret
The Ballantyne Billionaires
The CEO's Nanny Affair
Little Secrets: Unexpectedly Pregnant
One Night to Forever
The Nanny Proposal

Also by HelenKay Dimon

Pregnant by the CEO
Reunion with Benefits
Fearless
Ruthless
Relentless
Lawless
Traceless

Discover more at millsandboon.co.uk

THE NANNY PROPOSAL

JOSS WOOD

REUNION WITH BENEFITS

HELENKAY DIMON

MILLS & BOON

First Published in Great Britain 2018
by Mills & Boon, an imprint of HarperCollinsPublishers,
1 London Bridge Street, London, SE1 9GF

The Nanny Proposal © 2018 Harlequin Books S.A.
Reunion With Benefits © 2018 HelenKay Dimon

Special thanks and acknowledgement are given to Joss Wood for her contribution to the Texas Cattleman's Club: The Impostor series.

ISBN: 978-0-263-93606-3

51-0618

MIX
Paper from
responsible sources
FSC C007454

This book is produced from independently certified FSC™ paper to ensure responsible forest management.

For more information visit: www.harpercollins.co.uk/green

Printed and bound in Spain
by CPI, Barcelona

THE NANNY
PROPOSAL

JOSS WOOD

Dedicated to Rebecca Crowley,
who is leaving SA and heading home.
I'm going to miss you.
ROSACON is not going to be
the same without you!

Prologue

Eight months ago

Standing in the shadows of the balcony encircling the ballroom of the Texas Cattleman's Club, Kasey Monroe looked up at the clear night sky. Why had she thought attending a New Year's Eve Ball in Royal, Texas, knowing no one but Aaron Phillips—who might, or might not, become her new boss—was a good idea?

Aaron, as a member of the Texas Cattleman's Club, knew nearly everybody in the room. He'd introduced her to his gorgeous sister, Megan, and her equally good-looking husband, Will Sanders, CEO of Spark Energy Solutions. And while Aaron had made an effort to include her, she felt woefully out of place.

Even so, making small talk with strangers was still more fun than spending the night alone in her hotel room, obsessing about the party happening back in her home in

Houston. Throwing a New Year's Eve bash was a tradition she and Dale had started the year they'd gotten engaged and, for the first time in five years, she wouldn't be playing hostess to their friends. Kasey couldn't help wondering what Michelle was doing tonight. When last had she and her oldest friend spent the special evening apart? A decade? More years than that? Kasey rested her champagne glass on her cheek. It had been six months since she'd caught Dale and Michelle together in what was, as they'd explained, a drunken encounter that meant nothing. Pure sex, fueled by too much booze and a line of coke. Their combination of sex, drugs and rock and roll had broken her heart and, while she felt like her heart was slowly patching itself back together, she still felt like a fool.

Her husband and her oldest and best friend… In a million years, she would never have imagined that scenario. Would she ever be able to trust anyone again?

Five! Four! Three! Two! One…! *Yeah, Happy New Year to me. Husband-less, friend-less, in a new town and among strangers.*

Oh, boo-hoo, Kasey thought, irritated by her bout of self-pity and taking a defiant gulp of her champagne. The last six months had been tough, sure, but ending a marriage should never be *fun*. But there was light at the end of the tunnel: her divorce was final, she had money in the bank and *options*.

One of those options was Aaron Phillips's intriguing proposal to become his executive assistant. Known as one of the most innovative and successful hedge fund managers in the country, Aaron didn't have a large client base, but that didn't matter because his clients were all mega wealthy. He worked out of his office within his palatial house on the outskirts of Royal and, as Aaron explained, thanks to the wonders of modern technology, she could do her job from either her home in Houston or here in Royal. He was demanding, Aaron told her, but he wasn't a micromanager and as long as she produced the results, she could set her own hours.

Kasey felt a spurt of excitement; a hefty salary, flexible hours and working out of her own space would give her life structure and, hopefully, would stop her from dwelling on her failed marriage and the loss of a childhood friend.

Kasey lightly whistled to catch the attention of the waiter hovering by the ballroom entrance. She held up her empty flute and within a minute had a fresh glass of bubbly in her hand. This new year would be better, Kasey vowed. She was a strong woman and she was not going to allow the past to define her. No matter what it took, she was going to put this all behind her and get back to the person she used to be. Fun, happy, positive.

Change had to happen and she was the only one who could implement those changes. She could start by accepting the position at AP Investments and relocating to Royal. Even if she worked from home, a change of scenery, and leaving Houston, would be a good move. Tomorrow—*today*—was the start of a new year and a new life and, God knew, she desperately needed both.

Kasey looked into the ballroom and easily found Aaron's tall frame. She tipped her head, studying him. He was so very smart, so very well built and, pre-Dale, exactly the type of guy she'd look at twice. Or six times. Early to mid-thirties, with chestnut-brown hair cut short to tame the curl, he had the broad shoulders, long and powerful legs and narrow hips of a competitive swimmer. Unfathomable green eyes under—kill me now—wire-rimmed glasses. And light scruff covered his impressive jaw.

Sexy could be such a tame word, Kasey mused, feeling her stomach squirm. Then her skin tingled and she felt a slow burn that sent heat to that long-dead space between her legs. Wow…

Well, hello, sexual attraction. It's been a while.

In a room filled with some very fine eye candy, Aaron was handcrafted chocolate. Which meant, Kasey realized, the only way she could work for him would be virtually. There was no way she could spend eight or more hours a day with that gorgeous male specimen. At the *very* least, her keyboard would be perpetually covered in drool.

Kasey allowed a long slide of champagne to coat her throat and felt a small buzz. As if he could sense her eyes on him, Aaron slowly turned and scanned the ballroom. She really should look away, but Kasey, emboldened by the booze and the temptation of embarking on something different and a little bit wild, waited for his eyes to lock with hers. She'd met him twice before tonight and both times Aaron had been so professional and reticent, she'd found it impossible to read his emotions.

However, tonight there was desire and flat-out need in his eyes and on his face.

She turned around to check that there was no one behind her. No, she was alone and all that heat was for her. So…*hot damn.*

This certainly complicated the should-I-accept-his-job-offer question…

Kasey gripped the stem of her glass in a too tight grip and watched as Aaron walked, gracefully for such a big man, across the crowded floor. He was heading straight toward her, his eyes not leaving her face. Kasey swallowed and took another sip of champagne, hoping it would lubricate her dry mouth. One sip didn't help, neither did two. Hell, nothing would because a lava-hot man was looking at her like she was a pretty package he couldn't wait to unwrap.

Aaron stopped in front of her and lifted his hand. Kasey sucked in a breath, thinking he was about to touch her, then wrinkled her nose in disappointment when he plucked the champagne glass from her fingers and placed it on the edge of the railing. Aaron, still so close to her, looked down at her, his eyes drifting from her lips to her eyes.

"You look stunning, Kasey. Did I tell you that earlier?"

It had been so long since she'd been complimented on how she looked Kasey had no idea how to respond. When in doubt, and she was so in doubt, it was best to keep it simple.

"Thank you."

Unnerved by the warm appreciation in his eyes Kasey looked down at her tangerine halter-neck dress skimming her curves. Her two-inch heels just took her past Aaron's shoulder. He was a big man and his masculinity made her feel intensely feminine. Something else she was unfamiliar with.

"Happy New Year."

Kasey murmured the words back as a haunting melody drifted from the ballroom onto the balcony and swirled around them. Aaron's fingers touched her hip and Kasey felt heat pouring from him and burning through the thin fabric of her dress.

"Would you like to dance?" he asked, his deep voice raising goose bumps on her skin.

Aaron didn't wait for her reply. His hand slid around to rest on her lower back and he curled his other hand around hers, lifting it to hold it against his chest. Kasey felt his lips on her temple and wondered why, even though they were dancing outside, there was no fresh air. He was so warm, so solid, she thought as they swayed in place. Then Aaron's foot slid between hers and they were gliding across the empty balcony under the light of a Texas moon. The man sure could dance, Kasey mused as he spun her out and brought her back in, closer than before.

"You smell so good," Aaron whispered into her hair.

Her mouth curved into a smile. "I'm glad you approve."

Aaron pulled her hand up and raised her fingers to his mouth. His gentle kiss on the tips of her fingers sent heat skittering through her. "There's much I approve of, Kasey, and we both know that I'm not talking about your résumé and your references."

Kasey lifted her eyes to his face and saw his wry expression. She couldn't help noticing the desire in his eyes. And in his pants.

Aaron flicked the end of her hair with his index finger. "Since your arrival I've spent far too much time thinking about whether you'd feel as good as you look or whether your hair is as soft as I thought." He rubbed a strand of her shoulder-length hair between his fingers. "It is. And it's a fascinating color... I can't describe it. It's brown but not, red but not."

According to her stylist, her hair color was a rich, light auburn, but Michelle had always called it ginger spice. If all things were normal, if her best friend hadn't slept with her husband, Michelle would be the person she'd confide in about dancing with this sexy guy under the midnight blue Texas winter sky.

Don't think about her, them, the past!

Carpe diem, Monroe. Carpe diem...

Kasey laid her cheek on Aaron's chest and swayed along with him. *This is nice*, she thought. She felt relaxed and comfortable, *intensely* aroused, and pretty. She hadn't felt any of those things for a long time.

Aaron dropped her hand and his big arms pulled her closer. Every muscle in her body tensed as his hard length pushed into her stomach. Undeterred, he just gathered her against him, his hands flat against her lower back. "Relax, Kase, nothing is going to happen."

Damn, Kasey thought. It was the start of a new year and she really wanted something magical to happen. She wanted to feel his mouth on hers, to see if he tasted as delicious as he looked. She wanted those big, warm hands skating across her skin, wanted his mouth on her breast, on her stomach, maybe lower. She sighed. She wanted to feel what Aaron-induced pleasure felt like.

Bottom line? She wanted *him*.

"What if I want something to happen?" Kasey blurted out the words. She considered taking them back and forced herself not to. Aaron was a grown man. If he didn't want to get naked with her, he was adult enough to say so. But the action in his pants told her the thought had crossed his mind a time or two, as well.

This isn't a good idea, her overcautious brain insisted. *You want to work for him, you want to move to this festive town and to put some distance between you and your old life. Sleeping with your boss is not, on any planet or within any galaxy, a good idea. Besides, you're still sad, a little broken, still bruised.*Hopping into bed with Aaron, with *anyone*, wasn't a good idea. Feeling the twin urges of defiance and recklessness, Kasey's heart went to war with her head.

With Aaron, she didn't feel like the discarded wife, the foolish, naïve friend. In his arms, she remembered the confident woman she used to be. She felt desired and alive.

And they hadn't even got to the really good, rolling around naked, part yet.

Aaron put a little space between them. His expression turned contemplative, his eyes speculative. "What are you suggesting, Kasey?"

God, was he expecting her to draw him a picture? Suddenly feeling shy and out of her depth, Kasey placed her hands against his chest and tried to push him away, but he didn't move an inch.

"No, don't run away," Aaron said, his deep, husky voice soothing her agitation. "I just want us to be clear on what we are doing here. I want you to work for me, Kasey, and I don't want to lose you as an executive assistant because we want to scratch an itch."

She wanted to take the job. She did. The enormous salary would allow her to rent that fairy-tale cottage she'd fallen in love with in downtown Royal and would pay for her shoe and book habit. She wouldn't need to dip into her savings or the divorce settlement Dale agreed to pay for being a cheating douchebag dick. This job sounded interesting and challenging. But she really, really wanted to see what was under Aaron's perfectly tailored suit and blindingly white shirt.

"That's a sensible argument…" Kasey said, trailing off. Then she lifted her eyes to look into his. *Be brave, Kasey, take a chance. Start off the new year with a bang. Metaphorically.* And, maybe if the gods of good sex liked her, *literally.* "But on nights like these we aren't supposed to be sensible."

You're making a mistake—remember you can't trust your own judgment. You've made so many mistakes trusting men and people before.

Shut up, boring brain.

"One night, Kasey. A few hours to burn whatever we are feeling for each other out of our systems." Aaron's words echoed her thoughts. "I'm leaving for a skiing trip tomorrow and will only be back in Royal on the seventh. You can think about taking the job. If you do, this won't happen again. Ever. We'll be boss and employee."

Boss and employee. Kasey leaned back, knowing he'd

hold her as she forced herself to think. Difficult to do when she was so desperate to say "to hell with it" and feel.

But she was an adult and she had to walk into this situation, his arms and his bed, with her eyes wide open and her head on straight.

A week's break would give them some time to clear their heads, to practice their "I've forgotten what you look like naked" attitude. They were adults, they could do this.

Kasey nibbled the inside of her cheek. She wanted to burn the memories of Dale away, to finally exorcise him from her life, and she wanted to do that with Aaron. He was fantastically good-looking, successful and smart. But, more than that, she instinctively liked him.

Consider him as a welcome-to-your-new-life gift to yourself, Monroe.

"You're killing me here, Kasey," Aaron muttered.

Kasey draped her arms over his shoulders as she eased closer to him. "One night, no expectations, and when we meet again, we'll be all business?"

Aaron nodded. "That's the way I'm looking at this."

Kasey smiled. "One question?"

Aaron closed his eyes, exaggerating his anguish. "Did I mention that you are killing me here?"

Kasey's laugh mingled with the music. "Your place or mine?"

One

Eight months later...

Aaron Phillips pulled up to the curb outside Kasey's rental home and cut the engine to his luxury, German-engineered SUV. The car was fine but he missed driving his Vanquish with its bucket seats and a million horses under the hood. But he was, as of yesterday, Savannah's guardian and that meant a solid, dependable, safe vehicle with a booster seat and top safety ratings.

God, what had Jason been drinking when he'd named him as Savannah's guardian and not their younger sister, Megan? What did he know about raising a little girl? Zero. And that was why he was parked outside the house of the woman he'd tried, as much as possible, to avoid for most of this year.

They talked often during the day, their Skype connection was pretty much always open and emails constantly bounced between them. But despite living in the same town, he hadn't laid eyes on her more than six times over the last eight months. Every one of those meetings had been an exercise in curtailing his impulse to scoop her up and carry her off to his bed.

That night, God, it was still burned into his brain. His memories of her were so strong that he could almost feel her endlessly, addictively soft and fragrant skin, hear the small murmurs of appreciation she made, taste the spicy sweetness of her mouth. As for those pretty, feminine places she hid from the world, they'd rocked his world.

She'd been so tight, warm…ridiculously responsive.

Aaron banged his forehead on the steering wheel, trying to push the image of Kasey, naked and wanton, whimpering with desire and begging for him to push her over the edge, from his brain.

How bizarre it was that the hottest sexual experience of his life had been with his executive assistant at the start of the year. His best and last sexual experience…

Eight. Months. God, he really needed to get laid.

But finding a date and some bedroom action was the last thing on his mind.

Aaron glared at Kasey's pretty cottage, with its pitched roof, pale green cladding and bright pink front door. The house stood in the shade of two live oaks and was enclosed by a whimsical wrought iron fence. He didn't want to do this, Aaron thought. He didn't want to walk up that path and pound on her door. He didn't want his brother, Jason, to be missing, presumed kidnapped, possibly dead.

From the moment he first held his hours-old niece he'd been wrapped around her now over developed baby finger. But he was the fun uncle, the rule breaker in contrast to Jason being the rule enforcer. He was the *stay up late and eat sweets before bedtime* guy, Jason was her *brush your teeth, chase away the monsters and eat your vegetables* dad. Now he had to assume—please God, only temporarily— the responsibility of this precious little person and he felt utterly out of his depth. And soul deep scared.

What the hell did he know about raising a girl? Precisely nothing.

Damn, he wanted life to roll back eight months, to be the man he was before that New Year's Eve ball when life was relatively simple and not the complicated crap storm it was at the moment.

Whining and wishing isn't going to get this done, Phillips. Neither is it going to change a damn thing. And you've survived life's crappy upheavals before...

Slamming the heavy car door, his long legs ate up the distance between his vehicle and Kasey's front door. At the entrance he hesitated, his fist hovering as he was slapped, again, by the images of his assistant, naked and sprawled across his bed, her amber eyes foggy with desire.

With her reddish-brown hair spread across his pillow, and her slim legs trembling with need—for him—she'd looked at him like he was the fulfillment of every fantasy she'd ever had. Then she'd whimpered and moaned, screamed his name, completely caught up in the throes of pleasure. They'd spent most of the night together and Kasey had been a full-fledged participant who gave as good as she got.

When he woke the next day, the start of a new year, she was gone, leaving nothing behind but her lingering scent in the air. Ten days later she'd walked back into his life as his executive assistant and neither of them ever made the smallest reference to that wonderful, crazy, sensation-soaked evening.

Didn't mean he didn't think about it. Often.

Aaron rested his forehead on the ridiculously pink door. He couldn't think about that night now, shouldn't be thinking about it all. He had a favor to ask of Kasey, and re-membering her lusciously scented, velvety-soft skin and made-for-sin mouth was not helping matters.

Aaron ordered his junk to stand down, quickly adjusted himself and gave himself ten seconds to regain control. When he thought he was winning that battle, he rapped his fist against the door.

A minute passed and then another. Aaron glanced at his high-tech watch, his gift to himself for his thirty-third birthday, and frowned. It was after 9:00 a.m. Kasey should be up. His Saturday morning had already been jam-packed: he'd met with his lawyer, gathered the documentation to prove he was Savannah's legal guardian and filled Megan in on the big news.

It had been a brutal morning but, hell, that wasn't anything new. The past few months had been more of the same. It had started with the note Jason sent to Megan—accompanied by the urn containing Will's ashes—saying that he'd been with Will during the airplane crash and he needed time to grieve Will's death before returning home, something neither of them understood. Jason would never put his friend's death between him and his daughter, no matter how gutted he might be. Then Jason had stayed away, supposedly on business trips, and had failed time and time again to FaceTime with Savannah. As his fre-quent, albeit odd, emails had trickled to a stop, Aaron's and Megan's concern had mushroomed into genuine fear that something was *horribly* wrong.

Since Jason's disappearance—it had been too long to call it anything else—Savannah had been splitting her time between Aaron's and Megan's places. But they both agreed, with school starting soon, that Savannah needed permanence in her life. Megan was going through her own special type of hell—the man she'd married, and buried, was not actually the person she had thought he was. So until Jason came back, Savvie's place was with Aaron. *If Jason came back…*

His brother had to come back. He loved and adored his niece but Aaron wasn't ready to be a father to an almost-six-year-old girl who'd experienced more upheaval than any child should.

Jay, where the hell are you?

The front door opened and Aaron looked down into Kasey's heart-shaped, makeup-free face and, for an instant, he forgot how to breathe. She was dressed in a tank top, through which he could see the faint outline of her nipples, and the smallest pair of sleep shorts that skimmed the top of her thighs. His gaze drifted back up, drinking in those high cheekbones, that array of messy hair just grazing her shoulders, and those stunningly beautiful whiskey eyes groggy with sleep.

God, he wanted her. Still. Eight months of working with her hadn't cured him of that little affliction. He hadn't been so attracted to—*obsessed* with—a woman since Kate. And look how well that had turned out. His infatuation with Kate had had enormous consequences and was, in a roundabout way, responsible for his parents' death. His lack of a college degree, inability to trust and his emotional unavailability could also be traced back to *that* woman.

And here he was falling down that rabbit hole again, desperate to make Kasey his.

Your brother is in trouble. Your sister is heartbroken and confused. Your niece is a basket case and your world is falling apart. Is sex really what you should be thinking about, Phillips?

"Aaron…hi. Uh, what are you doing here?" Kasey asked, rubbing her fist in her eye.

Going slowly mad, Aaron silently answered. He looked

over her head, easy to do since he was nearly a foot taller than her, into her sunny, colorful abode. "I need to talk to you."

Kasey pushed her fingers through her hair and Aaron noticed the way her breasts rose and fell with the movement. And a part of him rose...*sheesh*.

"Can it wait until Monday?"

"I wouldn't be here at nine on a Saturday morning if it could," Aaron retorted.

Kasey narrowed her eyes at his bark and he recognized her play-nice expression. Kasey was tough and strong-willed, and never hesitated to put him in his place if she felt he was being too pushy. He disliked doormats and her unwillingness to take crap from a work-obsessed, demanding boss was one of the things he liked best about her.

Sighing, he softened his tone. "Let me in, Kasey. Please."

She stepped back, and Aaron walked into her bright, airy cottage. After closing the front door behind him, he jammed his hands into the back pockets of his jeans. Her furniture looked used but comfortable, covered in checks and stripes in shades of the sea. Yellow and orange cushions and vibrant vases of flowers created splashes of color in the sunny room.

"Kitchen's that way." Kasey's bare arm brushed his as she pointed to a door behind him. "Make coffee, will you?"

"Where are you going?"

Kasey glanced down and Aaron noticed her flushed face. She gestured to her clothing. "Not exactly the outfit I need my boss to see me in."

Aaron started to remind her that he'd seen her in much less but at the last minute pulled the words back. For eight months they'd pretended that night had never happened and mentioning it now, when she was halfway to naked, wasn't appropriate.

His brother was missing and his niece needed him. He was also one of the few people who knew that the man he'd thought was his old friend and brother-in-law was an impostor. Plus, he was trying to support his sister, whose life was even more of a tangled mess than his.

Which meant sex with Kasey should be the *last* thing on his mind.

Aaron swore and scrubbed his hands over his face. When he opened them again, Kasey was walking away from him. He ordered himself not to follow her—but, hot damn, those shorts did *not* cover her butt cheeks.

Coffee, Aaron thought. Coffee was the only thing that made sense right now. He slipped into Kasey's tiny kitchen, thinking he was far too big for this dollhouse. His house was huge—eight thousand square feet and seven bedrooms—but as he'd told Jason, who'd sarcastically called his house "the Shack," at six-three he was a big guy and he liked a lot of space.

A few minutes later Aaron saw Kasey standing in the doorway, wearing a pair of knee-length, cut-off denim shorts and a blue, white and red striped top. She was shoeless, her toes ending in slashes of hot pink. She'd brushed her hair, washed her face and, judging by the peppermint smell, brushed her teeth. Her face was still free of makeup, but she rarely wore much: her eyelashes were long and thick and her mouth a natural, deep pink. As always, she took his breath away.

"I need your help," Aaron stated, trying to get his mind off the bed down her hall.

Kasey picked up her mug, sipped and lifted her finely arched, dark eyebrows. "Okay." She glanced down at her clothes and grimaced. "Do we need to go to the office? Must I change?"

"Not necessary," Aaron told her. "You're fine as you are."

Kasey waved her coffee cup in a silent gesture for him to continue.

Should he tell her? Was he doing the right thing? Aaron wrestled with his doubt. He didn't trust anyone, not fully, but he needed Kasey's help and that meant sharing classified information, something he wasn't comfortable doing. He'd learned, the hard way, to keep his secrets, both business and personal, close to his chest.

"I'm trusting you not to repeat this, Kasey."

She nodded and Aaron continued. "It's a long, tangled story. You met Will at the ball. How much do you know about him?"

Kasey replied immediately, her business brain moving into high gear. "CEO of Spark Energy Solutions, a company with ties to oil, gas and solar. Recently passed away?"

"Yeah. A while ago, Will and Rich Lowell, his best friend, were in Mexico and they got caught up in a boating accident. Long story short, the boat exploded and we were told Rich died. Except that wasn't what happened. Rich escaped the brunt of the blast and Will's body was never recovered."

Kasey waited for him to continue.

"This is where it gets odd… Rich presumed Will died in that blast and he returned to Royal—but he returned as Will. Acting as Will, Rich took over Will's life and his business. Married my sister. Then, a few months back, Rich, still pretending to be Will, faked his own death… Following me so far?"

Kasey looked dazed. He didn't blame her; it was a hell of a story. "Meanwhile, the real Will also did not perish in that boat explosion."

"Seriously? So where was he while Rich was assuming his identity?"

"He was in Mexico, recovering from his injuries. He's

now back in town, laying low and quietly trying to unravel the mess." Aaron released a breath. "My brother, Jason, is Will's good friend and worked closely with him at Will's energy company, SES."

"Your brother didn't notice the difference between the real and the fake Will?" Kasey asked, sounding skeptical.

"Remember that boating accident? Acting as Will, Rich claimed he'd been badly injured, that he'd needed reconstructive surgery to both his face and vocal chords. Jason took his words at face value. Will and Rich had the same coloring and build, and they looked a lot alike, so none of us ever thought, not for a minute, that Rich wasn't who he said he was."

Kasey looked puzzled. "Okay, but I still don't understand how this relates to me doing a favor for you."

"Getting there… As I said, Jason worked for Will and he's gone missing. It's been two months since anyone has spoken to, or seen, him."

Sympathy crossed Kasey's lovely face. "I'm so sorry, Aaron. That must be awful."

That was one word for it. "My sister received a letter from him saying that he needed time away to recover from Will's death. But that letter was fake—it definitely wasn't his handwriting. Besides, no matter how upset Jason was, he would never abandon his little girl."

Aaron heard the harsh note in his voice and tried to tone it down, to find his control. "He's a devoted dad and he'd never neglect Savannah for this long. There have been emails, but on other trips Jason never connected with Savvie through emails—she's too little—he always FaceTimed with her." Aaron tossed his cold coffee into her sink and linked his hands around the back of his neck. "In short, Jason is officially missing, presumed kidnapped." He forced the words out. "It's possible that he's dead."

Kasey lifted her fist to her mouth, her eyes wide with shock mixed with horror. "God, Aaron."

He imagined himself in her arms, soaking in her strength, leaning on her, emotionally, for a minute, maybe two. But that wasn't what he allowed himself—he didn't fall apart, he couldn't. He had to be strong. For Jason. For Megan. For Savannah.

"Savvie is five, nearly six, and has been bouncing between Megan, my sister's house and mine. I remember Jason naming me as her guardian after her mom died a year or so back but I never expected to have to take full responsibility for her." First her mom, then her dad. No wonder Savannah looked and sounded shell-shocked. "I'm picking her up from my sister Megan's soon, but, while I can handle the occasional sleepover or a weekend here and there, she's going to be with me full-time."

Well, here went nothing. "I need reinforcements and I was hoping that you would, um, lend me a hand with her."

Kasey looked like he'd asked her to play with acid-covered playing cards. "Aaron, I'm your executive assistant, not a babysitter. You have an enormous disposable income, hire a nanny!"

A stranger in his house? No. Aaron folded his arms, prepared to argue. "On your résumé, you said that you spent a year in France as an au pair. And I'll double your salary if you take on the extra workload."

Kasey still looked doubtful.

"Yeah, I could hire a nanny but you're young, warm, and I think she'd relate to you better. I just need to get through the next couple of weeks, someone to help me until she goes to school. Then I'll make another plan," Aaron added.

"What about your sister? Can't she help you?"

Megan was trying to unravel her own messy life and

while he knew that she could occasionally help out, she wasn't available on a continual basis. "Megan has her own issues she's dealing with."

Aaron looked at Kasey, almost prepared to grovel. "I trust you, Kasey. I trust you with my business." Okay, that was a small lie. He trusted her as much as he could and only with parts of his business.

"The hell of it is that I need you. So, will you help me?"

I need you...

Kasey was still trying to make sense of his words when her cell phone buzzed with an incoming call. Seeing Michelle's name on her screen brought the usual wave of longing and disgust, regret and anger, so she did what she always did and let the call go to voice mail. She couldn't deal with her former best friend right now. She wasn't sure whether she ever could.

Kasey looked at Aaron, who dominated her small kitchen. She could see the worry in his deep green eyes; it was also etched into the grooves edging his masculine but still sexy mouth, painted in the dark circles under his eyes. He also looked like he'd lost weight, which in Aaron's case meant that he'd dropped muscle since there wasn't an inch of fat on him. She'd checked.

Despite working virtually and only seeing him within the confines of a computer monitor, she'd noticed that he was worried and, day-by-day, she saw his tension levels ratcheting up. Thanks to that amazing, glorious night that could not be mentioned, they were very careful to keep their relationship strictly professional, so she'd avoided asking him what was wrong and whether she could help.

And that raised the question, did she want to help? Should she help? She rather liked being on the outside looking in; it felt safer that way. But lately she'd started to think that maybe it was time to come out of her self-imposed hermit lifestyle, to start engaging with the world again. Meet some new people and, maybe, make a friend or two.

She wasn't looking for a new best friend or a new lover—she didn't trust herself or her judgment to go that far—but sharing a meal with a nice man or a cup of coffee with a girlfriend might be fun. But, God, she was so out of practice. She needed to dust off her social skills; Aaron was the only person she spoke to on a regular basis and that was all about business.

Looking after Savannah would pull her out of her rut and make her interact with someone new, even if she was only five years old. But she had to be careful, she'd made a promise to herself to protect what was left of her heart and she couldn't afford to become emotionally attached to anyone, let alone a little girl who'd lost her mom and maybe—God, she prayed not—her dad.

"It's a temporary gig, Kasey. Just until we find our feet," Aaron said.

Kasey tapped her nails against her fake granite countertop, fighting the urge to say no, to crawl back into the security of her quiet and lonely life. If she kept to herself, then no one could hurt her...

But they were talking about a little girl. What harm could she do?

Kasey thought she could handle Savannah but she had to remember that she came as a package deal with Aaron. And she definitely *couldn't* handle him!

To give herself some time to think, Kasey lifted her phone to her ear to listen to Michelle's message. "So, I know you're not too happy with me at the moment but it's been a while since we spoke. Kasey, we need to resolve our issues. I need to say sorry for my oops and you need to forgive me."

Oops? That was what her childhood friend was calling sleeping with her husband? An *oops*? Holy hell, now she'd heard it all.

"Anyway, I've tracked you down and I'm driving to Royal to see you. I should be there later this morning. And we're going to talk, Kasey. You can't keep running from me. I'm staying for the weekend, possibly longer if I can't get through to you, and we're going to thrash this out."

Like hell she was. Kasey's eyes flew to the clock on the wall—it was already ten and Michelle was super punctual. In fact, she was often early. She bit her lip and thought fast. "Would me helping you with Savannah mean me moving into your house?"

"It would make sense," Aaron replied, his voice as neutral as Switzerland.

Two hours ago the thought of sleeping down the hall from the hottest man in Royal would've sent her running for the hills. But dealing with Michelle, rehashing their torrid past, was more terrifying than dealing with a little girl and Kasey's raging but hopefully well-hidden lust for her boss.

Sold, Kasey thought. Michelle would arrive in Royal, not find her at home and, after a day, maybe two—because she had a low attention span and was easily bored—she'd hightail it back to Houston.

"I'll help you with Savannah this weekend, as a trial run," Kasey said. Not giving Aaron time to respond, she whipped around and headed down the hallway to her bedroom. Stepping into her tiny walk-in closet, she stood on her tiptoes and lunged for the suitcase on the highest shelf. A big, burly man from the moving company had placed it there for her; she'd thought it would be months before she needed it again.

Kasey jumped, her fingers grazing the edge of the suitcase, which wobbled and stayed put. Dammit, she hated being short. Kasey took a step back and hit a solid wall of muscle. She tensed and her brain ordered her traitorous body not to push her butt into his groin.

Aaron's chest connected with her back as his arm reached for the suitcase, easily lifting the case off the shelf. His muscles bulged as he held it in the air and Kasey felt his hard body press up against her back, thought she felt his warm breath fanning her neck. Kasey stared at a pile of her T-shirts, telling herself that she couldn't—*shouldn't*—turn around. That it wasn't a good idea to rise to her toes and slam her mouth against his.

Kasey heard Aaron's muffled curse in her ear, heard the suitcase hit the floor and then Aaron's big hands were on her shoulders and he spun her around to face him. She caught a glimpse of green fire in his eyes before he abruptly stepped back, holding up his hands, broad palms facing her, his chest heaving.

"Kasey." Her name was both a warning and a plea. As her boss he wouldn't initiate anything but she could, she had to. Kasey placed her fingers on his jaw and reached up to touch her mouth to his.

They both needed this connection…

Aaron made an appreciative sound in the back of his throat as his tongue slipped past her teeth to slide against hers, long, sexy strokes that heated her skin and made her head swim.

She'd missed this. She'd missed being the object of a man's desire, of being held and kissed, of feeling feminine and powerful and so, so sexy. Despite only sharing a few, pleasure-saturated hours with him, she'd missed Aaron. When she thought of pleasure and sex and desire, his was the face that came to mind, his hands, his kisses, his touch. And hadn't that been the point of that night so long ago?

She shouldn't be enjoying his kiss so much, her hands shouldn't be exploring the hard muscles under his bare skin. She shouldn't be pressing her breasts into his chest. And she most certainly should *not* be twisting her tongue around his, making those sounds of appreciation low in her throat.

My God. What was she thinking? Rationality filtered in as she remembered that he was her *boss*. What they'd had was a onetime thing. She was moving into his house to avoid Michelle, to help him with his niece, not to warm his bed. *Pull away, Kasey. Now.*

Just five minutes more…

Aaron jerked his mouth off hers, his fingers digging into her hips. He rested his forehead against hers and she was pleased to see that his face was flushed, that he, also, was short of breath. That they were both struggling for control. At least she wasn't alone in this madness.

"Kase—"

Kasey yanked her hands out from underneath his shirt and pushed the heels of her hands in her eye sockets. This man had the ability to shut down her synapses, to trip the power supply to her brain.

Kasey looked down at her bare toes, noticed a small chip in the nail polish on her middle toe. She didn't want to have this conversation but she needed to make sure of what she was walking into. "I'm going to be living and working in your house, Aaron. For a couple of nights at the very least."

She lifted her head to see Aaron's "Yeah, so?" look.

Man, this was embarrassing, but because her entire marriage had been based on lies, Kasey chose honesty over embarrassment. "Are you expecting more when I move in with you? Because that's not going to happen."

Irritation flickered in his eyes. "I never, for one moment, thought it would. You're still my employee and I'm still your boss."

"I initiated that kiss but you were as into it as I was, Aaron."

Irritation morphed into frustration and his muttered curse bounced off the walls of her bedroom. "I know. But we had an agreement and that agreement still stands."

"Then why didn't we stop?" Why was she pushing him on this? What did she want from him? Kasey didn't know. What she should be doing is laughing it off, ignoring buzz of sexual attraction between them. This was akin to poking a bear with a stick...

"I don't know what your excuse is but I had five feet plus of pure perfection pressed up against me. When you haven't been laid for eight long months, temptation is hard to resist!"

Kasey stared at him, trying to process his words. He thought she was perfect? He hadn't had sex since her? He was gorgeous and ripped, and she knew that when he walked down the street women stared at him, lust and appreciation in their eyes.

Aaron cursed again and started to walk away. At the door, he turned and those piercing green eyes pinned her to the floor. "My life is a mess, Kasey, and I don't need any more complications."

Kasey and reality collided with a hard thump and she nodded, embarrassed. "I shouldn't have kissed you. I'm sorry if I made you feel uncomfortable."

Aaron looked down at his tented pants and lifted an eyebrow. "In more ways than one." He then released a heavy sigh. "You started it but I got into it so we're both, equally, at fault and I apologize."

Aaron placed his hands on his hips. "Can we keep it simple? You're my assistant and temporary nanny, that's it."

Yeah, that was it. That was all it could be. It didn't matter that they had enough sexual chemistry to ignite the room, they needed to keep their distance. She respected Aaron's big brain—and, because she was still a woman, she also appreciated his very excellent body—but she was not prepared to jeopardize her job or to allow her heart to hope.

"So you're with me on this? From this moment on, our relationship stays strictly professional?" Aaron was giving her that steely eyed, hard-ass look he frequently used when dealing with a complicated work issue.

He was right. It was essential that they didn't make this situation any more complicated than it needed to be. Kasey capitulated to common sense. "It's a deal."

Two

From the balcony off his office on the second floor of his house, Aaron watched Kasey pull to a stop at the back entrance. Jumping out of her SUV, Kasey shoved her sunglasses to the top of her head and opened the back door. Aaron watched his niece leave the vehicle, all dark hair, sad eyes and long legs. So young, she'd experienced more upheaval than most people would in a lifetime. Aaron felt his stomach cramp and closed his eyes. *Crap, Jay, where the hell are you? What more can I do to find you?*

Look after Savvie, bro, he heard Jason's voice say in his head. *If you want to do right by me, look after my precious, precious daughter.*

I am. She's in my care until you come home, just as you wanted.

"I left a snack on the kitchen counter for you, Savannah." Kasey's voice floated up to him and Aaron opened his eyes to see her place her hand on Savannah's shoulder. "Then you can have a quick swim before your ballet lessons. That work?"

It was Wednesday and Kasey, without further discussion, was still here and doing a fabulous job with his niece. Her natural warmth and her non-pushy attitude endeared her to Savannah. They'd clicked the moment they'd met.

He tended to avoid talking to Savannah about Jason but Kasey faced that issue head-on, allowing the little girl to express her fears, holding her when she cried and answering her many questions about where her dad could be. Kasey answered Savannah as honestly as she could, never giving the child false hope or making any promises that no one could fulfill.

Savannah wasn't happy, far from it, but when she was around Kasey, she was more cheerful than he'd seen her in weeks. Both Savannah and Kasey were now living with him on a full-time basis. Sure, Savvie had been a frequent visitor to his house but it still felt strange to share his space with a woman and a girl, to find hair ties on his kitchen table and dolls on the floor. Kasey's perfume floated through the house and there were flowers on the dining table and on the desk she used in the corner of his office. Music filled his house and his fridge was filled with girlie foods like low fat yogurt, frilly lettuce and hummus.

"Will you swim with me, Kasey?" Savannah asked, and Aaron tuned back into their conversation.

"Sure thing, sweetheart. I just need to check in with Aaron to see if he has any work for me," Kasey replied.

Aaron saw the flash of disappointment cross Savannah's face. With her dark brown hair and green eyes, she was going to be beautiful. Hell, if he discounted the fear and sadness, she already was.

"Nothing that can't wait. Maybe I'll join you two,"

Aaron said, resting his arms on the railing of the balcony. Savannah's head shot up and she managed a small smile before running into the house. Kasey stood in place, her arms folded across the cotton fabric of her sleeveless sundress. He could see the concern in her eyes, could read her thoughts as easily as he could the stock market.

"You don't have to join us," Kasey said.

"It's fine. I'm hot and I need a break." Aaron knew she worried that shedding most of their clothes would crack open the door that kept their mutual attraction under lock and key.

It was a swim, he wanted to tell Kasey. They'd have an almost-six-year-old to chaperone them. Aaron ran his hand across his face, reluctantly admitting that if he and Kasey found themselves in a pool alone, their clothes would be shed in world-record-breaking speed. They were *that* combustible.

Despite it only being a couple of days, living together in the same house was torture. They shared his office. They shared their meals. They were constantly in close proximity and, when he went to bed, he was deeply conscious that Kasey was across the hall in the bedroom next to Savannah's. Every night he needed to talk himself out of slipping into her bed, of losing himself in her for an hour or two or most of the night.

He tried, he really did, not to think about her like that but at night, when the lights were off, he was ambushed by memories of how she felt…

God. Boss of the Year he was not.

Really, didn't he have better things to do than fantasize about his employee? Aaron turned away and walked back into his cool study, dropping into his leather chair. He had too many responsibilities to allow himself to be distracted by Kasey with her endless curves and catlike amber eyes.

First and foremost, he needed to find out what the hell had happened to Jason. His gaze drifted to the silver frame on his desk: two little boys held fish up to the camera, their toothy grins wide and free. He and Jason were only a year apart and nobody knew his brother better than he did. Yeah, they'd fought and they'd competed—girls, sports, business—but they were brothers, and blood always, always, came first. He'd been Jason's best man at his wedding, had handed him cigars and gotten him drunk when he'd become a dad. He'd kept his hand on his back and been a pillar of strength for him when he'd buried Ruth.

It had been more than two months since he'd heard from Jay and Aaron knew in his gut that something was wrong. Desperately wrong.

His brother was work obsessed but he'd never neglected Savannah. He was a good dad and, if Savannah was staying with Aaron or with Megan while Jay traveled, he made it a point to connect with his daughter every day, morning and night. Something terrible had to have happened because Aaron knew Jason would move heaven and earth to speak to his child.

Cole Sullivan, the PI his friend Will had hired, also believed that Jason was in deep crap. The note Megan had received—supposedly from Jason, stating he needed space to deal with Will's death—had been proved, through handwriting analysis, not to be Jason's.

Aaron could've told them that. Jason was a Phillips. They didn't run away from their responsibilities. His brother would never turn his back on his daughter. He wouldn't ignore his family's entreaties to get in touch just so he could wallow in his own pain.

No, something was very, very wrong.

Aaron heard the door to his study open and Kasey

walked in, heading for her desk in the corner. Instead of taking a seat, she bent from the waist down to peer at her monitor, her sundress perfectly delineating her heart-shaped ass, the same ass he'd slid his hands under to haul her against him as he'd lost himself in her eight months ago. He couldn't help his eyes traveling down as her short dress rode up in the back, allowing him a look at her slim, tanned thighs. Those spectacular legs had encircled his hips, had been draped over his shoulders as he'd—

God, he needed to get laid. Eight months was far too damn long, but whenever he considered finding a date, Kasey's face popped into his head. He didn't want sex with some random female. He wanted Kasey. Which posed a problem, because the woman worked for him and was helping him, temporarily, to raise his niece. He couldn't jeopardize either situation, or his honor, for sex. His neglected junk violently disagreed.

There was something—damn, what was the word?— *homey* about having his house and life invaded by two intensely girlie girls. Savvie's occasional visits didn't carry the same punch as having them here 24/7. The dolls and smells and music were comforting, and hearing feminine voices and the occasional trill of laughter made his house feel more like a home than the huge tomb he usually inhabited.

Aaron rubbed the back of his neck and reminded himself that this wasn't normal. Normal was Jay back at home with Savvie, Kasey in her house, he in his. He couldn't afford to get attached. All his relationships, romantic or not, tended to be messy and, as an added bonus, the people he loved tended to leave him. Sometimes both at the same time. No, it was better to stay emotionally detached.

But that resolve didn't help him with his need-to-get-laid problem.

Kasey stood straight and Aaron quickly looked up, glad that his desk hid his arousal. There were certain things Kasey did not need to know and his craving for her was one of them. "Aaron, I'm falling behind."

"How can I help?"

"Can you do Savvie's ballet run? I could use that time to catch up here."

Aaron nodded. It would do him good to get out of the house, away from the monitors and making financial decisions involving hundreds of millions of dollars. That took its toll and he could feel a stress headache building between his eyes.

Kasey opened the right-hand drawer to his desk and lobbed him a bottle of aspirin. "Take two and come for a swim, it'll help you unwind."

Aaron opened the bottle, shook the pills into his hand and tossed them into his mouth. He dry-swallowed the pills and ignored Kasey's wince. "How did Savvie do at day camp today?"

Kasey picked up a pen and threaded it through her fingers, something she often did. "She was better, I think. She told me that some boy brought in his guinea pig and that some of the girls were scared of it, but she'd loved it." Kasey sent him a look and he knew that something big was coming his way, something he might not like. "I think you should buy her a puppy."

Yep, there it was. "Kasey, do we not have enough on our hands without adding a puppy to the craziness?"

"She loves animals, Aaron, and she needs something to love."

"She has me and Megan."

"Her mom and dad have both left her, so she doesn't trust other adults not to do the same," Kasey argued, stubbornness settling into her expression.

She was not going to let this go. Damn, they were going to get a puppy, sometime soon.

He thought he should at least try to change her mind. "She's not old enough to handle the responsibility of looking after a dog, Kasey."

"This isn't about being responsible, Aaron. It's about her having something in her life she can hold on to," she reiterated. "Having something to love. Everyone needs someone or something to love and, God knows, dogs are a hundred times more reliable than humans."

And didn't that statement, Aaron thought as she walked out of the room, give him a glimpse into her soul.

Kasey stomped down the hallway and ducked into her room. Kicking off her sandals, she immediately walked over to the French doors and flung them open, allowing the heat of the hot Texas day to slide into her bedroom. For the last year or so she'd felt perpetually cold—a physical reaction to emotional pain—so she didn't mind a little heat.

Kasey rested her head against the door frame and closed her eyes. She was exhausted, which was the only reason she'd allowed those revealing words to leave her lips. *Everyone needs someone or something to love and, God knows, dogs are a hundred times more reliable than humans...*

And wasn't that the truth. Kasey looked at the small picture on her bedside table, her gaze focusing on the mixed breed she held in her arms. She'd found Rufus in Cleveland, the puppy half-starved, for food and affection. Because her parents were generally oblivious, she'd managed to keep him hidden until they moved to... God, what city came after Cleveland? Cincinnati? Boston? It was all a blur. But she did remember the screaming fight she'd had with her parents, that if they insisted on lugging her from place to place, school to school, then the least they could do was let her have one friend, even if it was a canine. Ru, like her, had endured the moves and loved the summer holidays at her grandparents' house in Houston. All she'd wanted was a stable home life, a place to settle down in, and she'd found that for three months of the year, in Houston.

Years later she'd believed that she'd found her place, her permanent home with Dale. Yeah, that hadn't turned out the way she expected it to.

Kasey walked over to the king-size bed covered in expensive, white Egyptian cotton and picked up her phone. There were two missed calls from Michelle, one from Dale. Knowing it was more of the same old, same old, she blew out a frustrated breath and tossed her phone back onto the bed.

Dale and Michelle were in a race to win her back. Both wanted to be the first to earn her forgiveness. They were both sorry...they'd made a mistake...could she forgive them?

Hell, no.

Their infidelity had not only left her unable to fathom being in a relationship again, but also riddled her with insane trust issues. She'd spent the last eight months rebuilding her life. She was starting to feel vaguely normal and she was so much stronger. She liked her job, she liked Royal and she liked not having to deal with their neediness and drama. At some point she'd have to meet with them, face them, but today wasn't that day. Tomorrow wasn't looking good for them, either.

"I'm ready, Kasey."

Kasey turned and smiled at Savannah, who stood in her open doorway, dressed in a pink-and-purple swimsuit, her swimming goggles high on her head.

Savannah noticed that Kasey was still wearing her sundress and her expression turned to resignation, her face crumpling. "Okay, well…if you're not going to swim, then I'll just go to my room."

So much pain, Kasey thought, her heart flipping over. Savannah was nearly six but she expected adults to disappoint her.

"Honey, I was just woolgathering. Of course I'm going to swim with you." Kasey walked over to the dresser and pulled open the top drawer. Yanking out her swimsuits, she held them up. "The blue racer or the orange bikini?"

Savannah, because she was a mini fashionista, tipped her head, giving the question her complete attention. "The orange bikini."

Damn, Kasey silently thought. The bikini was modest, but it was still four triangles and she didn't feel comfortable showing Aaron that much skin.

A little too late, Monroe, considering the man once managed to kiss every inch of your skin.

But she wasn't thinking about that, about him, about how his touch made her combust from the inside out… She remembered the taste of his mouth, his skin, how his fingers trailed over her—

No! Stop!

Enough. They'd had their one insanely hot night together and, as mind-blowing as it had been, it could never be repeated again.

She was permanently unavailable and he was her super-professional boss, so getting worked up about showing a little flesh was just…stupid. Apart from that kiss in her house days ago, Aaron never made any reference to what they'd done, how they'd done it and how hot it had been. He was so inscrutable that some days she even doubted that night had ever happened and she sometimes wondered whether Aaron naked was a very erotic, very sexy, figment of her imagination.

"Kasey!"

Kasey blinked and looked at Savannah, hands on her tiny hips, her green eyes frustrated. She clapped her hands and made a shooing motion. "You are wool-grabbing again."

Kasey started to correct her but smiled instead. "You're right, I am."

God, she really, really liked this kid. She had to be careful. After her marriage imploded, she'd promised herself she wasn't going to form emotional attachments again. She didn't trust herself enough to do that. Because trust and attachment led to a shattered heart and hers was only just starting to heal.

Aaron sat on a pool lounger a few yards from the pool. Kasey and Savannah were sitting in the water, on the wide, first step of the massive pool. Nearly every doll Savannah owned was in the pool with them and Kasey was helping Savannah to teach them to swim.

Kasey, long-limbed and slim, flipped a chubby plastic doll onto its back to make it float. Savannah, sitting between Kasey's legs, guided the doll through the water, her one hand on Kasey's thigh. They were lost in their own conversation, oblivious to his presence.

At one point in his life, while he'd still been at college, he'd dreamed of this: a big house, money in the bank, a hot wife and a cute kid. He'd been happy to play the field, but in the back of his mind he'd always been on the lookout for "the One." His perfect match. Instant recognition of his soul mate. God, for a guy who'd always had nerves of steel when it came to finance, he'd been such a damn romantic.

There was nothing romantic about being the direct

cause of his parents' car accident or having his fiancée run off with his client list six months after opening their investment firm together, nearly bankrupting him in the process. Kate had been six years older than him, sophisticated, and he'd hung on her every word. He'd believed her when she'd insisted he was bright enough to make it without completing his last semester of college, that he didn't need his degree in finance and that he needed to concentrate on their business. So in love with her, he'd dropped out of college, breaking his parents' hearts and ultimately causing their deaths.

Afterward he'd flung himself into their business, working crazy hours to get their company off the ground, to distance himself from the grief. How had Kate repaid him? The month after he'd made his first five-million trade, she'd visited every one of their clients and told them that she was the one reading the markets, that she was concerned about his emotional health, his youth. His clients, scared to risk their money on such a young trader, had moved their portfolios to Kate. He'd been left with the three clients she hadn't been brave enough to approach: his brother, Will Sanders and Megan. He'd taken his life savings, Megan's and Jason's modest investments and Will's larger investment, and made them all a damned fortune. His former clients, who had lost money with Kate, had reached out to him, asking him to manage their money again.

Because loyalty was everything to him, Aaron had refused. Besides, by that point—and thanks to Will's word-of-mouth advertising—he had more, far richer, clients than he could handle.

God, if only his parents had trusted his decision. If only they hadn't freaked and jumped into that car ten minutes after he'd told them he was dropping out of school. If only they hadn't driven through the night to confront him at Berkeley. If they had trusted him, just a little…

His heart had splintered into a million pieces when his parents died and what was left had been decimated by Kate's deceit. He would've given Kate everything. But she'd screwed him over, big-time, and, ten years later, his heart still wasn't capable of giving or receiving love.

Did Savannah sense that? Was that why she was so reserved around him? Did she subconsciously realize that he had nothing to give? God, he hoped not. If Jason— God… if his brother didn't come back, could he love Savannah the way she deserved to be loved, the way a little girl *needed* to be loved? He wasn't so sure…

Dammit, Jay, you'd better be doing everything you can to get yourself back here! I can't do this… Savvie needs you. She needs her dad.

And, hell, I need my brother.

He should be working, Aaron thought. There were markets to check, decisions to make. But he could take another five minutes to sit in the afternoon sun and soak up some rays. He tried to sit still but, feeling antsy, he reached for his cell and dialed Cole Sullivan's number.

The private investigator had assured him that he was doing everything he could to find Jason. But surely there was something Aaron could do, as well? Because, sure as hell, sitting around in the sun while his brother was missing wasn't it. Guilt, acidic and bitter, burned his tongue and the roof of his mouth.

"Sullivan."

Aaron asked whether Cole had any news.

"Nothing concrete since the last time we spoke, Aaron."

Nothing concrete… Did that mean Cole had found something? "Do you have a hunch about what happened?"

"I have nothing *concrete*, Aaron," Cole repeated. "I

make it a policy not to share my hunches or suppositions without anything to back them up."

Crap. Aaron gripped the bridge of his nose and ignored the burning in his eyes. "What can I do, Cole? Just tell me. I need to do something…the waiting is killing me."

"If there is anything, I'll let you know. Hang tough, Aaron. I'm hoping to have some solid answers for you soon."

"Okay. Keep me updated."

"You will be the second person I call," Cole promised him.

Aaron wanted to protest but remembered that Cole was working for Will. He wasn't calling the shots, wasn't Cole's client, and that burned him. He liked being in charge, but he was somewhat pacified by the knowledge that he was in the loop, that he'd get the information as soon as Will did. Besides, he instinctively trusted Cole. He knew he was doing everything he could to track down Jason.

Aaron saw the tiny feet next to his size thirteens and slowly lifted his head to look into Savannah's worried face. They shared the same green eyes, he thought, the Phillips chin.

"Were you talking to someone about my daddy?" Savannah demanded, fear and worry in her eyes.

Aaron felt like he was looking into his own soul. He thought about lying, then decided she deserved, and needed, the truth. "Yeah, Savvie, I was."

"Is he coming home soon?" Savannah asked, her bottom lip wobbling.

Aaron took her hand in his and sat straighter. His gut clenched at the mixture of hope and fear he saw in her eyes. "I don't know, honey. We're trying to find him."

"Something's wrong, Uncle Aaron. Daddy always calls me and it's been so long."

Tears just made the green of her eyes more brilliant.

Aaron reached up and touched her cheek with the back of his knuckle. "I know, honey. I'm worried, too." He gestured to his phone, conscious of Kasey standing a few feet behind Savannah, her body stiff with tension. Did she think he should be more upbeat? That he should be more optimistic? Was this one of those times when he should be lying his ass off?

He met her eyes and saw her concern for Savvie. She was clearly holding herself back, resisting the urge to sweep the little girl into her arms and soothe away her pain.

Aaron was grateful for her reticence. This conversation, as hard as it was, was the first real conversation he'd had with Savannah since she'd moved in full-time.

He picked up his phone and tossed it from one hand to another. "The man I was just talking to? His name is Mr. Sullivan, and his job is to find people who have gone missing."

"Will he find my daddy?"

Aaron lifted his broad shoulders in a weary shrug. "He's trying, honey. I just called him to ask him if I could help him, but there's nothing I can do. I would if I could, but this is his job."

Savannah moved so that she was standing between his legs. Aaron slid his arm around her, being careful to keep his touch gentle. His eyes burned when she laid her head on his shoulder. "Your job is to look after me... I heard you saying that to Kasey."

"It *is* my job. Nobody is more important to your dad than you and he'd want me to make sure that you are safe."

Savannah pushed her face into his neck and he felt her warm breath on his skin. "I miss him, Uncle Aaron."

"I do, too, Savvie." Aaron rested his cheek against her head and closed his eyes. *God, Jay, where the hell are you?*

He heard Kasey's footsteps and lifted his head to look at her. Her expression was pure sympathy and he managed a quick, half-baked smile.

Kasey placed a hand on Savvie's shoulder. "Hey, sweet pea, if you don't run upstairs now to change, you're going to be late for your ballet lesson."

Savannah pulled back and her eyes widened. "And if anyone is late, Mrs. Pitman goes red and her mouth goes all funny." Savannah made a face and both he and Kasey laughed at her squinty eyes and pursed lips. "I'm going to change real fast, Kasey."

"You do that, Savvie. Aaron is going to take you to your lesson and he'll pick you up, okay?"

Savannah looked at Aaron and, for a long moment, he thought she might demand that Kasey take her. "'Kay," she said before running across the outdoor living area and into the house.

Aaron stood and looked at Kasey, who was wrapping a piece of gauzy fabric around her hips and looking thoughtful.

"Should I have patted her on the head and told her that everything is going to be okay?" he demanded as Kasey pulled a strapless T-shirt over her bikini top.

He was annoyed to find himself holding his breath, waiting for her answer. He didn't want to mess this up and he didn't want Kasey to think that he had. Why was he concerned about her opinion? He didn't, generally, give a rat's ass about what people thought about him. But he respected Kasey…

"I think you did the right thing," Kasey said softly and his stomach unraveled an inch or two. "I'd far prefer that you hurt me with the truth rather than comfort me with a lie."

Aaron sent a glance to the empty house. "But she's so little…"

"Kids respect honesty, Aaron. You made progress with her by telling her the truth."

"Honesty is a big deal for me," Aaron said, looking into her lovely face.

"It's a big deal for me, too," Kasey replied, picking up the towel Savvie had left on the patio floor. When she straightened, Aaron caught the flash of deep-seated pain in her eyes, in the way her lips thinned, and wondered who'd lied to her and why. He opened his mouth to ask her but then remembered he had no right to go digging into her life. For eight months he'd managed—just barely—not to cross that line from business to personal, but since he'd kissed her in her bedroom, that line was out of focus and fuzzy.

Aaron picked up his T-shirt and pulled it over his head. "I'd better change."

Kasey folded the towels she was holding, paying the menial task much more attention than it deserved. "And I need to catch up on my day job." She turned away but Aaron caught her elbow and sighed at her soft skin, the scent of her perfume mingling with the chlorine smell of the pool. "Kase?"

Whiskey-honeyed eyes threatened to buckle his knees. "Yeah?"

He wanted to kiss her, to yank her to him, to plunder her sexy mouth and fill his hands with her plump breasts. He wanted to strip her out of her clothes and lay her down on that lounger and make love to her in the afternoon sun. Then he wanted to take her into the pool to see if pool sex was as good as he remembered.

Aaron noticed the tremble in Kasey's fingers, the way her pulse fluttered in her neck. She'd let him. He knew this as well as he knew his own handwriting. It was a fantastic fantasy but it was a crap idea. "Nothing. I'd better go."

Kasey nodded, started to speak, but then gave the tiniest shake of her head, clamped her lips shut and headed into the house without saying another word.

Three

Kasey sent the email, leaned back in her chair and rolled her head from side to side, trying to ease the tension in her neck.

She glanced at her messy desk, relieved that she was finally caught up. The work didn't stop because Savannah needed her. The clients, and her boss, still demanded their pound of flesh and their pint of blood.

Kasey looked out the huge window, noticed that the sun was starting to drop, and eyed her watch. Six thirty? Aaron and Savannah should've been home ages ago.

Where had the last two hours gone? Kasey closed down her computer and picked up the phone on her desk. She'd call Aaron and ask where they were. Savannah needed to eat, have a bath and be in bed by eight. She was almost six, not sixteen…

Kasey started to dial his number before remembering that Aaron was Savvie's guardian and if he wanted to keep her up all night, he could. She was just the temporary nanny, she had no right to phone and harangue him about his parenting skills. Kasey dropped the phone back into its cradle. Aaron was, possibly, the most responsible man she knew. Savannah would be fine.

The adults in Savvie's life—Aaron and Megan—were fully functional.

Her own parents were young when they'd had her and had no idea how to parent responsibly or how to parent at all. She didn't remember much of her early childhood but her few memories didn't place her parents in the best light.

Apart from the constant moves and the ten schools in twelve years, she remembered falling asleep behind a couch, her stomach cramping because her parents were too drunk to feed her, waking up in a stranger's house because they had forgotten to take her home with them when they'd left a party. Bedtime was when she was tired, supper was always takeout, bathing was optional.

The summer holidays spent with her grandparents had been blissfully normal. There were rules and those rules had made her feel safe and cared for. There was healthy food, plenty of sunshine, lots of time to play. Her grandparents were two stable, hardworking people who respected the hell out of each other, loved each other even more, and she'd desperately craved what they'd had. Love, friendship, stability…a proper home. She'd thought Dale could give that to her, which showed how ridiculously moronic she could be on occasion and how skewed her judgment was.

Kasey stood and pushed her chair back, stretching her back to work out the kinks. Through the open window she heard the low purr of Aaron's SUV coming up the long driveway and her mouth curved up… They were home.

Leaving the office, she hurried down the stairs, walked into the informal sitting room and headed toward the back hallway, which was almost as impressive as the main entrance. Instead of pulling his big vehicle into the five-car garage, Aaron stopped a few meters from her. He cut the engine, the back door opened and Savannah all but tumbled out of the car, hair a mess and eyes blazing.

Oh, God, what happened? Had they found Jason? Kasey darted a look at Aaron, who was walking around the hood of the car, and he shook his head, silently telling her it wasn't what she thought. "Kasey! Kasey!" Savannah hurtled toward her, flung her arms around her waist and buried her face in Kasey's stomach.

Kasey bent over the little girl, stroking her hair and lifting her eyebrows at Aaron. "What's going on?" she asked as Savannah wrenched herself off her and streaked to the back of the SUV.

"Kasey, come see! Quick! Come look."

Oh, dear Lord, Kasey thought, jamming her hands in the back pockets of her jeans. What had Aaron done? Whatever it was, it was earning big points with Savvie. Aaron tossed her a cheeky smile, opened the big back door of the SUV and turned around, a hairy ball of fur in his arms.

"His name is Kanga, Kasey, and he's a New-find-me," Savannah said, gripping the puppy's hairy face with both hands before kissing its nose. Kanga responded by licking Savvie's cheek.

"It's a Newfoundland puppy," Aaron corrected her, tucking the enormous puppy under his arm. He smiled at Kasey.

Kasey scratched the puppy behind his ears and lifted her eyebrows at Aaron. "When I said a dog, I meant a crossbreed from the pound."

"He is from the pound. Well, sort of. His mother's owner is facing financial difficulties. She asked the manager of the shelter to help her find a home." Aaron glanced down at Savannah, who still was nose to nose with the pup. "Savannah fell in love, what could I do?"

"Say no?" Kasey suggested sotto voce. "You do know that they are monstrous dogs, that they can reach one hundred twenty pounds and that they drool?"

Aaron's big, broad hand stroked Kanga's coal-black head. "She fell in love, Kase!"

Kasey's lips twitched. "Sucker. Good thing you have space and that you can afford the veterinary and food bill. He's going to cost a fortune, Aaron."

"They are."

Kasey sent him a puzzled look. "What?"

Aaron exchanged a conspiratorial look with Savannah and swung open the back door of the SUV. Another puppy, also a Newfoundland and even bigger than Kanga, but a rich, chocolate brown, sprawled across the cargo area. "Kanga and Roo came as a package deal, part of the reason why the shelter manager couldn't find homes for them."

The little girl leaned into the car and pushed her face into Roo's warm coat. When she lifted her head to look at Kasey, her eyes glistened with tears. "I love my puppies, Kasey." Pulling back, she turned around and hugged Aaron's hips. "Thank you, Uncle Aaron."

"My pleasure, kiddo." Aaron barely got the words out before Roo sat up and exploded to life. He barked once and barreled out of the vehicle, nearly mowing Savannah down in the process. Kanga wriggled and, because he was caught off guard, managed to slip from Aaron's grasp. Within ten seconds, two puppies the size of lion cubs and the dark-haired girl were streaking through the gardener's perfectly planted flower beds and across the manicured lawn.

Aaron placed his hands on his hips and watched Savannah fall to the grass, the puppies crawling over her, tugging her hair and licking her face.

"So, this is going to be fun," he said, sounding doubtful.

Kasey shook her head. "I have only one thing to say."

Aaron lifted an eyebrow. "Yeah?"

"I want a raise."

In the Royal Diner, Kasey looked at her watch, grateful that she had a little time to unwind before she needed to leave to collect Savannah from summer day camp. She relaxed against the back of the red faux-leather booth and looked out onto the busy road bisecting downtown Royal. It was a hive of activity; pickup trucks and sports cars were parked on either side of the road or were rolling down the wide boulevard. The residents of Royal ambled along clean sidewalks, lifting their hands in greeting and often stopping to chat. There was a sense of community here, Kasey realized, a small-town vibe she liked.

Amanda Battle, who Kasey knew to be the owner of the diner, stopped by her booth, holding a coffeepot. "Can I give you a refill?"

Kasey returned her open, happy smile. "Thanks, but I'm fine. I'm—"

"Kasey Monroe, Aaron's whiz of an assistant, temporary nanny to Savvie," Amanda replied, resting her hand on her hip. She laughed at Kasey's surprise. "This is Royal, honey, where gossip is the town's favorite sport. You're from Houston and you're either a snob or heartbroken, because you don't socialize much. In fact, this is the first time I've seen you in here for months."

"Not a snob," Kasey said.

"Heartbroken?"

"I was, but I'm better now," Kasey replied and realized

that it was true. She did feel better. Okay, so maybe with a broken marriage and a ruined friendship behind her, she wasn't living the idyllic, roses-and-champagne life she'd envisioned, but she was, temporarily, living in a fantastic house with a kid who thought she was pretty wonderful, two crazy dogs who kept her constantly entertained and her sinfully sexy boss.

"Finally!"

Kasey heard the familiar voice and every cell in her body tensed. Her world tilted. Kasey blinked, once, then twice, dimly aware that Michelle's red lips were touching her cheek, that she was sliding onto the bench opposite her and tossing her bag on the table between them.

Kasey felt Amanda's hand on her shoulder, heard her soft command to breathe. She did as she was told and the world refocused. Kasey looked into Amanda's sympathetic face and held up her cup. "Suddenly, I need a refill."

"And I'll have—"

"She's not staying," Kasey interrupted Michelle's carefree chirp.

Amanda's eyes bounced from Kasey to Michelle and back again. One arched eyebrow lifted. "Do you want her gone?" Amanda asked. "My husband, Nate, is the sheriff and he can be here in two minutes."

It was tempting, so tempting, but she really didn't want to cause a scene. "I'll let you know."

"You do that, hon." Amanda frowned at Michelle. "You, behave."

Michelle pouted, resting her forearms on the table. "Who does she think she is? She can't speak to me like that!"

Kasey matched her former friend's frown with one of her own. "What are you doing here, Michelle?"

Again, the pout. "You've never called me by my full name, it's always been Mish."

"That was before you slept with my husband."

"Are you still harping on that? God, it didn't mean any-thing! It was just sex! We were drunk and high."

"It meant something to me!" Kasey retorted. Why was this so difficult for her to understand?

"It was a mistake, Kase, I admit it." Michelle used one perfectly manicured finger to push her long blond fringe out of her eyes, then tapped the table with the fake nail of her index finger. "But I don't see sex the same way you do. Dale and I? We look at it differently."

Marginally interested in an explanation that made some sort of sense but damned if she'd ask her to elaborate, Kasey tipped her head to the side.

"Sex is a game, some fun, a passing fancy. It's an itch to scratch, a cool drink on a hot day. Add booze and drugs and it means even less."

Kasey heard the truth in Michelle's voice. She genuinely believed what she was saying but her lack of emotional intelligence was breathtaking. Had she always been this way? Had Kasey just been looking at her through rose-colored lenses?

Michelle's brown eyes met hers. "Can we get past this? I miss you so much."

"I miss you, too," Kasey quietly admitted. And she did. Michelle, with her devil-may-care attitude to life, could always make her laugh.

The other woman's eyes flashed with hope. "So, does that mean we're good?"

Kasey shook her head, her eyes burning with tears she refused to allow to fall. "I don't know. I don't think so. Because no matter what your attitude toward sex is, to me, it's an expression of love and I loved Dale. Booze or not, as my best friend, he was forever and ever off-limits." She swallowed hard. "I need more time to work through this, so…give me some space, okay?"

Michelle gnawed on her bottom lip. "I'm thinking about moving here, to Royal. With you gone, there's not much left for me in Houston…"

Kasey's stomach sank to her shoes. "Please don't, Michelle. I need distance from you, from what happened."

"But I need to be here, so when you do forgive me, we can be like we were."

Sighing, Kasey stood, grabbed her tote bag and slung it over her shoulder. Their friendship would never be the same again. Even if she managed to forgive Michelle, this would always be between them. "I need time. I need space. If you love me at all, please respect that."

Kasey looked at Amanda, who was heading toward her with a fresh cup of coffee in her hand. Walking away from Michelle, she reached into the back pocket of her jeans and pulled out some crumpled bills.

Amanda darted a look at Michelle and took the payment. "You should join our book club, we meet every couple of weeks."

Kasey felt touched at the offer. "I'd love to, but I don't have time to read at the moment."

Amanda laughed. "When I say book club, it's mostly just an excuse to ditch our men and drink wine. I'll let you know the next time we're getting together."

Kasey frowned, surprised at the generous offer. "Why me? You don't really know me."

Amanda darted a look at a sulky Michelle and raised her eyebrows. "Because, honey, you definitely need more options when it comes to friends."

"Kasey?"

She was driving Savannah home and lifted her eyes to

look at Savvie in the rearview mirror, sighing at the worry she saw in the little girl's eyes.

"Yeah, sweetie?"

Savannah sucked her lower lip between her teeth. "The kids at camp are asking whether I'm still having my party."

"What party, Savvie?"

"In two sleeps I'm going to be six and Daddy said that I could have my birthday party before I go to school. He said I could have a Princess Pool Party on Saturday."

Kasey blew air into her cheeks, silently cursing. This was the first time she'd heard about the party and her first instinct was to say that she didn't think it could happen, not with all the drama of her dad being missing. Kasey looked in the mirror again and saw the glimmer of hope in Savannah's eyes. Stuff it, she thought. The kid was going through hell and, sure, she had a lot to do, but how hard would it be to organize a princess party?

"I think your dad would've wanted you to have that party, Savvie." Kasey grinned at the whoop of joy coming from the back seat. "Let's do it."

"Yay!" Savannah shouted.

Kasey heard excitement and happiness in her voice.

She started to make mental lists, but her mind kept drifting back to her conversation with Michelle and the drama that seemed to follow her friend around. She was so over it…

It was easier to think about Aaron, who, on so many levels, intrigued her. Initially she'd been attracted to his looks but she quickly realized that he was so much more than a pretty shell. Aaron was phenomenally smart and she enjoyed, and appreciated, his quick mind.

But she'd known smart, handsome men before and they'd never caused her knees to shake and her mouth to water. His brain and body combo was distracting but his big heart, his integrity and his flat out honesty made him so very difficult to resist.

It would've been so easy for Aaron to pressure her to continue sleeping with him after she took the job as his assistant; they lived in the same town and they'd had spectacular sex. It would've been easy to carry on their affair and, because she'd been so vulnerable, she might've welcomed the distraction of a hot affair.

That never happened. From the day she started work, she kept expecting Aaron to make a reference to that night and how incredible it had been but he'd kept his word and had never so much as hinted to what they'd done to and with each other. Looking back, she was so grateful he'd been so professional. She'd needed that time to heal, to come to terms with her failed marriage and Michelle's betrayal.

The other day, when she kissed him, he'd been the one to slam on the brakes, to back off. He was her boss and to Aaron, kissing her was, at best, inappropriate. Kasey knew, on an instinctive level, that she could strip naked in front of Aaron, crawl all over him and be on the point of no return but if she changed her mind, said no, Aaron would back off.

And the next day he'd treat her with the same respect he'd always afforded her.

She trusted Aaron's honor and was completely convinced that she was, would always be, in control of their blazing attraction and that her job would never be used as a weapon against her.

She also knew that she really, really wanted to sleep with him again.

That night they spent together had been one of the most positive, life-affirming, healing experiences of her life. As he touched her, with reverence and care, she'd felt some of the fissures in her heart heal, her confidence seep back. There was something amazing about having a strong, masculine man worshipping her body that filled a woman with a sense of power and control. And knowing that Aaron enjoyed her touch as much as she did made her feel...what?

Potent, blissful, buoyant?

All of those, but Aaron also made her feel like herself, more like herself than she'd felt for a long time, possibly forever. When she was around him, she felt like the best version she could be...

But, despite the way he made her feel, she couldn't afford to become hooked on anyone again.

With a headache threatening to split her head in two, Kasey pulled into her designated spot in the garage, in between the very expensive Vanquish and Aaron's new SUV and wished that she could stay in the car, where it was quiet and cool. But Savannah needed a snack and she still had research to do for Aaron. And a party to plan.

She had to get her head on straight, to stop thinking about Aaron and the way he made her feel. She trusted him to not allow sex to influence her working life, she trusted him with her body, but it was smarter and safer to leave the situation as it was, to not rock the boat by suggesting that they explore the bubbling, roiling crazy chemistry between them...

Dale and Michelle had taught her that the only person she could fully trust, rely on, was herself. It was always better to keep her heart out of the firing line.

Kasey heard Savvie exit the car and closed her eyes. She desperately needed to get out of her head, to stop, for a few minutes, thinking and obsessing and remembering. Dale, Michelle, Aaron...all three of them, to some degree, frustrated and confused her. She needed to run off her frustration and as soon as she could, she'd put on her trainers, pull up her hair and hit the road. And if she shed a tear or two while she ran, nobody would know.

Kasey heard Savannah greet Kanga and Roo and she was off and running with her favorite friends. Walking around the car, she slung Savannah's backpack over her shoulder, picked up the bag of groceries and her bag, nudging the door shut with her knee. She went into the house through the garage door and into the utility room. Kasey frowned at the pile of dry laundry in the basket, now wrinkled and creased.

Continuing on into the kitchen, she placed the sack of groceries on the counter and Savannah's backpack over the arm of a dining chair. She wrinkled her nose when she saw a stack of dirty dishes in the sink. Aaron's housekeeper had taken a fall two days ago and was out of commission with a torn hamstring. It was rapidly becoming clear to Kasey that the two other occupants in the house assumed that the fairies—her—would magically make the mess disappear.

Taking a deep, calming breath, she glanced across the open-plan space, saw that Savannah had found the TV remote and was watching her favorite kids program, the puppies turning her into a Savannah sandwich. A glass holding an inch of juice stood on the side table, along with a side plate holding the skin of an orange. A sheaf of papers was on the floor and, even from a distance, Kasey could see that it was the twenty-page report she'd burned the midnight oil to compile for Aaron. And, on one of the pages, was that a paw print?

Seriously?

Kasey looked around and saw that the huge doors leading onto the outdoor area were open and that one of her trainers lay just outside the door. Temper bubbling, she hurried across the room and onto the patio, cursing when she saw that the shoe was not only ripped to shreds but soaking wet with puppy drool. Puppy drool and something yellow... God, they'd eaten her shoe and then peed on it!

No trainers, which meant no running until she managed to replace them.

"Kasey!"

She turned around slowly and saw Aaron walking into the room, his state-of-the-art tablet in his hand, his mouth taut with displeasure. With a final look at her mangled shoe—dammit!—she stepped into the house and looked at her grumpy but still sexy boss.

"Have you managed to source any information yet on that wind turbine company?" he demanded.

Aaron had given her the assignment as she was walking out of the door to collect Savvie, an hour earlier. She'd spent twenty minutes at the Royal Diner, picked Savannah up and then hit the grocery store to stock up on kitchen essentials. She'd come home and found the house a mess and her trainers in shreds. When would she have had the time?

It took all she had not to snap. "No, I haven't."

"I need that information, Kasey. The company is courting a few investors and I don't want to miss out on this opportunity because you can't do your job."

She knew that she should cut Aaron some slack. That he was desperately worried about his brother. That he wasn't sleeping. That he was struggling with the crazy reality that was now his life...

But with a now-throbbing headache, she was feeling less than tolerant. Kasey placed her hands on her hips and tossed him an irate look. "You're kidding me, right?"

Aaron finally looked up from his screen to glance at

her. "I need that information, Kasey. Like, in the next thirty minutes."

"Then go online and get it yourself," Kasey told him, anger roiling through her.

Aaron's eyes turned wintry. "Excuse me? Do you or do you not work for me?"

Kasey saw that Savannah was kneeling on the couch, looking at them with worried eyes. They couldn't fight in front of her, so Kasey told her to take Kanga and Roo outside to play ball. Savannah scrambled off the sofa, ran past the adults and out onto the patio.

"What is your problem?" Aaron asked, placing his tablet on the dining table before opening the fridge to pull out a bottle of water. He cracked the top and took a long swallow while Kasey tried to find the most diplomatic way to tell him that he was being an ass.

Nope, nothing. "You're an ass."

Aaron's thick eyebrows lifted.

"A demanding, selfish, annoying ass." Kasey pushed the words out between her lips. So much for diplomacy.

"Have you even noticed that the housekeeper isn't here? Clean laundry scrunched up in the basket, dirty dishes in the sink." Kasey pointed to her report on the floor. "I only got to bed at around one this morning because I was up compiling that report, which I find strewn on the floor covered in paw prints. The puppies have peed under the dining table and God knows where else! I am running myself ragged trying to keep Savannah busy. I am doing my job, Aaron, but which one comes first? Savannah or research? Housekeeper or puppy minder? I also now have to plan Savannah's party for Saturday!"

"What party?"

"Her birthday party!"

Aaron winced, guilt flooding his features. "Dammit,

I'd forgotten that it was her birthday soon. Maybe we should—"

Oh hell, no. They were not canceling! "She's having a party," Kasey said, sounding stubborn. "A Princess Pool Party, so don't argue."

"Okay but—"

Kasey, feeling overwhelmed, glanced around the room and her temper spiked again. "And those monsters you call dogs ate, and peed on, my favorite trainers!" she shouted. "All I wanted, Aaron—all that was keeping me going today, was the idea of getting out of this place, just for an hour, to run. To not think! Now I can't even do that!"

Kasey didn't realize that tears were running down her face until Aaron's thumb wiped the moisture away. "Ah, honey."

Still seething, Kasey smacked her hands against his chest, feeling like she was a pressure cooker about to blow. She was about to blast him but she made the mistake of looking into his eyes, at that sexy, masculine mouth descending toward hers. This wasn't the time for kissing. She needed to tell him that she couldn't do this, that she wasn't coping.

Then Aaron's lips claimed hers and the world shifted, tumbled off its axis.

The thought occurred to her that she should push him away—she was mad, dammit!—but Aaron was kissing her, his lips moving across hers, his tongue coaxing her to play, and the only thing she could think of to do was to wind her arms around his neck and press her breasts into his chest. Her lips parted and then Aaron took the kiss deeper, wilder, hotter. Kasey could feel that he wanted her, it was in the sin-with-me strokes of his tongue, the big hand cupping her butt cheek, the massive erection pressed into her stomach.

If she couldn't run, then sex would be an equally good way to burn off her frustration. It was just sex, Kasey told herself, deliberately ignoring her earlier sex and heart argument. People did it all the time. And Aaron was particularly skilled. She ran her hands down his broad back, pulled his cotton shirt up and slid her hand down the hot skin of his lower back. A bolt of lust shot straight to that hot place between her legs as she dipped her fingers beneath the band of his boxers. She wanted him, she wanted *this*, so much. She wanted to forget about past betrayals, sad little girls and missing brothers. She wanted to ignore the dirty dishes and the laundry and puppy pee. She wanted to step out of her life and feel, be the object of this big, sexy man's undivided attention.

Aaron pulled his mouth off hers and Kasey moaned her disappointment. She reached up to carry on kissing him, missed his mouth and kissed his cheek. Kasey felt his hands on her hips and then realized that he was lifting her…

Away from him.

Wha-at?

Again?

Not content to be a selfish ass around the house, he was also rejecting her. Kasey wondered if this day could get any worse, before quickly reminding the universe that her statement wasn't a challenge. She glared at Aaron, who was rubbing the back of his neck, looking uncomfortable.

"Savvie's around and the kid has been traumatized enough without seeing us getting hot and heavy."

Kasey looked out into the garden, saw that Savannah and the puppies were under the live oaks at the bottom of the property. The little girl wasn't paying them the smallest bit of attention. Kasey turned her attention back to

Aaron and frowned when he wouldn't look at her. Had he just kissed her to distract her from her rant? Was the kiss just a way to allow him to dodge the issue? Dale had used the exact same tactic all the time...all over her like a rash whenever they started to fight.

God, she was such an idiot. Kasey wanted to blast Aaron, but then she remembered that he was her boss, that she liked her job and, mostly, liked him. She'd agreed to be Savannah's nanny and, when she was feeling a little more rational, she'd tackle him about who was responsible for keeping the house from becoming a pigsty. But not right now. She needed to calm down, wash her face and head into the office to do some research on wind turbines. Work would help steady her and get them back on an even keel.

She needed to steady the ship.

"I want you, Kase," Aaron said, his voice tight. "Don't doubt that."

Even without his words Kasey knew that to be the truth. She saw it in the way his eyes connected with hers, the way he seemed to look into her soul. A muscle in his cheek jumped as if he were trying not to yank her to him and take her hard and fast. She didn't even need to drop her eyes to know that he was rock hard.

Don't, Kasey. Steady the ship, focus...do your job.

"Can you watch Savannah while I do my real job?" Kasey quietly asked, lifting her chin. If she had to work twenty hours a day, Aaron would never again accuse her of goofing off.

Aaron nodded. "Sure."

Kasey expressed her thanks, picked up her bag and started to walk out of the room. When Aaron called her name, she sighed. What now?

"In my desk drawer are some extra-strength aspirin. Take a couple. We'll talk when you're done."

"I'll have that report ready for you soon." She clipped the words out.

"Kasey—"

She didn't bother to stop but just walked away from him and hurried up the stairs.

Four

Well, hell.

Aaron watched Kasey walk out of the room, trying not to be distracted by the elegant sway of her hips and the fluidity of her long-legged stride. He started to follow her, realized what he was doing and slammed on brakes, attempting to push the idea of taking Kasey up against the wall or on the stairs out of his mind. Pulling away from her had been the hardest thing he'd ever done and, talking about hard, he needed a series of cold showers to settle the hell down.

Or sex. Sex with Kasey would take care of that problem. He couldn't ever remember wanting a woman this much.

She was driving him to the edge of lunacy.

Aaron gripped the bridge of his nose, cursing himself. He shouldn't have kissed her, but the combination of fire and pain in her eyes had aroused his protective streak and in that moment he'd wanted to kick anyone and anything that caused her even a smidgen of worry.

Even if it was his own ass he had to kick.

Exhaling roughly, he placed his hands on the kitchen counter, straightened his arms and looked around his house. Yeah, those were his dirty dishes on the coffee table. He'd meant to take care of them but he'd been distracted by an email and then a phone call.

Mrs. B had been injured and it had never crossed his mind as to who was keeping his palatial home clean, who was keeping him and Savannah organized. He'd been so caught up in his life, trying to keep his business on track and his niece happy—his concern for Jason a constant ache in the back of his mind—that he'd ignored the practical aspects of running a household. Or, worse, it had been easy to allow Kasey to pick up the slack.

He was, officially, a jerk. Kasey was working long hours and he'd been unreasonable with his demands and disrespectful of her work. Annoyed with himself, Aaron walked over to the sitting area and picked her report up from the floor. He'd been in the process of reading it when the puppies had jumped him and it had fallen to the floor, their paws landing on it. He smoothed the creases and placed the papers under his tablet. After straightening the cushions on the sofas, he picked up his dirty dishes, turned the TV off and headed back to the kitchen.

He was, mostly, a modern guy and believed that guys could do housework and girls could handle guns. Just because Kasey was acting as Savvie's nanny, that didn't mean she needed to cook and clean, as well. He should've been on top of this. He shouldn't have assumed that she would just take care of his niece and, by extension, him.

Besides, that wasn't the way he wanted her to take care of him. He wanted to feel the strands of her hair brush his stomach as she went down on him, her warm mouth wrapped around him. He'd allow her to build him up to a certain point before lifting her so that she straddled his hips, driving up and into her, her cries of pleasure slowing him down...

Yeah, thinking about sex is so helpful, Phillips. God, you are so screwed. Metaphorically.

Get your mind out of the bedroom and back on track!

To make life easier for Kasey, her role had to be more clearly defined and it was up to him to make that happen. And that meant that he had to get his raging attraction to her under control. No more kissing, no more lying awake, feeling guilty for fantasizing about having Kasey in his bed, in a number of explicit and erotic positions. He was unfocused; he should be worrying about Jason's welfare. And Savannah's. His sister, Megan's...

Aaron watched as Savannah walked to the house, a puppy on each side of her, one of her hands on each head. If Jason was dead—and with every day that passed that was becoming more likely—how was he going to cope with raising his niece on his own?

Kasey's help was temporary; he couldn't rely on her on a long-term basis. He'd have to hire a nanny, but the thought of a stranger moving into his house, replacing Kasey, who would leave his home and go back to her pretty little cottage in Royal, made his stomach churn. He liked seeing her face in the morning, walking down the stairs into the kitchen, seeing both his girls eating breakfast...

God, she wasn't *his* girl, she was his assistant. Why did these crazy images of a happily-ever-after keep popping into his head?

Savannah wasn't his daughter, Kasey was never going to be a permanent part of his personal life, and he was just making life that much harder for himself. Kate taught him that romantic dreams were nightmares in disguise, that loyalty was a fickle concept to most and that few people could be trusted.

His parents' death and Jason's disappearance reminded him that everybody he loved had a nasty habit of disappearing on him. So it was imperative that he keep his distance from Kasey. And that also meant keeping his hands off her. Not that Kasey would want to come anywhere near him anytime soon since he was a selfish jerk who only thought about himself.

For some reason, one Aaron didn't want to investigate, the notion of Kasey thinking badly of him left a sour taste in his mouth. And he had an idea of how to get rid of it.

Kasey sent a copy of her report to Aaron's email address and printed a hard copy, which she placed on his desk. Work, as it had for the last eight months, settled her emotions and she felt back in control. She wished she could sneak off to her room, exhaustion and embarrassment were a toxic combination, but she'd been upstairs for ninety minutes and she had a second job to do: a child to look after.

Ten more days until she could leave and go back to her cottage and her normal, albeit boring life, Kasey thought. Could she do it? Of course she could... Jeez, people survived not eating for ten days, she could cope with her attraction to her sexy but presently annoying boss and her fondness for a fairy child.

After brushing her hair and washing her face and hands, Kasey swiped on a layer of lip gloss and headed downstairs, thinking about what she could make for dinner. She wasn't keen on takeout—she'd had too much as a child—but the thought of whipping up something nutritious and filling made her want to whimper.

Stir fry? A chicken salad?

Kasey was taking a mental inventory of the fridge when she walked into the informal living area where they spent most of their time. Nothing came to mind and she was too tired to be creative.

But, since Savannah was setting the table, it had to be assumed that Aaron and Savvie were expecting food. She was going to have to cave and order takeout.

Kasey glanced to her right and saw the puppies lying by the door, both of them chewing on either end of a yellow, rubber chicken. The puddle they'd made earlier had been wiped away and her shoe was gone.

The room looked immaculate.

Aaron, she thought on an appreciative sigh. As if her thoughts had conjured him, he walked out of the utility room, wiping his hands on a kitchen towel. Kasey, feeling embarrassed, jammed her hands into the back pockets of her khaki capris. "Your report is on your desk. I also sent it to your email address."

"I saw that," Aaron replied, opening a cupboard and removing two large wineglasses. Gesturing to an icy bottle of white wine, he lifted his eyebrows in a can-I-pour-you-a-glass gesture. Kasey nodded and walked over to the kitchen counter to take possession of the glass of deliciousness.

"Savvie, shower time," Aaron said. "Can you manage by yourself or do you need some help?"

Savannah rolled her eyes. "Of course I can manage, I'm practically six, Uncle Aaron."

His lips twitched. "Okay, kiddo. Well, then, run upstairs while I have a chat with Kasey."

"Your pj's are under your pillow," Kasey told her. "Yell if you need me."

Savannah nodded, flashed Kasey a small smile and ran past them, Kanga and Roo at her heels. "No dogs in the shower, Savvie!" she called out, not wanting to deal with the mess one girl and two monsters could make in the bathroom.

"Aw…" Savannah groaned.

When Kasey heard her feet on the wooden stairs, she looked at Aaron. "I owe you an apology for earlier."

Aaron picked up their glasses and walked around the counter. "Let's take this outside, it's a nice night."

Kasey followed him onto the patio and sank into one of the comfortable wicker chairs. Aaron, still in his black cargo shorts and white T-shirt, kicked off his flip-flops and placed his big feet on the square coffee table.

He sipped his wine and looked over his garden before those mesmerizing eyes met hers. "I'm the one who owes you an apology, Kase. Mrs. B spoils me and I'm used to being waited on." He sighed. "I'm sorry. As you so eloquently pointed out, I've been a pain in the ass."

He had been, but she also knew there were extenuating circumstances. Jason's disappearance had to be killing him. She wanted to say something encouraging, to tell him that Jason would be walking through that door soon, back into their lives. But they would be empty words. Jason would've been here a long time ago if he wasn't hurt. Or worse. "Thanks for cleaning up."

"I also shoved the laundry back into the dryer. Packed the dishwasher."

Kasey smiled at him. "Thank you. If you tell me that you've thought about a plan for supper, I just might kiss you."

The words left her mouth and she blushed when Aaron sent her a wicked smile. "Since dinner is in the oven and a salad is made, I'll take you up on that offer."

Kasey grinned. "You made dinner? Awesome! What is it?"

"Lasagna from the Royal Diner," Aaron replied. "One of Amanda's waitstaff delivered a tray while you were upstairs. Oh, and I've arranged with Amanda to deliver a cooked meal every day until Mrs. B gets back."

Now Kasey felt guilty. "I just had a bad day today, you didn't have to do that."

"Cooking was never the deal and you have enough on your plate," Aaron conceded, his expression thoughtful. "Amanda asked after you. She said that you met someone at the diner, that you looked upset when you left the restaurant. Whose butt do I need to go kick?"

His tone was mild but Kasey could see the concern on his face and knew that if she said the word, Aaron would jump in and fight this battle for her. Being strong and independent, and not prepared to rely on a man again, she'd never let that happen, but it was a nice thought. "Just someone from my past."

Aaron dropped his feet, placed his wineglass on the coffee table and leaned forward, determination all over his handsome face. "It's obvious to me that the confrontation was a contributing factor to your meltdown this afternoon. Tell me what happened, Kasey."

Kasey held her wineglass to her chest, undecided.

Then he added a low-pitched "Please," and the words started rolling off her tongue.

"I saw Michelle at the diner. I've known her since I was ten. She used to be my best, closest friend."

"What did she do?"

Kasey sipped her wine before resting the glass on her knee. "She slept with my ex-husband. She says it was a drunken mistake. That it meant nothing." She released a pent-up breath. "She thinks I should forgive her, that what they had was just sex, that there weren't any emotions involved."

"But yours were." Aaron reached across the table, took her glass from her hand and put it on the table between them. It was only then that she realized her hand was shaking.

"You get that?" Kasey asked.

"Sure, I get that. It doesn't matter how they view sex. Whether it meant anything or not, fidelity, loyalty and monogamy mean something to you, so they should've respected that."

"Michelle doesn't understand that. She wants me to go back to how we were before."

"Can you see yourself doing that?"

Kasey thought about it for a minute. "A part of me does. I miss her, Aaron, I miss having someone to talk to, someone I believe in and who believes in me. Before I walked in on them, I really believed that Michelle was the one person I could go to if I had a dead body in the trunk, knowing that she'd grab a shovel. Without her, I feel lost. But so betrayed."

Aaron's big hand enveloped his glass. "And your ex? Is he wanting to come back into your life, as well?"

Kasey pulled a face. "There have been some calls, which I'm ignoring." Kasey shrugged her shoulders. "I was stupid. I thought he could give me the family and the stability I wanted. None of it makes sense to me."

Aaron's perceptive look sliced though her. "Do you want it to? Do you need to understand before you can move on?"

Kasey rubbed her hands up and down her arms. "I don't think I want to move on, not in the way I think you mean. I'm really not interested in a relationship, in commitment. My marriage and divorce stripped fifty layers off me and it's an experience I'd prefer not to repeat."

"So us sleeping together really was purely sexual?"

She blushed, remembering how erotic their night had

been. "Dale was the last person I'd slept with before you. I didn't want all my memories of sex being of him." Kasey looked down before flashing him a quick smile. "Thanks to you, I know that sex isn't insipid or boring."

Aaron just stared at her for a long time before shaking his head. "Seriously, some guys would be better off being neutered."

"No argument from me," Kasey replied, chuckling wryly. She swallowed some wine, enjoying the hot night, the deepening sky and Aaron's company. This was what she'd wanted with Dale—company at the end of a long day, unwavering support and a few laughs. Was that really so much to ask?

Aaron's big hand covered hers, sending that intense tingle up her arm, jerking her back to the present. "If you want to, we could talk to Nate—"

"Who?"

"Nate Battle, the sheriff? He's Amanda's husband and, if he sees your friend hanging around, he could warn her off. Or threaten her with a restraining order."

Kasey knew that he was just being Aaron, innately protective, intensely loyal. Within five minutes of starting to work for Aaron she'd realized it was dangerous to mess with her boss's family, his friends or his employees. He gathered everybody under his wing and would go to war for those he loved. Not that he loved her—of course he didn't—but she was an essential cog in his professional wheel. Since she was also Savvie's primary caregiver at the moment, she kept his personal life running smoothly, as well.

Kasey wondered what being loved by a man like Aaron would be like. And why hadn't any of the Royal females, Houston bachelorettes—hell, any single women in the state—bagged him? Like astrophysics and artificial intelligence, she simply could not comprehend why he was still single.

He was so damn sexy…

Kasey held Aaron's gaze and the moisture in her mouth disappeared as desire replaced concern on his face, his thumb stroking the inside of her wrist in a slow, sure, delicious slide. It took everything she had not to lean forward, to place her lips on his. Her fast heartbeat and flushed skin, the heat she felt between her legs and her jittery heart were just her libido telling her that she was a relatively young woman who had needs. Sexual needs. And pleasuring herself just wasn't cutting it anymore.

Sometimes the only thing that satisfied was a ripped masculine body and big hands, a sexy mouth and a long, smooth—

"Kasey!"

Thin arms wrapped around her neck and she could smell strawberries, meaning that Savannah had found, and used, her bodywash. Thoughts of Aaron's wonderful body and how he could satisfy her were banished when Savannah buried her face in Kasey's neck. Caught off guard by this open display of affection, she turned in her seat and pulled the little girl onto her lap. "You okay, cupcake?"

Savannah turned those vibrant green eyes on hers—her father's eyes, Aaron's eyes—and blinked slowly. "Uncle Aaron said that you are feeling a little sad and that we need to love you a little more than usual."

Kasey's heart bumped and her gaze flew to Aaron's face, but he'd slid down his chair, his head resting on the back, and his eyes were closed.

"I was a little cross earlier, Savvie, but I'm fine now," she told her.

"How fine?" Savannah demanded, and Kasey saw the

concern in her eyes. This little girl didn't need to worry about her, as well.

"Fine fine." Wanting to distract her, Kasey danced her fingers up her ribs and Savannah giggled.

"No-oo, I'm ticklish. And if you don't stop tickling me, you won't get your present."

Kasey's hands immediately stilled. "Present?" She loved presents, probably because there had been so few as a kid.

"Where did'ja put it, Uncle Aaron?"

He cracked one eye open, dropped his hand and pulled a shoebox from beneath his seat. It wasn't wrapped, so Kasey presumed that Savannah made something at school and Aaron found her a shoebox to house the gift. She looked at the designer brand of running shoes and sighed. One day, maybe, she might be able to afford a pair of these top-flight running shoes. Kasey scowled at the puppies, thinking since hers were in shreds, any trainers would be an improvement.

Savannah took the box from Aaron and pushed it against Kasey's chest. "Open it."

It was probably a drawing or a papier-mâché sculpture or something made from Play-Doh, Kasey told herself. No matter what it was, she had to be excited purely because Savannah was wriggling around, beside herself with anticipation.

Kasey lifted the box and shook it, surprised at how heavy it was. Savannah tried to tug the box out of her hands, impatient. "I'll do it! You're too slow."

Aaron sat up and placed a gentle hand on Savannah's small shoulder. "It's Kasey's present, Savvie, remember? To tell her that we'll do better?"

A tiny frown appeared between Kasey's eyebrows. It sounded like Aaron had been involved in this present, like it might have even been his idea. Her eyes slammed into his and the corners of his mouth tipped up in that sexy half smile that made her want to crush her mouth against his.

"I think you should open it before Savannah loses her mind," Aaron suggested, laughter coating his words.

Kasey placed the box on Savannah's thighs, lifted the lid and gasped at the multicolored trainers nestling in thin white paper. They were too small for Aaron's huge feet and too big for Savannah's and—Kasey peered at the shoe size—exactly right for her. She let out an undignified "Whoop!" before lifting one of the shoes from the box. It was a trail shoe, the one she'd wanted forever, in her size, and the color was perfect.

It had been two hours since she'd lost her sense of humor and in that time, Aaron had ordered supper, cleaned and tidied up, bought and had delivered a pair of running shoes? Her eyes slammed into his. "How? Why?"

Aaron smiled. "The why is easy—one or both of the demented duo ate your shoe and the shoes needed to be replaced. The how was as easy. I called the sports shop in Royal, spoke to the manager, and the kid who delivered the food from the Royal Diner picked up the shoes, as well."

Kasey cradled the box and the little girl to her chest, looking over Savannah's head to the man who kept surprising her. She didn't know what to say but… "Thank you. You didn't need to."

"I really did," Aaron assured her as he stood.

Kasey looked up at him, six foot plus of pure gorgeousness. With that wide chest, big arms, narrow hips, those long, long legs, he was the complete package. But more than that, he was also chivalrous. And kind.

And, dammit, while resisting his body had been torture, stopping herself from wanting to inch closer to him emotionally was, she was sure, going to be the death of her.

* * *

Since tomorrow was Saturday, Savvie had begged to stay up late.

Instead of heading up to his office to catch up on some work or to cruise the web for any sign of his brother, Aaron had stayed downstairs and spent ninety minutes watching an animated movie about cars and planes.

A quarter of the way through the movie, Savvie had crawled between them and fallen asleep, her head on Kasey's thigh and her legs sprawled over his. When he glanced over ten minutes later, Kasey was also asleep, her thick eyelashes dark against her creamy skin. Thinking they looked comfortable enough, he let them sleep, knowing that if Jason or Will knew he was willingly watching an animated movie, they'd take away his man card.

Well, maybe Jason wouldn't, but his other friend would. Sleeping girls, ice cream and animated movies were not a normal part of his life.

But hell, nothing was normal anymore. He couldn't keep his hands off his employee…he was the owner of two hyperactive puppies… Savannah was a little happier but…

Jason was still missing.

The credits started to roll over the huge flat-screen on the wall opposite them as Aaron picked his phone off the side table next to him. He swiped his thumb across the screen to wake the device. He had emails, but when he opened the program, they were all work-related. There was nothing from Will or Cole.

Aaron tapped out a quick message to Cole and cc'd Will.

There must be something we can do. Some lead we aren't pursuing.

Will replied first.

Richard Lowell has, literally, taken over my life. Jason is one of my best friends. Do you honestly believe that we aren't doing everything possible to find them both and get some answers?

Aaron read the message and tapped the face of the phone against his forehead. When Will put it like that...

But Jason was his family, his blood. And he deeply resented the fact that he wasn't part of the search, that he was relegated to the sidelines. He wasn't a sit-on-his-haunches type of guy: when he went after something, he threw his entire self into it. He'd dropped out of college, knowing he would be okay, convinced that he was making the right decision. Sometimes he regretted not having that piece of paper but it certainly hadn't affected his earning ability. It had been so much more important to his folks than it had been to him, hence their overreaction when he'd told them he was quitting.

He'd turned to Kate for comfort and she'd given him all the sex he'd wanted—he'd been young and stupid and assumed that love and sex were the same thing—while plotting how best to shove the knife into his back. He glanced over at Kasey, thinking they were a matched pair; they'd both been royally screwed by people who'd said they loved them.

Aaron gently bent Savvie's legs back so that he could stand. He turned to face his two sleeping beauties. A tiny frown puckered Kasey's brow and he rubbed the side of his thumb between her eyebrows, wondering what she was dreaming about. Her useless ex and her devious friend? Kasey had thought he'd been joking when he'd offered to kick someone's ass earlier, but he hadn't been. He'd gladly rain a world of hurt down on Kasey's ex-husband and ex–best friend.

Aaron lowered his hand to cup Kasey's cheek.

Keep it tidy, Phillips, she's not asked for your help, nor your protection. She would not appreciate, nor does she need, your interference. She's strong and independent.

Aaron smiled despite himself. She was also stubborn and had a temper that made all his blood race south.

Don't go there, Phillips. Not if you want to keep your sanity.

He bent down, scooped Savvie up and cradled her against his chest. She sighed, turning into him, and Aaron felt his heart contract when she nuzzled closer and then seemed to fall into an even deeper sleep.

A wave of emotion passed over him and he rested his lips in her hair as he walked her across the room toward the stairs that led to the upper floor. He'd been the cause of her grandparents' death and he couldn't find her father, but he'd be damned if he'd fail Savannah; she would have the best he could give her.

Unfortunately, Aaron wasn't sure that was enough.

Five

Aaron's footsteps descending the wooden stairs woke Kasey up. Keeping her eyes half-closed, she watched him walk past her on his way to the patio, then heard the click of puppy nails on the tiled floor.

"Outside, you idiots!" Aaron hissed.

Kasey opened her eyes fully and got an eyeful of Kanga's curly face before his warm and very wet tongue slurped her cheek, just missing the side of her mouth. Aaron grabbed hold of his collar and yanked him away as Kasey sat up and wiped the back of her hand across her face. *Eww.* Slobby kisses and puppy breath. What a way to wake up.

Cursing, Aaron clapped his hands, pointed to the door and both the puppies hurtled that way, mistakenly thinking it was playtime.

Kasey looked at the black screen of the TV and then at her watch. "How long have I been asleep?" she asked, trying to swallow her yawn.

"For most of the movie," Aaron replied. Standing by the folding back doors leading to the entertainment area, he jerked his chin. "Savvie is soundly asleep, so come for a walk with me."

Kasey bit the corner of her lip, thinking a smarter move would be to mosey on up the stairs and into the guest bedroom. Alone.

But suddenly she wasn't tired and, after months of a mostly solitary existence, the last thing she wanted was to be alone. She wanted to take a night walk with Aaron, to look up at the stars, to feel the night air on her skin. She wanted to inhale the smell of newly cut grass, and roses... and, if she was lucky, occasionally get a whiff of Aaron's unique scent. That combination of deodorant and cologne and soap that always made her knees liquefy.

She wanted *him*...

Releasing a deep, enervating breath, Kasey pulled on her sandals and walked past Aaron, her eyes bouncing across the dark grass to look for the hell-on-wheels puppies. "I can't see them," she muttered, her eyes slowly adjusting to the darkness beyond the entertainment area and the pool.

"They've bolted toward the live oak and the pond."

"Why didn't you put lights in the garden?" Kasey asked as they began to stroll down the path that snaked through his parklike estate.

"Because I like walking in the dark," Aaron said, placing a hand on her back.

Kasey felt Aaron's hand cover hers, and his fingers slid between hers. Her shoulder brushed his and Kasey resisted the urge to lay her head on his shoulder as they walked. Heat, want and need flowed through her, making her nipples tingle, her mouth dry and her core ache. This much temptation was dangerous. If she made a move, and she'd have to because Aaron's integrity wouldn't allow him to, would he reject her again? Could she stand it? She didn't think so.

Kasey tried to tug her hand away. "I don't want you to trip," Aaron said, keeping a firm grip on her hand.

Kasey left her hand in his, knowing she wasn't going to fall and thinking that Aaron knew that, too. Maybe he, like her, needed the physical connection as much as she did. Besides, how long had it been since she'd walked hand in hand with a man late at night? Too long, Kasey decided. Definitely long before Dale—

She wasn't going to think of Dale tonight, Kasey told herself. Or Michelle. She just wanted to hold Aaron's hand and stroll with him in the moonlight.

They walked on in silence, reaching the wood bench under the live oak that shaded a koi pond. Kasey looked down into the dark, still water but couldn't see any fish moving. "Are they asleep?"

"The fish?" Aaron asked, humor lacing his voice.

"Yes, the fish."

"I remember the landscape designer saying something about them hanging out on the bottom of the pond at night. They might be sleeping or they could be playing poker... who knows?"

Kasey grinned and bumped her shoulder into his. "Ha, ha."

Roo, not understanding the concept of said creatures needing their sleep, ran down the bank and belly flopped into the pond. Kanga followed two seconds later. Aaron yanked Kasey back to avoid the splash of water, his low laugh rumbling over her.

Kasey looked up at him and thought that he looked ten years younger, and, for a brief moment, that he looked like he didn't have a care in the world. She desperately wanted to keep him laughing. "What did the fish say when it hit a concrete wall?" Before he could answer she dropped the punchline. "Dam."

Aaron's lips twitched and, without missing a beat, he lobbied his own back. "When you have any really good fish jokes, let minnow."

"Not bad, cod do better," Kasey quipped.

Aaron wrapped his arm around her waist, pulling her close, and she felt laughter rumbling through him.

Kasey tipped her head up in a silent challenge but he shook his head, looking rueful. "I've got nothing."

"Lightweight," Kasey murmured, her hands on his biceps. "I have about a million stupid jokes."

"Save them for later, sweetheart. Right now I have other plans for that mouth," Aaron murmured. As she expected him to, he hesitated before asking. "Are you okay with that?"

Again, his integrity, his need to do right by her, took her breath away. She wanted to tell him how much she appreciated his offer, him, but the words stuck in her throat.

Unable to speak, she simply nodded.

Still feeling a little light-headed from seeing her normally oh-so-serious boss cracking up at her childish jokes, Kasey felt her knees buckle when he pulled her stomach into his hips and she felt the evidence of his desire. His right hand palmed her butt cheek, and Kasey sucked in a deep breath, lust scorching her nerve endings. Then Aaron's mouth plundered hers, taking her mouth in a kiss that was all about desire, about the need to possess, to conquer, to brand. A part of her—that spirited, independent part that rebelled at losing control—wanted to pull back, but the rest of her, the 90 percent that was totally turned on, slapped that thought away. She was a woman being kissed by a man who knew how to do it properly and, damn, she was going to enjoy it.

Needing more, needing to get closer, Kasey looped her arms around Aaron's neck and boosted herself up his body, her legs winding around his waist. He held her easily and, while his mouth devoured hers, she reveled in the feel of his shaft rubbing her core.

Aaron slid his tongue past her lips and she sighed into his mouth: he tasted like heaven, better than chocolate, smoother than wine. Of heat and spice and sex…

And then his mouth left hers as he pulled back, lifting one hand to tug her shirt out of her pants, to pull it up her body to reveal the lacy cup of her bra. Kasey looked down, saw her nipple trying to push its way through the lace and lifted her eyes to Aaron's. She gasped at the rapt fascination on his face, loving the power of being a woman, able to make such a strong, usually somber, man stare in wonder. Gripping him with her legs but trusting him to hold her, Kasey crossed her arms over her torso and pulled the cotton shirt up and over her head. She heard Aaron's gasp of appreciation.

"You are so damn beautiful," he muttered and Kasey, in that moment, believed him. She watched as his hand cupped her breast, his thumb pulling the lace out of the way so that he could stroke her, all his attention on that one erogenous spot. And suddenly nothing was more important than having Aaron between her legs, inside her, filling the empty, lonely spaces inside her.

Aaron lowered his head and sucked her nipple into his mouth, rolling the bud between his teeth before drawing it to the roof of his mouth. He used his lips and tongue and teeth in a way that was, Kasey was convinced, designed to drive her mad. She arched her back, her fingers stabbing his hair, holding his mouth in place. He couldn't stop, but if he had to, then he needed to take that mouth south, to kiss her in places that had been neglected for far too long...

"Baby," Aaron murmured, his mouth moving up, running his tongue along the cords of her neck, the scruff on his face propelling fire into her veins. He shouldn't shave, ever... "God, you feel so good."

Kasey dropped her legs to the ground and scooted her hands up and under his shirt, needing to feel his warm skin, to explore those hard muscles. She felt free out here, in the darkness next to the pond. In the house she was reminded of Savannah and that it was a place where she worked, but out here under the cover of night, she was just Kasey, and Aaron wasn't her boss but just a man she wanted with a depth that astonished her.

Kasey pushed his shirt up and over his head, her mouth on his chest, skimming over one flat male nipple, through fine chest hair that covered his pecs and channeled into a dark trail that disappeared beneath his cargo shorts. Kasey followed the arrow, her hand gliding over that hard, hard six-pack and over his harder erection. Man, even covered in fabric he felt so big, so virile, every inch of him screaming that he was a man in the best, most primal way.

Aaron's hands went to work on the button of her pants, pulling the zip down before sliding his finger over her and finding—how did he do that?—where she ached. Kasey tilted her hips up and hooked her calf around his for some additional stability while the world, and everything in it, disappeared.

Aaron's fingers dipped beneath the seam of her panties and pulled them to the side, allowing him easier access to her grooves and folds. One finger slid inside her and Kasey released a strangled cry, half swallowed by Aaron when his mouth covered hers. His tongue picked up the same beat of his finger and she knew that she was close to orgasm, about to tip into that firestorm with or without him.

Aaron freed himself and pushed her pants to the ground. Walking backward, he sat on the edge of the deep-seated bench, pulling Kasey upward so that she straddled him, her core sliding against his freed shaft, warm and perfectly hard. She gasped and slid across him again before encircling him, lifting him to hold him against her. Aaron's hand on her thigh stopped her from rising and she raised her head to look at him, not sure why he wasn't as desperate to reach completion as she was.

Aaron muttered a curse and looked in the direction of the house. "I have condoms at the house."

Kasey wiggled against his fingers, trying to get her tongue to form the words. "I'm safe...on the pill. And I'm clean. You?"

"Same." Aaron clasped her face with one hand and forced her to look at him. "Even so, we should stop—"

"You don't have to."

That was all the encouragement he needed. Aaron gripped her hips and pulled her down so that the hottest part of her pushed against the hardest part of him again. Kasey couldn't stop her whimper as her hips, without her permission, started to slide against him.

"Use me, baby. God, you're so hot," Aaron whispered, lifting his hands to her breasts, his thumbs playing with her nipples. "Yeah, like that...hot, smooth, sexy."

Kasey felt herself soaring again, as if she were an electrical current, flying along heated wires. Placing her arms behind her head, she writhed against him, needing more, just a little nudge to push her into that all-consuming heat.

Aaron provided that nudge when he dropped his hand and sank his finger into her folds, rolling her clitoris under his thumb. Kasey's small scream broke the night and she arched her back, remaining utterly still as wave after wave of pleasure crashed over her. Shuddering, she wrapped her arms around his waist, desperate to hold on to those last remnants of pure, golden pleasure.

Making Kasey come made him feel like he was Atlas and easily able to carry the world.

Aaron sat straighter and wrapped his arms around her, resting his face in her neck. Conscious that he was still full and hard beneath her, he sighed as she pushed her fingers into his hair and murmured in his ear, "You make me feel so good, Air. I want to do the same for you."

God, yes.

But, also, God no.

Aaron silently cursed himself, wishing he could switch off his brain and just be with her. He couldn't use the excuse of her being his employee, she'd told him, through her words and her actions, that she was fully on board with anything, possibly everything, he wanted to do to and with her.

No, Kasey wasn't the problem, he was.

Aaron placed his hands on her hips and lifted her off him, keeping his hands on her until she was steady on her feet. Rising, as well, he tucked himself back into his pants before picking up her pants off the grass and shaking them out. Kasey adjusted her panties, took her pants and stepped into them. She pulled her shirt over her head and looked around for her sandals.

A few minutes passed, Kasey frowned and Aaron knew that she was feeling uncomfortable, possibly pissed off. He couldn't blame her. After Aaron pulled his T-shirt over his head and jammed his feet into his flip-flops, he lifted his head and looked at her.

"I swear, if you mention our working relationship, I

might have to hurt you." Kasey said, sounding resigned and, well, sad.

"I'm sorry, Kase. I know I'm blowing hot and cold, but I can't do this."

Kasey looked irritated and gestured to the still-rigid erection tenting his pants. "Excuse me if I don't agree with that stupid statement."

Aaron pushed an agitated hand into his hair. "Of course, I can do it. I just don't feel like I should!"

"As far as I am aware, we are both consenting, unattached adults. There is no reason why we can't have wild monkey sex as often as we like."

Except that it wasn't just monkey sex, that he could handle. It was the emotional connection he was in danger of making during said wild sex that scared him spitless.

He couldn't take that risk. Not again.

But he couldn't tell her that so he used another, equally valid excuse. Aaron pointed to the end of the driveway and to the high ornate gates leading to the road. "Somewhere out there is my brother and he's in a world of hurt. In that house is his daughter, who is confused at best and whose world might be torn apart for the second time in two years. She's getting attached to you, and that's problematic.

"I need to find out what's going on with my brother. I need to make Savannah feel as safe and secure as possible. I do not need to lie awake veering between fantasizing about you naked and crawling all over me and what I'm going to say at my brother's funeral."

Aaron sank to his haunches, his forearm across his bended knee, his head bowed. It was the first time he'd voiced his biggest fear aloud and he prayed that Kasey wouldn't brush his fears aside or urge him to be optimistic. Kasey dropped to the grass, sitting cross-legged in front of him, and placed her hand on his arm. "Is that what you think, Air? Do you think he's dead?"

Aaron lifted his head to look at her. Empathy, not empty sympathy, thank God. "Yeah." His voice sounded like he'd used sandpaper on his vocal cords. "I think he's dead."

Kasey just dropped her forehead to his arm, somehow knowing that small gesture of comfort was all he could deal with.

This amazing woman deserved his honesty, it was all he could give her.

"It would be so easy to lose myself in you, Kase. If we slept together again it would be so easy to pretend that this situation—you in my bed and living in my house—is real and the rest of it isn't." Aaron touched her head, unable to stop himself from playing with her hair. "It's a stressful situation and it's too easy to use you, to use the attraction between us, to hide. And there's the chance we'll start to think that something built on stress and sex and lust is real, when it's not. I can't do that. It's too dangerous. I have a child and a business to protect, a new normal to find.

"What I have to give isn't enough for you, Kasey. You deserve better."

Kasey didn't say anything and Aaron stared down at her head, waiting for her to respond, to chew his head off or to tell him that she understood. Kasey eventually lifted her head and sat back, the balls of her hands pushing into her temples. "One of the things I most admire about you is your honesty. After all the lies of the last few years, and despite the embarrassment factor of throwing myself at you, I am grateful for that."

"So, we're okay?"

Kasey shrugged. "Yeah, we're okay, Aaron."

He wasn't completely convinced but, feeling completely shattered, he'd take her half-hearted assurance.

Aaron stood and held out his hand in a silent offer to help her up. Kasey placed her hand in his, allowed him to tug her to her feet and immediately pulled her hand from his. "It's getting late and we ought to head back."

Aaron nodded. "Yeah, I still need to read your wind turbine research and make a decision about investing in that copper mine."

Back to business, Aaron thought glumly, a safe, neutral topic.

They started walking toward the house and Aaron whistled for the puppies. When the two bandits didn't appear, he whistled again and released a concise, one-word curse. "Dammit! Where the hell are they?"

He looked toward the house, saw two dark forms in the lounge and that they were fighting over a brightly colored shoe box. The box that held Kasey's brand-new trainers. Aaron released a curse and started to run.

Aaron pulled himself through the water, his arms aching and his thighs burning. After less than two hours' sleep, his normal gym session and forty-five-minute swim was punishing.

Reaching the side, Aaron did a quick, professional turn and flipped over onto his back, glaring up at the blue sky as he pulled himself through the water. Swimming was normally the time when he could check out, but all he could think about was the bliss on Kasey's face as she rode him, the moonlight on her creamy skin, the warm, sexy smell of her arousal, that keening sound she made when she came. Not throwing her over his shoulder and running her back to the house and straight into his bed was the hardest decision he'd ever made, but it had been, was still, the right one.

Aaron knew that Kasey wanted him, possibly as much

as he wanted her, but they were both adults and, as such, were old enough to realize that you didn't, or shouldn't, always get what you want.

Aaron slapped the wall, turned and belted back down the pool. Kasey intrigued him, made him want to dig beneath her layers to see what was below. And when he hit that layer, he wanted to dig down another... He suspected that Kasey was the type of woman you could spend a lifetime exploring and never be bored. For a man with a low tolerance for boredom, she was exactly the type of woman he'd look for...

If he was looking. Which he absolutely wasn't. He freely admitted that she was a confusing mixture of smart and sassy, vulnerable and proud, all contained in a very pretty package.

She also had the ability to melt his defenses, to decimate his control. And, maybe, that was the real reason he'd stood on the brakes last night, why he'd walked away from the offer in her eyes.

She made him lose control and forget, or dismiss, the hard lessons he'd learned about women and commitment and why he should keep himself emotionally detached.

His attraction to her wasn't only physical, he was fascinated by her brain, her past, and wanted to learn about how she came to be the person she was. Curiosity and attraction were a volatile combination and, as he'd learned with Kate, he'd be the one caught up in the explosion. Aaron had survived one blast, he wasn't fool enough to look for another.

Besides, a woman and a relationship was so far down his list of priorities it wasn't even on the page.

Out of the corner of his eye he saw Kasey walk onto the pool deck, dressed in a pair of denim shorts and a white, billowing cotton shirt that edged down one shoulder, showing off a pale pink bra strap. Last night's creation had been pale green. Aaron wondered how many matching sets she had and in what colors…

Kasey took a sip from the cup in her hand and waited for him to power his way to the end of the pool. When he reached the wall, he dropped his legs and stood.

"Hey."

Aaron pushed his hair off his face and nodded. "Hey." *Scintillating conversation, Phillips.*

"I just came down to tell you that I have to run to town. I need to pick up Savvie's birthday cake and supplies for the party later."

God, he'd forgotten that it was Savannah's sixth birthday party and that his house was about to be invaded by twenty giggling girls for a Princess Pool Party. How the hell had that slipped his mind since it was all Savannah could talk about lately? And, talking about his niece… where was she?

Kasey answered his question. "Hannah's mom offered to take her this morning so that we could run errands. Apparently trying to set up a kid's party with an excitable six-year-old running amok requires the skill of a five-star general or years of practice," she said, sitting on the closest lounger.

Aaron boosted himself out of the pool, his eyes on her face. Twin blue stripes ran under her eyes and her face looked a little pale. So he wasn't the only one who hadn't gotten much sleep last night.

He snagged a towel from behind her, beads of water from his body dropping onto her thighs and feet. Looming over her, and thanks to her blousy top, he had a perfect view down her chest. Yeah, yeah, he shouldn't, but he couldn't resist.

Kasey slapped her hand against her chest and cut off

his view. His sighed his disappointment and looked into her irate, whiskey-colored eyes.

"Seriously?" she asked, jumping to her feet.

Aaron shrugged as he wrapped a towel around his waist. "I'm a guy, it's what we do. And you're beautiful."

Kasey threw up her hands and Aaron jumped back as warm coffee hit his stomach and chest. Kasey released a low "Dammit!" and banged her cup onto the closest table, slapping her hands on her hips. Aaron saw determination cross her face and wished he'd kept his mouth shut.

"I'm done, Aaron. This isn't working."

Oh hell, no. If she told him that she was leaving, she would drop him, and Savannah, in a world of hurt. He was normally reticent to the point of rudeness and never ran his mouth, so what in the bloody hell had gotten into him?

"We need to come to an understanding," Kasey stated, her tone suggesting that he not argue with her. "This hot and cold can't go on."

Fair point. Aaron held her eyes and rolled his hand in a gesture for her to continue. "I haven't slept, Aaron, partly because I felt so damn guilty about last night. That I... had, um—you know!"

A small part of him was amused at her blush, at her incoherence when talking about sex. God, her husband had to have been a selfish prick. "Because you came and I didn't?"

Kasey didn't look grateful at his attempt to help her out. "Yes, *that*. You were left high and dry."

Aaron shrugged. He was a big boy, he'd coped. Taking care of himself wasn't much fun but it had helped...sort of.

"And, judging by the fact that you can't resist looking down my shirt and I am standing ten feet away from you because I can't jump you from here, this crazy attraction isn't going away!" Kasey pushed her hands into her hair and scowled. "Why now? We've had eight months together, why didn't it happen sooner?"

That was a no-brainer. "We didn't eat, work and live together, Kase. We hardly saw each other."

Kasey pulled a face. "Oh…right. And now the opposite is true."

Aaron nodded. "Seeing you in those sexy shorts and your flirty sundresses doesn't help," he added.

Kasey pointed a finger at him, waving it in the direction of his chest. "And I see you half-naked every morning. God, you're ripped."

Aaron saw the heat in her eyes and under his towel his junk jumped to life. Yeah, he liked the fact that she thought he was hot, but it didn't help in his quest to keep his hands to himself. Dammit.

"Aargh!" Kasey wailed. "You see, we both do it! You look down my shirt and I get distracted by your abs and those sexy muscles."

Aaron frowned. "What muscles?"

"These sexy hip muscles…" Kasey slapped her hands against her edges of her flat stomach before closing her eyes in frustration. "Seriously, I need a filter on my mouth."

Aaron picked up the T-shirt he'd left on the back of the lounger and pulled it over his head. When the shirt covered his stomach and his, apparently, sexy hip muscles, he quirked an eyebrow at her. "Better?"

Kasey glared at him. "Careful, your ego is showing." She gripped the edge of the wooden table behind her and nodded. "But yes, thank you. Marginally better. So, as I was saying…this can't go on, Aaron. As you know, from last night and my inability to construct a decent sentence this morning, I want you. And I'm pretty sure that you want me, too."

Only with every damn breath he took. "I shouldn't, but I do."

Kasey tipped her head to the side. "And we both agree that this is just about physical attraction, that neither of us needs, or wants, anything more?"

Aaron nodded, not trusting himself to speak. Was she really going there, about to suggest that they have a no-strings affair? Did he want that? Hell, yes. Could he handle it? Could he do a no-strings with Kasey?

That, he didn't know. That was his biggest fear. He didn't want to become emotionally entangled with her and it felt like he could, if he let himself. Sleeping with her would be like opening the door to that possibility. And man, he'd hate it if this fling caused her any pain down the line.

"What if we just explored this, did it a couple of times, let the fire burn itself out?" Kasey said. "And maybe try to do it in a bed this time?"

Only Kasey could find the humor in this awkward situation. Only Kasey would be brave enough to lay her cards on the table. Aaron appreciated her unflinching honesty, her ability to look at the situation and find a way to deal with it.

Kasey tossed her hair, her eyes still holding that fierce light of determination. "Because it will burn itself out, Aaron. It has to."

Aaron folded his arms and just looked at her. Yeah, the determination blazed hot and true, but beneath that emotion he could see want and need and more than a little fear. She wanted him but she was scared to feel this way. She spoke easily of a sexual relationship, but he had to make it very clear that there would never be anything else, that he had nothing to give her more than some hot nights and explosive pleasure. Or was he trying to convince himself?

Hell if he knew. But the words needed to be said; he didn't want any misunderstandings down the line.

Before he could find his words, Kasey plowed on ahead. "If we do this, then it's on the understanding that there will be no hard feelings if one of us calls it quits. No sulking, no temper tantrums, no snide comments. Just a promise to respect the decision and to go back to normal."

Would anything be normal afterward? He wasn't banking on it. He just planted his feet and lifted his eyebrows, knowing she had more to say.

"We still have a child in the house, so, by sunrise, we're in our own beds."

"Obviously," he replied.

"No one knows about this but us."

"That goes without saying."

Kasey shook her head. "I just don't want everybody to know that I'm sleeping with my boss, and you're the one who is connected to the people in this town. Hell, you're a member of the Texas Cattleman's Club."

Despite the wave of anticipation and excitement coursing through him at the thought of, finally, having her again, her comment irked him. "I'm not in the habit of blabbing about the woman I'm sleeping with, Monroe."

"Good to know," Kasey replied, ignoring his irritation. "No spooning when we're clothed. No casual physical affection. No flowers or pet names."

The demands kept sliding off her tongue, as easily as if she were reciting facts she'd garnered for him on a company or a stock. The thought hit him like a bolt out of the blue. Had she researched this? Taken advice from the internet on how to conduct a no-strings affair? Aaron narrowed his eyes. Yeah, he suspected that his very efficient assistant had spent part of the night doing online research. Aaron was partially amused and partially pissed off.

"No expectations, no commitment, no fighting." Kasey kept rolling through her list.

"Are you done yet?" Aaron interrupted her, keeping his voice neutral.

Kasey thought for a moment and nodded. "I think that's it. Is there anything you want to add?"

"Oh, do I actually get a say?" Aaron asked and waited until she nodded. "I'm honored."

Kasey's eyes flashed with indignation. "Don't be snippy."

"Don't be bossy," Aaron retorted. She didn't like taking orders, he suddenly realized. She did it, it was part of her job description, but Kasey preferred to be the one calling the shots, leading instead of following. He'd always been attracted to strong women. He became easily bored with people, men and women alike, who blindly followed where he led. Actually, come to think of it, since Kate, had he deliberately chosen women who were submissive, subconsciously giving himself an excuse to bail? Hmm, interesting.

"Well, what are your conditions? Once we know where we stand, we can talk about when and where," Kasey said, sounding impatient.

Oh, no, that wasn't the way this was going to happen. Their affair was not going to be something scheduled and monitored. If sex didn't happen organically, as a natural consequence to whatever situation they were engaged in, it wasn't happening. Kate had tried to control him using sex, there was no way he was going to let that happen again.

"Two things," Aaron said, walking over to her and only stopping when he was close enough to smell her delicate scent, to feel the tips of her breasts against his chest. He caught her chin in his hand and tipped her face up so that she had to gaze into his eyes. Her mouth looked so damn

inviting and her scent enveloped him, his hands wanting
to pull her shirt up and over her head, to drop those shorts
and plunge inside her. Telling himself not to be a complete
moron, he miraculously managed to tamp down his desire.

"This isn't a business deal or a stock trade. We'll sleep
together when it feels right, when we are so hot for each
other that we can't stand not to," Aaron told her.

Kasey tried to pull her chin out of his hand but he held
firm. He looked for any signs of her feeling intimidated
but her eyes only flashed annoyance. And underneath the
aggravation was hot and potent desire. And maybe, or was
he imagining this, the smallest hint of amusement at his
grasp for control of this situation. Reassured, he dropped a
hard, openmouthed kiss on her lips before speaking again.
His second statement was designed purely to annoy her,
a small punishment for forcing the issue, for making him
face up to the fact that he had no hope of resisting her.
"And I'm the boss. In bed and out."

He heard her exasperated gasp as he dropped his hand
and stepped away from her, turning to walk into the house.
At the doorway, he stopped and turned to look at her, still
gripping the table like her life depended on it. She looked
frustrated and irritated and turned on and pissed off, a
combination that nearly had him heading back to her. He
knew she was hot and wet and knowing that he could,
within a minute, be sliding inside her warm, secret places
filled him with awe.

Kasey held his hot look but Aaron could see the flutter
of her pulse in her neck, the heated flush on her cheeks.
Aaron wasn't even sure whether she knew that she licked
her lips. Was she imagining him picking her up, tossing
her over his shoulder and storming up the stairs with her?

It was a hot fantasy, and one he intended to play out in
the near future, but unfortunately that would have to wait.

He wanted to smile at her sour-lemon face but he kept his expression inscrutable. Just to keep her off balance, he tossed another conversational grenade at her feet. "I'll come with you and help you with your errands. Shall we leave in thirty minutes?"

"Do I have a choice?" Kasey demanded.

He knew she was really asking about his previous statement, about being the boss in the bedroom. He grinned. "Not even a little one."

Six

The journey back to Aaron's house was quiet and Kasey leaned forward to adjust the stream of cold air pouring out of the air-conditioner vents. She darted a look at Aaron and saw that he was looking at her, that infuriatingly sexy half smile on his face.

He looked confident and relaxed, everything Kasey wasn't feeling since she was having second, and third and fourth, thoughts. Should she tell him that she was unsure? She opened her mouth to speak but then he placed his hand on her bare thigh, his thumb drawing patterns on her bare skin.

Nope, she wanted this, she wanted him. No doubts allowed…

Kasey heard her distinctive ringtone, surprised to see that her phone had synced with the onboard display on Aaron's dashboard. She immediately recognized the number on the screen. Before she could tell Aaron to disconnect the call, he hit the button on his steering wheel and answered, his voice as steady and calm as always. "Phillips here."

After a beat of silence, Dale's voice filled the car. "I'm looking for Kasey. Who the hell are you and why are you answering her phone?"

Irritation flashed across Aaron's face and Kasey dived for her bag, trying to find her phone to cut off the call. "I'm her boss. Who the hell are you and what do you want?"

"I'm her husband. I want to talk to Kasey."

Kasey pulled the bag onto her lap as Aaron whipped the SUV into his driveway, stopped in front of the gates and pressed the remote control on his visor. The gates opened and Aaron steered the car up the long driveway. Anger suffused his face. "I thought you were divorced," he muttered, looking at her.

"I am," Kasey replied. Giving up her search for her phone, she ran a hand over her forehead. "What do you want, Dale?"

"Just a damned conversation. Is that too much to ask?" Dale tacked on a foul curse at end of his statement and Aaron's hands tightened on the steering wheel.

"Watch your mouth, moron," he growled.

"Dale, I'm hot and tired, and I really don't want to spoil my day talking to you," Kasey said.

"Listen, we need to discuss what happened, why our marriage ended. You need to understand that—"

Kasey looked at Aaron and slashed her hand across her neck. Aaron immediately disconnected the call and then pulled his car into his huge garage. He shut off the engine and sent Kasey an inscrutable look before getting out of the car and walking around the hood. However, instead of opening the back door to pick up the bags of supplies, as she'd expected, he yanked open her door, put his hands around her waist and physically lifted her from the vehicle.

Not allowing her feet to hit the floor, he leaned her up against the side of the car and crushed his mouth to hers, silencing the protest she was about to make. His tongue invaded her mouth, and all thoughts of Dale and what he wanted, or could want, and the heat and frustration of the day, melted away. There was only Aaron and he was kissing her, his hand moving up and under her short dress, long fingers digging into the soft skin on the inside of her thigh.

Aaron lifted his head and bent his knees so that he looked directly into Kasey's eyes. "You and me, Kase. I don't want you thinking about anything else except the way I make you feel."

Kasey nodded and Aaron went in for another kiss but her fingers on her lips halted his progress. "That goes for you, too. For a couple of hours, you have to stop worrying about Jason and Savannah." She repeated his words back to him. "There's just you and me."

Aaron pushed a strand of hair off her forehead and tucked it behind her ear. She saw gratitude in his eyes and tenderness. "Deal."

Kasey lifted her mouth to his, tracing her lips across his, the scruff of his beard tickling her in wickedly sensuous ways. "Let's get inside where it's cool," she suggested.

"I know the best place, and it's been a fantasy of mine since you first moved in." Aaron grabbed her hand and tugged her toward the entrance to the house.

Kasey looked back at the car, thinking of the birthday cake and Savannah's party supplies. "The cake will melt," she protested.

Aaron sighed, released her and opened the back door. Handing her a grocery sack, he lifted the Princess cake with one tanned hand and picked up the handles of the other bags. Jerking his head in a follow-me-and-hurry-the-hell-up gesture, he strode into the house. Putting the cake

in the cool oven where it was protected from the psycho canine twins, he took the bag from Kasey and dropped them
all on the granite surface of the island. Then, holding her
hand in his, he led her onto the outdoor patio.

Kanga and Roo barked their hellos and danced around
them, but Aaron ignored the puppies, tugging Kasey toward the pool. At the edge of the pool, he kicked off his
shoes, swooped Kasey up into his arms and jumped into
the refreshing water. As her head broke the surface, before she had time to protest, Aaron pulled her into him, his
mouth on hers, startlingly hot compared to the cool water.
Realizing that Aaron was standing, Kasey wound her legs
around his hips, ignoring the furious barks of the puppies,
who had no idea what they were doing.

She did and that was all that mattered. Kasey's dress
billowed in the water and she broke their kiss to pull the
fabric up and over her head, looking down to see that
her white bra and panties were now transparent. Aaron's
head was also bent and his hand cupped her left breast,
his thumb swiping her nipple through the fabric. Bending
his head, he drew it up into his mouth, the fabric an ir-
ritating barrier between her and his clever mouth. Kasey
used one hand to snap open the front clasp and her breasts
were freed to be loved by him.

Wanting him as bare as she was, Kasey pulled Aaron's
shirt over his head and allowed it to float away as she ran
her hands over his big, broad, muscled shoulders and down
his thick biceps. It had been so long since she'd had her
hands on him, she wanted to explore every inch of him.

But if he didn't stop tonguing her, driving her wild as
he switched from one breast to the other, she didn't think
she'd last long enough to touch him at all. Pushing her
hand between the band of his cargo shorts and his stomach,
Kasey felt Aaron suck in his breath as her hand slid down

his pants to encircle his thick shaft. Aaron went statue-still, sucked in a deep breath and laid his forehead on hers.

"God, I want you."

Kasey rubbed her thumb over his tip. "I can tell."

Aaron's hand pushed beneath the fabric of her bikini panties and his long fingers moved between her legs from behind and delved into the hot space between her legs. "You want me, too."

Kasey groaned as he found her bud and gently rubbed it. She arched her back and closed her eyes. "So much," she admitted, her voice low and hoarse. "I can't wait to have you inside me."

"Same here." He pressed a kiss to her forehead. "Do you trust me?"

With this, she did. She trusted him to make her feel wonderful. But she didn't trust him, or anyone, with her heart. "God, yes."

Aaron didn't waste any more time. He released her to undo the button on his pants, then kicked them away. Grabbing Kasey's wrist, he moved her to the side of the pool, to where the water came to his waist. He pushed her panties over her hips and when they were free, he placed both his hands behind her knees, spread her open and pushed into her. Kasey hooked her legs around his back, her heels digging into his butt cheeks.

The shock of pleasure danced through her as he filled her, quickly to be replaced by those insistent waves of pure bliss. Kasey felt herself building up, Aaron's sure, hard strokes taking her to the edge of the abyss. As soon as he felt she was about to tip over, he pulled back, keeping his hips still as he teased her mouth and her breasts. He was taking his time, driving her crazy, building her up and pulling her back. When she thought she had to come or lose her mind, Kasey wound her fingers in his hair, jerking his head back so that he had to look into her eyes.

"Now. Take me now," she ordered.

"Who said you were the boss?"

Kasey tried to come up with a smart-aleck reply but before she could, Aaron was pounding into her, rubbing the base of his shaft along her most sensitive spot and lifting her up, up, up. She was about to scream her frustration when he stilled, thinking he was pulling back, but then he lunged up and into her and Kasey felt herself tumbling, tumbling, exploding, realizing.

Stars exploded behind her eyes, galaxies formed and dissolved as the Big Bang started and ended along every one of her nerve endings. Aaron groaned and from a place far, far away, Kasey felt him tense and then release himself inside her. Holding him tight, she rode another wave of pleasure before dropping her head back and encountering the edge of the pool.

A warm, wet tongue licked her from the edge of her mouth to her temple and Kasey opened her eyes to look up into a pair of quizzical brown eyes. Kanga barked in her face and Kasey felt, and smelled, his warm puppy breath on her face.

Aaron's laugh rumbled over her as he placed his hand under her head and pulled her face into his neck. "I think the puppies had quite a show," he said, amused.

"I hope they aren't scarred for life," Kasey replied as he detached himself from her.

"I'm sure they'll be fine," Aaron said, turning his head to softly kiss her lips. "Kase, that was…"

He didn't seem to be able to find the words but his face told her that he'd loved making love as much as she had.

"I know, it was amazing," Kasey whispered, her breasts rubbing against his chest. She dropped her feet to the floor of the pool and slicked her hands over her head, pushing her hair back. Aaron reached for her hand to pull her back into his embrace, tucking her against his side as he rested his back against the wall off the pool, bending his knees so that the water covered his shoulders. "This water is divine."

Kasey placed her head on his shoulder, laughing when Kanga pushed his snout into Aaron's neck before resting his chin on Aaron's tanned shoulder. She grinned. "Aw, he just wants to cuddle." She sent him a teasing smile. "I like the way you cuddle, Phillips."

Aaron grinned as he lifted his arm to hook his hand around Kanga's head. "Well, I am a really great cuddler."

Kasey dropped her hand to his thigh and rubbed it in a long, smooth stroke, loving the long, hard muscles under his skin. "You really are. So, would you like to…cuddle… me again?"

Roo, the maniac, barked once before launching himself into the pool, quickly followed by Kanga. Aaron shook his head before turning to look at her. "If by cuddle you mean make love to you until you are boneless, then hell to the yes."

Well, all righty, then, Kasey thought, resting her arms along the side of the pool, laughing as she watched Aaron referee the fight between the puppies over his shorts.

He was, after all, the boss.

Not that she'd ever admit that to him.

Later that afternoon Aaron stood in the doorway to Kasey's bedroom, watching her shove pins into her hair and smiling at the occasional curse that slipped past her lips. A black, silky dressing gown hit her mid-thigh and was belted at the waist, giving him hints of a strapless lacy bra and that spectacular cleavage he'd tasted and teased. Kasey pulled a pin out of her mouth, jammed it into her hair at the back of her head and whipped around, slapping her hands on her hips.

"He gave you twenty minutes' notice?" she demanded, although she already knew the answer to her question. "Who does he think he is?"

"He's Mark Ward," Aaron replied, leaning his shoulder into the door frame. "He's an investor I've been courting for two years, one of the richest men in the country, and I want to put some of his cash to good use." For the second time in five minutes, he looked at his watch. If they didn't leave in the next fifteen minutes, they were going to be late, and he'd heard that tardiness irritated Ward. "I'm lucky that he called while Megan was still here and that she was happy to take Savvie for the evening."

"I really like your sister," Kasey commented.

"She likes you," Aaron said, thinking about how Kasey and Megan had worked so well earlier to make Savannah's party one the little girl would never forget.

"C'mon, Kase, hurry it up," he muttered. Partly because he didn't want to be late but also because looking at her in that curve-hugging dressing gown was a temptation he was finding very hard to resist.

Kasey glared at him. "You told me we were going out twenty minutes ago. In fifteen minutes, I have showered and dried my hair and even managed to do something with it."

Aaron looked at her piles of meticulously arranged curls and wished he could blow off this dinner, pull her onto that bed and scatter those damn pins all over the room. Rich investor, Aaron reminded himself. Important. He'd had her twice before the party and once during the party when they'd left Megan on kid duty for ten minutes and, God, it had been so damn hot. He should be able to keep his hands off her for a few hours but…nope. Not happening.

Get your head in the game, Phillips.

Kasey sat on the stool in front of the dressing table and picked up a square black box, flicking it open with practiced ease. Picking up a tiny brush, she stroked gray powder across her eyelids. "Why am I involved in this madness? You can go on your own and I can watch an adult movie while working my way through a massive bowl of popcorn."

Aaron lifted an interested eyebrow. "An adult movie?" he teased.

Kasey sent him another scowl. "Something that isn't PG-rated. Something with a lot of ass-kicking and a couple of explosions."

She was an action-movie type of girl. Good to know.

"Mark's wife is a foodie and she's been wanting to eat at the Glass House for a while. He thought that while he was in Royal, we could meet to see if we click enough for us to explore the possibility of doing some deals together."

Kasey continued to work on her eyes and Aaron was happy to watch her. He just wished she'd hurry it up. "And you couldn't handle him by yourself?"

"I could, but he invited me to bring someone, made it very clear that this was a social evening."

Aaron wanted to ask her why women opened their mouths when they applied mascara but didn't want to hold up the process by talking.

"Where are we going again?" Kasey asked, dabbing her cheeks with blusher.

"The Glass House is an upscale farm-to-fine-dining restaurant situated within the Bellamy, which is Royal's newest, and hippest, resort. It's reportedly getting rave reviews."

"Well, if I don't get to see a hot hero kicking butt, at least I'll get a good meal," Kasey grumbled. She stood and

Aaron sucked in a heated gasp. Kasey didn't normally use much makeup—she was naturally gorgeous and didn't need to—but her smoky, sexy eyes were a punch to the stomach. She looked sophisticated and timelessly alluring.

Standing in the doorway, shoulder pressed into the door frame, watching her applying her makeup felt normal; worse, it felt right. It was almost as if he was watching a clip advertising what his future could look like, complete with a stunning woman and a precocious little girl. Aaron rubbed his hands over his face, annoyed with himself. One afternoon of stunning sex and he was already a basket case, allowing himself to fantasize over what could never be.

They'd agreed, made a friggin' pact! They'd agreed to not become emotionally attached, this was a no strings affair, something that would end. Not even twelve hours had passed since that discussion and he was already looking for a ball of twine. No. He wasn't going to let that happen, he wasn't going to put himself in the position of needing her and relying on her.

As much as he liked Kasey, and he also respected the hell out of her, he couldn't trust her, or anyone, with his heart or his life.

"Are you okay?"

Aaron's head shot up at Kasey's quietly stated question. "Fine, why?"

"No regrets?" she asked, looking down at her tube of lipstick.

Kasey had the uncanny ability to sense his unease and he didn't like feeling that exposed.

"I'm fine."

Aaron saw her quick frown at that overused word and knew that he had to distract her from asking a follow-up question. They didn't have the time, and he certainly had no inclination, for any non-superficial conversation. "I'm just regretting that there's no time to make use of your bed."

Kasey smiled and his heart flipped over. Aaron sighed, he still really, really wanted to put that bed to good use. To keep from walking across the room and ruining her hard work by kissing her senseless, he glanced at his watch again. They really needed to leave, mostly because he was five seconds away from blowing Ward off altogether.

Kasey walked into the huge closet, pulling the door closed behind her. God, wanting her was killing him, inch by heated inch. Despite their earlier interludes, he wanted to spend the night taking his time, rediscovering every creamy inch of her. It had been ninety minutes but it seemed much longer since he'd touched her. Feeling, attraction, flat-out desire slapped him with the force of a sonic boom. He loved the tender skin behind her ear, hearing her sharp intake of breath when he nibbled her collarbone. Her birthmark low on her back that looked, and tasted, like a strawberry. Her long, finely muscled legs, her sensitive, pretty toes. And all those feminine secret folds that held her passion, her essence, that seemed to crave his touch.

Aaron rested his forehead on the door frame, conscious of the throbbing and rock-hard pipe in his pants. Yay, all he needed was to meet Ward with a hard-on—that would make a good impression.

Forcing his thoughts elsewhere, Aaron recalled the day, and remembering Kasey's devastated face when she'd heard her ex's voice in his car was an effective way to diminish his hard-on. He believed her when she told him that she was over her ex but she was still dealing with their betrayal. Hey, Aaron wasn't about to judge her, a decade had passed and he still hadn't come to terms with his parents' deaths and Kate's duplicity. But Kasey only allowed him glimpses of her pain, only revealed the first layer of her despair but refused to allow him to dig any further.

That he wanted to know more, a lot more, about her irritated him. She fascinated him, always had, right from the beginning, and he'd only managed to keep things professional because he'd valued her sharp mind and business skills. And because they had, despite working closely together, worked out of separate premises. The few times they had met Kasey had walked around with a *Don't go there, it didn't happen* attitude, utterly and completely professional at all times.

But things had changed since she'd moved in here, into his space, and he'd felt the ropes keeping her so tightly controlled loosening. Maybe it was Savvie. Maybe, like him, Kasey had tired of fighting their attraction, but she was thawing...

And, by sleeping together, they'd just stoked the raging fire between them. It had the potential to become an uncontrollable wildfire but he didn't have the faintest idea, or the smallest inclination, to put it out. If he ended up burned to a crisp, it would be his own damn fault.

Kasey stepped out of the closet and Aaron felt his heart quicken. The dress was sleeveless, skimmed her curves and was covered in gold and bronze sequins. And it was short, showing off a lot of her long, slender, spectacular legs. Those legs, the ones he wanted—again!—wrapped around his hips ended in gold-and-black, super-high spiked heels.

Aaron couldn't decide whether to howl his approval or to beg her to change into a nun's habit. He couldn't breathe, but then again, who needed air when he had Kasey to look at?

Kasey picked up a small bag off her bed, tossed in a tube of lipstick and her phone, and tucked it under her arm, a tiny scowl appearing between her eyebrows. "If you don't like what I'm wearing, then tough because I don't have anything else and I would love an excuse to stay here and stretch out in front of the TV."

He wasn't about to say anything. How could he since he'd lost the ability to suck in air? Kasey walked up to him and tapped the watch on his wrist. "Half an hour from soaking wet to ready to rock. You should be impressed, Phillips."

Aaron opened his mouth to tell her he was, that she impressed the hell out of him, but then he saw her bare back and noticed the glittery sequins ended low on her back, just before the flare of her delicious ass.

It was official, the woman was trying to kill him.

Seven

Aaron so owed her, Kasey decided, looking down at her exquisite plate of rare Wagyu beef. Apart from the fact that he didn't make a comment on how she looked—and, dammit, she looked pretty fine—he was also quieter than usual, leaving her to carry the conversation with Mark and his wife. Although naturally quiet, when he needed to, Aaron could work a room with charm and flair and she knew that he was a hell of a conversationalist. The Wards were funny and down-to-earth, despite having squijillions in the bank, and they were a captive audience as she told them what little she knew about Royal and the surrounding countryside.

Kasey took a tiny bite of her beef, sighing her appreciation, as she saw the restaurant manager approaching. While he answered Fiona's questions about the menu and the chef, Kasey took the opportunity to grind her heel into the side of Aaron's foot. As she expected, he pulled away abruptly and narrowed his eyes at her. "What the hell was that for?" he demanded on a low whisper.

"Can you please focus? I'm running out of conversation here!" Kasey muttered, keeping a smile on her face. "What is wrong with you? You need to impress this man and you can't do that if you don't show him that you have a brain underneath that pretty package."

Aaron's mouth quirked up. "You think I'm pretty?"

"Pretty? No. Infuriating, annoying and gorgeous? Yes," Kasey replied. "Just get your head in the game! You're going to lose this opportunity if you don't."

Kasey kept half an eye on the manager and their companions, prepared to give her attention back to them in a heartbeat.

"It's your fault, you know," Aaron said, blotting his mouth with a fine linen napkin to cover his low-pitched words. "That dress could be used as weapon."

Kasey smiled slowly. "You like it?"

"Sure, I like it. But the body inside it is nuclear."

Kasey met his molten green gaze. In his eyes, she could see him naked, rolling her over and sliding into her. "Will you stop doing that?" she demanded, blushing.

"Doing what?" Aaron asked, making a stab at looking innocent. At six-three and built like a running back, it wasn't a look he could pull off.

"Seducing me."

Aaron's big hand covered her thigh, his warm fingers an inch or so from her happy place. "Yeah, that's a problem. Not sure I can do that."

Wanting to throw her arms around his neck and press her mouth to his—something that the smart and sophisticated patrons within the restaurant, and the Wards, wouldn't appreciate—Kasey folded her napkin and laid it on the table. She needed to take a walk, to get some air, to calm the hell down. Bathroom break, she thought. That would give both of them a chance to remember that they were responsible adults and why they were here.

Kasey excused herself, ignoring Aaron's raised eyebrow, and proceeded to saunter across the restaurant, utterly unaware that every male eye in the place was watching her long-legged walk.

And Aaron didn't like that... At all.

"Charming girl," Mark said, swirling the red wine in his glass.

His words only made sense to Aaron when Kasey's heart-shaped butt, long legs and slim frame disappeared from view. Dammit, Kasey was killing his brain cells one chunk at a time. Aaron gave himself a mental punch to the head and met the older man's eyes. He was about to say something innocuous when, surprisingly, another set of syllables left his mouth. "She's driving me nuts."

Fiona laughed and Mark grinned. "We can see that."

Aaron started to apologize and Mark held up his hand, still smiling. "No, please, that wasn't a criticism. Actually it was reassuring to know that you are not a work-obsessed, driven clone. I meet so many of them. Basically they are robots walking around in suits."

He could be like that, Aaron thought, he normally *was* like that. However, in his defense, he didn't think that any man could sit next to Kasey and think of business when she was wearing a dress like that. Feeling his phone vibrate in his jacket pocket, Aaron automatically reached for it, his thoughts immediately going to Jason and then to Savannah.

"My apologies, I do have to check this message." His heart lifted when he realized that it wasn't Megan and that meant everything had to be fine with Savannah. But it sank a second later when he realized the message was from Will. Could it be about Jason? Had they found him? Only one way to find out, Aaron decided, and anxiously opened the message.

Cole and I are at the ranch, brainstorming Jason's disappearance. Care to give your input? Maybe you'll catch something we've missed.

Aaron fought the impulse to stand, call for the bill and head out to the ranch. However, as much as he wanted to do that, he still had a responsibility to his business and he had to drop Kasey off at home. Aaron typed a quick Sorry, could come by later message and tucked his phone away.

He pushed his hand through his hair. "That was rude. I'm sorry, but let me assure you that it is necessary to keep my phone on.

"And I apologize if I've been rude and distracted tonight," he added, keeping his voice even and genuinely apologetic. "It's been an…unusual time and I'm a little unfocused." Not wanting Ward to think that his brain turned to mush at the sight of a pretty girl, he held up his hand. "It's not an excuse but I've had some personal issues that have cropped up."

"Your brother's disappearance for one," Mark said. Aaron was surprised when the gentleman leaned back in his chair, looked him in the eye and murmured, "I wish there was something I could do to help, but I suspect you've done all that you could. I just hope you find him soon."

"Not knowing must be hell," Fiona said, briefly touching his hand with hers.

"It is," Aaron replied. It was easy to talk to these people, he thought, nearly as easy as it was to talk to Kasey. "I'm looking after his daughter, with Kasey's help, and I lie awake at night, wondering what or how I'm going to tell her…"

"Do you think he's in danger?" Mark asked him, straight-out and to the point. Aaron appreciated his not dancing around the issue.

He should just shut up but the steadiness and genuine empathy in their eyes kept him talking. "My heart doesn't want to think that, but my head is telling me otherwise. There's been no activity on his cards, none on his phone. I start thinking the worst and then I feel guilty for losing the faith, telling myself that I can't think like that until I have proof. It's a mess."

Aaron tried to smile and tugged at his collar, wishing he could just stop the words from tumbling from his mouth. It was because these people reminded him of his parents, he realized. They listened to him the same way, both of them tuned in and focused. Damn, that was the first good memory he'd had of his parents in a long, long time.

Aaron sighed. "Honestly, I shouldn't have agreed to dinner tonight. Coupled with Kasey in a sparkly dress… and I'm distracted. I'm better at investing money than my performance tonight shows."

Mark shook his head. "Your reputation and résumé speak for themselves, Phillips. I never doubted your ability to manage my money."

Fiona sent her husband a loving look and leaned forward. "Mark likes men who are real, Aaron. He's researched you, as you have him. I can promise you that if you were effortlessly charming, all over him like a rash, he would've walked away from you in a heartbeat. He prefers genuine to fake and the fact that you are sensitive enough to be worried about your brother and confused by a pretty girl is reassuring, not disappointing. My husband doesn't like robots."

Good to know. Aaron ran his finger around the collar of his open-necked shirt, now feeling more than a little uncomfortable at the turn of the conversation. He was happy that it didn't seem like he'd totally blown this meeting but he wasn't thrilled at being called sensitive.

Looking away from Fiona's warm brown eyes that seemed to see way too much, he suppressed his sigh of relief when Mark changed the subject, taking the spotlight off him. His potential client asked him to identify some of the people in the restaurant and Aaron leaned back in his seat, his eyes skipping over the strangers he didn't know. He pointed out a few of the members of the Texas Cattleman's Club, giving Mark a brief background on the movers and shakers in the room.

Aaron looked into the far corner of the room, idly noticing a tall man rising to his feet. Will's back was to him and he thought that his friend must've had a haircut since he'd last seen him, his hair was army short. The rest of his table rose to his feet and, through the crowd, Will turned his head and Aaron noticed that he was wearing glasses with a heavy black frame. Haircut and glasses, Aaron mused wryly, they were definitely getting old.

"More wine, Aaron?" Mark asked.

He looked back to his host, who was holding a bottle of Château Latour Pauillac, one of his favorite vintages. He started to nod, then covered his glass with his hand. "I'm driving us back home so I shouldn't."

And he needed to have all his wits about him if he was going to look at Cole's case notes, discuss Jason's disappearance—

Aaron frowned and looked across the room again, not seeing the tall man he'd thought was Will. The group had left the restaurant, the man he'd mistaken for Will had probably left with them. Because Will was at the ranch, with Cole, talking about the investigation. Last time he checked, Will couldn't be in two places at once.

Too much sex, stress and too little sleep, Aaron thought. He was seeing things.

"Everything okay, Aaron?" Mark asked, looking concerned.

From somewhere deep inside him Aaron pulled up a smile, but seeing that Mark's expression didn't change, he didn't think he was fooling anyone. He shook his head, glanced across the dining area once more and shook his head again. "I think I might be going mad," he said.

"All the best people do," Fiona reassured him, laughter in her voice. "Here comes your girl."

A couple of hours later Kasey thanked Mark for supper and was surprised when, instead of shaking her hand, Fiona held her arms and dropped a light kiss on her left cheek and then her right. "It was so lovely meeting you, Kasey. I do hope we do this again soon."

"I hope so, too. I had a lovely evening, thank you."

Aaron offered to walk the Wards to the entrance of the restaurant, where the valet had their car waiting, so Kasey excused herself to go to the restroom to freshen up. Like the rest of the venue, the restroom was beautifully decorated and in the corner were two wingback chairs covered in what looked to be silk, a delicate table between the two chairs. Her feet were aching and the chairs looked terrifyingly comfortable, but Kasey knew that if she sat, she might never get back up. She was exhausted, mentally and physically wiped out.

Kasey washed her hands, saw that her makeup was holding up and reapplied her lipstick, jumping when she saw Michelle's reflection in the mirror next to her own. Instead of turning around, Kasey frowned at her reflection. "Are you stalking me?"

"Oh, get over yourself! I was having a drink at the Silver Saddle—"

"Where?"

Michelle looked impatient. "It's the bar adjacent. I heard that Aaron and you were eating at the restaurant and you always visit the restroom before leaving a restaurant, so I took a chance. See how well I know you?" Michelle replied, moving to stand next to Kasey and placing her butt against the counter holding the basins.

Kasey sighed. "Why are you still in town, Michelle?"

"I told you that I was thinking about relocating to Royal for the short term."

"So that you can win me back?" Kasey dropped her lipstick back into her bag and tucked it under her arm.

"Partly." Michelle shrugged. "I like the town and I'm interviewing at Pure, they have an opening for a specialist masseur. I'm waiting to hear whether I got the position."

"Well, if they were interviewing for someone who slept with her best friend's husband, you'd already have the job." The words left Kasey's mouth and she immediately regretted them because tears filled Michelle's eyes and hung, like perfect little jewels, on the bottom row of her eyelashes. When Kasey cried, her eyes swelled and she looked like a piglet, but Michelle looked as perfect as ever.

"When are you going to forgive me, Kase? It was one time. We were drunk. I don't remember any of it. It just happened." Michelle placed her hands on the counter and stared down at the floor. "You've been my best friend since I was ten. I love you and I miss you, but you're so damn stubborn!"

Was she making too big a deal of this? she asked herself yet again. Was she throwing away her best friend because she was making this out to be more than it was? Was she being naïve?

"I was wasted. I remember climbing next to him on the sofa, thinking that I just wanted to be held. I don't remember much else."

Kasey shifted from foot to foot, wanting to walk out but unable to. She rubbed the back of her head. "I don't think you realize how much you hurt me, Mish. What you did was inexcusable."

"I didn't mean to and I was parrot-face drunk. Surely that counts for something? Don't you miss me at all? Is one night worth throwing away everything we meant to each other? We spent every summer together, we chose the same college so we could be together. We shared an apartment. We did *everything* together."

Dale used to complain about the excessive amount of time she and Michelle had spent together, along with frequent barbed comments about the fact that Kasey carried Michelle financially. Michelle was always short of cash and Kasey had bailed her out more times than she could count.

But having Michelle in her life, someone who knew her inside and out, the only link to her past and her grandparents, had been worth the money she'd thrown in her direction. She was funny, loving and kind, and such fun to live with.

Kasey hung her head. "I can't just wipe it away."

"Don't you miss me, miss us?" Michelle whispered.

Kasey couldn't answer her, knowing that if she did, she might just forgive her. She wasn't ready to do that, not just yet. Or maybe she was and that was what scared her more.

Michelle sent her a teary smile, squeezed her hand before walking toward the exit.

Kasey slumped against the counter and winced when she heard a toilet flush and then a door to a stall opening. Blushing, she looked to her right and saw the beautiful and sympathetic face of a woman with her long hair tucked under a white ball cap. Her chocolate-brown eyes radiated sympathy.

Kasey waited for the gorgeous stranger to make a comment but when she stayed silent, she shrugged. "Sorry about that. As you heard, I have the worst taste in men."

The woman nodded as she approached the basin to wash her hands. "And friends."

Kasey couldn't argue with that.

"I'm Danica Moore, by the way, Dani to my friends. I'm the executive chef here at the Glass House."

"I'm Kasey," Kasey told her. "That Wagyu beef was extraordinary."

Pleasure flashed in Dani's eyes. "Thank you, I appreciate that." Dani hesitated before asking her next question. "So, let me get this story straight—your friend slept with your man?"

"Yep, my best friend had a drunken encounter with my husband. They both said that they were too wasted to know what they were doing."

"Ouch." Dani rinsed her hands, her face thoughtful. "But she was sober enough to remember that she was lonely, that she wanted to be held? Forgive me, but that explanation sounds fishy."

Huh, Kasey thought, she hadn't thought of that.

"Her actions hurt you more than your husband's infidelity did," Dani said, drying her hands.

Kasey blinked back her tears. "I want to forgive her and I want her back in my life, but I can't pull the trigger and tell her that."

Dani shook her head. "You don't really want to forgive her. What you really want is for life to roll back to what it was like before."

Kasey thought of being married to Dale and shuddered.

No, she far preferred to be around Aaron, big, and self-contained. And so damn honest. She always, always knew where she stood with Aaron. But yes, Dani was right in that she wanted to obliterate any memory of what Michelle had done or for it to have not happened at all.

Dani touched her shoulder. "Listen, one thing I know is that you can't look back, you can't live in the past. You have to deal with reality, today. Now."

"Reality blows," Kasey whispered, knuckling away a tear. She glanced at herself in the mirror and just from a few tears her eyes were horror-film red. *Perfect*.

Dani smiled. "Yeah, sometimes it does. But you look like a strong woman who can handle whatever is sent your way."

"I need to get back to work," Dani added as they walked out of the restroom. She glanced at Kasey and grinned. "You really don't cry well, honey. You look all blotchy and orange-eyed."

"Thanks," Kasey retorted.

Dani smiled and held up her hands. "Sorry, I call it as I see it. On that note, I know that you don't want to hear this…but your friend? She's playing you. Be careful, Kasey."

Yeah, that was exactly what she didn't want to hear.

Aaron woke up with the early-morning sun in his eyes and buried his face in the crook of Kasey's neck, holding her naked body close to his. She was his perfectly matched puzzle piece, her head under his chin, her bottom curled into his groin, his legs tucked beneath hers. After more than a decade of waking up alone, holding her, breathing her in, felt good, Aaron thought. It felt *right*.

The last time he'd felt this content, even happy, with a woman was in those early days with Kate, before she'd screwed him over. Kasey was Kate's intellectual equal but his ex didn't have a fraction of Kasey's natural warmth. Kate had only one priority, her own well-being, while Kasey put everyone else's needs before her own. Kasey wanted to believe the best of people. Why else would she be trying to find an excuse to reboot her friendship with her best friend?

Aaron was a black-and-white type of guy while Kasey saw the world in shades of gray, he thought, cupping her soft, warm breast in his hand. Despite being hurt and betrayed, she was far more tolerant than he was and that made her vulnerable. Something about her friend moving to the same town Kasey had relocated to, the way she kept "bumping" into Kasey, made him leery and suspicious. It was almost stalker-ish...

Aaron frowned, acknowledging there was a strong possibility that her friend might hurt her again. And if that happened, he would kick some ass. Nobody, including him, would hurt Kasey if he could prevent it. There had been too much failure in his life: he'd hurt his parents, he'd allowed Kate to play him, he'd failed to protect Megan from Will's impostor...

Well, Kasey *would* be protected, no matter what it took. Maybe he could get Cole, or one of his associates, to look into Michelle and her life, to see if there was some ulterior motive behind her behavior...

But was that going a step too far? They were sleeping together, just having sex, she didn't need or want him interfering in her life and snooping into her friend's motives was way over the line they'd drawn in the sand.

Aaron sighed, thinking that, as per usual, nothing was ever simple. He and Kasey were supposed to sleep together and extinguish his fire for her, but his desire for her was nowhere near close to burning out. Yeah, sex was a brilliant distraction from his fears about Jason's safety and raising Savannah on a full-time basis, but every time he slept with Kasey he felt closer to her, emotionally as well as physically. With every kiss, he wanted more, wanted to sink into her strength, open up to her about his past and his fears...

He didn't know if he had it in him, but for the first time in...well, forever, he felt the urge to trust *somebody*.

Kasey wiggled in his arms and he heard her yawn.

"I can hear you thinking," she complained.

Aaron placed his lips in her hair. "Sorry, baby."

Kasey stroked his forearm. "Don't apologize, I know how much you have on your mind."

"Actually, I was thinking about you and your friend," Aaron admitted.

Kasey rolled over onto her back, her whiskey-colored eyes puzzled. "Why?"

Aaron pushed a strand of hair out of her eyes. "I don't trust her."

Kasey's smile didn't reach her eyes. "You don't trust anyone."

Aaron opened his mouth to tell her his earlier thought, that he was on the point of trusting her, but self-preservation had him pulling the words back. "Just like you."

"I trust you more than I do anyone else," Kasey admitted, turning on her side to face him. Her hand drifted over his hip and he felt the blood drain from his head.

"Ditto, honey." Aaron dropped his mouth to hers, pushing the words out against her lips, knowing that they had to be said. "But I'm giving you as much as I can."

Or, he silently amended, as much as he'd allow himself to. Because if he handed over his trust, his heart... if he laid it all at her feet and she stomped on it, he didn't think he would recover. Kasey wasn't the kind of woman a man recovered from.

She curled her arm around his neck, sadness in her eyes. "I know you are and I'm not ready for more, personally. But professionally…?"

Aaron frowned at her, puzzled. "Yeah?"

"This is probably the wrong time to bring this up, seeing that I am naked and we're not in the office, but—" Kasey wrinkled her nose and shook her head. "Forget it, it'll keep."

Aaron shook his head, intrigued. "No, go for it. Say what you think."

Kasey sat up and pulled the sheet over her chest, hiding her pretty breasts from his view. Holding the sheet with one hand, she tucked her hair behind one ear, then the other. Taking her time, she wiggled her butt before blurting out the words. "It hurts that you don't trust me with the names of your richest clients. Every time I enter their stupid code words into the system, when I'm capturing data, it's like standing on a rusty nail. I would never release that information, Aaron. Those names are safe in my mouth, in my hands."

Aaron pushed himself up, surprised by her vehemence. "I didn't realize it bothered you so much."

Kasey lifted her slim shoulders. "It shouldn't but it does. I'm big on honesty. I pride myself on my integrity and I've worked for you for eight months. You not trusting me fully, on a professional basis, stings."

Aaron rubbed his stubble-roughened jaw, turning her words over in his mind. If he was in the same position, would he feel the same? Probably, he admitted. "It's not you, Kase, it's me."

Her amber eyes darkened with annoyance at what she thought was a cop-out. He held up his hand, silently asking for her to wait, to listen. He'd never told anyone about Kate, preferring to keep his broken heart and dented pride to himself. He just needed a minute to work out what, and how, to explain.

"I was trading in the last year of college and my—" how to describe Kate? "—*partner* and I were very successful, very quickly. About six months before I was due to graduate, I dropped out to focus on the business. My folks died unexpectedly and a few months after that, my partner absconded from the business, taking our clients and leaving me with nothing." He released a breath. "Long story short? I've worked with numerous people over the years, done many deals, had a few employees. I've never told anybody who my top ten are."

Kasey smoothed the sheet over her thighs, her head bent. After a long time, she lifted her head and tried to smile. "I understand. I do, I know what it feels like to be betrayed. But…"

"I'm sorry." Aaron placed his hand on her knee. He dropped his head to place an openmouthed kiss on the bare skin of her shoulder. "I want to, Kase, but habits die hard. I don't know if I'll ever get there."

Kasey nodded and when she averted her gaze, regret twisted through him. Desperately wanting to wipe the pain from her eyes, he pushed her onto her back, his mouth touching her lips, her chin, her jawbone. He'd had her a few times last night and he wanted her again. He wanted to make love in the early-morning sunlight, to watch her fall apart in his arms. Because when she left, and she would leave, because nothing wonderful in his life ever lasted, he'd have this memory of her in his bed, sunbeams on her skin.

Kasey's fingers were tap dancing down his spine when he heard his phone ring. He turned his head to look at the offending object and decided, just this once, to let it go to voice mail. He pulled a pink nipple into his mouth, heard

Kasey's low murmur of approval and cursed when his phone rang again.

Kasey stretched out her hand, snagged the phone from the bedside table and handed it to him. Aaron looked at screen, saw Cole's name and grumbled in exasperation as he rolled off Kasey. He snatched the device from her hand and barked out a quick hello.

It took Aaron a few minutes to make sense of what Cole was saying. He turned to look at Kasey, who'd wrapped her arms around her bent knees, her expression quizzical. Thinking that he might need her help to make sense of this latest craziness, Aaron told Cole to hold on, switched the phone to speaker mode and asked the PI to repeat himself.

"I was just informed by one of my contacts in law enforcement that there is a link between Rich and a small aircraft crash in the Sierra Nevada mountains a few weeks back. A body was recovered from the wreckage but because the local sheriff deemed it to be an accident, the victim was identified and quickly cremated."

Aaron's eyes met Kasey's, as puzzled as she looked. "What's the connection to Rich?"

"The aircraft's registration number. It matches one in Will's fleet," Cole replied.

Aaron saw Kasey's eyes widen and felt the earth shift beneath his feet. He held out his hand to Kasey and when her fingers gripped his, the room stopped spinning. "Who was the victim?"

"Said to be a Bob Smith," Cole replied. "Apparently he has no next of kin, no friends and was all but broke."

That didn't sound right. "Yet he was flying an expensive light aircraft?" Aaron asked.

"Sounds awful convenient, doesn't it?"

Damn right it did.

"The sheriff did the bare minimum to investigate the

crash, the body was cremated without doing an autopsy and the sheriff is being supremely uncooperative," Cole continued.

"His remains?" Aaron asked.

"The sheriff said he and his friends conducted a small ceremony and dispersed of the ashes. I call BS," Cole said. Aaron felt his stomach knot. God, he knew what Cole was implying...

"I'm going to make my way out there, but it's going to take me some time since I'm out of state," Cole stated. "Thanks to jurisdictional crap and territory disputes, it's going to take some time for the red tape BS to be waded through. But if you went up there and nosed around, because you are a civilian, you might get more out of the sheriff."

Finally, he could do something to help. He looked at Kasey. "Get hold of my pilot, tell him to file a flight plan for—"

Cole told him the name of the town and Kasey scrambled out of bed, all long legs and creamy skin. Aaron shook his head—*concentrate, Phillips!*—and turned his attention back to the logistics of their trip. "—Durango City and that I want to leave as soon as we get to the airport, which should be within the next half hour or so. We should reach Durango City sometime after lunch."

"Good enough," Cole said. "Let me know what you find. And, Aaron?"

"Yeah?" he snapped, impatient.

"Watch your back."

Aaron disconnected the call, walked over to his closet, pulled down an overnight bag and a change of clothing. When he turned back to look into the room, he saw Kasey wrapping a towel around her torso. "I need a five-minute shower and another ten to pack, I'll meet you downstairs," she told him, looking determined.

Aaron shook his head. "You're not coming with me."

Kasey didn't react to his no-nonsense tone. "Of course I am. Savannah is at Megan's and your sister will keep her until we get back. I am not letting you fly out on your own, not knowing what you might find."

Stubbornness settled over his face. "You don't know what you are talking about."

"Don't insult my intelligence, Aaron. I know what you are thinking… Air, could the remains from this victim be the same remains in the urn supposedly sent by Jason to Megan with the note saying they are Rich's remains?"

Yeah, Kasey wasn't a fool and she'd made the same connections he and Cole had.

"You thought you saw Will at the Glass House last night but if it wasn't Will, then who looks enough like Will to momentarily fool you? Rich. And if Rich is in Royal, then who died in that airplane crash?"

Aaron couldn't say it, didn't want to think it. "It can't be Jason, Kase. I don't think I can handle it."

Kasey walked over to him and wound her arms around his waist, placing her lips against his heart. "I hope it's not, Air. I pray it's not. But just in case there's a small chance it is, you can't be alone. I won't let you do this alone. I'm going, Aaron, and you're going to let me."

Aaron took a minute to hold her, to suck in the support she offered, thinking that this one time, this one time, he'd allow someone in. And he'd take her prayers and add a few of his own.

Not that he believed, not for a minute, that his prayers would change the outcome.

Eight

Kasey followed Aaron into the small building housing the sheriff's office, trying to keep up with his long-legged stride. It had been a long day already and she was bubbling over with frustration, but her boss, and lover, was a tightly coiled string about to snap.

They'd planned to be in Durango City by midafternoon but thanks to a violent thunderstorm lashing the Sierra Nevada mountains, they'd needed to divert to an off-the-beaten-track landing strip that was just long enough to land Aaron's Gulfstream. Finding a vehicle to rent had been their next challenge. When they finally did, they'd made the journey to Durango City in lashing rain, finally arriving, tense and snappy, in the small town situated in the foothills of the mountain range. Kasey knew that Aaron wanted to visit the crash site but it had also been many weeks since the plane had gone down and Kasey wasn't sure what Aaron was hoping or expecting to find.

Kasey, who was a little more detached from the situation, thought that talking to the sheriff and the game warden who'd happened upon the crash would be more constructive. Maybe they'd stumble onto something, but Kasey wasn't holding her breath. This whole trip was a massive fishing expedition and she doubted they'd hook much, or anything, at all.

Kasey looked at Aaron's tight face and sighed at his bleak expression. *God*, she prayed, *please let there be something, anything.*

Standing at the counter waiting for the young deputy who was also acting as a dispatcher to finish her call, Kasey leaned into Aaron's side. He was as stiff as a plank. She linked her fingers in his and squeezed. "Why don't you let me do the talking? Honey will work better than vinegar or, in your case, homicidal frustration."

He managed a tiny smile and nodded his agreement. Aaron allowing her to take the lead, to do something for him, was a small victory, Kasey realized. He didn't release control easily and when she was alone, later, she'd savor the fact that he trusted her enough to do this for him.

Kasey placed both her hands on the counter and sent the young woman a smile. "Hi, we were wondering if we could speak to the sheriff. Is he in?"

The deputy tossed a look at the closed door across the room and frustration flashed in her bright blue eyes. "It's quitting time and the sheriff doesn't like problems at the end of the day."

Kasey suspected she was trying to contain a massive eye-roll. Her disdain for the sheriff's adherence to office hours was easy to discern.

Feeling Aaron's bubbling anger, she squeezed his hand in warning. "It's about that plane crash up in the mountains a few weeks' back. We won't take much of his time."

"Victim's been identified, case is closed."

The female deputy left the room as Kasey turned around to see a slim man, well-groomed, standing across the room, in front of a door with large writing emblazoned across the glass. Sheriff Billy Orson, she presumed, wearing very nice threads for a small-town cop. Cold-eyed and tense, Kasey thought. And, judging by the long up-and-down he gave them, not at all happy to see them. Kasey pasted on a smile and walked across the room, Aaron by her side. She held out her hand for him to shake but Sheriff Orson kept his hands in his pockets, rudely ignoring her gesture.

Well, then. "My name is Kasey Monroe and we'd like to ask you some questions about the plane crash."

"Nothing to say. It crashed into the side of the mountain. The victim's wallet was in his pocket. Body and photo ID looked alike. Did a search, no next of kin, no fixed abode, no money."

"You didn't find it strange that someone with minimal resources was flying an expensive aircraft?" Kasey asked. "And that the aircraft wasn't registered to him?"

The sheriff looked bored. "People hire planes all the time."

"Can we see your reports? The photo ID, pictures of the man who died in the crash?" Kasey persisted, annoyance at his lack of cooperation turning her voice as sharp as a knife blade.

"No."

"What else can you tell us?"

"Nothing."

Before she could blink, Aaron stepped up to the sheriff and slammed his hand on his chest, pinning him to the door of his office. "Start talking."

Something cold and malicious appeared in the sheriff's eyes. "Take your hands off me or I'm going to arrest your ass!"

"You and whose army?" Aaron growled, not dropping his hand. "You know more than you're saying and I want to know what you're hiding."

"Get your hands off me." The sheriff dropped his hand, pulled out his weapon and placed the barrel against Aaron's chest.

Kasey sucked in a horrified breath but Aaron, nerves of cold steel, just held his eyes.

"Aaron, back off before you get hurt," Kasey snapped.

Aaron kept the sheriff pinned to the door with just the force of his hand on his chest and ignored the gun. "If he shoots me, he has to shoot you, and two dead bodies would be tricky to explain. Drop the gun, moron."

The sheriff dropped the gun to his side but Aaron's hard eyes didn't waver from his face. "Tell me about the crash."

Kasey saw fear flash in Sheriff Orson's eyes. She thought he was about to speak when he closed his eyes and the color disappeared from his face.

"Nothing to tell." Kasey had to strain to hear his words. "Nothing I *can* tell."

The sheriff was scared of Aaron but there was someone else who scared him more. Kasey looked at Aaron and placed a hand on his arm, silently encouraging him to release his hold on the lawman. They'd get nothing more from him. When Aaron finally dropped his hand and stepped back, she knew that he'd come to the same conclusion.

"You're as shady as hell and you'd better find yourself a damn good lawyer because, if I find out that you are in any way complicit in what happened to my brother, I will chase you into the depths of hell."

This cold, hard man didn't sound like Aaron but it was

him; ruthless, determined, dogged. A little scary but ridiculously sexy. Was it weird that his badass attitude made her insanely hot? Yeah, Kasey thought, it was weird.

"We're staying at the local inn tonight, room 14, and we leave at the break of dawn. If there's anything you want to tell me, it had better be before then." Aaron bent his knees and glared into the sheriff's worried eyes. "Trust me, you don't want to mess with me."

Sheriff Orson opened his mouth to speak, abruptly shook his head and forced his lips to sneer. "Get the hell out of my town."

Aaron didn't react, his hard expression didn't change. "Break of dawn. Don't make me come looking for you."

Kasey, hearing the knock on the door to the honeymoon suite at the Durango City Inn, lifted her head off Aaron's shoulder and frowned at him. He looked at his watch and Kasey turned his hand to squint at the dial. "It's after midnight."

Aaron pulled away from her, stood and quickly pulled on his jeans. He waited at the door until Kasey was dressed in a sweatshirt and yoga pants before pulling it open. She looked past him to see the young deputy from the police station standing in the hallway.

"Can I come in?" she whispered.

Aaron stepped back and the girl slipped into the room, her arms folded against her chest. "I don't have much time. I'm Jen, by the way."

Aaron shut the door behind her and leaned against the wall. "Why are you here, Jen?"

Jen rocked on her heels and Kasey thought she looked like someone had shot her dog. "My dad was the sheriff of Durango City for a long time. When he died, Sheriff Orson was elected."

Kasey exchanged a look with Aaron, neither of them understanding the relevance of her statement.

"My dad was a good cop who believed in justice. Orson is as dirty as an old barn," Jen stated, her eyes flashing with anger. "I grew up with my dad and he spoke to me about his cases, and everything Orson did on this investigation was wrong."

Aaron straightened, his interest piqued. "What do you mean?"

"From the beginning, this case was…fishy. If there's an accident on the mountain, the search-and-rescue team gets called out to recover the body, but Orson and a friend brought the victim back down, on their own. As per policy, I met Orson at the funeral home to collect evidence, but there wasn't any. No photos of the scene, no personal effects, nothing. I heard Orson tell the funeral director that there was no family, no one to contact, and that he should be cremated as soon as possible, and that he would, personally, pick up the cost."

Aaron rubbed his hand over his lower face. "Holy crap."

Jen pulled a face. "It gets worse and that's why I'm here."

Kasey knew that whatever she was about to say was going to rock Aaron's world and there was nothing she could do or say to protect him.

"Later that night I went back to the funeral home and snuck into the room holding the two-man body fridge. My gut was screaming at me to do something. Everything about this situation was wrong and I needed to do right by this victim. I didn't believe, for one second, anything that Orson said."

"What did you do?" Aaron asked, sounding choked.

"I swabbed the vic's mouth for DNA and pulled some strands of hair from him. I sent those samples off to the state forensics lab, faking Orson's signature. I hid the results when I got the DNA report back." She tossed the envelope onto the closest chair. "There's the report, you can compare his DNA against whoever you are looking for." Jen rocked on her heels, looking miserable. "I'm sorry to tell you this, but the man who died in that crash looked a lot like you."

Kasey saw Aaron's knees buckle and his hand reach out to grip the door frame to steady himself. She wanted to go to him but his quick glance warned her to keep her distance.

"There's more—" Jen said.

God, Kasey thought, how much more would Aaron be able to take? "He wore a ring on his finger. It was pretty distinctive," Jen said, looking at the bed where they'd held each other a little while before, back when life still made sense.

"Black tungsten edged with rose gold. Two intertwined hearts engraved on the inside band. He wore it on the ring finger of his right hand, not left," Aaron said, his voice breaking.

Kasey then noticed that Jen held an evidence bag in her hand, filled with two medicine vials and, in the corner, a black-and-gold ring. She lifted it up. "Additional samples of his DNA, in case you want to run more tests. Do you want to keep this? I don't know what to do with it and if I'm found with it I'll lose my job."

Aaron just stared at the bag, so Kasey, her heart breaking for him, took the bag Jen held out. "Thank you," she murmured.

Jen nodded. "I'm so sorry," she said before turning to walk toward the door. "If, at some point in the future, you need me to speak to your local cops, or any other law enforcement, I'm prepared to do that, even if it means losing my job."

Kasey placed the evidence bag on the table, conscious

that Aaron's eyes hadn't left the clear plastic packet. "We so appreciate this, Jen."

"There's one more thing I thought was strange. You're from Royal, Texas, right?"

Aaron nodded.

"Well, that's where Orson sent the urn containing the ashes."

Kasey shut the door behind Jen and turned back to look at Aaron, desperately wishing she could find the right words to comfort him, if comfort was at all possible. As she looked for something to say, Aaron sat on the edge of the bed and started to pull on his shoes.

"Where are you going?" she asked him.

"Out."

Kasey looked toward the window and, although it was pitch-dark outside, she could hear the heavy rain slamming against the windowpane. "Okay, give me five minutes to get dressed and I'll come with you."

"I don't need you," Aaron said and, without looking at her once, walked out of the room.

Kasey rested her forearms on her knees and closed her eyes. It was a special type of hell when you wanted to be there for someone you loved but they wouldn't let you in. Kasey tunneled her fingers through her hair and groaned as the full impact of that thought hit her.

She loved Aaron. She did. She loved him unconditionally, probably had from the moment they first met but her brain had taken a while to take on board what her heart, and body, already knew.

She simply loved Aaron with a depth of feeling that astounded her: no strings, no provisos, no conditions. It was something that just was…

Loving Aaron, a man who didn't need or love her back, was now her new reality.

* * *

Kasey, despite her efforts to stay awake, drifted off to sleep around 4:00 a.m. and when she woke at seven, Aaron was standing in front of the window, his shoulders up around his ears. Walking over to him, she placed her hand in the middle of his back and rested her forehead on his spine.

"How are you doing, Air?"

It was such a stupid question—he was obviously gutted at the news of his brother's death—but she had to say something. Kasey felt his chest rise and fall with his intake of breath. "I'm…as good as it gets."

Kasey moved to stand in front of him, so that she could see his face. His beard was long past his normal sexy stubble and she could barely see his lips, his mouth was so tightly drawn. And his eyes, his beautiful green eyes, were flat and dull. Kasey placed her hand on his big biceps. She followed his gaze and looked out the window. The clouds had moved on and the mountain range loomed in the distance.

"I faxed the DNA report to Cole. He's going to get the DNA compared to Jason's, and the ashes in the urn Meg received, but there's no question in my mind that it's him. Hearing that he's dead isn't a surprise. Since the moment I heard that he hadn't contacted Savvie, I think I knew in my gut that he wasn't coming home."

"I'm so sorry."

"I have to tell my niece and my sister…" Aaron said, his voice as bleak as those mountains in the winter.

"That's going to be tough," Kasey murmured. She knew it was a long shot but she had to try to keep his hopes up. "The DNA testing might still prove that it's not him, Aaron."

"He never took that ring off, Kasey." Aaron rubbed his

face with his hands. "After my folks died, I thought I'd never have to be the bearer of bad news again. I thought that once was enough."

"What do you mean?"

Aaron looked utterly miserable. "I told Jason and Megs that they were dead, that they both were killed in a car accident." The lack of emotion in his voice scared Kasey. He wasn't an unemotional man, he loved deeply, but she sensed that he had to shove down his emotions to function.

"They were on their way to see me and were killed about twenty miles from Stanford. That's the basics, but I never told Jay and Megan that the reason they were in Stanford was to see me."

Kasey sat on the seat of the bay window and looked up at him, puzzled. Aaron kept his eyes fixed on the mountains and Kasey knew that not looking at her was his way of coping. "I was interning at a small investment firm and I was sleeping with my older boss. I was also in love with her. We were about to open up our own investment firm, she had a couple of clients and I had wealthy contacts back in Royal. I told my folks and they lost it. They jumped into the car to talk some sense into me and they called me to tell me they were nearly in Stanford. The argument started up again on the telephone—I said something about them staying the hell out of my life and then I heard the crash, heard my mom scream."

Kasey shuddered, desperately fighting her tears. But if Aaron could stand there dry-eyed, then she wasn't allowed the luxury of falling apart.

"I not only caused their death—" God, Aaron, no! "—but I also failed them by not taking care of my siblings."

Kasey frowned, trying to work out the meaning of his words. "I don't understand, Aaron."

"I encouraged Megan to marry 'Will.' I walked her

down the damn aisle! I didn't spend enough time with Jason, I didn't keep close enough tabs on him."

Kasey understood his irrationality: when things went wrong, blame had to be assigned and Aaron, with his overly heightened sense of responsibility, was blaming himself. "You're not being fair on yourself, Aaron. Megan is an adult as was Jason. They made their own decisions."

Aaron shook his head, his expression pure stubborn pride. "I'm the oldest, I could've done something to prevent all this."

Kasey stood and wrapped her arms around him. "It's not your fault, Aaron. *None* of this is your fault. Not your parents' death, not Megan's marriage, not Jason's death. This isn't your burden to shoulder." Yet, even as she uttered the words, Kasey knew that nothing she could say would penetrate his grief. He needed to mourn, to let go, to feel. Blaming himself was, she thought, maybe easier than dealing with the solid reality that his brother was dead, probably by another man's hand.

He needed to break, Kasey realized, and he needed to expel some of this acidic, corrosive guilt and tension. There was comfort in sex—in being wrapped in warm arms, folded into a heart that loved you. Sexual intimacy might help ease his grief. Like she'd needed sex eight months ago when she'd felt unloved and undesirable, Aaron needed sex right now to disconnect, to release some tension and to be with someone who loved him. He'd deny that need with his very last breath, but Kasey knew that he needed that connection to someone; he'd been alone, truly alone, for far too long. It wasn't a long-term solution, of course, but sex would be a balm on his open, weeping wound, temporary stitches to his broken heart.

Without giving herself time to talk herself out of what she was about to do, she placed her hand on his crotch and felt shock ripple through Aaron. He didn't move but under her fingers, through the denim fabric of his jeans, she felt him harden and knew that he was about to pull away.

Kasey kept her hand on him and stood on her toes to look into his eyes. "You need this, Air. Let me give this to you. Let me take away a little of the pain. It'll come back with a vengeance, but for now… Let me take care of you." She wanted to tell him that she'd always be there for him, as little and as much as he needed, but now wasn't the time or place.

"God, Kase, I—"

Kasey rubbed her thumb up his long length. "You need this, let me give you this."

She pushed her hands under his T-shirt and lifted the material up his chest and over his head. Aaron just watched her, those emotionless green eyes warming slightly as desire temporarily swamped grief. Kasey kissed his sternum, his collarbone, the flat circles of his nipples, her hands tracing the hard ridges of his muscles.

"I love the way you touch me," Aaron muttered.

"I love to touch you," Kasey assured him, knowing her statement to be pure truth. She could do this for the rest of her life, touch this one man, forever. She loved him: it was inconvenient and possibly disastrous, but she'd do anything for him.

Kasey opened his belt, flicked open the top button of his jeans and, one by one, separated the rest of his buttons of his fly. Sliding his jeans down, she quickly discovered he wore no underwear and was glad there were no more barriers to her touch.

She wrapped her hand around his shaft and looked up at him, his eyes closed and the muscles in his neck and shoulders loosening. She cupped his balls and stroked him from shaft to tip, hoping her touch was all-consuming, allowing him a measure of distance from his grief. Ironic that keeping his distance was what she least wanted from him—she wanted his hopes and dreams and thoughts and worries—but right now, detaching from all those emotions was what she could give him.

Kasey felt his hands on her breasts, thumbs running over her nipples. This was about him but she felt the tug of desire, the need for more. Tilting her head up, she watched as his eyes opened and clashed with hers. Desire and lust collided and then Aaron sprang into action, like a big panther who'd been Tasered. He grabbed her sweatshirt, yanked it off her body and dragged first one nipple, then the other into his mouth, his hands diving between her legs. Then his fingers stilled and he pulled his head back to look at her.

"You're so wet."

Kasey nodded. Giving him pleasure made her hot. "I want you."

Aaron growled and pushed her yoga pants and panties down her hips, commanding her to step out of them. She was just free of her clothing when he lodged an arm around her butt and walked her over to the bed, laying her down. In one smooth movement, he wrapped his hands around the backs of her knees, lifted her up and pulled her open. Without waiting, he plunged inside her, filling every inch of her. There was no finesse or skill, this was pure sex, unleashed and as powerful as a summer storm. Kasey gripped his hips and held on as he whipped her higher and then higher still.

"I can't wait much longer. Dammit, Kase, come!"

His command flew over her skin and Kasey felt the explosion, the cosmic bang from deep inside her. She felt Aaron's thrust, felt his crown against her womb, and then he froze before she felt the jerks deep inside her that told her he'd followed her into the blast.

Kasey held him while he shuddered, his face in her neck, his big body covering hers. Taking shallow breaths, she wrapped her limbs around him, holding on as his shudders turned to sobs and she felt his tears on her skin, rolling over her collarbone.

She cradled him, wishing he knew that this place, in her arms, was where he belonged but knowing that Aaron, being Aaron, didn't believe he belonged anywhere.

Nine

Despite having his back to the door, Aaron knew when Kasey stepped into the downstairs living area of his house. It had something to do with the way the air stirred, energy moved. He'd never been so in tune with anybody, emotionally or physically, as he was with Kasey Monroe, and her holding that much power scared the crap out of him.

Aaron felt her eyes on him, reproachful and sad. Since their arrival back in Royal this morning, he'd barely spoken to her except to ask her to contact Will Sanders and Cole Sullivan and tell them to meet him at the house. Kasey had faxed Deputy Jen's reports to Cole and a few minutes after he and Will arrived at his house, Cole had confirmed his worst fears: Jason's DNA matched that of the sample taken from the body recovered from the plane crash, it was his ashes in the urn at Megan's house. Jason was dead.

The rest of the day had been equally hellish. Will

fetched Megan and Savannah from Megan's house on the outskirts of town and, while Kasey distracted Savvie, Aaron had broken the news to his sister that their sibling was dead, probably by her husband's hand. He'd braced himself for Megan's grief, had expected her to throw herself onto his chest, but she'd, instinctively, turned to Will for comfort, folding herself into his big arms and quietly weeping against his chest. Aaron felt both upset and relieved that she'd turned to Will; upset because he knew that he wanted to be the one to comfort his only sibling, relieved because he didn't know if he could.

Aaron turned around and saw that Kasey was now standing by the kitchen counter, and he resisted the urge to cross the room to her, to step into her arms. Instead, he looked into her eyes and saw her need to comfort him, to hold him tight. A part of him wanted her to do exactly that but he knew that if he allowed her in, if he leaned on her, he might never let her go again.

And he knew that he had to let her go.

He was in crisis mode, had been since he'd first heard about Jason's disappearance and that he needed to care for Savannah. He'd been scared and out of his depth and, not used to feeling either of those things, he'd started to look to Kasey for support. It was natural but it was also stupid. Because, in a few months, when the rock on his chest had lifted a fraction and he had a little distance between his grief and, yeah, this clawing anger, he'd revert back to being the man who preferred to be on his own, to walk his own path, alone.

It was better if they parted company now, before she started to think there was a chance that she might move in here permanently, that she would be the mom Savvie so desperately needed. And, Jesus, this hurt to admit but... yeah. She needed to go before he fell in love with her and found himself unwilling—or unable—to let her go. As he well knew, losing people hurt, dammit! Whether it was by death or breakup, having someone be an integral part of your life and then not having them in that space sliced and diced one's heart. It was smarter to not put yourself in that position in the first place.

"Savannah's finally asleep," Kasey said, her voice sounding infinitely sad. "Megan is just washing her face, she'll be down in a minute or two. Will is in your office, making calls."

Aaron turned to face her, pushing his hands into the front pockets of his jeans. After telling Megan about Jason, and after her first bout of tears had passed, he'd asked her to help him tell Savannah. It was Megan's suggestion for Kasey to be with them and it had been the right decision. Like he'd anticipated, Savvie had turned to Kasey for comfort. The little girl had wrapped her arms and legs around Kasey's body and sobbed and then sobbed some more. Megan had tried to take her but Savvie had refused to relinquish her hold on Kasey. It was Kasey who'd taken her up to bed, who'd coaxed her into sleep.

He was mourning his brother, angry over what had happened to him, and all the while he was fighting his feelings for Kasey. Which meant Savvie's attachment to her temporary nanny was becoming a problem. The little girl was going to be heartbroken, again, when Kasey left. He should put some distance between them and Kasey, and the best way to do that would be to tell her to leave, to send her back to live in her own house. But it was too soon, Aaron thought, way too soon. He couldn't do that to the distraught little girl.

And let's be honest here, you want her to leave because it would be easier for you. You're not acting in Savannah's best interests, Phillips.

Telling Savvie that her best friend was leaving her life just after hearing that her father was dead would be a double blow to Savvie…

God, he couldn't do it. He *wouldn't* do that. He wasn't that much of a selfish prick.

Savannah's needs came first and he'd just have to find a way to live with Kasey. Maybe in a month or two, when Savannah felt settled, he could start easing Kasey out of their lives. Would that work or would Savvie be even more attached to Kasey than she was now? Would he?

God, he just wished someone would tell him what the hell to do!

Megan walked into the room, Will on her heels. It was obvious that Megs had been sobbing, her eyes were fire-engine red and swollen. Her face was pale and her hair was a mess but, Aaron noticed, his sister was still a beautiful woman. Aaron started to cross the room to pull her into his arms, to give her the comfort she so obviously deserved, but Will cut him off, yanking Megan into his arms, holding the back of her head to his chest. His eyes met Aaron's over Megan's head and Aaron read the back-off command in his eyes.

And, judging by the way Megan's hands gripped Will's hips, she wanted comfort from Will and not from him. Fair enough, Aaron conceded, ignoring the bitter taste in his mouth. For the last decade, up until Jason's disappearance, he and Megan hadn't been much more than casual acquaintances, so he wouldn't be the one she turned to in a crisis. But it hurt, dammit. He was her older brother, she and Savannah were the only family he had left.

Aaron felt Kasey's hand on his back—he hadn't seen her move across the room—and it felt natural to lift his arm to pull her closer, to absorb some of her strength. However, he came to his senses at the last moment and stepped away from her, lifting his shoulder to make her drop her hand. He couldn't rely on her. Not now, not ever.

Aaron saw the flash of hurt on Kasey's face and felt his stomach knot. He had to start the process of distancing himself at some point and he might as well start now. After all, he couldn't possibly feel more crap than he currently did.

Or maybe he could, who the hell knew?

Cole, thank God, broke the tense silence by clearing his throat. He'd forgotten that the private investigator was still there. "Shall we all sit down?"

Aaron nodded, perched on the arm of the closest chair and noticed that Kasey took the seat as far away from him as possible. Anger-tinged hurt flashed in her whiskey-colored eyes as she crossed those long legs. She also looked wiped, Aaron thought, noticing the dark circles around her eyes.

"As you know, Jason's DNA matches the body found in that crashed plane," Cole said, and Aaron appreciated his calm demeanor. "The DNA is also a match to the ashes in the urn you received, Megan, the ashes we originally thought were Will's. If you aren't convinced, we can send the samples to another lab for a second round of testing. Is that what you want to do?"

Aaron looked at Megan, who shook her head. Jason was dead. No amount of DNA testing would change that. "There's no point, Cole. The dispatcher saw the body, she commented on his resemblance to me. It's definitely him." Megan, tucked into Will's side, released a small sob. Aaron stared at the floor. After a minute of listening to Megan cry, Aaron looked at Cole, then Will. "There's something I haven't told you. I haven't had the time. I don't know if it's important but it's definitely odd."

He looked at Kasey and she gave him a small nod, encouraging him to continue. Cole's eyes locked in on him and Will, his arms still around Megan, cocked his head. "Kasey and I were at the Glass House on Saturday night— God, is today only Monday? It seems like a month ago." Feeling bone-tired and emotionally shattered, he looked at Kasey, wishing he could touch her because the world was starting to slide out from under his feet again.

"Glass House. Dinner…" Cole prompted him.

Right. He looked directly at Will. "You sent me a text earlier that evening saying that you and Cole were at the ranch, discussing the case. I replied back that I might try to meet you later, but it was a crazy evening."

Between Kasey looking like a sex goddess and him trying not to act like an idiot around Mark Ward, he'd tucked his worry about Jason away for a few hours.

Aaron felt the wave of guilt and grief swamp him but he kicked his way to the surface, knowing this was important. "I was looking around the restaurant and a group in the far corner stood up and your back was to me."

Will lifted his eyebrows. "Me?"

Yeah, this was where it got tricky. "Or somebody I thought was you. Shorter hair, wearing glasses, but your height and weight. I wanted to excuse myself to have a word with you, then I remembered that you said you were at the ranch. It had been a long and confusing day and I thought I was seeing things."

Cole and Will exchanged a long glance before Will shook his head. "I never left the ranch that night."

"So, someone was at the Glass House on Saturday evening who looked like you, Will," Cole said, folding his big hands and widening his stance. "Let's connect the dots…" Cole took a sip of whiskey and placed his glass on the stone mantel. "Abigail Stewart saw Jason and Fake Will, aka Rich Lowell, fighting and it's common knowledge that Rich and Jason boarded that plane together. Nobody filed a flight plan. Shortly thereafter, a small-town sheriff gets a report of the crash and, instead of launching a proper search and rescue, retrieves a victim from the crash. One victim, not two. What happened to the other person on the flight?"

Will started to speak but Cole held up his hand to stop him from interrupting. "Let's go for the most logical explanation, which is that passenger number one incapacitated passenger number two, exited the plane—probably by parachute—and the plane, flying on autopilot, crashed into the mountain. Then Sheriff Orson goes against all protocol to retrieve the body, doesn't order an autopsy, falsely identifies the body and arranges for it to be cremated. His deputy, following protocol, reported the crash to the aviation authorities and that's how I stumbled on the call sign."

Will nodded. "Sounds to me like the sheriff was paid off."

Well, yeah. Aaron had already worked that out for himself.

"Rich, acting as Will, was the last person to see Jason, the last person with him. If Jason became suspicious of who he was and what he was doing, then Jason would've had to be—" Cole hesitated "—dispersed of. It makes sense that Rich set up Jason to die in that crash and he walked away. Rich, with Sheriff Orson's help, pretended that Jason was still alive, sent the urn and the letter, supposedly from Jason, to Megan announcing his own—Will's—death, allowing him a new start."

"But if Aaron's eyes can be trusted, and I believe they can, Rich is still on the loose and back in Royal."

But why? Aaron wondered. Why come back to the place where everyone thinks you are dead? It made no sense.

Megan leaned away from Will, furious. "Rich is back in Royal? I swear to God, I'm going to kill him!"

"Settle down, honey," Will murmured, pulling her back to his side. "You are staying out of this."

"We have to play it cool, Megan." Cole sent her a sympathetic look. "If Rich is back, there has to be a damn good reason why he'd risk his neck to show his face here. Something has pulled him back here, because he's taking a hell of a risk. That tells me that he has unfinished business, and that makes him dangerous."

Aaron frowned. "What would be important enough to him to pull him back here?"

"Knowing Rich, money or revenge," Will said, anger in his eyes.

"Could it be connected to the money he stole from the Texas Cattleman's Club?" Aaron asked.

"Maybe. But revenge can't be ruled out, it's probably a combination of both," Will replied. "So, who is potentially in danger? Me. Megan…and you, as well, Aaron, if he thinks that Jason confided in you about his suspicions."

"I agree that you and Megan could be in danger, me not so much," Aaron replied. "But we shouldn't take any chances. Megan can move in here, with me."

"Megan will move into the main house at the Ace in the Hole," Will said, his tone suggesting nobody should argue with him. "I'll protect her there."

Aaron saw that Megan was about to argue and lifted his hands. "You two work it out and let me know."

He looked at Megan. "We need to think about making a death announcement, holding a funeral for Jay."

Cole held up his hand. "Until we know where Rich is and what he's planning, I strongly suggest that the news of Jason's death stays in this room."

"Our brother is dead, Cole!" Megan cried.

Cole looked sympathetic but still tough. "He'll still be dead next week and the week after that, honey. I know it's hard but keeping his death a secret will make it easier to catch Rich, we don't want him bolting. You want him caught, don't you, Megs?"

"Damn straight I do," Megan retorted before nodding. "Okay, we'll keep it a secret, for now."

Aaron nodded his agreement and turned to Will.

"You need to take this to the FBI." He felt a burst of impatience at Will's suddenly blank face. "I know you are working with the FBI and other law enforcement, Sanders. You, too, Cole."

"I can talk to them until I explode, but it's all supposition, Aaron," Cole said, his voice calm. "And it all hinges on your sighting of Rich, which you admit was very short and fleeting. Add to the fact that you have been under enormous stress and that you are grieving, the assumption will be that you are clutching at straws."

"I saw him!" Aaron shouted and, out of the corner of his eye, saw Kasey jump a foot high in her chair.

Cole didn't back down. "I'm not arguing with you. I'm just telling you that your word isn't proof, that your story would be easily dismissed. We need more."

"Our brother slammed into a mountain!" Aaron roared, losing his grip on his temper.

"I need solid proof that Rich was involved, Aaron," Cole insisted.

His calm demeanor infuriated Aaron. Feeling like he needed to punch something, or someone, he shot to his feet and headed to the sliding doors. He needed air. He needed the silence of the night. He needed to walk to the end of his property and to scream, maybe to cry.

What he didn't need was to be in this room, listening to this crap.

He felt Kasey following him and as he stepped out onto the patio he whirled around to glare at her. "Will you goddamn give me some space? You are Savannah's nanny, not mine! Leave me the hell alone!"

Kasey nodded once, folded her arms against her chest and planted her feet. She blinked back her tears, nodded and spun around, holding her head high as she walked past his sister and the men. Aaron, feeling like a total dick and regretting his temper, tracked her movements until she disappeared into the hallway and, in the pin-drop quiet, he heard her feet on the wooden stairs. Without looking back at the rest of his guests, Aaron whistled for the dogs and disappeared into the night.

"I've had enough."

Kasey looked down at the plate Savannah pushed away and saw that she'd eaten a healthy portion of her breakfast, not as much as she'd like, but enough. She wasn't going to nag Savannah into eating more on her first day back at school after hearing about her father's death.

It had been hard enough for Kasey to coax her out of bed, coax her into dressing, into eating something. Savannah hadn't wanted to go back to school but after talking to the school principal and school counselor, Kasey realized that it was best for Savannah to be with her friends, to have a few hours of distraction. School was where Savannah needed to be, so it was Kasey who had made that happen.

She made everything happen, at the moment, Kasey thought as Savannah went to brush her teeth. For the last week she'd answered calls from both Aaron's friends and business associates, asking why Aaron wasn't taking their calls or answering his emails. She interacted with Savannah, keeping the little girl busy and entertained. Savannah was clingy and, naturally, weepy and on the other end of that scale, Aaron was cold, distant and non-communicative.

She was everything to Savannah and nothing to Aaron.

Something had to give and soon... Savvie wasn't the only one who'd had enough.

Kasey checked her watch and noticed that it was nearly time for Megan to collect the little girl for school. Megan had been wonderful over this past week, picking Savannah up most afternoons and taking her back to Megan's house. Will hadn't succeeded at convincing Megan to move to his ranch for protection from psycho Rich—at least not yet. Kasey knew Will might not let go of the argument until Megan relented.

The doorbell rang and Kasey hurried into the hallway to greet Megan. As she opened the door, Savannah ran down the stairs, looking a little excited.

"Anything interesting happening at school today, Savvie?" Kasey asked as they walked out of the front door and down the stairs to Megan's vehicle.

"Puppet show," Savvie answered, sliding her hand into Kasey's and resting her head against her biceps. Savvie looked up and her eyes filled with tears. "Is it okay if I laugh a little today, Kasey? Would Daddy mind?"

Blinking back tears of her own, Kasey bent so that her eyes were level with Savannah's. "Savvie, of course he wouldn't mind if you laughed."

Out of the corner of her eye, Kasey saw Megan leave her car and then her hand was on Savvie's shoulder. Kasey flicked a quick glance at Megan and saw her concerned expression. "Savvie? Why would you think that it's not okay to laugh?"

Savannah stared down at her pink sneakers. "Yesterday, I was watching cartoons and I laughed. Uncle Aaron heard me and he slammed his glass down, said a bad word and stormed out of the room. He looked mad."

Kasey heard but ignored Megan's low hiss of angry surprise. Placing both her hands on Savannah's shoulder, she pulled in a deep breath and met the child's amazing green eyes. Like Aaron's eyes, they were chock-full of grief and guilt. "Honey, I know your daddy would be fine with you laughing. He loved you more than anything in the world and he only ever wanted you to be happy."

"But Uncle Aaron was mad because I laughed," Savvie protested. "And he is sad and mad because Daddy's dead, so I should be like that, too."

A classic example of kids watching what adults do, taking their cues from them on how to cope.

And Uncle Aaron was going to have six layers of skin stripped off him for being an insensitive ass, Kasey silently told her. "I'm sure he was mad about something else and that it had nothing to do with you."

Kasey pulled Savannah in for a hug, resting her cheek on Savannah's head. "If you don't hurry now, sweetie, you're going to be late for school. And while you're driving maybe Meg can tell you some funny stories about when she and your daddy were kids and the silly things they did."

Savannah's eyes lit up. "Daddy was silly?"

"I think he was. And remember, Sav, that you can talk to Meg and me and Aaron about your dad being dead, but no one else, okay?"

"'Cause you're trying to catch the bad man?" Savvie asked as Kasey opened the door for Savannah to climb into the car.

Kasey watched as Megan pulled away, catching a glimpse of Savannah leaning forward in her seat to hear Megan's stories about Jason. The child needed to talk about her dad, she needed to express her grief and keep his memory alive. Megan would try to do that but Savannah needed Aaron to step up to the plate, as well.

The silent, surly beast was ripping the little girl in two and it stopped, right now. Kasey hurried through the house, almost running by the time she hit the patio. Standing at the end of the pool, she waited for Aaron to stop, but instead of acknowledging her presence, he just turned and headed in the opposite direction.

Oh hell, no. He wasn't going to brush her off. She could cope with Aaron giving her the cold and silent treatment but she was damned if she'd let him hurt his niece, the child of her heart. When Aaron ignored her a second time, Kasey looked around, her eyes landing on a pile of fashion dolls Savannah had left on the outdoor table. Picking up a handful she resumed her place at the edge of the pool and hurled a doll at Aaron. It bounced off his shoulder and, because she could, she let fly with another three.

Two missed but the third hit him in the head. Aaron dropped his feet and, standing shoulder-deep in the water, glared at her.

"What the hell was that for?"

"You knew I was trying to get your attention and I don't like being ignored!" Kasey let the last doll fly and Aaron jerked his head out of the way at the very last minute. Pity, Kasey thought.

"What the hell is wrong with you?" Aaron yelled, swimming to the side of the pool and easily hoisting himself out. Kasey felt heat rush to between her legs as her eyes skimmed over those hard muscles and acres of masculine skin. God, she missed him. In her bed and out. She missed being in his arms, being the recipient of those half smiles, the desire in his eyes.

"Well?" Aaron asked, standing in front of her, scowling.

"Well, what?"

Aaron pointed to the plastic dolls floating facedown in the pool. "Want to tell me why you brained me with those?"

Oh, right. Kasey whirled around, picked his towel up from the lounger and tossed it at his chest. She couldn't think properly with all that skin on display, skin and muscles she wanted to glide her hands over, that surly mouth she wanted to kiss more than she wanted to breathe. But she wanted more than the great sex, she wanted his fears, his laughter, his grief. She wanted to comfort him and love him…she wanted to be a part of his life.

But this wasn't about her, it was about Savannah. Looking past him, Kasey stared at the pool.

"I can cope with your surly attitude and the silent treatment, Aaron. You haven't spoken more than a sentence to me since the day we flew back from Durango City." Kasey saw that he was about to object but she silenced his response with a fierce scowl. "You don't owe me a damn thing, but your silent and broody attitude is affecting your niece and *that* I won't tolerate!"

"You won't *tolerate*?" Aaron lifted a supercilious, I-am-the-boss eyebrow. "Last time I checked, you were working for me, Monroe."

"Oh, get over yourself!" Kasey retorted. "I am the only one interacting with Savvie, the one who holds her at night, who dries her tears, who damn well talks to her, so don't you dare pull that I-am-the-boss crap with me! She's scared to laugh at a puppet show today because she thinks that her dad wouldn't like it."

Aaron, admittedly, looked genuinely horrified at that. "Why would she think that?"

"Oh, it might be because you slammed down a glass, cursed and then stormed out of the room when she laughed at something she saw on TV."

Aaron shook his head. "I don't remember doing that and if I did, I'm sure I wasn't angry because she was laughing!"

"It doesn't matter whether you did or didn't, she thinks that. She thinks that she has to be mad and sad because you are. She's hurting, Aaron, and she sees you hurting and she thinks that she has to act like you do." Kasey rubbed her hands up and down her face before looking at Aaron again, suddenly feeling utterly vulnerable. "It's been five days but that little girl needs you, she needs to know that she'll be okay, that you'll be okay, that she isn't going to be living with a surly, broody man for the rest of her life."

Kasey pulled in a deep breath, thought, *What the hell?* and plowed on. "She misses you, Aaron, and I do, too. I miss being with you, touching you, talking to you. I miss my friend and my lover."

Aaron pushed his wet hair off his face and Kasey saw the misery in his hard eyes, the brief tremble in his bottom lip before he firmed his lips. "Yeah, I've been meaning to talk to you about that."

Oh, God, that didn't sound good. "But first, Savannah." He rubbed the back of his neck and nodded. "I'll try and do better with her. Be more open, more interactive."

"She needs your affection, Aaron. She also needs to talk about Jason."

Aaron immediately shook his head. "I don't think I can. It's too hard."

Kasey slapped her hand on his chest and pushed. "This isn't about what you need, Aaron, this is about Savannah. She's the child, you're the adult, and her needs come first."

Aaron sent her a hot look, like he was prepared to argue, but then stepped back, putting space between them so that she had to drop her hand. He stared down at the pool and eventually nodded. "Okay, I hear you. I'll do better with Savannah."

Kasey lifted her eyebrows, knowing her will-you-do-better-with-me question was all over her face. Aaron cursed and shook his head. "I'm not going there, Kasey, not with you."

"Going where?" she asked, feeling the chambers of her heart starting to separate.

"Wherever your fantasies are taking you, there's not going to be a happy-ever-after for you and me. Not the way you envision. There's not going to be a you and me and Savvie living here with two ridiculous dogs, being the perfect family."

Kasey just stared at him, trying to hold her heart together, unable to respond.

"Savvie needs you right now, but I don't, not the way you want me to. I need you to help me with my business, to help Savannah through this horrible period of grief, but when our lives find a new type of normal, Savannah and I will live here on our own and you'll go back to being my virtual secretary."

Really? It seemed that Aaron had this all planned out, knew exactly what the future held and that he expected her to toe the line. The hell she would. She was damned if she'd fall into line just because some man said so.

"I love you, Aaron, more than you'll ever know and at the moment, because you're being an ass, probably more than you deserve."

She saw the horror on his face and rolled her eyes. "Oh, relax, I'm not asking you to love me back, my love isn't conditional. But what I won't accept is you tossing out commands about my life and what I do with it. You're not my boss, Aaron, from the moment I stepped into this house I've been working with you, not for you." Kasey suddenly knew exactly what to do. "I'll take Savannah to school and then I'll go back to my house and work from there, reliev-

ing you of my company. When *I* think Savannah is emotionally stronger—and it will be my decision because you
are emotionally constipated—I will start spending nights
at my cottage, extending the time apart until she feels like
she can do without me on a day-to-day basis. I will stay
in touch with her and God help you if you try to stop me,
Phillips. That's my girl in there and I will fight you, bil-
lionaire bucks or not!

"When Savannah is stronger, I'll resign and find something else to do. I didn't need Dale and I sure as hell don't
need you. Yes, I love you and I'd love a family, a man who
can treat me with the respect I deserve, who can love me
through thick and thin. I'm a good bet, Aaron, and you're
the idiot for not being brave enough to see that!"

Kasey registered the shock on his face but she was too
angry to enjoy it. "I'm going inside before I do, or say,
something I really regret. Or before I brain you with a
chair."

Because the urge to do exactly that was strong, Kasey
thought it best to walk away.

Ten

Aaron rubbed his towel over his head and watched Kasey's beautiful, slender frame cross the entertainment area and disappear into the house. Dropping to sit on a lounger, he reluctantly admitted that he'd screwed up and he'd done an awesome job at it.

Kasey loved him. Or she thought that she did. For an instant he'd been desperate to believe her, to allow himself to hope but then, just in time, he remembered that he'd heard it all before and declarations of love were easy to make. Despite what Kasey said, love was conditional, nobody loved without wanting something in return.

Despite longing for what she offered, the family he once thought he wanted, he was right to walk away.

And, although he'd been lost in grief and anger and guilt, Kasey was right to pull his head out of his ass. He had left her to do the heavy lifting with Savannah, partly because his niece was so much more responsive to Kasey than she was him and, yeah, because it was easier to let

Kasey deal with Savvie's emotions. He was having a hard enough time dealing with his own.

But Savannah was, ultimately, his responsibility and not Kasey's, and he'd never shirked his responsibilities in his life...until now. Aaron, seeing Jason's disappointed face in his mind's eyes, rubbed the moisture off his face, not all of which was pool water, and made a promise to his brother to do better. Jay was relying on him, wherever the hell he was, to make sure that Savvie had the type of childhood, life, Jason would've given her. And that meant that she needed a father and not the shadow man he'd been these past few days.

I'll try, Jay. It might take me a while, but I'll get there. Be patient with me, okay? I've got to learn to be a dad.

He could, and would, learn to be the best dad he could be for Savannah and to honor his brother's memory. But that was as far as he was prepared to go. He meant what he'd said to Kasey, as soon as he got a handle on being a dad, and to some extent, a mom, Kasey would need to move out. They had to go back to normality.

Whatever normality was.

He wanted to protect himself, of course he did, but he needed to protect Kasey, as well. He couldn't give her what she wanted, what she needed. Oh, he had the big house and he'd acquired a cute kid she adored through tragic circumstances, and they had this insanely hot chemistry, but that didn't a future make.

Kasey would never settle for the little he could give her. He was a solitary man, an independent guy, someone who didn't need the reassurances and comfort love brought. He didn't trust easily—no, he didn't trust at all. As she'd pointed out, Kasey, nearly a year after working for him, still didn't know the identity of his core group of investors. She worked closely with him yet he couldn't fully trust her with his business. And if he couldn't trust her with that, how could he trust her, or anyone, with his heart? And it wasn't like he was overreacting or being melodramatic, he had good reason not to trust, to guard himself against the vagaries of life.

And his fear. Because, dammit, he was damned terrified that he would love and lose again.

He wouldn't be able to bear it if he fell in love with Kasey—as he was a hairbreadth away from doing—and he lost her. He'd survived his parents' death, had coped with Kate's betrayal and he would, sometime in the future, be able to cope with Jason's death.

There wasn't a shadow of doubt in his mind that loving and then losing Kasey, through death or a breakup or divorce, would destroy him. He'd gamble with tens of millions of dollars in the workplace and not break a sweat, but tasting the dream of Kasey at his side, raising Savvie as their own, possibly with more kids later on, living, laughing and loving her and then losing her and them and the dream…

Aaron felt his heart rate accelerate, noticed that his breathing was shallow.

No. He couldn't do it. He couldn't trust it to last and if—when!—it disintegrated, he'd fall apart too. He couldn't take that risk.

No, it was better for him, better for Savannah, in the long run, for them to part ways. Despite Kasey calling him an idiot, he still believed it was the smarter option.

It really was. It had to be.

It was a special type of hell to finally realize what you really wanted and know that you were never going to have it. Kasey lifted her coffee cup to her lips, barely registering that the liquid was cold. Although it was only lunchtime, storm clouds were building up outside, casting a strange green light over the neglected garden outside her cottage in Royal.

After Aaron's hard, cold, speech, she'd made good on her promise to put some distance between the two of them. Every morning she dropped Savvie off at school and instead of heading back to the office she shared with Aaron, she drove to her cottage, where she and Aaron communicated virtually.

Kasey picked Savvie up from school and ferried her to and from her after-school activities. Back at "the Shack," she ate supper with the Phillipses, trading as little conversation with Aaron as possible, put Savvie to bed and retreated to spend the long night in Aaron's guest suite.

Rinse and repeat.

Kasey didn't know how much longer she could operate within the confines of their own Cold War. Being around Aaron and only talking to him via email and the occasional video call was more difficult than she imagined. They'd lost the easy way of communicating they'd enjoyed before she'd moved into his home and every conversation was short, stilted and underlined with sadness and regret. Well, it was from her side. She had no idea how Aaron was feeling because he hid his feelings behind his inscrutable mask.

Kasey thought that she knew heartbreak, that she'd experienced the pain of failed relationships, but nothing compared to loving and losing Aaron. Dale's cheating and Michelle's betrayal still hurt but it was now an oozing scratch compared to the open-heart surgery she was currently experiencing.

She wanted Aaron, ideally as her life partner—she wasn't brave enough to dream about being his wife—but she'd settle for being his friend. Unfortunately, she wasn't even that anymore, she was just a woman he'd slept with during an awful period of his life, who'd helped him out during a jam and whom he now wanted to shove firmly back into a take-out-at-work-only box.

A part of Kasey wanted to rail at him, scream at him for being so dense—didn't he see how good they could be together?—but another part of her sympathized with his fear of being hurt. He'd endured more pain than one man should in his lifetime and she couldn't blame him for running from anything, or anyone, who might cause him more.

The hell of it was that she wouldn't. She realized how rare it was to find someone as brutally honest as Aaron, a man who was a curious combination of sensitive but strong, and loyal to a fault. She felt totally secure with Aaron; with his mile-wide streak of integrity she knew that he would never cheat on her, that when he gave his word he would never renege on it.

But he'd never given her his word. Or anything else, and the sooner she accepted that irrefutable fact, the sooner she could start rebuilding her life.

Kasey stretched and, seeing how dark it was outside, flicked on her desk lamp. The wind rattled the window-panes and thunder rumbled in the distance. She hoped the late summer storm would blow away her misery but knew that it might take a couple of summers of storms to feel marginally human again.

Melodramatic much, Monroe? Damn, this being in love—properly in love, grown up in love—wasn't any fun at all.

Her computer buzzed with an incoming call and Kasey's heart flipped when she saw that Aaron was calling. Stupid heart, being so excited to see him, even if it was by a computer screen.

Kasey touched her keyboard and Aaron's beautiful,

much loved face filled her screen. He was in his office, dressed in a pale green T-shirt that matched his eyes. The scruff on his jaw was thicker than normal and worry deepened the creases around his eyes.

"There's a storm coming in," Aaron told her.

Kasey placed her forearms on her desk. "Yeah, I noticed that."

"They are predicting lashing rain and the possibility of hailstones the size of tennis balls," he stated. "Your house might get nailed."

Since there was nothing she could do, Kasey just shrugged.

"Savannah is safe at school, but I think you should come back here," Aaron commanded.

Kasey shook her head. "I'm not getting into my car now to run from a storm, Aaron. I'll be fine."

"Kase—"

"Don't!" she snapped. "Don't pretend you are worried about me, you're just worried that something might happen to the nanny and executive assistant you profess to need so much."

"I do need you!" Aaron shouted, looking angry. And worried.

"Pity that you don't need me the way that I want you to need me," Kasey said. The sound of her doorbell chiming reached her over the rising wind and drumrolls of thunder. "I've got to go, someone is at the door."

"Kase! Just get in your car and come home."

"Conversation's over." Kasey shook her head and pushed her chair back, wondering if he'd noticed how miserable she was. God, she couldn't do this much longer. The doorbell pealed again and she muttered a curse as she headed into her tiny hall to yank open her front door.

Wet and shivering, Dale stood on her porch. Her first

thought was that he was going to catch a cold—he always did—quickly followed by the wonderful realization that her ex being sick wasn't her problem anymore.

Lightning crackled and Kasey pulled Dale into her hall. "What are you doing here?"

"I've been trying to talk to you for weeks," he told her, pushing his hair off his wet forehead. "I drove up so that you and I could have a conversation."

Kasey thought about pushing him out the door, then decided that maybe it would be better to let him get whatever he had to say off his chest so that they could move the hell on. She was so over him.

Wanting to make this quick, Kasey didn't invite him to sit. She just stood in front of her desk and lifted her eyebrows.

"Speak."

Dale looked down at the floor and shuffled his feet. "I know that you won't believe me since I did what I did, but I love you, I always have. I need you to know that."

Kasey snorted and then a sudden thought occurred to her that rocked her world. *No. Freaking. Way.* "Are you trying to tell me that you want me back?"

The hope on his face gave her her answer. Kasey shoved her hands into her hair and laughed, the sound filled with genuine amusement.

"What's so funny?" Dale demanded.

"You are." The lights flickered as the storm threw a temper tantrum outside. "Dale, you don't know what love is and, honestly, neither did I. Love is honesty, it's reliability, it's responsibility. Love is steady, calm, it's inextricably linked with integrity. I now know what love is and it isn't with you and the life I left behind. It's here, in Royal. Love, for me, is Aaron and Savannah."

Dale lifted his lip in a sneer. "Well, I suppose it doesn't hurt that the guy is loaded."

"I would live in a tin shack with him if he asked me to!" Kasey slapped both her hands against his chest and shoved him, making Dale stumble back. "He doesn't want me, you moron! But that's the thing about love, you can't just turn it off and on. I will always love him because love doesn't fade when it's inconvenient, when there's something better to do!"

She swallowed a lump in her throat, forcing herself to go on. "He's in the process of moving me out of his life and my heart is breaking, but worse than that, I know his heart is breaking and there's nothing I wouldn't do to take his pain away! If he had to ask me the smallest thing, or the biggest, today, tomorrow, ten years from now, I would move heaven and earth to give it to him because there's nothing—*nothing!*—I wouldn't do for him. He, and that little girl, are my world. Just because I am not his, doesn't change a damn thing because love isn't selfish, dammit!"

Dale shrugged. "I'll give you some more time, it'll blow over with him."

"It won't and you should consider us completely done, Dale."

His face hardened as her words sunk in. Then his expression changed, becoming harder and meaner. "You mean that, don't you?"

"You have no idea how much."

Dale's lips tipped up in a nasty smile. "Then there's something you should know…" Kasey didn't nibble on that bait, but he carried on regardless. "It wasn't just once."

The wind had kicked up and hard rain started to lash the windows, and Kasey heard the sharp ping of hail on her roof. Dammit, the storm had arrived.

A crack of lightning lit up the room and highlighted the

spiteful look on Dale's face. "Michelle and I didn't sleep together just once, it wasn't just one drunken encounter. We had an affair while you and I dated, again shortly after we were engaged. It carried on, on and off, the entire time we were married."

Kasey stared at him, waiting for the wave of hurt, the jolt of pain. When none came, she looked inside herself and checked. Nope, nothing.

Well, huh.

"Nothing to say?"

Kasey took a moment to find the correct response to adequately convey how little she cared. Dale and Michelle were firmly in her past and she intended to leave them both there. She winced at the expensive sound of glass shattering in her back bedroom courtesy of a big hailstone. Dammit! A crack of lightning sizzled through the air, quickly followed by angry thunder.

"Kasey?"

"I deserve better than this. I'm tired of being tired and I'm tired of giving you and her my energy. I'm done," Kasey stated, as calm as the storm outside was vicious. "I don't care anymore. About you. Or her. Or what you did together."

Somewhere close, a bolt of lightning made contact with the earth, the exclamation point at the end of her sentence and, as if to drive her point home, she and Dale were plunged into darkness.

Great, Kasey thought, being caught in a storm with her less-than-useless ex was exactly what she *didn't* need!

Aaron cursed as the picture of Kasey's nice ass and the sound of their voices faded from his screen. A loss of power was the most logical explanation for the abrupt lost connection and he knew that area of Royal was prone to electrical failures in big storms.

But dammit…

Aaron found himself staring at his monitor, not seeing the icons on his desktop or the ticker tape of stock prices rolling across the bottom of his screen.

She loved him? She'd always be there for him? Today, tomorrow, in ten years' time? She'd do anything for him? Sure, Kasey had told her that she loved him but he hadn't believed her, hadn't realized the depths of her feelings. It hadn't been an off-the-cuff statement, she'd meant every word. More than he realized.

Tin shack? Nothing she wouldn't do for him? Unconditionally? Her words bounced in and out of his brain. She loved him?

Holy crap.

Kasey loved him. Loved him loved him. Properly. Genuinely. Forever.

Aaron felt his breath catch in his throat, felt his heart expand. That amazing, wonderful, giving, sexy woman loved him? He felt like he'd been dropped to the floor by a right hook from a world heavyweight boxer.

He needed to hear her say those words to his face again, to fall into that space where he felt… God, safe. Kasey made him feel safe. He trusted her.

Aaron rubbed his hands over his face, trying to get his heart to restart and his breathing to slow down. He trusted her, he could finally admit that out loud. He probably always, subconsciously, had. He couldn't imagine handing over Savannah's care to anyone he didn't trust, allowing someone he had doubts about into his business, into his bed, his mind…his *heart*.

He'd tried hard to fight it, to fight her, but it was no use—he trusted her with everything he had and the final barrier to love, to being in love, falling in love, was removed. He didn't have an excuse anymore to be alone, to stay alone.

To raise Savannah alone.

This wasn't about Savannah, he realized, and if he found the courage to lay his heart on the line, he had to make it very clear to Kasey that he did need her, and not because he needed help raising Savannah. He needed her because he could be utterly authentic with her, brutally honest. She valued honesty and loyalty as much as he did.

Today, tomorrow, in ten years' time—Kasey made a pledge and he knew that she'd stick to it. And the fact she didn't need him to love her to make that promise floored him. She loved him unconditionally, utterly...*honestly*.

Unconditional love...not love based on his money or earning capacity, on whether he had a college degree. She loved him for who he was and not what he did.

God.

Realizing that the storm had tapered off, Aaron jumped to his feet, determined to get to her, to drop his heart at her feet. He snatched up his keys and when he reached the door, he stopped, halted by a powerful thought. He was running to Kasey because she loved him, she was prepared to give him what he needed, to fill the holes in his life. But could he give her what she needed? This had to be a two-way street...

What did she need?

A husband, a family, security...emotional safety. He'd never cheat on her, they enjoyed each other's company and would have a rocking sex life. Children? They already had one, they could cope with a couple more. So far, so good. Could he love her?

Aaron looked deep inside himself and suddenly realized that it wasn't a question of could, he did. He wasn't sure when he'd started to love her but he thought it was pretty soon after she moved into this house. Did the *when* matter? Wasn't the *how* more important?

He'd move mountains for her, given the chance. If that wasn't something she required of him, then he vowed to make damn sure that she knew, every day of her life, that she was the center of his world. That he'd love every day, every moment, they had together, grateful for the gift she was.

Aaron slapped the frame of the door, switched off the light in his office and headed for the stairs, determined to start this new chapter in his life as soon as he could.

The storm had been fast and furious and over within a half hour. In that short time, it managed to turn her lawn into a lake, punch a hole through her spare bedroom window and uproot the small live oak next to her driveway.

Kasey stood on her driveway and ignored Dale as he crossed the road to climb into the driver's seat of his car. He was leaving her life for the final time and she couldn't be happier about it. Right now she had bigger problems than Dale—and Michelle—to deal with, she had a little girl to collect from school and a house and a yard to clean up.

Kasey heard the low purr of a familiar engine and sighed as she noticed Aaron's familiar SUV turning the corner onto her street. Ah, crap. Now she also had her grumpy, bossy boss to handle.

Really? Couldn't she catch a break? Not willing to rumble with Aaron, she pulled her car keys out of the back pocket of her jeans and pressed the remote control to open her garage door. Hurrying into the small garage, she thought that, if she was really, really lucky, she could be in her car and halfway down her driveway before Aaron pulled up. She'd yell something about collecting Savvie and she'd manage to avoid him for another couple of hours.

Kasey had started to back down her driveway when she saw Aaron in her rearview mirror, pulling... God, what was he pulling across her driveway? Slamming on the brakes, Kasey yanked on the handbrake and flew out of the car. She stopped a little way down her driveway and spent a minute watching Aaron as he pulled a heavy branch across the driveway, directly behind her car.

"What the hell are you doing?" Kasey demanded.

Aaron didn't look at her and Kasey's eyes bounced from his face to the bulging muscles in his arms. "Pulling this damn branch across your driveway."

"I see that. Want to explain why or have you just lost your mind?"

That half smile she'd missed so much touched Aaron's mouth. "To stop you running away from me."

He could've just parked his SUV behind hers to stop her from driving away... Okay, none of this was making a lick of sense. "I do have to collect Savannah at three."

"Depending on how the next fifteen minutes goes, I'll either move the branch or ask Megan to collect Savannah," Aaron said. He looked toward the road where Dale was still sitting in his car, looking at them.

"Why is moron-head still here?" Aaron demanded, glaring at Dale.

"I don't know." Kasey narrowed her eyes at him. "Not that him visiting me has anything to do with you."

Aaron tipped his head. "Really? Actually, I think it has a lot to do with me."

Tired, sad, confused... Kasey wished he would just go. Spending a little time with Dale made her realize how unsuited he was for her and how well she and Aaron gelled.

And knowing that hurt because Aaron didn't want her in his life...

Kasey pushed her hair off her face and looked up at the gray sky. "Just go, Aaron," she begged. "I'm tired and I have the insurance company to call, damage to sort out."

"I'll help you do all that...later," Aaron told her, stepping up to her. "Right now we are going inside and we're going to have a chat."

She couldn't bear to hear the repeat of his "we'll be okay on our own" speech. Of course they would be okay but if they were together they could be a million times stronger and better. Kasey shook her head and lifted her chin. "Just go home, Aaron."

"Okay, then, if you're going to be like that." He placed his hands on her hips, hoisted her over his shoulder in one easy, fluid move, and Kasey found herself dangling down his back. From her upside-down view of the world, she saw Dale's car driving off.

Forgetting about him, she tried to smack Aaron on the ass. "Put me down, you jerk! What the hell!"

"We need to talk," Aaron told her, walking through her front door and kicking the door closed with his foot. He pulled her down and Kasey found herself sliding along his body, his very hard, very "hey, I'm excited to see you" body.

Kasey looked up and her eyes collided with his, amber clashing with pure green. Kasey opened her mouth to say... something but before she could speak the words she was still forming, Aaron's mouth covered hers in a kiss that was as tender as it was sexy, as hot as it was loving. Beneath the shimmer of lust, the layer of desire that always flooded them whenever they touched, she felt something deeper, wiser, infinite in his kiss.

Something she'd never experienced before.

Pulling back, unsure whether her imagination was running wild, Kasey yanked her mouth from his and lifted her fingers to her lips, feeling bewildered.

"What the hell was that?" she murmured.

"That was me, kissing you, the way I intend to kiss you for the rest of our lives."

The rest of their...*what?*

Confused, Kasey allowed Aaron to tug her over to her desk and watched as he picked up a permanent marker, yanked the top off with his teeth and, turning her wrist over, scrawled a few random letters and numbers on her arm.

"What is going on with you?" Kasey demanded, her eyes bouncing from her arm to his face.

"Master code. To my client files, my bank accounts, pretty much everything. With that code you have all the access I can give you to every aspect of my life without compromising my clients' privacy."

"Okay." Kasey frowned. "Why?"

Aaron bent his knees so that his eyes were level with hers. "Because I trust you, Kase. With everything I have, everything I love, I trust you."

Uh... Kasey knew that she was repeating herself but...

What. The. Hell?

She stared at Aaron, wide-eyed and slack-mouthed. "Have you lost your mind?" she asked.

Aaron clasped her face in his big, warm hands, his eyes drilling into her. "Did you mean what you said to your ex? That you loved me, would always love me and that your love wasn't conditional on whether I loved you?"

Kasey frowned. That was the way she felt but she'd never said those exact words to his face. "Why would you think that?"

Aaron looked impatient and jerked his head at her computer screen. "You answered the door but didn't kill the call. I was still there."

Kasey frowned at him. "You listened to my conversation with Dale? That was rude, Phillips!"

"I don't give a damn!" Aaron snapped back. "I want to know if it's true."

Kasey tossed her hair. "What part?" she demanded, stalling for time, conscious of heat filling her face.

"All of it. Specifically, the part about you loving me unconditionally."

Crap. Kasey sighed and looked down at the floor. She'd hoped to keep her pride, hoped to have kept that salient little piece of information to herself.

Kasey felt Aaron lift her chin. "Kase, look at me. Did you mean what you said?"

Kasey nodded. "Yes." She stared at his pale green T-shirt. "Sorry," she added, shrugging.

Aaron pulled her to him and wrapped his arms around her, his big body enveloping hers. "Don't be sorry, Kase. Please don't be sorry for loving me."

"I'm more sorry that you can't love me back." Kasey spoke the words into his broad chest, into the fabric of his T-shirt.

From above her Kasey heard the sound of a soft laugh. "Well, now, that's not completely true."

Kasey pulled back and scowled up at him. "What is that supposed to mean? You love the sex, you love the way I love Savannah, my cooking? What?"

Aaron looked contemplative. "The sex is earth-shattering, I do love the fact that you love Savannah and your cooking is meh at best."

Kasey rolled her eyes before trying to remove herself from his strong grip. "Let me go, Aaron."

"Not in a million years," Aaron told her. Placing his one

hand on her lower back, he pushed his fingers into her hair, holding the back of her head so that she had no choice but to look up. "No more games or wordplay, Kase. Here it is, as forthright and as honest as I can be."

Kasey's eyes widened as she lost the ability to speak.

"I'm utterly, crazy, wildly, in love with you and I only realized it when I heard you tell your ex what I mean to you. I refuse to apologize for my eavesdropping because that conversation changed my world, it opened up my eyes and freakin' ripped me apart, in the best possible way."

Kasey blinked once, then again, but Aaron was still gazing at her with love and adoration in his eyes. "Uh—"

"And I'm not telling you I love you because I need a mom for Savannah or because you are a kick-ass assistant or because I need you in either capacity. I'm telling you I love you because you are… Everything. You are my everything."

Kasey felt tears burning her eyes as she lifted her hand to hold Aaron's much loved face. "Air…"

"Yeah." Aaron closed his eyes briefly, opened them and looked bashful. "I don't have the words, Kase, but I trust you, with everything. With Savvie, with my secrets, with my clients—all of them." He tapped the writing on her wrist. "But most of all, I trust you with my battered, mangled heart."

Kasey, knowing Aaron's issues with trust, got how big those words were, how massive his declaration. If he had told her he loved her but still couldn't trust her, then his love wouldn't mean much; with Aaron love and trust were inextricably intertwined.

Aaron lifted her hand and kissed her knuckles. "Don't go, Kase. Stay with me. Be mine."

Kasey nodded once and the tears she'd been trying to blink away rolled down her cheeks. She wound her arms around Aaron's neck and buried her face in his shoulder, her own shaking with love and relief.

Aaron rubbed her back before releasing her, his thumbs stroking the tears off her cheeks. "Kasey, honey? I love you. You, amazingly, love me. Isn't this supposed to be a good thing?"

Kasey nodded. "I just didn't know how I was going to say goodbye to you and Savvie."

Aaron pulled her back into him and it felt natural to boost herself up, to wrap her legs around his waist, confident that he would support her, in any way she needed, for the rest of her life. "Warning—I'm never letting you go."

"I don't want you to," Kasey told him, her smile on his lips. "I love you so much, Air."

Aaron's face softened as love and adoration danced in his eyes, across his face. "I love you, too, baby." Holding her, he lifted one arm to look at his watch. "I really want to tell Savvie that we are going to be a family but we have a little time." He pretended to think. "I wonder what we can do until then?"

Kasey grinned impishly at him. "Move the branch blocking my driveway? Board up my broken window? Call the insurance company?"

Still carrying her, Aaron started to walk down the hallway to her bedroom, his smile pure sexiness. "Yeah... screw that."

Epilogue

Late the next afternoon, after spending the day in Royal, Kasey walked into Aaron's office to find him on the phone. She smiled when she saw Savannah lying on the floor next to Aaron's desk, coloring, the puppies sitting at her feet.

"Scar, how are you? How's California?" Aaron asked, leaning back in his chair and speaking via speakerphone. His eyes softened as he looked at her and Kasey's heart filled with love. Everything that mattered to her was in this room at this exact time.

Aaron held out his hand to her and she crossed the room.

"All good, Aaron. I'm so sorry to hear about Jason. How's the peanut?"

"I'm okay, Auntie Scarlett," Savannah piped up. "Sad but okay. When are you and baby Carl coming back to Royal? You need to meet my New-find-me puppies."

"Soon, honey. I miss my animals and my friends and my family. I have some news, Aaron. Luke and I were married a few days ago, on the beach, but we're going to settle down in Royal."

Aaron grinned as he pulled Kasey onto his knee, lifting his head in a silent demand to be kissed. Kasey brushed her lips across his before curling up against his chest. He smiled as he congratulated Scarlett and Kasey heard his happiness for his friend in his voice. Who was she again? As if reading her mind, Aaron picked up his pen and jotted Scarlett McKittrick, Veterinarian, and Paradise Ranch across the piece of paper in front of him. Ah.

Aaron's hand moved under Kasey's dress and up her thigh. She shivered and he smiled at her, heat and promise in his eyes.

In the background, Kasey heard the sound of a male voice calling Scarlett's name. "I've got to run. When I'm back, bring the new additions to the family to the clinic so that I can check them over and give them their shots. And bring your new girl, too," Scarlett said.

"There's a deal," Aaron said, smiling as he disconnected the call.

Kasey wound her arm around Aaron's neck and was about to give him a proper, missed-you-like-hell kiss when she saw Savvie scrambling to her feet. Savannah rolled her eyes and placed her hand over Kanga's and then Roo's eyes. "Ugh, more kissing. Let's go, boys."

Kasey blew her a kiss and Savvie smiled before running out of the room, the dogs on her heels. Instead of kissing Kasey, Aaron picked her up and perched her on the edge of his desk. "Sit there for a minute so that we can talk without me getting distracted."

Kasey smiled. They got distracted a lot lately and, currently, not a hell of a lot of work was happening at AP Investments. "Okay."

Aaron stood and placed his hands on his hips. "How did your meeting go with Michelle?"

Kasey shrugged. "It's done. She begged a little, cried a little, tried to lie her way out of it, but I think she's finally accepted that she's no longer a part of my life."

Aaron looked relieved and then concerned. "Are you okay with that?"

Kasey shrugged. It still hurt but she was okay. "I'm making new friends so I will be."

Aaron smiled. "The book club crew. Those women are dangerous."

"But so much fun," Kasey replied.

Aaron's wonderfully green eyes turned serious. "When you walked in just now, I realized that my life started when you walked into it." He bit his bottom lip and shook his head. "But as happy as I am, I have to ask you, again, if you truly know what you are taking on. Savvie and I are a package deal, Kase. Are you ready for that? For her? For me?" Aaron stared down at his feet, his expression a little tortured. "I wouldn't blame you if you wanted some time to think about this."

Did he really think she'd walk when he needed her the most? Kasey placed her hand on his arm, waited until he looked at her. "I love you and I'm not going anywhere, Aaron."

He looked relieved but still a little stubborn. "If you're here because you're worried about me jumping into investigating Jason's death, I told you I wouldn't. I know that I have to leave it to Cole and Will to manage. It pisses me off but my priority is Savvie. And you."

Kasey knew he wanted to, that he was as frustrated as hell standing on the sidelines. "Good to know, but I'm still not going anywhere."

Aaron pushed an agitated hand through his hair. "I need

you to be sure, Kase. We're talking marriage, making us a family…it's all serious stuff."

So serious and *everything* she wanted. Kasey stood and placed her hands on his hips, tipping her head back to look up into his face. "Air, I can't wait for the future…our future. You and me, together. We are a team, we're stronger together than we are apart. As for Savvie, I love her, Air. She's the child of my heart. Even if we have a dozen more, she'll always be my first."

Aaron rested his forehead on hers, tension seeping out of his body.

Kasey kissed him once, then again. "Are we good?"

"Yeah. I love you," Aaron murmured, his smile as warm as sunshine against her lips. Aaron's arms pulled her closer and his mouth brushed hers, full of love and desire. Kasey felt her heart settle and sigh, she was home and all was good with her world.

Then, from outside the door, Kasey heard Savannah admonishing one, or both, puppies. "Kasey's going to be so mad… Why do you guys have to eat her stuff? She's not going to let you be flower dogs when they get married if you don't learn to behave!"

"No dogs at the wedding," Kasey told Aaron.

Aaron used one finger to push a strand of hair off her cheek. His voice was pure tenderness when he spoke. "You say that but we both know that you will walk up the aisle to me with a little girl and two crazy dogs at your side."

He was right and, frankly, Kasey couldn't imagine it happening any other way.

* * * * *

REUNION
WITH BENEFITS

HELENKAY DIMON

One

Spencer Jameson wasn't accustomed to being ignored.

He'd been back in Washington, DC, for three weeks. The plan was to buzz into town for just enough time to help out his oldest brother, Derrick, and then leave again.

That's what Spence did. He moved on. Too many days back in the office meant he might run into his father. Eldrick Jameson was the family patriarch, a recently retired businessman on his fourth wife…and the main reason Spence wanted to be anywhere but the DC metro area most of the time.

But dear old Dad was not the problem this trip. The new wife had convinced him to move to Tortola, an island over fifteen hundred miles away. That was almost enough distance, though Spence would have been fine with more.

No, Spence had a different target in mind today. Abigail Rowe, the woman currently pretending he didn't exist.

He used the keys he borrowed from the office manager to open the door to the abandoned elementary school in northeast DC. The building had been empty for two years, caught in a ball of red tape over government regulations and environmental concerns. Derrick wanted the company to buy it and do a complete internal rebuild to turn the massive property into something usable. Spence was on-site meeting the head of the team assigned to make it happen...the head being *her*, and she actually didn't know he was attending.

He followed the sound of voices, a man's deep laughter and the steady rumble of a lighter female one. Careful not to give away his presence, Spence leaned against the outer hall wall and peeked into what he guessed used to be the student dining hall. Paint peeled off the stucco walls. Old posters were half ripped down and half hanging by old tape. Rows of luncheon tables and benches had been replaced with one folding table and a couple of chairs that didn't look sturdy enough to hold an adult.

A woman stood there—*the* woman. She wore a sleek navy suit with a skirt that stopped just above the knee. She embodied the perfect mix of professionalism and sexiness. The flash of bare long legs brought back memories. He could see her only from behind right now but that angle looked really good to him.

Just as he remembered.

Her brown hair reached past her shoulders and ended in a gentle curl. Where it used to be darker, it now had light brown highlights. Strands shifted over her shoulder as she bent down to show the man standing next to her—almost on top of her—something in a file.

Not that the other man was paying attention to whatever she said. His gaze traveled over her. As she talked and pointed, he leaned back slightly and stared at her legs then up higher.

Spence couldn't exactly blame him, but nothing about that look was professional or appropriate. The lack of respect was not okay. The guy's joking charm gave way to something much more territorial and heated. As far as Spence was concerned, the other man was begging for a punch in the face.

As if he sensed his behavior was under a microscope, the man glanced up and turned. Spence got a full-on view of him. He looked like every blond-haired, blue-eyed guy in his midthirties who hung out in bars around the city looking for young Capitol Hill interns to date. Good-looking in a still-brags-about-his-college-days kind of way. That sort of thing was big in this town, as if where you went to school defined you a decade or so later.

Point was, Spence knew the type. Charming, resourceful and looking for an easy lay. He knew because he'd been that guy. He just grew out of it well before he hit thirty.

The other man's eyebrows rose and he hesitated for a second before hitting Spence with a big flashy smile. "Good afternoon."

At the intrusion, Abby spun around. Her expression switched from surprised to flat-mouthed anger in the span of two seconds. "Spencer."

It was not exactly a loving welcome, but for a second he couldn't breathe. The air stammered in his lungs. Seeing her now hit him like a body blow. He had to fight off the urge to rub a hand over his stomach.

They'd worked together for months, every day with him wanting to break the office conduct rules and ask her out. He got close but backed off, sensing he was crossing a line. Then she made a move. A stolen touch here. A kiss there. He'd battled with his control and waited because he needed to be careful. But he'd wanted her from the first moment he saw her. Now, months later, the attraction still lingered...which ticked him off.

Her ultimate betrayal hadn't killed his interest in her, no matter how much he wanted it to.

"Spencer Jameson?" The guy walked toward Spence with his arm extended. "Excellent to meet you."

"Is it?" Spencer shook the guy's hand as he stared at Abby. He wasn't sure what was going on. Abby was supposed to be here with her team. Working. This felt like something else.

"I didn't realize you'd be joining us." Her deep voice stayed even, almost monotone.

If she was happy to see him, she sure hid it well. Frustration pounded off her and filled the room. The tension ratcheted up to a suffocating degree even though none of them moved.

Spence tried not to let his gaze linger on her. Tried not to show how seeing her again affected him. "Where are the others?"

The man did a quick look around the empty room. "Excuse me?"

"Derrick told me—"

"Rylan Stamford is the environmental engineer who is performing the site assessment." She even managed to make that sentence sound angry and clipped.

The job title didn't really explain why Rylan looked ready to jump on Abby a second ago. Spence sensed Rylan's mind wasn't only on the job. "Our assessment?"

"The city's," Abby said. "Rylan isn't employed by us."

Rylan's smile grew wider. "But I've been working very closely with Abby."

Yeah, Spence kind of hated this guy. "I'm sure."

Abby exhaled loud enough to bring the conversation to a halt. She turned back to the table and started piling the paperwork in a neat stack. "Did you need something, Spence?"

She clearly wanted to be in control of the conversation and them seeing each other again. Unfortunately for her, so did he. And that started now. "We have a meeting."

She slowly turned around again. "We do?"

"Just the two of us." The idea was risky and maybe a little stupid, but he needed to stay in town until his soon-to-be sister-in-law gave birth. Derrick's fiancée's pregnancy was high-risk and Spence promised to help, to take some of the pressure off Derrick.

"Oh, I see."

That tone… Abby may as well have threatened to hit him with her car. She definitely was not happy to see him. Spence got that. "No, you don't."

She sighed. "Oh, really?"

If words had the force of a knife, he'd be sliced to pieces. She'd treated him to a prickly, unwelcome greeting and, if anything, the coolness had turned even icier since then.

The reaction struck him as interesting, infuriating even, since *he* was the injured party here. She cheated on him. Well, not technically, since they weren't officially going out back then, but she'd done the one thing he could not stand—she used him to climb the ladder to get to a stronger, more powerful Jameson: his father.

Spence glanced at Rylan. He stood there in his perfectly pressed gray suit and purple tie. He had the right watch. The right haircut. He'd shined his shoes and combed his hair. Nothing—not one damn thing—was out of place on this guy.

Clearly Rylan hoped this was a date or the prelude to a date and not an informal afternoon business meeting.

Well, that was enough of that.

"Are you done here?" Spence asked Rylan, making sure his tone suggested the answer should be yes.

"Absolutely." Rylan's sunny disposition didn't dim one bit. He put a hand on Abby's arm and gave it a squeeze. "I'll call you tomorrow so we can go over the list of concerns." His hand dropped as he faced Spence again and nodded. "Mr. Jameson."

Yeah, whatever. "Rylan."

Spence watched the engineer leave. He'd never had such a sudden negative reaction to a person in his life. Rylan could have said anything and Spence would have disliked him.

Abby leaned back with her hands resting on the table on either side of her hips. "Heavy-handed as always, I see."

Facing her head-on, without a buffer, tested the defenses he'd thrown up against her. He shouldn't care. It shouldn't mean anything. If only his brain and his body would listen to that order.

Despite standing ten feet apart, Spence felt a familiar sensation spark inside him. Desire mixed with lust and a bit of confusion. The intensity hit him full force.

"Did I interrupt your date?"

She rolled her eyes. "Right. Because I'm incapable of meeting with a man without crawling all over him."

"You said it, not me."

She exhaled loud enough to let him know she had better things to do. "What do you want?"

She didn't back down. He'd always loved that about

her. The boss-employee boundaries didn't mean much to her. If she had a thought, she said it. If she disagreed, she let him know. She'd been tactful in not making angry announcements in the office lunchroom, but she wasn't the type to coddle a man's ego, either.

He'd found that sexy. So sexy even as his life crumbled around him and his relationship with his father, which had never been good, disintegrated.

"Is that how you talk to your boss?" He figured he may as well try to reestablish the lines between them. Like it or not, they had to figure out a way to tolerate each other.

For him, it meant ignoring the way she walked and the sound of her voice. Forgetting that he once was willing to go against his father to be with her. But he had to smash all of those feelings, all that vulnerability, now.

"Is that what you are? Last I checked, you ran out of the office and never looked back. If this were a cartoon, you would have left a man-size hole in the wall." She smiled for the first time.

"I'd had a surprise." As if that was the right word for seeing the woman you wanted locked in the arms of a father who turned out to be a constant disappointment.

She pushed away from the table. Without looking at him, she finished straightening the stacks of files. Made each edge line up. "You still think you're the victim then?"

"You were kissing my father."

She glanced over at him again. "Why are you here, Spence?"

No denial, but just like the last time they'd talked—yelled and argued with each other—and a hint of sadness settled in her big brown eyes. Her shoulders fell a bit and for just a second, she didn't look like the confident, in-charge woman he knew her to be.

He had no idea what that meant. But he did have a job to do. "This is an important project and—"

"I mean in DC." She picked up the stack of files and hugged them tight to her chest. "Are you back permanently?"

He hated that question. Derrick had asked it. People at the company had asked. The guy at the rental car company wanted to know. Spence gave her the same answer he'd given to everyone for three weeks. "Derrick needs some help."

"Huh." She frowned at him as her gaze wandered over his face. "I don't really think of you as the type to drop everything and come running to assist someone else."

Charming. "It's not as if we know each other all that well, do we?"

"I guess not." She bent down and picked up her bag. She looked cleaned up and ready to bolt.

"Derrick's fiancée has a health issue," he said.

The anger drained from Abby's face. So did some of the color. She took a step forward with her hand out, but dropped her arm right before she touched him. "Did something new go wrong with the pregnancy?"

"You know about that?" Sure, the pregnancy had been on the gossip sites. One of the playboy Jameson heirs settling down was big news. Their lives had been followed and dissected for years. Every mistake highlighted. Every girlfriend photographed. The rumors, the lies. But the family hadn't confirmed the pregnancy because it was too soon and too personal. "Are you two friends?"

Abby's expression went blank. "You sound horrified by the idea."

Admittedly, he was acting like a jerk, as if everything was about him. Ellie, Derrick's fiancée, needed support. Spence got that. But still… "Well, it will be a bit uncomfortable, don't you think?"

"As uncomfortable as this conversation?"

For some reason, the response knocked the wind right out of him. He almost smiled, but managed to beat it back at the last minute. "Look, we're going to need to get along."

She shrugged. "Why?"

Man, she had not changed one bit. *"Why?"*

"You've been back for three weeks and we've successfully avoided each other. I say we keep doing that."

She sounded aloof and unaffected, but he could see her white-knuckle grip on the files. Much tighter and she'd cut off circulation to her fingers. In fact, this close he saw everything. The flecks of gold around the outside of her eyes. The slight tremor in her hands.

He could smell her, that heady mix of ginger and something sweet. It was her shampoo and it floated to him now.

He inhaled, trying to calm the heartbeat pounding in his ears. "Now who's running?"

"Do you really want to have this conversation? Because we can." She took one more step. The move left little more than a whisper of air between them. "I'm not the one who saw something, misinterpreted it and then threw the mother of all hissy fits."

The air in the room closed in around him. He could actually feel it press against his back. "Misinterpreted?"

"You're offended by my word choice?"

"You were kissing my father!" He shouted the accusation loud enough to make the walls shake.

A sharp silence descended on them right after. In

the quiet, she retreated both physically and emotionally. The air seemed to seep right out of her.

"That's what you think you saw." Not a question.
Not really even a statement. She said the words and let
them sit there.

The adrenaline shooting through him refused to ease
off. "Hell, yes!"

"You can let yourself out." She walked around him
and headed for the door.

"Hey." His hand brushed against her arm. He dropped
it again when she glared at him. "Fine. No touching."

"None." Which sounded like *not ever.*

Regret plowed into him. He came here for them to
talk this out. He'd gone into the computer and looked
up her schedule. Came here unannounced, thinking
he'd have the upper hand.

"I want us to be civil toward each other," he said
as he struggled to bring his voice back under control.

She shook her head. "No."

"What?" He'd been the one to offer the olive branch.
He hadn't insisted on an apology or that she take responsibility. But she still came out swinging and didn't stop.

"You lied to me," she said in a voice growing stronger with each word.

For a second, his brain misfired. He couldn't think
of a response. "When?"

"You let me believe you weren't *that guy*, but you
are. Rich, entitled, ready to bolt, tied to his daddy and
desperate for approval." She counted out his perceived
sins on her fingers.

That fast his temper skyrocketed again. Heat flushed
through him "That's enough."

"The suggestion still stands. We ignore each other."

"Does that mean you're going to leave every room I enter? Get off projects I'm overseeing?"

She shrugged. "That all works for me."

No, he was not going to be pushed into a corner. He was the boss. He wasn't the one who screwed everything up.

He pointed at her. "You did this to us."

Her mouth dropped open. For a second, she didn't say anything, and then she clenched her teeth together. "You're unbelievable."

She slipped by him a second time. Got the whole way to the doorway.

"Stop trying to storm off, and talk to me." He didn't try to grab her but he did want to.

She was absolutely infuriating. Every word she said pushed him until the frustration mixed with the attraction and it all pounded in his head.

"Okay." She whipped around and faced him again. "You want me to talk, try this. You're no better than your father."

The words sliced through him. Ripped right through the layers of clothing and skin.

"I guess you should be the one to compare us since you kissed both of us." When she just stood there, staring at him, he wanted to lash out even harder. "What, no comeback?"

"Stay out of my way."

"Or?"

"Don't push me, Spence. Other people might be afraid of you or want to impress you, but I know better." She shook her head. "What you need is for someone to kick your butt. Keep talking and I will."

Two

Everything was weird now. For the last few weeks, Abby didn't think twice about heading over to Ellie's house on the tree-lined street in Georgetown for a visit. She lived with and was engaged to Derrick Jameson and their high-risk pregnancy had people at work, their friends—everyone—on edge.

Derrick was Spence's older brother, and Spence was the nightmare that just wouldn't go away, so Abby was torn. Being friends with someone tied that closely to the man who broke her heart promised more pain. That was the last thing Abby needed.

Ellie and Abby met by accident, really. Someone wrongly suggested Abby and Derrick were having a "thing" and Ellie stopped by Abby's office to apologize for getting her dragged into their personal business and someone else's vendetta. Abby still didn't understand what happened, but she was grateful for the warning and the show of trust from Ellie, a woman who didn't know her at all at that point. That was three weeks ago and they'd been friends since.

Trust was more than she ever got from Spence, the man she'd planned to date, sleep with, before he stormed off refusing to listen to her months ago. The awful day played out so clearly on a loop in her head.

Panic and frustration whirled together in her mind. "It's not what you think."

"I have eyes, Abby." And that furious gaze switched back and forth between her and his father...and his hand on her waist. The noise rumbling out of Spence almost sounded like a snarl. "You want the top of the Jameson food chain? He's all yours. Good luck."

She tried to follow him but Eldrick held on. "Spence, wait—"

"I told you." Eldrick smiled down at her as she yanked her arm out of his grip. "You're going after the wrong Jameson."

"I'm so happy you came..." Ellie's smile fell as she talked. "What happened?"

The memory blinked out at the sound of Ellie's voice. Abby snapped back into reality as she stood in the doorway to Ellie and Derrick's bedroom, holding a box of brownies from that place in Foggy Bottom that Ellie had raved about a few days before.

Abby had no idea what conversation she missed as her mind wandered, but both Derrick and Ellie stared at her. Ellie was cuddled up in a blanket in the center of the gigantic never-seen-a-king-size-bed-that-big bed with pillows tucked around her body and the television remote control in her hand. Derrick, still wearing his dress pants and button-down shirt, sat next to her. Not on top of her, but close enough for the intimacy, the closeness, to flow around them. His only nod to being home and not at work came in the removal of his tie. It lay over the armrest of the overstuffed chair by the bed.

"Nothing." That seemed like a reasonable response to most things, so Abby went with that as her answer.

"Huh." Ellie made a face. "You look furious."

Derrick let out a long breath. "So, Spence."

"Definitely Spence," Ellie said with a nod.

Well, they weren't wrong. Derrick and Spence were brothers and her bosses. But still. "I don't know how you two are related."

"We're actually a lot alike." Derrick smiled at first but when Abby stood there, not moving, Derrick bit his bottom lip. "But I can see that's the wrong answer."

"Did something happen?" Ellie patted an empty space on the bed, inviting Abby farther into the room to take a seat.

Seeing the two of them, with Derrick's arm resting on the pillows behind Ellie and his fingers slipping into her hair and massaging her neck, struck Abby with the force of a slap. A pang of something…jealousy, regret, longing…moved through her. She couldn't identify the feeling or grab on to it long enough to assess it. But the idea that she was interrupting did crash on top of her.

She was about to drop the brownies and run when she saw both of their faces. The concern. Derrick was the big boss and he deserved to know Spence hadn't really done anything wrong. This time.

She shook her head. "Nothing, really. He walked onto my job site unannounced."

Derrick winced. "Yeah, about that."

Ellie's head slowly turned and she pinned Derrick with a you're-in-trouble glare. "What did you do?"

"With you being on bed rest—"

"Don't blame me," Ellie warned.

"Let me try again." Derrick, the tough, no-nonsense boss who sent employees scurrying, cleared his throat. "Since I can't be in the office as much as usual right now—"

Ellie's sigh echoed around the room. "You're still blaming me."

They were so cute, so perfectly in sync, that Abby took pity on Derrick. "Let me guess. Spence is overseeing some of the projects now that he's back in town."

Derrick closed his eyes for a second before opening them again. Relief poured off him. "Thank you and yes."

She wasn't willing to let him *all* the way off the hook. "Like the one I'm in charge of."

"The key phrase there is that *you are in charge.* Spence watching over the project is in line with office procedure. It's purely a we-need-to-know-what's-happening check. You know that."

"That was a lot of words," Ellie said in a stunned voice.

"I wanted to be clear."

This time, she rolled her eyes at him. "Uh-huh. You're sure you're not doing something else?"

Derrick smiled. "I have no idea what you're talking about."

Abby got it. Derrick rarely explained himself. He'd gone into an office-manual description with his answer. That immediately put Abby on edge. The idea of Derrick playing matchmaker or trying to push people together to talk…forget it. That was ridiculous. He wasn't that great with people, which is why his assistant, Jackson Richards, worked nonstop and everyone ran to him for everything.

It also explained why the entire office celebrated when Derrick fell in love with Ellie. Everyone hoped love would soften him. It had, except for the palpable panic that now hovered around him due to the endangered pregnancy.

Still, shortly after Spence left town, Abby had been promoted. She'd seriously considered turning the offer down out of fear of it being perceived as a payoff to get her to keep quiet about the Jameson men shenanigans. Then she decided she qualified for the position and needed the money because there was no way she was staying at Jameson for long.

She went from assistant to project manager. Now she had a seat at the manager's table. She didn't need a full-time babysitter, and certainly not *that* full-time babysitter. "Spence showed up at a site meeting unannounced."

"He does have access to your calendar," Derrick said.

Ellie patted Derrick's knee where it lay curled on the bed beside her. "I love you but you're not very good at this."

Loyalty. Derrick and Spence had it. Abby got that.

"No, it's fine." She tried to keep her voice even but knew she failed when Derrick frowned and Ellie's eyes widened.

"Really?" Ellie snorted. "Because that tone did not sound fine."

Derrick had stopped massaging Ellie's neck but he started again. "I think she's afraid she'll upset you if she launches into her why-I-hate-Spence speech."

Ellie waved the concern away as she turned the television from muted to off. "Nope. Jameson family gossip is ridiculously delicious. I'm always happy to hear it."

Hate Spence. If only. Abby's life would be so much easier if she did hate Spence. She'd tried. Her mind spun with all the ways he'd failed her. How he hadn't believed her or let her explain. She could call up a ton of hate for the elder Mr. Jameson and heaps of anger and disappointment for Spence, but that was it. And seeing him again...her normal breathing still hadn't returned.

She'd heard his deep, rich voice in the hallway at work and ducked into the closest office to avoid him. Then there was his face. That gorgeous face. The straight black hair and striking light brown eyes. He'd been blessed with those extraordinary Jameson genes, including a hint of his Japanese grandmother around the nose and cheeks. Tall, almost six-two with impossibly long legs and a trim waist, Spence was a bit more muscled than Derrick. Spence's shoulders, and that pronounced collarbone, cried out for kisses.

Not that she noticed.

She was trying really hard not to notice.

With a shake, she forced her mind back to work and the best way to survive being in the same building as Spence. "Well, hopefully it was a one-time thing and I can submit reports or tell Jackson and make Jackson talk to Spence."

Derrick frowned. "That sounds like an efficient use of office resources."

"It might keep Spence alive." Ellie slipped her fingers through Derrick's as she spoke. "Just saying."

The gentle touch seemed to spark something in Derrick. He sat up a bit straighter as he looked at Abby. "If it's a problem to deal with Spence, I'll switch projects with him. I'll be the silent Jameson looming in the background on yours."

As if she could agree to that. Saying yes to the offer suggested she couldn't handle pressure, and that was not a message Abby wanted to send.

Ellie visibly squeezed his hand. "That's not really how you run the office, is it?"

"No," Derrick said.

Abby shrugged. "Sort of."

For a few seconds, no one spoke. They all looked at each other, back and forth, as the tension rose. Abby wasn't clear on what was happening. Maybe some sort of unspoken chat between Ellie and Derrick. But Abby did know that the cool room suddenly felt suffocating. Even the cream-colored duvet cover with the tiny blue roses—an addition she would bet money moved in with Ellie—didn't ease the mood.

"Everything okay in here?" Spence's firm voice boomed into the silence.

He hovered right behind her. Abby could almost feel the heat pulse off his body. When he exhaled, his warm breath blew across the back of her neck.

Time to go. That phrase repeated in her head until it took hold.

"Spence." Ellie smiled. "Look, it's Spence."

"I do live here. Temporarily, but still."

In the bedroom down the hall. Abby knew because she'd walked by it a few days ago and glanced in. Saw a bag and hoped it meant nothing. Then she recognized Spence's tie from the day before flung over the unmade bed.

"For now." Abby meant to think and not say it, but she managed to mumble it.

Of course Spence heard and placed a hand on her lower back. "Meaning?"

The touch, perfectly respectable and so small, hit her like a live wire. Energy arced through her. She had to fight the urge to lean into him. To balance her body against his. "I'm sure you'll be on your way again soon."

Spence's exhale was louder, more dramatic this time. "That's not—"

Derrick stood up. "As fun as it is to see you two work things out by lobbing verbal volleys at each other, Ellie does need her rest."

"I'm having fun." Ellie caught Derrick's hand.

Abby silently thanked Derrick for giving her the easy out. Once she maneuvered her way through the three-story brick mansion, she'd be gone.

She put the box of brownies on the bed and pointed to them. "I just wanted to drop them off. Don't eat them all at once."

"You're very sweet." Ellie went to work on the tape holding the sides of the box down. "I make no promises about how fast they'll be gone." She shot Derrick and Spence a serious look. "So we're clear, I'm not sharing."

"No one would dare defy that order." Abby could not escape fast enough. "I'll text you later."

She pivoted around Spence and practically raced down the hall. Moved as fast as her stupid spiky heels would let her without wiping out in an inglorious sprawl. The humming in her head blocked out all sounds. She didn't realize she'd been followed until she reached the bottom of the intricately carved wooden staircase and heard footsteps behind her.

She turned around just as she left the steps. Spence was there. Of course he was.

With his palm flattened against the wall and his other on the banister, he stopped. She couldn't help but stare. His body was an amazing mystery to her. A package she ached to unwrap. How long were his arms, anyway?

His expression stayed blank as his gaze searched her face. "What are you doing here?"

"Visiting Ellie." Not a lie. She'd brought a treat and everything.

Spence finished coming down the stairs. Slipped his body by hers until they stood side by side. "How do you even know her?"

He still towered over her. She stood a good five-eight and with the heels could talk to anyone without feeling as if someone was trying to intimidate her. But Spence still towered, though he did stand a few steps back, giving her space.

"I do work at the company," she pointed out, not knowing what else to say.

"A lot of people work there. None of them show up at the boss's house." Spence folded his arms across his middle and stared her down. "What's really going on?"

He had to be kidding with this. "Do you think I'm stalking you?"

"Are you?"

She was doing the exact opposite, whatever that was called. Hiding from him? Sort of. Trying to find breathing room to center her control and ease the disappointment that clawed at her every time she thought about him and what could have been. "Lately, when I come over I text first to make sure you're gone. Happy?"

His arms slid down until they hung at his sides again. "Isn't that a bit extreme?"

"No." It was self-preservation.

She refused to get snared in another Jameson trap. She trusted Derrick. He'd delivered on every promise he'd made to her back then, when he begged her to stay with the company after... Spence.

"Sooner or later, we're going to need to talk to each other," Spence said.

"I disagree." Not her most mature answer ever but probably the most honest one.

"Abby, come on."

The tone of his voice suggested he was done playing games. Well, that made two of them. "It's fascinating that you ran off without saying a word months ago, but now you want some big chatty moment with me. I guess us talking is fine so long as it's convenient to you."

"We're adults."

Lecturing. Great. Just what she wanted from him. "One of us is."

With that, she turned and walked out. She'd reached her maximum load on Jameson testosterone for one day. She needed her shoes off and her feet up. Some wine. No Spence.

A Spence-free zone. The idea made her smile as she walked down the hall then closed the front door behind her.

"She's not wrong," Derrick said as he slowly walked down the stairs.

"You want to clue me in here?" Because Spence felt deflated and empty. The gnawing sensation refused to leave him. He'd blown out of the office all those months ago. Traveled around. Helped out on random building sites across the east. Lived a life so different from the spectacle he'd grown up in. All that competition. How his father pitted the three of them against each other. How Derrick always tried to protect them from Dad's wrath, especially Carter, the youngest.

They lost their mom to cancer. Their father didn't even have the decency to let her live out her life in peace. No, he moved her to a facility then marched in there one day and demanded a divorce so he could marry his mistress. He thought she was pregnant but she wasn't, so he quickly dumped the mistress, too. Then he ran through others. He was on wife number four and insisted this one had changed him. Yeah, right. The man treated women as disposable and his sons as property.

All that playing, all that acting at being a Big Man, and he let the business slide. Derrick had stepped in and saved it years ago. They all had to work there from the time they were teens. It was a family requirement, but Derrick was the one who rescued them all—including their father—and restored the family checking account when he took over the day-to-day operations four years ago.

That incredible turnaround was one of the reasons Spence stood on Derrick's first floor now. He owed Derrick. He also loved Derrick and wanted to help. That meant sticking around. Worse, it meant facing his demons and dealing with Abby.

Spence wasn't good at standing still. He'd always been the brother to keep moving. Go away to school. Go farther to a different school. Try to work somewhere else. Delay full-time work with the family as long as possible.

The Jameson name choked him. He didn't find it freeing or respectable. Forcing his feet to stay planted was taking all of his strength. He didn't have much left over to do battle with Abby.

"Are you admitting you're clueless? That's a start." The amusement was right there in Derrick's voice.

At the sound, some of the churning in Spence's gut eased. He had no idea how to handle Abby, but he could do the fake fighting-with-his-brother thing all day. "Don't make me punch you while your fiancée is on bed rest. She shouldn't see you beg and cry right now."

"Are you quoting from a dream you once had? Because that's not reality."

They'd physically fought only once. It was years ago, over their mother. Spence had been desperate to keep her in the house with nurses. Derrick, barely in his twenties, had tried to make it happen but couldn't. Spence had needed an outlet for his rage and Derrick was right there. The perfect target.

There was an almost three-year age difference between them, but Spence still got his ass kicked. And he'd deserved it because his anger really should have been aimed at his father. Spence was thirty-three now. In theory, he knew better.

"Spence, she's one of the best we have." Derrick sat down on a step a few from the bottom and started counting out Abby's attributes on his fingers. "She can multitask and oversee projects, keep things moving. She's smart. She's a great negotiator."

It was an impressive list, but Spence already knew it by heart. Every time he tried to run through her sins in his mind, the image of her face would pop up and his thoughts would stumble. "I feel like you're reading her résumé to me."

"Don't scare her away."

There was no amusement in his tone now. Spence got the message. "You do understand she screwed me, right?"

"I don't know what happened back then because you bolted and when I tried to talk with her, in part to make sure we weren't going to get sued, she refused to say one single negative thing about you." Derrick threw up his hands before balancing them on his thighs again. "Hell, I can name twenty bad things just sitting here and without thinking very hard, but she protected you."

"She sure has no problem listing out my faults now."

"Do you hear what I'm saying?"

"That you're nosy as hell." Spence dropped down on the step two down from Derrick and stretched out sideways so he could look at Derrick. "What's your actual point?"

"Maybe you got it wrong back then."

Spence leaned his head back against the staircase railing and stared up at the ceiling. "I saw her kissing Dad."

"Right, because our father never set anyone up or did anything to mess with us."

That got Spence's attention. His head lowered and he looked at Derrick. "I don't—"

"When rumors were going around about me in an attempt to convince Ellie to dump me, Abby's name came up."

"What?"

"Some people think the two of us had a thing. There are whispers, none of them true, but they're out there." Derrick shrugged. "Ellie heard, wanted to apologize to Abby for dragging her into our personal mess, they met and, honestly, it's like they've known each other for years."

Derrick and Abby. Fake or not, there was an image Spence never wanted in his head. But Abby and Ellie? No one was safe if those two put their powers together. "That's just great."

"For you, no. Abby is going to be around here for Ellie. And she's a big part of the managerial team at work." Derrick dropped his arm and touched the step right by Spence's shoulder. "I want you here and I will do anything to keep you in the office and in town, but even I can't work miracles. You have to fix this because I can't."

"I've never heard you admit that before."

"You're going to run into her."

Derrick sounded so serious. Spence wanted to make a joke or ignore the whole conversation. He knew he couldn't do either. "I can handle it."

"I'm wondering if the rest of us will survive it."

Suddenly, so was Spence.

Three

Abby sat in a conference room on the fifteenth floor of the swanky office building where Jameson Industries was located. A glass wall with the glass door fronted the room, facing into the hall. The room was reserved for relatively few people in the company because it connected to Jackson Richards's office next door. He used it. Derrick used it. Today, she used it.

She looked at the stack of papers in front of her, then to her laptop, then across the small round table to Jackson. He was Derrick's right-hand man and the most accessible person on the management staff. He was also tall and lean with a runner's body and, if rumors were correct, the one every single woman in the office named as the most eligible and interesting man in the office. There hadn't been an actual poll, to her knowledge, but she got asked at least a few times a week if he was dating anyone. Not that Abby saw him in a romantic way. She didn't.

She considered Jackson one of her closest friends, if not *the* closest. After a relatively solitary existence growing up—just her and her mom and the apartment manager who watched her when her mom worked the night shift at the diner—dating here and there, keeping attachments light in case she needed to get up and go, Jackson acted as a lifeline for her. They even lived in condos next door to each other, which was more of an accident than anything else. But when you heard about a good deal on a downtown DC property with a doorman and reasonable monthly fees, you jumped on it. Jackson sure had.

But right now she was at work and out of patience. She beat back the urge to knock her head against the table. "If I have to read one more email from Rylan, my brain will explode."

The man sent her the most mundane emails. The status check today, which he sent a day earlier than he said he would, was to tell her nothing had changed. Yeah, she guessed that much. But with emails clogging her inbox and her mind on constant wandering mode these days, she needed something solid. Jackson was it.

"Good thing we have good health insurance here," Jackson said as he closed the file he was reading.

She snorted. "I'm pretty sure head explosion isn't covered."

"He is persistent." Jackson glanced at the conference room door as it opened. "Speaking of which..."

"Hello." Spence stepped inside. He didn't make a move to sit down. He stopped and rested his palms on the back of the chair nearest to him.

That fast, the oxygen sucked out of the room. The easy banter with Jackson gave way to suffocating tension. It pressed in on Abby, proving what she already knew. Seeing Spence grew harder each time, not easier.

Jackson smiled as he moved some of the files and papers around to make room in front of an open chair. "Hey, Spence."

As far as Abby was concerned, all of that accommodating was unnecessary. She had no interest in sitting there, explaining her projects to Spence. She had a file made up with the relevant information and emailed him the rest. She'd done her part to keep the machine running.

"Right." She shut her laptop, careful not to slam the cover down, and stood up. "I'm going to head back to my office."

"I need to talk to you for a second." Spence's gaze moved from her to Jackson.

Jackson sighed. "Why are you looking at me? I'm supposed to be in here. I'm not leaving."

"Help me out," Spence said.

Jackson shook his head as he stood up. "Did you not hear my dramatic sigh?"

"It was tough to miss."

"That's because I spend half my life rescuing Jamesons from certain disaster." Jackson ended the back-and-forth with a smack against Spence's shoulder.

Some of the tension drained away as Jackson and Spence fell into their easy camaraderie. That sort of thing always amazed Abby. Men could argue and go at each other, but if they were friends or related, they seemed to have this secret signal, heard only by them, that triggered the end of the battle. Then all the anger slipped away.

She wished she possessed that skill.

She glanced at Jackson. "You deserve a raise."

"Hell, yeah." Jackson winked at her as he walked out of the conference room through the connecting door to his office.

A second later, Spence slid into the seat Jackson abandoned. He flipped through a whole repertoire of nervous gestures, none of which she'd seen from him before. He rubbed the back of his neck. Shifted around in his seat. Put a hand on the table then took it off. But he didn't say a word.

After about a minute, the silence screamed in her head. "You're up, Spence. You're the one who wanted to talk."

Fight was probably more accurate. They couldn't seem to be civil to each other for more than a few minutes at a time since living in the same town again. They verbally sparred. Every conversation led them back to the same place—he believed she came on to his father. The idea made her want to heave.

He let out a heavy sigh that had his chest lifting and falling. "We got off on the wrong foot."

"When?"

He frowned. "What?"

"Now or back then?" She was having a hard time keeping up, so he was going to need to be more specific. "Maybe when we were starting to go out and had plans for our first official date that Friday. You left on Thursday without a word."

The memories flashed in her brain and she blinked them out. She refused to let the sharp pain in her chest derail her. This close, right across the table, she could see the intensity in his eyes, smell that scent she associated with him. A kind of peppery sharpness that reeled her in. In the past. Not now. She wouldn't let it happen now.

"You are determined to make this difficult." He had the nerve to look wounded.

She pushed down her anger and lifted her chin. "Do you blame me?"

"Actually, yes." He sat back in the chair. The metal creaked under his weight as he lifted the front two legs off the floor. "You kissed my father."

And there it was. The only point he could make, so he did it over and over until it lost its punch. "So you've pointed out. Repeatedly."

"Okay. Enough." A thud echoed through the small room as the front legs of his chair hit the floor again.

"I agree." She stood up. Her vision blurred. She struggled through a haze of anger and disappointment to see the stacks of documents and folders in front of her.

"Please, sit." His hand slipped over hers. "I know you think I'm an ass, but I'm here because I am worried about Ellie and the baby. The chance of my big brother running himself into the ground is really good. He may be acting cool, but he's a panicked mess."

Part of her wanted to throw his hand off hers. The other part wanted to grab hold. Her life would have been so much easier if she could have hated him. She begged the universe to let that happen.

Instead, she slipped her hand out from under his, stopped moving her things around and looked at him. "Of course he is. He loves Ellie."

Spence's gaze traveled over her face. "You like Derrick."

All the blood ran out of her head. "You're not accusing me—"

"No!" Spence held up both hands as if in mock surrender. "I mean, respect. Friendship. Deeper than a boss, but not romantic."

Her heartbeat stopped thundering in her ears. It was as if he opened his mouth and her body prepared for battle. The whole thing gave her a headache. "That's fair. Yes."

"Any chance we could get there? I'd like us to be friends." His hand rested on the table, so close to hers.

She stared at his long fingers. She'd always loved his hands. They showed strength. Seeing them made her wonder what they would feel like on her.

She pushed the thought away. "No."

"Abby, come on."

"I have that level of trust and understanding with Derrick because there is nothing else in the way. Nothing else between us because I don't have any other feelings for him." The words echoed in her head. She closed her eyes for a second before opening them again, hoping she'd only thought them. But no, there he was. Staring at her. Clear that he heard every syllable.

His eyebrow lifted. "But you do feel something for me?"

The look on his face. Was that satisfaction or hope? She couldn't tell. Didn't want to know. She never meant to open that door. Thinking it and saying it were two very different things, and she'd blown it. Now she rushed to try to fix the damage. "Did. That's over."

"Is it?"

He stood up then. Took one step toward her. Not too close, but enough to cut off her breathing. To make her fight not to gasp.

"I want to kiss you." He put his hands on her arms and turned her slightly until they faced each other. "Tell me no if you don't want me to."

They'd kissed before. Gone to dinner, stolen a few minutes in closed conference rooms now and then.

But this one was lined with windows on one side. She looked over his shoulder, thinking someone would be out there. That her brain would click on and common sense would come rushing back. For once, no one rushed up and down the hall.

She opened her mouth to say no, sensing he actually would stop. But she couldn't get the word out. Not that one. "Yes."

With the unexpected green light, he leaned in. His mouth covered hers and need shot through her. The press of his mouth, the sureness of his touch. His lips didn't dance over hers. They didn't test or linger. No, this was the kind of kiss where you dove in and held on.

His mouth slipped over hers and her knees buckled. She grabbed on to the sleeve of his shirt. Dug her fingers into the material as desire pounded her. Her brain shut down and her body took over. She wanted to wrap her legs around his and slip her fingers through that sexy dark hair.

Voices in the hallway floated through her. She heard laughter and the mumbling. The noise broke the spell.

"Stop." She pushed away from him. Still held on but lessened her grip and put a bit of air between them. "Don't."

Her gaze went back to the glass wall. She heard talking but didn't see anyone. Not unusual at this end of the hall since only Derrick and Jackson had offices there. But she took the sound of voices as a warning. Forcing her fingers to uncurl, she dropped her arms and stepped back another step, ignoring the way the corner of her chair jammed into the side of her thigh.

"Sorry." Spence visibly swallowed. "I know I'm your boss and it's weird."

She looked at him then. Really looked. Saw the flush

on his cheeks and his swollen lips. That haze clouding his eyes. He had been as spun up and knocked off balance as she was. It was tempting to shut it all down and let him believe this was about Human Resources and office rules, but it wasn't. Employees could date and this wasn't about that.

"We both know this isn't workplace harassment. You asked permission and I said yes. I know my job doesn't depend on kissing you. There's no big power play here." She laid a lot of sins at his feet, but not that one. His father? Yes. But not Spence.

"I guess that's something."

"You hated me and ran away but never threatened my job. You're not that guy." She waved a hand between them. "But this—us—we've proven it doesn't work. We're miserable around each other."

"I never hated you."

No way was she going to dissect that and examine it. "Okay."

"And are we? You make me feel a lot of things, Abby. Miserable isn't one of them."

And she was ignoring that, too. She had to. Believing, even for a second, that he might trust her, that he might get what he did when he sided with his father months ago, was too dangerous. He'd been clear about what he thought of her back then. They needed to stick with that and stay away from each other.

She grabbed her laptop. Almost dropped it. "I need to prep for another meeting with Rylan."

Spence watched the fumbling. Even tried to help when the laptop started its dive, but when she pulled it all together, he stepped back again. Slipped his hands in his pants pockets. "When is it? I'll come with you."

"To the meeting? Do you think I can't handle it?" He

really was determined to babysit her. Thinking about that killed off her need to unbutton his shirt and strip it off him. Mostly.

"That guy's interest in you is not entirely professional."

Her brain cells scrambled. She didn't understand what he was saying or why now. "And you're worried I'll kiss him, too?"

"I'm concerned he won't know where the line is. I don't want you to be put in an untenable position." Whatever he saw on her face had him frowning. "What?"

"Where was this Spence months ago?" She would have done anything to have him stick up for her then. To be on her side.

"What does that mean?"

She retreated back behind her safe wall. Her mother had taught her to be wary. She'd learned the hard way from the man who never stuck around to be a dad. Then her mom taught the ultimate lesson when she died in that diner shooting. Abby had to be stronger, smarter. Always be ready. Always be careful.

"I'll be fine." Somehow, she made her legs move. The shaking in her hands had her laptop bouncing against her chest from the death grip she had on it. She ignored all of it, and Spence, as she walked out.

But that kiss she would remember.

Spence couldn't forget the kiss or that look on Abby's face. It was as if she expected him not to believe her, not to stick up for her. Then his mind slipped back to another office. Another kiss. He'd walked in and his life had turned upside down. All that hatred for his father manifested itself in one horrible second, and he'd taken it out on Abby. She knew about his father's charm and his effect on women. He'd just hoped she would be different.

That realization brought him to Derrick's office. Spence didn't want to talk, but hanging out with Derrick generally calmed him. He was a reminder that the Jameson men could turn out to be decent. Their grandfather was a disgraced congressman. Dad was considered a big-time successful businessman who always had a beautiful woman on his arm. Spence and his brothers had spent too much time in the public eye as props for family photos and public relations schemes.

But Derrick was the real thing. He didn't see it, but Carter and Spence did.

As soon as Spence walked in, Derrick motioned for him to take the seat on the other side of his massive desk. Without saying a word, Derrick opened the top drawer and took out a large envelope. "Here."

Spence wasn't exactly looking for work talk but he sensed that's not what this was anyway. "Do I want to know what this is?"

"It's from Dad."

The damn agreement. Despite all of Derrick's hard work, Eldrick owned the majority of the company. He promised to turn it over, but not before he put his boys through another set of tests. It was his way of holding on to power and exerting control.

Derrick had been given a specific time to clean up his reputation. He was also supposed to lure Carter and Spence home, which proved easy enough once Derrick admitted it to them. But he did more than that. He managed to run a multimillion-dollar company, expand its holding, meet their father's conditions and land the best woman for him.

For Derrick—easy. For anyone else? Likely impossible.

Spence hated to guess what his task was. "Lucky me."

Derrick dropped the envelope on the desk. "Rip it up without opening it."

The suggestion didn't make sense. "What?"

"Walk away from this."

"Isn't this my stipulation, the things I have to do? The way you explained it to me before, Dad only turns over the business if we all do his bidding. You had the biggest part and finished. Now it's my turn." Still, Spence couldn't bring himself to touch the envelope.

"Don't let him do this. It's manipulation."

It was. No one debated that. Not the lawyers who drew up the documents. Not Jackson, the only person outside of the family who knew other than Ellie. The requirements were personal and not likely to be legally enforceable, but with controlling interest, dear old Dad could sell the company and take the company that meant everything to Derrick away from him at any time. Spence refused to let that happen, even if it meant staying and working there.

"You deserve to run the company. You saved it." To Spence, it was that simple. He'd talked to Carter, their younger, California-living brother. He agreed with Spence. Whatever it took to beat the old man and get Derrick the business, they would do it.

Derrick shrugged. "I'll find another way."

"I'm thinking it's time I stepped up and took responsibility." Something even Spence had to admit he should have done before. Stopped running long enough to help.

"Are we only talking about the job?" Derrick smiled as he asked the question.

"This isn't about Abby." It was infuriating how she

was the first thing that popped into his mind—always. Spence couldn't kick that habit.

"Right, Abby." Derrick made a humming sound. "Do you notice how you brought up her name, not me?"

Spence was not touching that. He knew he had a weakness for her. There was no need to pretend otherwise. "I was talking about being more engaged here, at work."

Derrick sat back in his chair. "I can't say I hate that idea."

"Yeah, well, don't get excited. I might suck at it."

This time, Derrick laughed. He'd so rarely done that in the past, but he did it now that he'd found Ellie. "I like the positive attitude."

Spence never had one of those before. Maybe it was time he tried. "I'm being realistic."

"I'll take whatever I can get."

Four

Abby kicked off her high heels and dropped down on her sectional sofa. Next, she propped her feet up on the round leather ottoman in front of her. If she had the energy, she'd change out of her work clothes. She picked dropping her head back against the cushions and closing her eyes instead.

The condo was on the seventh floor of a securebuilding that sat a block off of Logan Circle. The trendy area became trendy during the last decade. Now galleries and restaurants and fitness studios lined the streets. Several parks nearby provided great places to run and bike, but she tried never to do either. She preferred walking the city and turning her muscles to mush in kickboxing classes.

She picked the building because of the location. She was able to get in on the newly refurbished space before the prices skyrocketed and used a work bonus to do it. Now she laughed when she heard what people were willing to pay for studios on lower floors in the building. It was an odd feeling when the place you lived became a place you likely could no longer afford if you were trying to buy *right now*.

There were four condos per floor and those were serviced by a private elevator. A penthouse stretched the full length of the building on the floor above but there was never any noise up there except when the couple who lived there threw one of their lavish rooftop garden parties. She'd never been invited but she loved sitting out on her tiny balcony and listening to the music and laughter as it spun through the DC night.

The best part of the building was her neighbor—Jackson. His two-bedroom also had a den. She didn't need the extra space or the bigger price tag, but she loved having him close by. The man appreciated takeout. One of his many fine attributes.

The door opened after a quick knock. She didn't get up because she didn't have to. She'd texted Jackson as she walked in the door. She wanted Chinese food and could almost always convince him to share with her.

"You're drinking wine already?" He laughed as he relaxed into the corner seat of her sectional.

She opened her eyes and looked at him. He'd stripped off his tie and rolled up the sleeves of his shockingly white dress shirt. His hair showed signs that he'd run his fingers through it repeatedly during the day.

He really was attractive. Those big eyes and the athletic build. Decent and smart. Hardworking and compassionate. Funny. And she felt nothing but a big loving friendship for him.

Clearly there was something wrong with her. She knew what it was and didn't try to hide it. "Spence."

"Ah." Jackson reached behind him to the table that sat there. "Here's the bottle."

Abby watched Jackson fill a glass for himself then put the bottle on a wooden tray on the ottoman for easy reach. If they were going to talk about Spence, and they were because she needed to blow off some of the frustration pinging around inside of her, then she might need a second glass.

She skipped over the kissing part of the afternoon and how that rocked her so hard she'd spent the rest of the day brushing her fingertips over her lips. "He talks and I want to punch him in the face."

"That sounds like a healthy reaction."

She ran her fingers up and down the stem of her glass. "Doesn't it make you frustrated, having to deal with the Jamesons and their money and power and bullying behavior?"

His eyebrow lifted. "Are we still talking about work?"

"He makes me…" She couldn't even find the right word. Hot, angry, spun up, frustrated. They all fit.

"Want to punch him." Jackson toasted her with his glass. "Yeah, I got it."

"I love Ellie. She's funny and smart and charming and doesn't take their crap."

"Sounds like someone else I know." When she frowned, he kept talking. "It does. You don't get onto the managerial team at a family-owned company unless you're good. You're damn good."

"Like you?" She knew the truth. Jackson was a star at work. Derrick depended on him. Everyone did. Even she did. If you needed an answer, he likely had it.

He acted as if he were thinking something over. "Maybe I do deserve a raise."

"I'm tired of all of it."

"Wait." He put down his glass, took hers and did the same with it. "That sounds suspiciously like you're thinking about finding a new job and leaving."

She felt a little lost without the glass to grab on to and started talking with her hands. "Don't you toy with the idea? Leave, open your own place. Do some consulting."

"Sounds risky but potentially rewarding, except for the part where you'll work round the clock, be panicked about finances and eat peanut butter for every meal so you can stockpile cash." He shook his head. "I've already lived that life. I really don't want to go back."

They shared a similar background, having been raised by single moms who barely earned enough money to keep the lights on. But he hadn't been alone. He had a sister, a twin. But it had just been Abby. She depended on her mom until the day she lost her, and she'd mourned her every day since. Missed the vanilla-scented shampoo she used. Her smile. The way she laughed at bad horror movies. That loss, so deep and raw, never disappeared. Moving forward became easier but was never easy.

But this was about her, and her work life and figuring out the best choice for her, separate from the Spence piece of the puzzle. "Me, either, but I'm not afraid of putting in the hours."

"I don't doubt you at all." Jackson studied her for a second before picking up her wineglass and handing it to her again. "Not to bring up a rough subject, but you know Eldrick is coming to town, right?"

Spence's dad. Abby despised the man.

"What?" The glass slipped in her hands and wine splashed over the side and dribbled down her hand.

She caught it before it hit her light gray couch or her silk blouse.

"I had a feeling you didn't know."

"Are you sure it's happening?" Because that was her nightmare. Dealing with Spence was rough. Not smashing a computer over Eldrick's head might prove impossible.

He'd left shortly after he'd kissed her all those months ago, made it clear he did it to teach Spence a lesson. Since then, he'd married another wife and left the country. Abby seethed every day since. She'd hoped he'd stay on that beach in Tortola forever, but no such luck.

"Found out today." Jackson kept watching her, as if he were assessing if he should shut up or provide more details. "It's for Ellie and Derrick's engagement party. They postponed it when Ellie fainted and figured out she was pregnant. Derrick told his dad to stay away, but now the shindig is back on and father Jameson is flying in with the newest wife."

"Ever met her?"

"No, but Derrick had her investigated, so I learned too much." Jackson made a you-don't-want-to-know face.

Abby rolled her eyes. "Of course he did."

"The Jameson men are somewhat predictable."

"It's scary."

"Eldrick Jameson is…" Jackson made a humming sound. "I can't actually think of a decent thing to say about that man."

"Me, either. But go back a second. Ellie is still on bed rest." Abby didn't want her friend confined, but she didn't want a reason to see Eldrick, either.

"I don't think that means we tie her to the bed and keep her there. She's allowed to move."

"But a party? Isn't that stressful?" It would be for Abby.

"They're being extra careful." Jackson shrugged. "Getting the doctor's okay and all that. Trust me, Derrick isn't happy about it, either. I think after all the rumors in the paper about them, Ellie wants the party to stop any whispers."

That meant this was happening. It sounded like Derrick was throwing up roadblocks but none of them showed any promise in stopping the party. "Ugh."

Jackson laughed. "I can hear the excitement in your voice."

He might as well have said *funeral*. "I hate parties. Derrick hates parties."

"But he loves her."

That made Abby smile. "They really are too cute. I mean it. *Too* cute."

"Well, if it's any consolation, they were a mess at first. Derrick nearly blew it about a hundred times." Jackson shook his head. "It was kind of pathetic."

"Maybe there's some relationship malfunction in the Jameson gene pool."

Jackson drained his glass and poured another. "I've often thought that."

"I'm supposed to go over and see Ellie at lunch tomorrow." Abby wanted to cancel, or at least get some sort of promise that Spence would not show up. He seemed to be doing that a lot these days.

"Business?"

"Girl talk."

Jackson made a face. "Do I want to know what that means?"

"I don't know." It wasn't exactly Abby's strength, either. She'd grown up with few friends and kept that streak going most of her life. That's why when Ellie

took her in and insisted they get to know each other, and
then introduced her to her best friend, Vanessa, Abby
didn't balk. She took the risk this one time and it had
paid off. Spending time with Ellie made Abby smile.

"She texted. I'm going."

"The things we do to make the pregnant woman
happy."

Abby lifted her near-empty glass. "I'll toast to that."

The next afternoon, Abby arrived at Ellie's house,
weighed down with bags of food. Derrick had to go
into work for a few meetings, so Abby used the code
and slipped through the layers of security to get inside.
Then up the stairs. A few minutes later, she unloaded
the salads and caprese-on-focaccia sandwiches onto the
tray set up on the edge of Ellie's bed with drinks and
what looked like a bowl of pretzels.

Ellie sat propped up in the chair next to the bed with
her legs stretched out on the ottoman in front of her.
Abby guessed she wasn't on the bed because it was covered with envelopes and papers.

"The sandwiches smelled so good on the walk over
from the deli that I almost ate one." Abby pushed some
of the paperwork to the side and sat on the edge of the
bed. "What is all this?"

Ellie smiled as she grabbed a sandwich out of the
bag. "It's party time. Two and a half weeks."

"Really?" Abby tried to keep the dread out of her
voice but she was pretty sure it seeped in. "You know
you're supposed to be in bed, right?"

"The doctor gave the okay. I have to sit for most of
it, some of it with my feet up, which is really boring.
The party has to be in the afternoon and not long." Ellie
unwrapped the paper and ripped off a piece of focac-

cia. "I'm pretty sure Derrick will carry around a timer and make sure I don't stand for more than three minutes at a time."

"Because that sounds reasonable."

"He's ridiculous." But a huge grin formed on Ellie's lips as she shrugged. "It's kind of adorable."

"I'm surprised he didn't fire the doctor and find one who forbids parties." Abby felt bad that the idea sounded so good to her. "The man is not a great socializer."

"As opposed to you."

She had to cut this off. Spence was going to be Ellie's brother-in-law, which meant whining about him would put her in a terrible position. Abby didn't want to do that. "We're not talking about Spence."

Ellie's hands dropped to her lap and her smile grew even wider…if that was possible. "Look how you jumped right to him. Interesting."

"Don't make me grab the food and run." Abby took her time digging around in the bag, looking for a napkin.

"That's just mean." Ellie barely let the words sit there before she launched into her next point. "But I would say—"

"Oh, here we go." Abby gave up. She could only fake interest in the inside of a bag for so long before it seemed weird, and she feared she was nearing that line. "I'm listening."

She also twisted the paper napkin between her fingers. In, out and around. Tight enough that she heard the paper rip.

"The sparks between you two? Whoa."

Oh, man. That couldn't be true. She'd tried so hard to hide it, to fight it off.

Abby refolded the mangled napkin, then turned to the sandwich. Unwrapped each edge. But the grumbling in her stomach from before had vanished. This topic seemed to zap the hunger right out of her.

She dumped the uneaten sandwich on the tray next to her. "What you're sensing? That's anger."

"Babe, I know anger. That is not what I see." Ellie took a bite, then another.

"We may have some…unresolved issues."

"The queen of understatement."

Yeah, no kidding. But that led to a bigger issue, one Abby was not totally sure how to discuss. "I need you to know that I might not be at the engagement party."

"Wrong." Ellie smiled and reached for her bottle of water. "But why are you under that incorrect assumption?"

Abby tried to pick up anger, anything in Ellie's voice that suggested disappointment. She sounded more resigned to prove Abby wrong than anything else.

"Those unresolved issues relate to Papa Jameson and—"

"The kiss?" Ellie's eyebrow lifted. "Yeah, I don't blame you there. My father-in-law-to-be deserves a good kick."

Apparently there was an office memo no one bothered to tell her about. As far as Abby knew, Derrick had kept the kiss information limited to a very few in the office. The idea that someone other than a small circle and Ellie might know made Abby's stomach roll. She didn't want to be viewed as someone who lied and schemed her way to the top. She didn't care what choices other people made, but she'd earned this position by working her butt off.

Abby picked up the napkin then put it down again. "You know about that?"

"Of course. It's the kiss heard 'round the family." Ellie looked at Abby's face and her smile disappeared. She waved a hand and shook her head. "No, don't panic. Actually, I made Derrick tell me, but he wasn't all that forthcoming with juicy details. All I know is Spence thinks you were playing a power game and kissed his dad."

Abby's stomach refused to stop somersaulting. If this kept up, she could forget about lunch because she'd be seeing her breakfast again. "He's an idiot."

"Which one?"

And that's why she liked Ellie so much. "Good point. Both of them."

Ellie winced. "I haven't met father Jameson yet."

"Lucky you."

"How bad was it back then?"

Intolerable. All hands and creepy looks. Word was Spence's father liked to pick interns by their looks— young, pretty and blonde. A practice Derrick immediately stopped once he figured it out. But there was no reason to completely terrify Ellie during her shaky pregnancy. "Bad enough that I'm considering skipping a party and missing cake, which is sacred food in my book."

"If I let you punch him, will you come?" Ellie sounded excited by the idea.

So was Abby. "Which him?"

"Either. Both."

So tempting. "That might be a deal I can't pass up."

"Believe it or not, I really like Spence," Ellie said.

Some of Abby's amusement faded. "Let's not go there."

"Of course, I've only know him for a few weeks."

"I worked with him, was wildly attracted to him. Fought it off and lost. And then I *really* lost." That was more than Abby usually admitted. Jackson knew pieces of the story and a bit about her feelings, about how hurt and torn apart she'd been. Derrick had made it clear back then he'd collected some of the facts but not all of them. It didn't matter because Abby didn't want to relive any of it.

"Any chance Spence can redeem himself?" Ellie asked.

Abby had asked herself that a thousand times over the last few months. She dreamed about Spence showing up and apologizing. Ran through all these scenarios on what she would say. But Spence stole that opportunity away from her, too, because he never came back for her. He came back for Derrick and Ellie. Abby vowed not to forget that.

She cleared her throat, swallowing back the lump that had formed there. "I have to be smarter than that, more self-protective this time around."

The memory of the kiss flashed in her mind. Not the one that destroyed everything. The one from yesterday. The new one that carried a note of hope and a hint of desperation. The feelings had thrummed off Spence. And she'd been trying to forget them, talk herself out of the way her heart leaped and her body turned all mushy when his lips touched hers, ever since.

Ellie shook her head. "Men. They do ruin things sometimes."

Abby suddenly felt like eating again. "No kidding."

Five

She'd ignored him for three days. Spence wasn't great about being shut out of anything. He also didn't trust Rylan, and that's exactly who Abby was meeting with today. Right now.

The door stood open. Papers were strewn across the conference room table. Maps and documents with official government seals. A thick binder filled with information Spence knew would bore him.

Spence waited until the last minute to slip into the room she'd reserved for the meeting. Rylan stood by the window, looking down into the street. The only noise in the room came from the sound of the automatic room fan. That and the squeak of Abby's chair as she moved it back and forth while studying the paper in front of her.

She glanced up as soon as the door clicked shut. "You're sitting in on all of my meetings now?"

The refusal to back down... Spence found that so sexy. "I actually work here."

She treated him to the perfect eye roll. It almost shouted *you're a jerk*. "For now."

Spence kept walking until he got to her side. Then he slid into the seat next to her with his arm resting on the table. "This idea you have that I'm ready to bolt? Get it out of your head. It's not happening."

She slowly lowered her pen. "It did before."

Shot landed. Spence felt it vibrate through him. The truth really did suck sometimes.

"Derrick needs me here." That was also true. He'd come back for his brother and his growing family. Spence had repeated that to himself during the entire journey to DC. Now he wondered if something else pulled him there. An invisible thread that bound him to Abby. A need to come home and resolve the seemingly unresolvable.

She tapped her pen end over end against the table. The clicking sound turned to a steady thump when she started to hit it harder. "And no one needed you before?"

"Didn't feel like it." He'd felt betrayed, yet not. Almost as if he'd expected Abby to disappoint him back then.

Man, that was not something he wanted to examine too closely. At least not there, in an office conference room.

Rylan picked that moment to turn around and face the room. "Is everything okay between you two?"

Abby lifted her hand without looking in Rylan's direction. "You remember Rylan."

"Hard to forget." Rylan was the kind of guy who lingered. Maybe not dangerous but not honest, either. Spence knew the other man was stringing the approval process out. He was either receiving a payment from a competing company under the table, or he had a crush on Abby. Spence hated both options. "Do we have the final okay to proceed?"

Rylan stepped up to the table. "Soon."

A pounding started at the base of the back of Spence's neck. "What does that mean?"

Rylan's mouth opened and closed a few times before he actually stumbled and got a few words out. "There is still some work to be done."

Ah, work. Sure. "Then why are you here instead of off doing it?"

Rylan glanced at Abby but she just smiled at him. That told Spence that she was sick of the stalling, too.

"This is a status meeting," Rylan finally said.

"Didn't you two meet about a week ago?" Spence leaned back in his chair, enjoying the line of sweat that appeared on Rylan's forehead. "I'm asking but, see, I know that answer because I was there."

"I also needed to deliver some documents to Abby." Rylan picked his briefcase off the floor and took out a white envelope. He handed it to her without breaking eye contact with Spence.

She took it and tucked it into her file. "Thank you."

Since she wasn't balking at his heavy-handed behavior, Spence figured he had the green light to continue. Rylan stood frozen with his hand on the back of one of the chairs. He didn't make a move to sit down or do anything that looked like work.

"And now you can go." Spence made the words sound like an order.

It worked because Rylan took off on a frenzy of activity. He loaded up his briefcase and reached for his suit jacket. He nearly tripped over his own feet getting to the door. "I'll call you as soon as I have the answers you need."

The door slammed behind him. Then Spence was alone with Abby. He hoped this round would go better than the last few. Except for the kiss. He'd be happy to repeat that.

Abby flicked the pen back and forth between her fingers. She seemed calm, maybe even a little amused.

Spence was smart enough to know quiet sometimes meant dangerous. He seriously considered ducking.

She waited a few more minutes, drawing out the tension and letting it build before she talked. That pen kept twirling in the air. "Is your plan to walk into every meeting I have and bully people?"

The tone. So judging. "Have you always been this dramatic?"

She eyed him up. "Yesterday you sat in on a meeting at the office and never said a word."

He suddenly felt sorry for the people who worked under her. She knew how to use that voice, that look, to set the tone. No one had to guess her mood. "I'm confused. You want me to talk, then you don't."

"It made people uncomfortable."

He knew the feeling. "You mean you?"

The invisible hold pulling between them broke. She looked away as she shook her head. "Your ego is amazing."

"Thank you." He stretched his arm out along the table. Almost touched her but was smart enough not to try. "About Rylan."

She straightened up the stack of papers in front of her. "We need him to sign off on a variety of environmental issues. He's dragging his feet, but it will happen. You know that."

So professional. Every word was true. That's how the process worked, but Spence was talking about something very different. He sensed she knew that. "And you know he's interested in more than hazardous waste."

"He's still within a reasonable time frame for getting the work done."

An interesting answer. One he decided to hit head-on. "Are you ignoring his crush in order to smooth the way for our approvals?"

"You didn't actually accuse me of using my looks to get what I want, so I'll let that pass." She stood up.

"I'm not a total jerk, Abby. I'm concerned that he's making you uncomfortable or that he's harassing you. Neither is okay." Not liking the way it felt to sit while she loomed over him, he stood up, too. Kept his distance, or as much as being around the corner from each other at the table would allow. "I don't want him crossing a line."

Her eyes narrowed. It looked like she was studying him, trying to figure out if he was lying or not. "Women in the workplace have to maneuver through a labyrinth of ridiculous male behavior to get things done. But I have hard limits. I don't sleep around to get what I want."

The words struck right at the heart of their issues, but that's not where he was going, and digging into the past would only shut down the conversation. "I wasn't suggesting that."

"You did before."

He could not go back over that ground one more time. Part of him wanted to forgive and forget and move on. He didn't know if he could, but he was sure she was not up for the "forget" part. "Abby."

She went back to the papers. Stacked and restacked the same group twice before looking up at him again. "I'm just making my position clear since you think this has been an issue for me in the past. Don't want to be wrongly accused again."

"You'll tell me if you need me to—"

"That's the thing, Spence." She dropped the papers she was holding and they fell against the table with a whoosh. "You can't swoop in and fix this."

"First, I do not swoop."

She snorted. "If you say so."

"Second, I don't want any woman in this office to deal with nonsense." And he meant that. The last few generations of Jameson men had issues with women. He was determined to break the cycle and he knew Derrick and Carter wanted that, too.

"That last part is a responsible and appropriate thing for a boss to say, and maybe even a little sweet, but it's also impossible. There will always be some level of nonsense."

The words deflated him. "I'm sorry."

"For?"

The list was so damn long and went far beyond the topic they were discussing. "Everything? I'm really not sure, but I hate this feeling. The wall between us. The anger. The broken trust."

She blew out a long breath. "It's in the past. We should let it go."

He knew that made sense but it sounded wrong. They kept going at each other, but under all that anger, all the frustration and disappointment, something else lingered. Something he wasn't ready to let go of. "What if I don't want it to stay in the past? We could go over it now."

The color left her face. "Sometimes you need to move on."

"And sometimes you need to stick around and fix things." He stepped in closer and took her hands in his.

"You're saying…"

He wasn't even sure. "Finish the sentence."

His thumb rubbed over the backs of her hands. A light caress over her smooth skin. Then his hand slipped up. To her wrist, then a bit higher. Fingers on bare skin.

She jerked away, pulling back and putting space between them again. Her hands visibly shook as she grabbed for her files and her phone. "Thanks for the offer of help with Rylan, but I've got this."

He thought about stopping her, but now wasn't the time. When she walked out the door, leaving it hanging wide-open behind her, he wondered if the time would ever be right.

An hour later, Spence turned up in Derrick's office. He'd gotten back to his desk after the run-in with Abby and another half hour walking around the building, trying to make sense of the conflicting messages bombarding his brain, and saw the note. A summons of sorts.

Derrick started talking the minute Spence crossed the threshold to his plush corner office. "We have a problem."

"Our father plans on visiting, so we have more than one." Spence still hadn't figured out how he was going to handle seeing him. They hadn't spoken since the infamous kiss that ruined everything. Eldrick had tried in his usual smart-ass bragging way. Spence had ignored him and his envelope.

Derrick looked up as he settled back in his chair. "For once I'm not talking about him. I'm talking about you."

Spence stopped in midstep across the room. "Excuse me?"

"There's been a lot of talk in the office. Gossip."

There always was. That was the nature of an office.

People locked into a confined space all day. They were bound to get bored and start talking about nonwork things. Spence was sure Derrick hated that reality, but it was a fact. "Since when do you care about that?"

"People have noticed the tension between you and Abby. It's been weeks and it's not getting better."

Spence felt something twist inside him. He made it to the chair across from Derrick but didn't sit in in. He stood, gripping the back with a white-knuckled grip.

"What people?" Because Spence couldn't tolerate people whispering about Abby. No matter what had happened between them now or back then, she was great at her job. She deserved the office's respect. It was not as if the past was anyone else's business anyway.

"People who work in this building. People with eyes."

"Come on." Spence refused to believe it was that widespread. He hadn't even been home a month and except for the glass-walled office kiss, he'd been careful.

"You really don't have any idea, do you?" Derrick rocked back and forth in his chair. "Well, the people who work here need to think that management is at least somewhat competent."

Fair enough. "Isn't it your job to install that faith?"

"When I'm not here, it's yours." Derrick leaned forward with his elbows balanced on the edge of his desk. "Which brings me to my point."

Spence knew they'd get there eventually. "Feel free to skip any part of this lecture."

"You need to get yourself in line." Derrick dropped that bomb then stopped talking.

Figured, his brother picked now as the perfect time to get cryptic. Spence had that sort of luck. "That's it?"

"Yes."

"Your pep talks suck, Derrick."

Light streamed in the window. Before Ellie, Derrick kept the blinds closed. Not anymore. That realization made Spence smile when nothing else about this talk did.

"You have a thing for Abby. That's not new. It's not a great idea in an office environment either, but with consent, open communication and ground rules it's workable." Derrick exhaled. "That's direct from Human Resources, by the way. I needed to be able to sleep, so I checked."

"This is about you now?"

"The point is you're avoiding how you feel about her." When Spence started to respond, Derrick talked right over him. "Unfortunately, that's not new, either. But the mess is making people twitchy, so fix it."

Spence's fingers tightened on the back of the chair. "Is this some new Human Resources program I don't know about? A sort of tough love thing?"

"The engagement party is back on. Business associates will be there. People from the office will be there. And Abby will be there." Derrick looked less happy the longer he talked.

Spence heard about the party from Ellie, so this wasn't exactly news. "Okay."

"Inside and outside of the office, you need to either deal with the fact you have feelings for Abby or bury them deep enough that they're no longer an issue."

Burying them. He'd give anything to be able to do that. "We're trying."

Derrick shrugged. "I have no idea what that means."

That made two of them. "To get along. We're trying."

Derrick laughed then. "How's that going for you?"

"It's a work in progress."

* * *

Abby sat at her desk. She'd finally stopped shaking. Spence did that to her. Got her churned up then broke her down. She didn't know how much more she could take.

With her door closed for a bit of privacy, she leaned back in the leather chair. Spun it around until she faced the windows. She looked out over the traffic. Watched a car weave in and out, riding right up on the bumpers of the ones in front of it. Talk about anxiety. It was enough to make her happy she took the metro or walked to most places.

After a few minutes, she spun her chair again. Looking at the files and the light flashing on her desk phone signaling messages, she thought about those brownies she got for Ellie. Those sounded good right now. Always, actually.

Her gaze fell on the school project file and a memory tugged at her. It took a few seconds, and then she remembered the envelope from Rylan. She reached into the folder and grabbed it. Tore the closed tab. The whole time she hoped this was work-related and not some sort of weird date invitation.

She slipped her fingers inside and took out the white piece of paper. The stationery made her heart stop. Her involuntary gasp filled the room. Berger & Associates. She knew the name all too well. Jameson's direct competition on most prestigious commercial build-out jobs.

They'd once made her a job offer. Very lucrative. All she had to do was sell her soul and spill all the proprietary information she knew about Jameson's financial dealings. Things that would give Berger the edge in bidding on jobs. Never mind that telling those secrets would likely get her sued by Derrick and make her an outcast in the DC business community.

But the timing had been interesting. Berger swooped in right after the kiss with Eldrick happened. It was as if they'd sensed her rage and vulnerability and pounced. Still, she turned them down. Angry or not, she would always turn that kind of offer down.

They'd tried a few times since but never with much enthusiasm. A call here. A stray comment at this meeting over there. Now this.

She scanned the note. It was terse and unsigned. Basically just a date and time for a meeting and the name of a restaurant in Foggy Bottom. Then there was the last line: "You don't have a choice. Make this happen."

For the fifth time today, she got dizzy and the world flipped upside down on her. The game never ended… no matter how tired she was of playing it.

Six

The next two weeks passed in a blur. The office was on fire with work and party details. Derrick came in and out, looking and sounding grumpy and tired. The only thing that made him smile were the calls from Ellie. Spence seriously considered setting up a video system where Derrick could watch Ellie all day and maybe relax a little. Jackson told him no because he was pretty sure that crossed a line.

But Ellie had come through the weeks with little pain and no bleeding. The pregnancy was still considered high-risk and would be until the end, but Ellie had just moved into week ten and found some comfort in that, even though twelve seemed to be some sort of magic number for her.

Derrick hadn't found any peace. Spence was pretty sure Derrick would never be calm and not panic where Ellie was concerned.

At least the party had started. Spence looked over

the green lawn that stretched out behind the family's Virginia estate. Set in the country, it consisted of acres of rolling hills outlined by tall trees for privacy. A rectangular pool that no one had been in for years lay perpendicular to the house. The pristine water glistened, as did the intricate inlay of stone surrounding it.

He grew up here but hadn't been back for more than a year. Walking inside required that he exorcise more than one ghost, so he stayed outside.

His father hated anyone stepping on the lawn. The house rules were pretty strict. No one in his locked office. No one could eat dinner until he did. No noise in the house once he got home. Feet off the furniture. No running in the house. And those were the easy ones. He could go on for hours about how his property must be respected.

With that history, Spence couldn't help but smile when he saw how Derrick had set up tall tables in the grass and all along the brick pathways that led from the house to the pool, then branched off to the pool house and over to the guesthouse. People mingled and servers passed food and drinks. Soft music blasted from the outdoor speakers and lights that had been strewn above him twinkled even though the sun had not gone down.

The place had a festive air. For the first time, in what had to be more than a decade, laughter floated around the property. People smiled and looked at ease. Everyone seemed to be having fun, including the mother-and wife-to-be who sat in her light blue dress at a table closest to the back patio area with Derrick hovering over her shoulder. She wore her hair back and greeted guests. If an internet gossip site hadn't announced her pregnancy prematurely, people likely wouldn't guess.

Everything looked perfect. The party took place in

the backyard, which consisted of acres of rolling hills and a perfectly manicured green lawn. From where Spence stood in the rear of the soaring three-story redbrick main house, he could watch people bustle in and out of the four sets of French doors outlined by columns, leading into what his father always called the great room.

Ivy covered most of the first floor's exterior walls. And there, standing on the second-floor balcony overhang above the house's back entrance stood Abby. She wore a purple cocktail dress. Sort of a lacy material that slipped over her impressive curves, highlighting each one. Her brown hair down fell unbound and free. When she turned to point out something on the far lawn to Jameson Industries' head of sales, the sun caught the strands, turning them a lighter caramel color.

A second later, she leaned in and the older man on the other side of her said something that made her laugh. That open, genuine smile stole his breath. He put his hand against his stomach without thinking. Her body made him ache to settle the anger that lingered between them and move on to touching.

"Is it wrong that I want this over?" Jackson asked as he joined Spence at one of the high tables.

Spence forced his gaze off the woman who snagged every thought out of his head and onto the friend he'd missed as he traveled around, away from DC. "Not having fun?"

"Your father is coming. Carter is supposed to finally breeze into town. Derrick is a damn mess and there is no way Ellie is going to sit for her own engagement party." Jackson shrugged. "So, yeah. Everything is about normal around here."

"When you put it like that, I'm wondering why the

two of us didn't go on an impromptu vacation and skip this." Spence saw a flash of purple and looked up again. Abby was talking to a business associate now. Someone Spence considered forgettable. But her? No. She stood out in any crowd.

Her memory lingered. Seeing her here, out of the office, lighter and not bogged down by their arguments or a stack of work, eased some of the tightness in his chest. She put in almost as many hours as Derrick usually did, but now she looked relaxed. Or she did until she started talking to this new guy.

"Well, you're in love and fighting it. I'm guessing that's your excuse."

Spence barely heard what Jackson said but he could tell from Jackson's amused expression that he needed to. He shook his head and focused in on the conversation in front of him. "What?"

"Unless you're okay with the idea of Abby dating…" Jackson spun around and pointed at a random blond-haired guy Spence had never seen before "…that guy. He was sniffing around her earlier."

The words came together in Spence's head and his insides froze. Heat washed through him, a kind of fighting preparation where his body switched to high alert and his brain kicked into gear.

"You seem pretty protective. Are you interested in her?" Because Spence had no idea what he would do then. He'd walked away from her and she was a grown-up. Next to his brothers, Jackson was his closest friend. They all considered him family. But damn.

"Hold up." Jackson put up a hand and looked like he was trying to swallow a smile. "Don't start swinging. I care about Abby as a friend. Only a friend."

Spence felt the tension ease out of him. "Oh, right."

"A friend who will beat you to death if you hurt her again."

Spence fumbled with his drink, almost dropping it before setting it down. "I didn't see that coming."

Jackson moved the glass out of spilling range. "You know Abby and I hang out all the time, right?"

"Well…no. You…you do?" Spence stammered his way through the response but his mind went blank. He didn't even remember Jackson and Abby talking all that much before he left town.

"That will teach you to go away and not visit."

Another apology Spence needed to make. He just wasn't sure how to admit that he had to go away because seeing her chipped away at him until he couldn't think straight. That he stayed gone until Derrick called because that's how he'd learned to deal with personal conflict: he stepped away from it.

"Ellie's brother is here. He seems to be behaving," Jackson said as he gestured toward a nearby table.

Noah had a history of issues, just two of which centered on decision-making and controlling his anger. He had been a huge issue in Derrick and Ellie's relationship at the start. But the twenty-year-old was brilliant and Derrick had become a mentor to him. Things were smoothing out on that front. "He's doing better. Fitting in at work and is opening up a bit to Derrick, which is kind of funny to watch."

Jackson nodded. "I love sitting in on meetings between the two of them, even though I rarely understand what Noah is saying."

Spence cleared his throat as he searched for the right words. "About me leaving—"

"She's been nervous lately, and that's not her style. I'm not sure if it's because of you or—"

"Wait a second." The conversation kept rolling and Spence had yet to catch up, but he couldn't let this part pass. "I have no intention of hurting her."

Jackson lifted his glass and took another sip. "Because you love her."

The words skidded across Spence's brain. He wanted to deny but that's not what came out. "Stop saying that."

Jackson slowly lowered his glass again. "I notice you haven't told me I'm wrong about the love thing. Not even a 'get out of here.'"

"And I notice you waited to ambush me with this topic at a very public event."

Jackson took a sip of his beer. "I'm a pretty smart guy."

"You are." Carter stepped up to the table out of nowhere. "And trouble. Six-foot-something of pure trouble."

Seeing his baby brother, hearing that familiar amused voice, stunned Spence for a second. Carter looked the same except for the short scruff of a beard. He'd always possessed the clean-shaven baby face look. Not now. The straight black hair and black eyes were the same. He loomed tall and strong. None of that had changed.

"Carter," Spence greeted his brother then stepped back for Jackson to take a turn.

More than one head turned as the three men shook hands and hugged. Spence saw a few people point. He glanced up to the second-story deck and saw Abby watching rather than paying attention to the man talking to her.

"Who takes more than four weeks to drive across the country? How lazy are you?" Jackson asked as he flagged down a server and grabbed a glass of water for Carter.

He downed it in one sip. "I was hoping Dad would come and go before I got here."

Jackson shook his head. "You're not that lucky."

"None of us are," Spence said.

Carter reached for another glass of water from a passing tray and scanned the area. "There are a lot of people here. Do we even know this many people? I sure don't like this many people."

None of them were that great with crowds, but Carter had "it"—the charm that allowed him to talk to anyone about anything for a good twenty minutes. The sunny smile and ability to chime in at the right times. After all that interested listening, he could slip away without crushing feelings.

Most people who met him described him as the kind of guy who really listened. Spence doubted that was actually true. Carter had perfected the art of faking it. A good skill to have if you wanted to survive in the Jameson family.

"Ellie insisted if this was going to be a big party, it had to include friends, family and work people." Jackson shook his head as he spoke.

"She also demanded cupcakes," Spence said.

Carter's gaze traveled over the crowd, hesitating a few times before he spied Derrick and smiled. "Where exactly is my cupcake-eating future sister-in-law? I'm dying to meet the woman who managed to tame Derrick. She's like a miracle worker."

"You'll like her." Spence did. He couldn't imagine anyone not liking her.

"She's there." Jackson pointed at the same table Ellie had been sitting at for an hour. Derrick had moved back, but not far. "The pretty brunette talking with my sister. The other woman at the table is Ellie's best friend, Vanessa."

"Who Jackson finds very attractive." Spence had heard Jackson talk about Vanessa a few times, which was a few times more than he usually spoke about any woman in his life.

He shrugged. "I do have eyes."

"Wait a second." Carter's smile widened. "Your sister is here?"

"She's off-limits to you." Jackson grumbled something about the Jameson men being nothing but trouble.

"You've been saying that for years." Carter slapped Jackson on the back and took off. "I'll be back. Try not to burn down the house while I'm gone."

Spence watched as Carter stopped in front of Ellie and Zoe, Jackson's sister. He picked Zoe up and spun her around. After some whispering with Ellie, he pulled her to her feet and hugged her, too.

Spence shook his head. "The charmer."

"In case you were wondering, I saw Abby go into the house." Jackson peered over the top of his glass at Spence. "Just helping."

"She's free to move around."

"How very open-minded of you."

"I mean…" Yes, he wanted to talk with her. Spence could at least admit that to himself. Seeing Derrick happy and Carter at home had Spence longing for something he couldn't quite name or describe. The sensation hit him in waves and each time it crashed in, her name formed in his mind. "Fine."

"That's what I thought."

Spence reached over and polished off the rest of Jackson's drink. "You're not as smart as you think you are."

Jackson laughed. "Yes, I am."

* * *

Abby was now very clear on what the phrase "made my skin crawl" meant. Ten minutes ago, she'd turned to leave the balcony and go down and check on Ellie. Got two steps before Jeff Berger slipped in front of her. She hadn't known he was invited but she guessed she should have assumed. His company often went up against Jameson Industries on bids. Management from both companies joked about a friendly competition between the companies. She now knew that carried with it a seedy underbelly.

"It's been a long time. I've called and haven't heard back from you." Jeff swirled the liquor in his glass. "I'm beginning to think you're ignoring me."

"Weird, right?"

"Honestly, I'm not used to that type of response."

She guessed it would cause a scene if she tossed his sorry butt off the balcony of this sweet house, so she refrained. "From women?"

"From anyone."

Lovely. But she was not surprised to hear it. Jeff had *that* look. The typical DC dude-with-money-and-connections look. He was older than Derrick by about ten ears, maybe forty-five or so. He had twin boys in private school. They played lacrosse because Jeff had. They'd probably go to some Ivy League school because Jeff did. Grow up to take over Daddy's company like Jeff intended to do.

He walked around in a fog of privilege, once commenting that it was amazing how far the Jameson family had gotten, what with having a Japanese grandmother and all. As if their background should have discounted them from making money or fitting in with the old-money boys who liked to drink their lunches on Capitol Hill restaurants.

Jeff wasn't old. There was nothing infirm about him. The receding hairline did nothing to dim what Abby supposed were his objective good looks. At least that's what other people said. He did nothing for her.

He played golf and belonged to a country club because he was supposed to, but he stayed fit. Every time there was a charity run in town, he was there with his sneakers on…making sure to get his photo taken for the newspaper. He put on a hell of a show. Abby had to give him that.

She sensed he also secretly despised Derrick and his success. "I'm surprised you're here."

Jeff's phony smile faltered a bit. "Derrick and I are business acquaintances."

"Not friends."

He made an annoying tsk-tsk sound. "What does that word even mean?"

No surprise he wouldn't be familiar with the definition. She decided to cut through the garbage and get straight to the only issue between them. "Despite the covert agent thing you did with the note—and I will be talking with Rylan about that, by the way—I won't be showing up to the meeting as ordered."

"Of course you will." Jeff took another swallow as he watched the activity on the grass below. "And do you know why, Abby? Because you are a very smart woman. You also have a lot to lose."

The anxiety churning in her stomach took off now. She'd gone from wanting to see Spence and hating how much she wanted to see him, to dreading this conversation. Life kept whizzing by her and she could not grab on and slow it down.

But she wasn't about to buy into whatever nonsense Jeff had planned. "Threats?"

"Think of this more as a conversation. One that will benefit you, if you play the game right." He leaned down with his elbows on the banister and surveyed the property as if he owned it. "After all, you wouldn't want Derrick or Spence to think you betrayed them."

The word twisted in her head. Now that he'd planted it, she doubted she'd think of anything else. "I didn't."

Jeff stood up straight again and stared down at her, letting his gaze wander all over her. "You will."

The look wasn't predatory. This was a power play. Another one she'd walked into the middle of thanks to her work. "Don't even try it, Jeff."

His eyebrow lifted. "Word is Spence is sniffing around you again. You wouldn't want to mess that up."

"Go to hell."

He winked at her. "We'll talk soon."

Spence started up the carved staircase running up the middle of the house. It rose then stopped at a landing and split with separate staircases going off to the right and left. As kids, he and his brothers would race cars down the steps, but only when his parents weren't home to yell about the game.

This time when he looked up at the landing, he saw strappy high-heel shoes and long legs. Amazing legs. Like, killer those-things-should-be-insured legs. The edge of a purple cocktail dress. A little higher as his gaze slipped over her hips then on up.

Abby.

His heart revved. He could feel his blood pressure spike. All that talk about her and love, and there she was.

She walked down the stairs, taking her time. Enticing with a slight sway of her hips. Mentally slicing his control to shreds as she took each step. She stopped on the one above him but didn't say anything.

"There you are." His gaze met hers and the picture in his head—the one of them together, him stripping that dress off her shoulders—screeched to a halt in his head.

She smiled but it didn't reach her eyes. She scanned the downstairs as if looking for someone and not wanting to see them. His dad, maybe? Whatever was happening inside her had her looking uncharacteristically shaky and unsure.

He reached out for her hand and was surprised when she grabbed on. "Hey, are you okay?"

He guided her down to the floor, hearing the click of her heels against the polished hardwood. He slipped her hand under his arm and touched her fingers. Ice-cold.

With the fake smile in place, she cleared her voice before answering. "Fine."

"That's not really believable."

She shook her head. "Spence, I can't discuss this right now."

"Okay, wait. You're obviously upset." He guided her around the banister and into a hall. It ran the length of the right side of the house.

Leaning against the wall, he tried to block their view from the people walking in and out of the house. Many stopped and stared at the artwork trailing up the staircase and the massive chandelier hanging in the center hall. Others smiled on the way to one of the house's nine bathrooms a few doors down.

A thousand thoughts streamed through his head. He blamed his father for putting her in this state. He also played a part. So did too much work. There was a lot of responsibility to go around, but he wanted to lessen the burden. "Talk to me."

"I'm on edge and…" She shook her hands in front of her, like she was trying to get the feeling back in them.

He had no idea what was going on in her head but the aching need he had for her turned into something else. "What is it? Tell me so I can help."

She looked at him then. Met his gaze straight on. "I have all of this energy bouncing around inside me. Add in alcohol and, well, it's a combination for bad decisions."

"Am I a bad decision?" He knew the answer but asked anyway.

Her gaze traveled over him. Hesitated on his mouth, then dipped lower. To the base of his throat. "The absolute worst."

That look. It was almost as if… What the hell was happening? He grabbed on to the last of his common sense. Something was wrong. She didn't seem like herself and there was no way he was going to take advantage of that. "Maybe you should go upstairs and rest and then we can—"

"Kiss me."

That fast the world flipped on him. Tension ratcheted up. Not the I'm-worried kind but the let's-get-naked type. "Excuse me?"

"Where does that door lead?" She pointed at the one over his shoulder and when he didn't answer, she reached across him and turned the knob. A quick flick of the wall switch and the oversize pantry was bathed in light. "This will work."

He was pretty sure he was having a stroke. His muscles refused to work. He couldn't form a sentence. It was a struggle just to get out her name. "Abby…"

She backed him up against the packed shelves lining the wall. Their bodies barely touched as they brushed over each other. It was enough to set off an explosion in his head. The good kind. The kind where he wanted to touch her and taste her and do everything he'd dreamed of doing with her but figured he would never get the chance.

"I'm tired of wanting you and fighting it." She grabbed the post behind his head with one hand. The other went to the top of his shirt to play with the buttons there. "I'm tired of trying to do the right thing."

Wanting you? He was half-sure he made that part up in his head. "Abby, what's going on?"

"I'm here in this beautiful place. Watching you. Seeing all these people. Thinking about my choices." She dropped her head down to rest on his chest.

Her scent wound around him. Soft hair slid over his skin. He was pretty certain she could hear his heartbeat because it hammered loud enough to fill his ears.

Knowing he could pull back if she asked him to, because that would always be the answer for him, he slipped his fingers through her soft hair. "Is this the alcohol talking?"

"I've only had one half-filled glass of Champagne."

Her voice vibrated against his chest. Warm breath skipped over his bare skin.

There was no way he was going to survive this.

His fingers continued to gently massage the back of her neck. "I don't want to take advantage of you."

Her head shot up. "You're not your father."

"What?"

"Kiss me."

Her eyes were clear and he didn't smell alcohol. But the stench of regret would be sickening and strong if he got this moment wrong. "I'm trying not to be a jerk here."

She undid his top shirt button. Then the next. "I'll sign a release if you want or go tell a witness I asked for this or—"

"Stop talking."

He left her for a second. Didn't go far. With his hands shaking, he turned the lock on the door, grateful there was one. The mumble of voices rose and fell outside the door as people walked down the hall. No one tried to come in, but there really wasn't a reason to. At least he hoped that was true.

He looked at her, studied that stunning face and saw the heat move into her eyes. Still, they had to be clear because this could go so wrong. "Be sure."

"Spence, you are never going to get a greener light."

She stood there in that sexy dress with her hands crossed over her chest. She wasn't hiding from him. No, he got the sense she was ready. Very ready.

"You'll tell me if—"

She reached out and hooked her finger through his belt loop. Pulled him close. "Green light."

Seven

Spence's mouth covered hers and the last of her doubts blinked out. Thoughts and unwanted feelings had been whirling in her head since he stepped back into town. They came together in one blinding certainty when his hands slid up her sides—she wanted this.

Those palms cupped her breasts through her dress and her skin caught fire. She waited for the material to melt away, for her knees to give out, but somehow she stayed upright and dressed.

Those amazing fingers massaged and caressed. It took all of her control not to reach behind herself for the zipper and strip the top down. Feel him skin to skin.

"Spence…" She didn't know exactly what she wanted, so she let the whispered plea sit there.

Backing her against the shelves, he trapped her between his arms. He grabbed on to the bars on either side of her head and leaned in. Rubbed his body against hers as his mouth treated her to a heart-stopping kiss. The kind that knocked common sense far into next month.

"You are so sexy." That hot mouth traveled down her neck.

A shiver raced through her. And when those lips slipped to her ear and his tongue licked along the top edge, the shiver turned to a full-body tremble. She held on to his waist to keep from falling down.

His muscles tensed under her fingers and his breathing came harder. It thudded under her fingertips as need flashed in his eyes. He didn't do anything to hide her effect on him…and she loved that.

They broke into a wild frenzy of touching and she was knocked harder into a shelf behind her. A can crashed to the floor. Then another. She kicked them out of the way and blocked every sound, including the whooshing of her heartbeat in her ears. Her focus centered on his mouth and the energy spinning around them.

Expert hands traveled over her and around to her back. The screech of her zipper rose above the other sounds a second before his palm brushed over her bare skin. Fingers slid under her bra. The cool air hit her as the front of her dress fell down. It heated again when he lifted his head and stared at her.

Fingertips skimmed over the rounded tops of her breasts. The touch was so reverent, so loving, her breath hiccupped in her throat.

"Touch me." She breathed the order against his neck. He already was but that didn't matter to her. She wanted the imprint of his fingers all over her.

That amazing mouth kissed a trail along the top lacy edge of her bra. Her head fell back as his lips went to work. His tongue licked over her nipple as one hand slipped down the front of her in a slow slide that ignited every cell.

Needing to get closer, to bring him in, she opened her legs as wide as her dress allowed. When that didn't bring her relief, she shimmied, tugging the material up to the top of her thighs.

It was all the invitation he needed. His hand tunneled under her dress to skim along the elastic band of her underwear. The tiny bikini briefs were no defense against his fingers. They pressed up and under. Then he was touching her. Swirling his finger over her.

Need walloped her. It pressed in on her from every direction. She lifted her leg and wrapped it around his thigh. The position gave him free access and he didn't hesitate. His finger slipped inside her. Pumped back and forth until her lower body matched its rhythm.

Relief at being touched gave way to a new tension. A pounding need to feel him everywhere. "Spence, now."

A warning flashed in her mind. She was on the Pill but they should take more precautions. But the minute the thought entered her mind it left again. All of those weeks of fighting amounted to foreplay. The talking, the kissing…she was wound up and burning for him.

Her throat felt scratchy and her skin hot. She couldn't move fast enough, rip the buttons on his shirt open with enough force. Once her fingers touched the firm muscles of his chest, she dragged them down.

The shelves rattled behind her as he picked her up and wrapped both legs around him, low on his hips. Her dress bunched around her waist. He tugged on her underwear. Pulled and yanked.

"Rip it." She almost yelled the order.

"I'll buy you ten pairs," he said through harsh breaths.

His hands shook as the material tore, shredded in his hand. She didn't know if he dropped it or stripped it away. Didn't really care. She was too busy craving the weight of his body. It anchored him but she wanted more.

She fumbled with his belt as tension thumped around her. She got the zipper down and shoved the material out of the way. When she wrapped her fingers around his length, he swore then took in a big gulping breath. His control seemed to snap. With jerky movements, he put a hand over hers and squeezed and the resulting groan vibrated through him.

Between his finger inside her and his mouth on her neck, her body flipped to ready. She arched her hips, trying to drag him inside her. When that failed, she slipped her thumb over his tip. His body actually fell forward. The shelves clanked behind her as they moved, but she didn't care.

They could have been screaming, drawing the attention of everyone at the party, but none of that mattered. Just the man wrapped around her and the feel of his mouth on her skin.

"Now, Spence." She was two seconds from begging.

She opened her mouth to do it when she felt him. Just the tip, rubbing over her. Back and forth, moving deeper with each pass. Then he pushed inside her. Slow, in a seduction that had her hips bucking. As he shifted, her internal muscles adjusted and clamped down on him, clinging to him.

"Damn, Abby." He was panting now as his arms supported her and his mouth traveled to that sensitive space right behind her ear.

When a noise rumbled up her chest, she put the back of her hand over her mouth and bit it. But her control faltered with each delicious thrust. The steady in and out had her body tightening. Every cell pulsed. After one last push inside her, she came apart. The orgasm screamed through her as her hips continued to move back and forth.

He kept plunging as the sweat broke out at the base of his neck. When her body started to wind down, she concentrated on him. Kissed that sexy collarbone and dragged her teeth along his neck.

That's all it took. He moaned as his hips tipped forward one last time. His fingers tightened on the back of her thighs. She held on as the orgasm hit him. His body rocked against her and she felt it all. Finally, his head dipped until his forehead rested against her chest. The pulses continued for a few more seconds before his body relaxed and his weight pressed heavier against her.

His labored breathing blew across her chest. The sleek muscles of his back tensed as she traced her fingers over them. She tried to soothe him with gentle kisses on the top of his head.

After a few seconds, he turned his head to the side and rested his cheek against her chest. "Well, that was amazing."

She had no idea where he found the energy to speak. She couldn't even manage to use that breathy voice like he did. Her muscles refused to listen as her body curled into his.

"Yeah." That took all she had but at least she managed to whisper something into his hair.

He lifted his head and stared down at her. Those sexy eyes, all intense and unreadable, watched her. "Any regrets?"

His voice sounded scratchy and oh-so-sexy. She

knew she could be coy or play games, but she couldn't muster up the energy for that, either. "None."

A second later, the doorknob rattled and they both jumped. Their bodies hadn't separated or cooled. They both held their breaths. After a second shake of the knob, the voices in the hall died down and whoever was out there seemed to move away.

"That was close," she said, even though she didn't care.

She knew she should slide down, enjoy the friction until their bodies separated. She rested her head against his instead.

"Abby?"

With all the stress and worry gone, exhaustion hit her. But her eyes popped open again just as they were beginning to close. "Yeah?"

"Next time, we use a bed."

It took another fifteen minutes for them to break apart. Spence couldn't stop kissing her while they straightened their clothes and cleaned up a bit. He didn't even try to hold back. The last one came as he pulled up the zipper to her dress. Before finishing the last inch, he leaned down and pressed a kiss on the bare skin of her shoulder. Tried to remember every scent and feeling so he could relive this moment later.

When she turned around to face him, he expected regret and maybe a little shyness. Instead, she smiled up at him. "Does my hair look like we just had sex?"

Every part of her did, but he figured that had more to do with his needs and his perception than with the state of her clothes and makeup. "You look amazing."

"We need to leave this room." She sighed. "I'm sure someone has been looking for us."

Knowing his family, many *someones* were. Maneuvering through the next twenty minutes might not be that easy. It would help if he could forget that he carried her ripped panties in his pocket. "I envy you being an only child at the moment."

She smiled and opened the door. Peeked out while he stole one last look at her perfect butt. The woman filled out a slim-fitting dress better than any woman he'd ever known. She was curvy and sleek…and he would have to concentrate very hard not to think about what she could do with that mouth.

They'd just stepped into the hall when Carter appeared in front of them. That grin. The way his gaze wandered over both of them.

This was not going to be good. Spence would bet money on that.

"Where were you two?" Carter asked as he glanced into the dark pantry behind them.

Abby's eyes widened. "What?"

"Hmm?" Spence asked at the same time.

Carter's grin only grew bigger. "Was that a hard question?"

Leave it to his baby brother to pick this moment to come home after months away. Now he was showing up everywhere. The guy's timing sucked. "Of course not."

Carter gestured for them to go into the library two doors down the hall. Since complying struck Spence as the quickest way through this situation, he followed. They all stepped inside and were immediately surrounded by walls of books. A desk sat in the corner by the large floor-to-ceiling window. There were a few other chairs scattered around the room but they stood there, with the door closed behind them.

Carter looked from Abby to Spence and back again. "You missed the toast to the happy couple."

"Well…" Yeah, that's all Spence had. His brain refused to jump-start after the mind-blowing sex.

"Ellie can't drink anyway," Abby said, piping up to fill the silence.

"Yes." Spence nodded. "Good. That's right."

Carter shook his head, looking far too amused by the stilted conversation. "Because that was my point."

"We're just…" It happened again. Spence started talking, then nothing. His mind went blank.

Abby touched the back of her hand against his chest. "Walking."

"Wow." Carter crossed his arms over his chest. Looked pretty impressed with himself, as if every minute was more fun than the last. "You two aren't very good at this. Maybe you need practice."

"What are you talking about?" Abby asked.

The door opened behind them and Jackson slipped inside, sparing Spence from whatever answer Carter might have come up with to Abby's question. Jackson's shoes clicked against the buffed hardwood floor as he walked. He'd picked up a piece of cake at some point and now balanced that plate along with his glass. With his fork raised halfway to his mouth he started talking.

"I heard you guys were in here. Where did you…" His gaze switched from Abby to Spence. "Oh."

Carter snorted. "Right?"

"I give up. Are we wearing a sign?" Abby finished the question by glaring at Spence.

He wasn't sure what he did to warrant that, or maybe he did, but he knew no matter what had happened in that pantry, this embarrassment was going to be his fault. No way would Carter let this opportunity pass.

"Kind of." Carter cleared his throat as he pointed at Spence's chest. "Your shirt is—"

"Buttoned wrong, genius." Jackson shook his head as he put his drink on the edge of the desk and scooped up a forkful of cake.

After a quick look at Spence, Abby rolled her eyes. "You had one job."

A guy could not catch a break around here. Spence went to work on fixing the misbuttoning. "Excuse me, but my brain is not working at top-speed right now."

No one said anything for a few seconds. Spence knew he should jump in and clean up his last comment but what the hell did he say?

When the quiet dragged on, Carter rubbed his hands together. "So, how do you want us to handle this?"

"With a little dignity would be nice," Abby mumbled as she threw them all a men-suck glance.

"We're all grown-ups." Jackson's gaze moved around the group before landing on Spence. "For the most part."

"Right. We've all had sex. Not together, of course." Carter was just revving up, speaking faster as he went when he glanced at Abby and his words sputtered out. "What? Are we dancing around the word? At least I hope it was good sex. You were both smiling a few minutes ago."

"I can think of a thousand places I'd rather be right now," Abby said in an emotionless voice.

"So that it's official and since I know introducing myself shouldn't get me in too much trouble compared to whatever else I might say, I'm Carter Jameson." He held out his hand to Abby.

She took it as she frowned at him. "We've actually met before."

Carter's eyes narrowed. "We have?"

Spence thought back to the calls he shared with Carter all those months ago. The complaints about Dad and his behavior. Talks about the kiss and how sick he felt at seeing it. He hoped Carter forgot every last word. "Be careful."

"I'm Abby Rowe." She finished shaking his hand, then dropped her arm to her side again. "I work for your company. On the management team, actually. We used to pass in the halls. Not often but sometimes when you were in the office visiting your brothers."

"I don't... Oh." Carter's eyes widened. "Okay, yeah."

Jackson nodded. "Subtle."

"You'd be less annoying if you didn't smile so big right now." Abby shot Carter her best watch-it look as she talked.

"Sorry." Carter had the grace to wince as he looked at Abby. Then he turned to Spence. "So, is she why you came back home so fast when Derrick called for help?"

This discussion just got worse and worse. It was as if Carter didn't have a filter. Spence wanted the talk before Abby unleashed and kicked them all. "Hey, Carter? Shut up."

The noise from the hallway grew louder right before the door pushed open. Spence's vision refused to focus...but then it did. He saw a couple—him in his sixties, tall with a regal look to him. Her in her forties with shoulder-length auburn hair and a smile that looked like it was plastered on her face against her will.

Eldrick and the newest missus. All dressed up with her in flowing off-white pants and a matching shirt, and him in navy pants and a blazer. The type of outfit that suggested he'd rather be on a boat.

The only thing that made the unwanted meeting tolerable was that Eldrick's newest wife looked even less excited to be there than any of his children. Spence almost felt sorry for her. Officially meeting the family for the first time like this couldn't be easy. Especially *this* family.

"I see your behavior has not improved since we last saw each other, Spencer." That familiar stern Dad voice floated through the room.

All of the amusement drained from Carter's face. "Dad."

"When did you get here?" Spence didn't mean for it to come out like an accusation but even he heard the edge to his tone.

"I just arrived. You remember Beth." Eldrick gestured toward his wife.

For a second, Spence thought he missed a marriage. They'd eloped and Derrick and Spence had only seen her once, even then only briefly and as she stepped on a private plane at the airport. Carter never had. But that wasn't the name Spence remembered. "I thought your name was Jackie."

She nodded. "Jacqueline Annabeth Winslow Jameson."

That was quite something. Spence felt a headache coming on.

"She prefers…" Eldrick smiled as he looked around the room, and then his mouth fell into a flat line. "Abigail."

Without a word, Abby picked up Jackson's glass and threw the contents in Eldrick's face. They all jumped back, and Beth or Jackie or whatever her name was this week gasped.

Abby didn't even blink. "Welcome home."

Eight

Abby's brain had clicked off. Just seeing Eldrick pushed her into a killing rage. He stood there, smiling while he acted as if everyone around him should jump to his command. When he said her name, her brain snapped. All those months of seething backed up on her and she grabbed the drink. Not her usual move but she refused to regret it.

She'd heard people whisper about his good looks. They hadn't faded as he'd aged. He still possessed that country-club air. The salt-and-pepper hair matched his trim frame. The Champagne dripping down his shirt and stuck in tiny droplets in his hair, not so much.

She hated every inch of his smug face.

She looked around the room. No one seemed angry, but Eldrick sputtered as he wiped his hands down his shirt. His wife patted her hand against his chest, as if that would somehow dry the material.

Well, they could all stare at her or be furious—even kick her out—Abby didn't care. Eldrick deserved to be drenched. That and so much more.

"What in the world was that about?" Jackie-Now-Beth asked.

"Ask him." Because Abby wanted to see if he would say it to her face. Spew his lies with her standing right there, ready to pounce.

"Okay." Jackson put out both hands as if trying to calm down the room. "Let's all relax for a second."

"Jackson is right. Let's not get excited. It isn't as if that's the first time someone doused Dad in a drink in this house." Carter shook his head. "I can think of at least two other wives who used that trick."

Abby liked him.

"Carter, not now." Spence issued the order without moving his gaze from her.

He still didn't get it. That realization moved through Abby, nailing her to the floor. After the sex and the flirting, even the fighting, he didn't see the truth. He still believed she was a willing participant in that kiss with his father back then.

Some of the fight ran out of her at the thought but she would not back down. Eldrick could not weasel out of this confrontation by throwing his weight around or running away to get married. She stood right in front of him because he needed to face her. He owed her this moment.

"That was unnecessary." Eldrick kept his voice even as he threw a scowl in Abby's general direction.

That ticked her off even more. "You made my life miserable."

"Who are you?" Beth asked. There wasn't any heat in her voice. More like a mix of confusion and concern.

Abby didn't know what to think about Beth. In her shoes, if she were married and in love, she'd go ballistic if someone attacked her husband. Then in private, she would shake him until he told her the truth.

But she asked, so... "I'm Abby. I work at Jameson Industries and—"

"Not if you keep behaving like that." The anger edged Eldrick's tone now. The threat hovered right there but he didn't drop it. "Do you understand me?"

He talked to her like she was a child. Dismissive. The man was completely annoying. She had no idea how he'd produced or had any part in raising his otherwise decent sons.

"No one is firing her." Spence's tone was clear and firm. The underlying beat of don't-test-me rang in his voice.

Abby couldn't figure out if that was aimed at her or his father...or both. She tried to ignore the part of her that cared what he thought. She had to block every memory of his touch and the way his mouth felt against her skin to get through this. Fury fueled her now and she couldn't back down. She needed all of her focus now. She'd waited for so long for this moment. It was happening.

She turned to Beth, not sure if the woman was an ally or not. "Your husband, on those occasions when he bothered to come into the office, would corner me. He talked about how we should have private dinners. Commented on my skirt length."

Carter's mouth dropped open. "What?"

"When was this?" Beth asked as she shifted a bit. One minute she was tight up against her husband's side. The next she put a bit of space between them.

Abby had expected the other woman to lash out and

aim all of her disbelief right at Abby, not believing any accusations. But Beth looked engaged. Maybe she'd always suspected her husband could cross the line. Abby wasn't sure. Beth's eyes had narrowed but she wasn't yelling or shouting about Eldrick's imaginary good points.

That was enough to encourage Abby to keep going. "It happened right up until the time he left to marry you."

"That's not true." Eldrick took a step in Abby's direction. "You stop this."

Spence blocked his path. "Let her talk."

That's exactly what she intended to do, with or without their permission. She'd laid this out for Human Resources at the office right after it happened. They'd called Derrick in and then she'd shut down. She knew she needed to own that piece, but back then the idea of going up against a wall of Jamesons had panicked her. She needed to hold on to her job, at least until she'd found something else.

It took her months to realize Derrick wasn't his father. Derrick would have believed her, but by then the damage had been done and Spencer was gone. She'd lost all she could tolerate losing and Eldrick was no longer around to cause trouble, so she let the complaint drop. But now he was back, and that meant he was fair game. She refused to let anyone else suffer because of him.

Which mentally brought her to the hardest part of her story. The part she once tried to tell Spence but he was too busy storming off to listen. "You kissed me. Grabbed me in my office and told me that Spence was wrong for me."

Carter moved then. He turned to face his father. "You did what?"

She couldn't stop now. The words spilled out of her. "He bragged about how Spence would never believe me. How he'd see us together and immediately blame me and bolt."

"Oh, man. That's messed up."

She was pretty sure that comment came from Jackson. She didn't look around to see, but Carter and Spence seemed frozen. Neither of them moved. The only sign of life she could pick up in Spence was the way his hands balled into fists at his sides.

"Okay, look." Eldrick held up his hand as he stepped into the center of the group. "You're exaggerating this a bit, don't you think?"

She refused to stop now or let this slide. This time he needed to face the consequences, even if they only amounted to her yelling at him. "You thought it was funny to see Spence back down."

When Eldrick took another step, Spence grabbed his arm and pulled him back. "Funny? How could you possibly think that?"

"I was saving you, as usual."

Spence made a choking sound. "You can't be serious."

"She worked for you. It was too risky for you to make a move. I was proving a point. It all worked out." Eldrick had the nerve to shake his head.

Between what he said and the patronizing tone in which he said it, Abby wanted to punch him. Worse, open that door and yell her accusations into the hall so that everyone in that big house, on that massive property, knew the kind of man Eldrick really was.

Eldrick stared down at Spence's hand on his arm. "It was a matter of containing the potential damage. We both know you weren't in it for the long term, so why endanger our position? Dating was too risky. The potential liability outweighed whatever feelings you thought you had."

Before Abby could say anything else, Beth turned to her husband. "Eldrick?"

Abby couldn't read the other woman. She stood tall and her voice never wavered. Abby knew almost nothing about her. No one at work talked about her. Jackson had said something about her being different from the other wives. Not as young. Not demanding or the type to run through money, except for her request that they move away and enjoy life on the beach.

One look from his wife and Eldrick's stern I'm-in-charge-here glare faltered. His tone morphed into a lighter, more cajoling sound. "Beth, it's not—"

"We were engaged when this happened. You hadn't announced it to your family, but you had asked. I wore the ring."

Eldrick shot a look in Abby's direction. She sensed a hint of desperation. He no longer stood there as if he could kick them all out at any minute, even though he likely could.

Good, let him squirm.

He shrugged. "Help me out here."

"You've got to be kidding." Abby crossed her arms in front of her to telegraph the very simple message that the man was on his own.

"She could have sued you." Beth took a step closer to Abby. "It sounds like she should have. And hurting your own son? Your behavior was appalling."

The move was so sudden that Abby lost her balance. She leaned against Beth for a second before straightening up again.

"I figured he was protected. It's his company, after all," Abby explained.

An odd sound escaped Spence. "Abby, you can't believe that his behavior would have been okay with us. With me."

She almost said words that would cut him down. The sentence was right there. *You were too busy running away to care.* The only thing that stopped her was Spence's pained expression. "He was in charge, Spence. He'd *been* in charge, had that big corner office that Derrick now uses. I didn't know how many other women—"

"None." Eldrick practically yelled the response.

Carter snorted. "That's doubtful."

Abby blew out a long breath and spilled the last of the truth as she looked at Spence. "I didn't know who to trust."

The hit didn't land any lighter because of her softer tone. She saw Spence wince. So did Jackson. But she wasn't aiming at either of them. Her target, the man she ached to hurt, stood right in front of her.

In the last few seconds he seemed to have lost some of his height. His shoulders fell and he stared at his wife as if he wasn't sure how to approach her.

"Beth, listen to me." Eldrick's hand brushed against Beth's arm.

"Did you really say those things to Abby?" When he didn't immediately answer her, Beth's eyebrow arched. "Well?"

She sounded like a mom now. A really ticked off one. Abby remembered that you're-in-trouble tone from her childhood.

Finally, Eldrick exhaled. "I don't remember exactly what I said."

Relief soared through Abby. Some of the tension eased from her body, leaving her feeling lighter. "Which means yes."

Eldrick snapped at her. "This isn't your business."

"How can you say that?" Carter asked in a voice that still sounded stunned and confused. "This is about her."

"And Spence is your son, Eldrick." Beth shook her head before glancing over at Abby. "Were you and Spence actually dating back then?"

Before she could answer, Spence jumped in. "We were starting to. I was hopeful."

Those words… Abby never expected to hear him admit that out loud, because that moment had passed. She'd spent so much time being angry and hurt because he didn't believe her. Because he didn't stick around long enough to listen to her. She'd never stopped to think about what he saw. That didn't forgive any of his behavior, but it meant something to see how broken he looked and sounded now that he knew the truth.

He did care.

Beth turned back to her husband. "What is wrong with you?"

"I've been asking that for years," Carter said half under his breath.

Eldrick shot Carter a withering look before answering. "Beth, this is a family matter."

"I am your wife now."

For once, Abby thought that was a good thing. This woman did not back down or buy into Eldrick's ramblings. But she clearly deserved a better husband.

After a few seconds, Eldrick seemed to mentally calm down. His shoulders relaxed and the ruddy color on his cheeks vanished. "We should talk in private."

Beth nodded. "Let's go."

"I haven't seen Derrick and his fiancée yet." One look at Beth's face and Eldrick nodded. "Fine."

Without another word, they walked across the library and opened the door. Eldrick didn't look back or say anything as they stepped into the hallway and closed the door behind them.

Abby didn't realize she'd been holding her breath until it seeped out of her. She suddenly felt dizzy and her throat ached. She'd been feeling off for a few days but chalked that up to all the energy she was using trying to tamp down on her attraction to Spence. Now she figured the draining fatigue came from finally letting all of her frustration out.

Carter smiled at her in a way that looked almost like an apology. "Happy?"

"I'm not unhappy." Tired and out of words, yes.

Spence stepped in front of her then. His face was pale and the sexy grin from the pantry was long gone. "Abby."

He probably wanted to talk it out, but she couldn't do it. She needed a break. A few minutes of quiet. "I want to go home."

He nodded as his voice stammered. "Of course. I'll take you."

"No, I will." Jackson backed Spence away. "You Jamesons probably need to talk this out."

"I don't—"

"Hey." Carter caught Spence's arm and pulled him back. "Give her a minute, Spence."

She appreciated the support. With her head spinning and her knees weak, she doubted she could get out of there without falling down. She'd never appreciated Jackson's supportive arm as much.

But a part of her did ache for Spence. For the grief

and pain she saw in his eyes. For the way his mouth dropped open and stayed there, as if he didn't know what to say.

She tried to smile at him but couldn't quite get there. "We'll talk soon."

She gave his arm a quick squeeze, and then she was gone.

Spence couldn't move. His brain screamed to go after her. Forget Carter's well-meaning warnings and Jackson's small head shake. He'd screwed this up in every way possible. Let his history with his father ruin his chance with Abby.

Back then it had seemed so simple. His father made moves on women all the time. Married or not, he was always looking for what else was out there. He'd flirted with women Spence dated until he learned never to bring them around the house or work. Having a thing for Abby, who was right there in the office, threw Spence's usual routine out of whack. He couldn't keep her away from his dad.

That was his one defense. He'd been using it since high school when Spence walked into the kitchen one night and saw his dad standing at the sink with his hand on Spence's then-girlfriend's lower back. They were whispering and laughing. He doubted anything actually happened, but it was so wrong. Dominating and sick.

Spence had been wary and on the lookout ever since. So, when he walked in on that kiss he thought… Bile rushed up the back of his throat at the memory.

"What is going on?" Derrick burst into the library, frowning and wide-eyed with confusion. "You all disappeared and Abby just ran out of here. Not actually, but she sure looked spooked."

Carter frowned. "Dad."

"Eldrick is here?" Derrick's mouth fell and his tone flattened. "Lucky us."

"He and Beth—"

"Wait." Derrick held up a hand. "Who is Beth?"

"Yeah, that's a confusing piece of the story. Apparently, we call his wife Beth now. Believe it or not, you'll like her." Carter shook his head. "But the point is Dad admitted to sexually harassing Abby and setting her up with that kiss to scare Spence off."

Spence appreciated Carter's explanation because he wasn't sure he could get one out right now. He wasn't sure of anything. He glanced at his watch, trying to calculate how much time he should wait before going to see Abby. Jackson might have the answer. Spence half hoped Jackson also would know what to say because Spence was clueless. There wasn't an apology big enough to handle this.

"I can't…" Derrick slipped his fingers through his hair. "I asked her back then, but…" He looked at Carter. "Is she okay?"

Carter shrugged. "She unloaded, so hopefully she will be."

"What about you?" Derrick glanced at Spence. "You okay?"

"No."

Carter gave him a reassuring pat on the shoulder. "You will be, too. Give it time."

Spence wasn't convinced.

Nine

Spence waited for two days. Sunday dragged by with him texting Abby and not receiving a response. Carter had convinced him to wait a little longer and Ellie agreed. Jackson fed him some updates. On Monday, she didn't show up for work and Spence's nerves were shot. He had this image of her packing and leaving town. That was his thing and he was desperate for her not to repeat his mistakes.

The sick thing sounded like subterfuge. Derrick said that never happened. He couldn't remember a day Abby had missed since starting with the company. And that did it. Spence spent the afternoon trying to come up with a plan that didn't come off controlling and rude like his father. Spence didn't want to be that guy. Ever.

But she was in hiding. Not her style and not something Spence had expected, but that's what he got. He had to deal with it. True, she deserved some peace and time to think. He tried to give it to her. He really did. But at seven on Monday night, he stepped into the lobby of her condo building and met up with Jackson.

"I hope I don't regret letting you in," Jackson said as they walked to the elevator.

Yeah, that made two of them. "Get in line."

The fact Jackson was comfortable there, that he got in and out and on the security-protected elevator without trouble had Spence's mind spinning. He grabbed on to the bar behind him in the elevator as the car started to move. He hoped the stranglehold would keep him from doing or saying something stupid.

After a few seconds of silence, he opened his mouth anyway. "She's—"

"Not expecting you," Jackson said.

Spence couldn't figure out if that was a good idea or not. Showing up unannounced might be a jerk move. Honestly, he'd pulled so many with her he couldn't tell where the line was anymore.

"Are you planning to stick around and referee?" Part of Spence didn't hate the idea. Strength in numbers and all that. Having reinforcements might not be bad, either, since he expected Abby to be furious.

The rest of him wanted Jackson out. The majority part. This was private, or it should be. The unloading, the telling of what happened back then, played out in front of an audience. She deserved an empty room for whatever else she needed to say. And he would take it. He owed her that much.

"You really have been gone a long time." A mass of keys and security fobs jangled in Jackson's hand.

"What?"

Jackson shook his head as he smiled. "I forgot we've

been hanging out over at Derrick's place or going out to eat since you've been back. So, you don't know."

The elevator bell dinged and the doors opened. Spence stepped out into the hall, not sure where to go or how to interpret Jackson's unusual ramblings.

"Any chance you're going to explain?" Spence asked.

Jackson nodded. "Follow me."

He turned left and started down the hall. Stopped in front of the first door and pointed at it. "She lives here."

Then he kept walking. Got to the next door and stopped. "This is mine."

Spence's heart stopped. For a second, he couldn't breathe. "You live in the same building? On the same floor?"

Next to each other. That struck Spence as convenient and frustrating, and his anxiety spun out of control inside him.

"Abby told me about a good deal. I jumped in, bought low and became her neighbor." Jackson winked at him. "But before you panic, and I can see it welling up in you already, I'm still only her good friend. Nothing more."

"Why?" Spence couldn't imagine another man not wanting her. Not making a move. Loyalty, sure, and none of the brothers or Jackson had ever tried to ask another's ex out, but still. The proximity, their clear chemistry.

"It was never going to happen." Jackson shook his head. "Because you love her."

There was that word again. Spence kept waiting for his brain to reject it, but it didn't happen.

The lock clicked and Jackson opened his door. "Don't mess this up."

When the bell bonged, Abby glared at the front door to her condo. She'd just sank down into the corner seat of her sectional. Arranged the blankets and pillows just right around her. Had a box of tissues on one side. The remote control on her lap. Medicine, water bottle and a cup of lemon tea right in front of her.

When the bell rang out a second time, she cursed under her breath. This could only be a handful of people. No one buzzed to come upstairs. The phone didn't ring from the front desk to ask her permission to send someone to her. Jackson had a key. That left someone in the building or maintenance.

She stomped across her living room, ignoring the way her bright purple slippers clapped against the hardwood floor. She wore sweatpants and a shirt. No bra. Someone was about to get a show.

She peeked in the peephole and froze. Clearly the bad cold or the medicine or just life in general was making her vision blur. There was no way Spence stood out there. None.

"What?" She shouted the question through the door.

"Abby, please let me in."

Yep, same silky voice. A defeated muffled tone, maybe, but that probably had something to do with him standing in the hallway.

But there was no use in ignoring him. That was easy on the phone. Harder when he hovered outside her door. She opened it and stared at him. "What?"

Whatever tough stance she was trying to take likely was ruined when she sniffled. Stupid cold.

He frowned at her. "You really are sick?"

Of all the things he could have said, that one was unexpected. "Of course. I don't hide. Like I'd give your father that satisfaction."

Oh, she'd wanted to. She'd even toyed with the idea. When the fever hit her on Saturday night after the big showdown with Eldrick, she'd chalked it up to frazzled nerves. By the next morning when she couldn't lift her head off the pillow, she realized it was something else.

Needing to sit down, she left Spence at the door and walked back to her sectional. The cushions had never looked so inviting. She flipped off the slippers and slid into her cocoon of covers. Didn't even look at him again until her head rested against the pillows propping her up from behind.

He stood over her, watching her. His gaze traveled over her. Not sexual. No, this felt like he was conducting an inventory. "When did you get sick?"

"I'd been fighting it off for about a week." She lifted her head in the direction of the pill bottle on the ottoman. "I took some medicine I happened to have here and thought I caught it in time, but no."

He sat on the edge of the couch. About a foot away from her. "It's not healthy to self-medicate."

"You sound like my doctor." She was kind of tired of men telling her she was wrong about things. Not a rational response, she knew. But still.

He looked around the condo. His gaze zipped to her modern kitchen and the sleek white quartz countertop. To the dishes piled in her sink. "Have you eaten?"

She cuddled deeper into the cushions and let his deep voice wash over her. "It's amazing what you can have delivered in this town."

"True."

That's all he said. He didn't move or try to get closer. She sensed he wanted to say something and she was not in the mood to make any of this easier on him. Now wasn't the right time and she didn't have the strength to carry on much of a conversation, but she could sit there and listen.

"I'll handle these." He stood up and stripped off his suit jacket. Threw it over her chair. The stupid thing hung there like it belonged in her condo.

She hated that.

"What are you talking about?" she asked as she watched those long legs carry him to the other side of the condo.

He stepped into the open kitchen and rolled up his shirtsleeves. "The dishes."

Did he just say... "Are you kidding?"

He shrugged. "Seems like the least I can do."

"You know how to do dishes?"

He looked up at her. "I'm not totally useless."

"No one said *totally*."

She thought she saw him smile at her joke as he went to work. Those long fingers soaped up the dishes. She considered reminding him she had a dishwasher, but it was right there. Surely he could see it.

No, she sensed this was something else. As if he were paying penance.

He cleaned in silence for the first five minutes. Then he started to talk. "I learned young to shut down. My dad would yell because nothing was ever good enough for him. I'd take myself out of the middle of it. Some days, he and Derrick would go at it." Spence shook his head as if he were reliving a memory in his mind. "Unbelievable."

She didn't say anything. The cadence of his voice comforted her. Getting a peek into his childhood seemed to chase some of the germs away.

"Eldrick Jameson is not a good man. He was a terrible, distant, mean father. Hell, he wasn't even much of a businessman. Derrick had to rescue the company from Dad's overspending and bad choices." Spence folded the towel and hung it on the bar on the stove. "Other kids had it much worse. I get that. We never wanted for anything. Dad kept up the outside appearances. Played the role of family man."

Abby thought about Eldrick's series of marriages. Of all the goodwill he'd run through in his life.

Spence walked back into the living room. She moved over a bit to silently tell him he could sit next to her.

He took the hint. Dropped into the cushions and snaked his arm along the back of the sectional. Didn't touch her. Didn't even come close, but having him near felt reassuring in an odd way.

"You weren't the first girlfriend he approached…and I know I'm taking liberties with that word." He waited until she nodded to continue. "But he'd made passes before. Sometimes the ploy worked, sometimes not. It chipped away at my trust of him and the women I was attracted to. Of myself."

Spence picked at a spot on the cushion. Sat in silence for a few seconds before continuing. "He knew I was likely to run if he pushed too hard and tested me all the time. Made it clear I didn't deserve anything in the company or in the way of a home life because I hadn't proven myself."

"He really was terrible." She hadn't meant to say that. It slipped out but it wasn't wrong.

"Still is, though Beth might turn out to be one of his better choices." Spence exhaled. "He's currently sending us through this list of tasks we have to perform in order for him to turn the company over."

"What's yours?"

"I don't know." Spence barked out a harsh laugh. "He gave Derrick an envelope for me but I never opened it. I was too busy trying to figure out where we stood."

We? She had no idea but she wasn't ready for this conversation either. "Spence, I—"

"I'm not asking. It was just an explanation." His hand dropped and his fingers moved closer to her shoulder, but he still didn't touch her.

She sensed he might not unless she gave permission. And that was not going to happen…yet.

"I learned this defense. Carter and I both did. We took off. Carter traveled. I tried to forget everything here and all my regrets."

She tipped her head back and looked at him. Let her gaze linger over his tired face and the dark circles under his eyes. "Am I a regret?"

"You are amazing. Smart and beautiful, funny and quick." He shot her a cute smile. "Sexy as hell. That pantry was basically every one of my fantasies brought to life." His smile faded. "But I messed up before. I do regret running out on you, not believing you. Breaking your trust before I really had a chance to earn it."

"I guess you had a reason not to trust so easily." She'd never admitted that before. Never even let it enter her head. In every scenario that ran through her mind, she was the sole victim in Eldrick's schemes. But now she saw that wasn't quite true.

"Don't give me an out, Abby." His fingers slipped lower then. Right next to her shoulder. Brushing against it in a soothing gesture. "I'm a grown man. I was done playing Eldrick's games but that doesn't excuse leaving you here to deal with him."

"He bolted soon after." She had been so happy that day. Happy every day since when he stayed gone.

Spence shook his head. "That's not my point."

She lifted her hand and covered his. Let their fingers tangle together. "I know."

They sat there in silence. Images ran across the television screen. She'd turned the sound off when the doorbell rang and hadn't turned it back on. Now they both watched the show, some detective thing with a lot of running, without any noise or talking.

She tugged him a bit closer. Felt the cushion dip when he slid over and wrapped an arm around her shoulders. The sex had been so good. Not smart, because she hadn't insisted on a condom and at some point they needed to talk about that, but hot and right and almost cleansing in the force of it. But this felt pretty great, too. The silence. The calm.

Her fingers slipped over the remote, but she still didn't turn on the sound. She didn't want to break the mood. Not when she could concentrate on the way his breath blew over her forehead, and how every now and then, he would turn his head to place a chaste kiss on her hair.

"I know I need to earn back your trust," he said into the quiet as darkness fell outside the windows behind the couch. "I just want you to think about giving me the chance to do that."

Hope soared inside her and her heartbeat kicked up. The traitorous thing. The answer *yes* screamed inside her head but she didn't say it out loud. Not yet. Not when Eldrick was still in town and Spence's propensity to flee hadn't been resolved. And she still needed to deal with Jeff Berger and whatever stupid thing he had planned for her.

She glanced up at Spence. Let her gaze wander over his lips. "I actually am hungry."

A smile broke out on his lips. This one genuine and warming. "What do you want?"

She turned just a bit under his arm so she could see him better. "You mean you can cook, too?"

"I order things." He suddenly looked so serious. "I'm really good at ordering."

The joking almost did her in, but she held on to her control. This would take time to fix. "You just ruined my image of you as this big domestic guy who could do anything in the house."

His eyebrow lifted. "Oh, I have skills. When you're feeling better, I'll show you."

Her heart jumped. "Interesting." Man, it so was.

"But for now..." He lifted his hips and slid his phone out of his back pocket. Started clicking on the keys. "You're getting soup."

It was the right answer but she wrinkled up her nose at the suggestion anyway. "I want a burger."

He shot her a side-eye. "I'll buy you as many as you want as soon as you're feeling better."

"That's a pretty good incentive to get well." So was he, but she didn't mention it.

"Then soup it is." He dropped a quick kiss on her forehead. "We'll get back to the good stuff soon enough."

For the first time in months she believed that. "You're on."

Ten

The next week passed by in a happy blur. They didn't get naked again, which Spence regretted, but it was the right answer. He was willing to give Abby as much time as she needed and hoped the answer wasn't forever.

She was feeling better and back to work, having missed only one day. Her so-called easier schedule quickly gave way to long meetings and even longer workdays. They went to dinner, talked, watched movies on her sectional, and then he went home each night after a lingering kiss. That was the new cycle.

Since Beth had dragged Eldrick right back out of town after the scene in the Virginia estate library, it was easy to ignore his calls. Even easier to ignore the stupid envelope with his To Do list for keeping the business. It sat unopened on the dresser in the bedroom Spence still used in Derrick and Ellie's house. She was still resting but up more. Keeping Carter entertained and Derrick smiling.

It was all so normal. Well, normal for other people. Spence didn't know what to do or what to think. He stayed on edge, waiting for the bad news to come. Because it always did.

In her second week back, they had a morning status meeting, covering several projects, and then Abby had a business lunch. Something she'd been putting off and moved on her calendar twice. He didn't know what it was but he trusted her. They were...*dating*. He guessed that was the right word, but who knew. He wasn't about to ask, because he didn't want to scare her away. Not when things were going well.

Right now she was sitting in a conference room chair, pummeling Rylan with questions. "When will the report be done?"

He shifted the papers around in front of him on the conference room table. Abby had insisted on scheduling them for the big room. The one with expensive artwork hanging on the walls and the blackout curtains. It spoke to the company's success and provided a level of intimidation.

The whole thing was wildly enjoyable for Spence to watch.

"I need—"

"Rylan, I am done playing with this." Abby leaned back in her chair. "You know I am."

Something had changed in the relationship between Abby and Rylan. It had always been professional, respectful and still was, but Abby's patience had seemingly expired. There was a charged energy in the room. Gone was Rylan's flirting and Abby's gentle coaxing. She was going in for the kill.

"I finished," Rylan said in a flat tone. "You set a deadline and I met it."

He pushed a report across the table. A letter attached to a thick binder with folded blueprints tucked inside.

Abby didn't touch it. "I thought so."

"The project has been approved. There are no more impediments to getting started on the work." Rylan couldn't have sounded less excited if he were talking about toothpaste.

Spence was pretty sure he'd missed a step. No question the Abby-Rylan dynamic had flipped. Rylan actually looked a little afraid of her, which was probably a wise choice. Abby walked into the meeting looking all professional and no-nonsense in her trim black suit. Rylan usually let his gaze travel a bit. He'd wait until she turned and would sneak a few peeks. Not today.

Spence found the outfit sexy as hell. That little bit of light blue stuck out from the top of her buttoned jacket had sent his control careening into a wall. He'd seen the jacket unbuttoned earlier in her office. He knew the shirt was silky and thin and all he wanted to do was get his hands under it.

He really hoped he earned that right back soon.

"If that's all?" Rylan stood up before he finished the sentence.

"You've signed everything?" Abby just stared at the man, still not touching the paperwork she'd pushed so hard to get completed. "I don't want any surprises."

"No, we're done."

She nodded. "Good answer."

A minute later, he was packed up and Spence showed him out the door. Handed him off to an assistant, then stepped back into the conference room. The satisfied grin on Abby's face suggested she liked how that battle ended.

"Want to clue me in?" he asked.

Her head jerked up. "What?"

"That was a big change in attitude. You were coddling him, letting him take the maximum time to ensure the project got approved. It's exactly what I would have done since Rylan seems like the type who craves attention." Minus the flirting, of course. Spence was pretty sure Rylan wouldn't have tried that tactic on him. Spence leaned against the table and faced her where she still sat in the chair. "He went from drooling over you and dragging his feet to jumping to your every demand."

She shrugged. "We had a chat and I made my position clear."

"Which means?"

"I told him he had misstepped if he thought he had a chance at something with me. Also made it clear I wanted the job done."

"Uh-huh." That sounded like half a story to Spence. "Did he actually make a pass at you?"

A week ago that question might have sent her temper spiking. It could have led to a fight, with one of them storming out. But that had changed, too. Spence no longer weighed every word. He was careful but not wary.

She stood up. Let her hand trail over his thigh. Low enough to be decent but with enough pressure to pull his mind away from the office. "Abby…"

"I made it clear that it would be stupid for him to try anything." She rubbed her thumb back and forth over a crease in his pants.

"Are you trying to prove to me that you can handle him?"

"Didn't I?"

"You did, but I already knew that you would." His hand went to her waist and he toyed with one of the buttons holding the sides of her jacket together. "Any chance I can convince you to skip your meeting and have lunch with me?"

By "lunch," he meant not eating. He'd settle for an actual meal, but his control was wavering. The more he watched her in action at work and cuddled with her on the couch at night, the more he wanted everything. And the more Jackson's use of the word *love* didn't seem so misplaced. Not that he was ready to talk about that, because he wasn't.

"Derrick would be impressed with your work ethic," she said.

Spence and Derrick had an understanding. Spence knew his strengths and Derrick didn't try to redirect those. "My skills tend to be best used in going out and getting us new projects to bid on, or better yet, just win outright."

"Always the salesman."

"It takes a lot of time and study." He stood up, letting his hand linger on her stomach. "Weeks, sometimes months, of reviewing everything to find the right course of action."

"Are we still talking about work?"

Not really. "Of course."

She tugged on the bottom of his tie. "How about this. We both be good employees this afternoon, then we'll meet up for dinner."

He liked the way her mind worked. "I can make a reservation."

"At my place." She skimmed a finger down the buttons of his shirt. "We'll stay in."

All the blood rushed from his head. The idea of a night with her, even just holding her, sounded so good. "You sure?"

"I hear you're very skilled at doing dishes."

He had to smile at that. She could charm and seduce him into just about anything. "Not to brag but I'm good at a lot of things."

"I plan to let you prove that to me."

With one battle done, Abby moved on to the next one. Last week, as soon as her bad cold passed, she'd called Rylan. Made it clear to him that passing notes to her from other businessmen was both juvenile and a move guaranteed to haunt him. She mentioned filing a complaint. Then she talked about telling Spence about what really happened and how Rylan let Jeff Berger use him.

She'd dropped every threat she could think of to teach him a lesson. Once she had his full attention, telling him he had exactly one week to finish his work and deliver his report had been easy, and he beat her deadline by a few days.

She suspected this meeting with Jeff would not run as smoothly.

They met in a noisy restaurant. One of those impossible-to-get-reservations type in a building that used to be a bank or a warehouse or something. It had soaring ceilings and the bar stretched out along one side with an open kitchen in the back.

The servers shared a similar look. She thought of it as unshaven, hair-in-a-bun male Pacific Northwest vibe. It fit with the decor and the all-black serving outfits. They seemed to know Jeff and hovered around the table, trying to please him. Even called him by name.

She wrote the whole scene off as more of his power-play antics. He wanted to impress her, make her think he controlled everything. Whatever.

What he didn't understand is she'd already taken on Eldrick and Rylan this week and somehow managed to tame Spence into potential boyfriend material at the same time. Whatever threats Jeff had planned would be just one in a long line she intended to bat down.

She ignored the menu in front of her and reached for the water glass. Taking a sip, she glanced around the main dining room. Saw the plates of salad and bottles of wine being delivered to tables. Heard the clink of silverware as she tried to decipher the mumble of conversation around her.

Jeff's heavy sigh broke through the action. He slipped an envelope across the table. "Here is an explanation of what we need and compensation for your time. Just as we discussed."

"We never discussed anything."

He frowned at her. "Don't play hard to get."

The man was savvy. Abby guessed there was a typed note and cash in there. Didn't matter because she didn't intend to open it and find out. She slid it back across the table in his direction. "Not interested."

Jeff made a big show of folding his menu and putting it aside. He leaned in with his elbows on the edge of the table. "Now, Abby. You don't even know what I'm offering."

Turned out this meal was exactly what she thought it was about—trying to get her to spy on Jameson Industries. She wasn't interested in anything from Jeff but she sure wasn't interested in that.

"A trip to nowhere." She looked around for the restroom. From there she could make an easy escape. That sounded smarter than risking Jeff making a scene. "No, thanks."

She turned in her chair and started to get up.

Jeff's hand clamped down on her wrist. "Sit down."

She didn't jerk back or start yelling. Didn't give him

the satisfaction of knowing his touch made her want to throw up the stale protein bar she'd choked down before coming into the restaurant fifteen minutes ago. "Amazing how you become less charming when you don't get what you want."

"I tried this the nice way. I offered you a job months ago, and you said no. I just offered you an easy way to make extra money and you pushed it away." He dropped her wrist and sat back again. "Do you see what I'm saying?"

She refused to rub her wrist to alleviate the burning sensation of his hold. "That you can't take no for an answer."

"You're the problem here, Abby."

She was just about done with overbearing businessmen. Seeing how others operated made her appreciate Derrick and Spence's style even more. No wonder Eldrick had thought he could get away with bullying. Apparently, it was the go-to move for many just like him.

But the comment did intrigue her. She gave in to her curiosity. Maybe this way she could prepare for whatever he had planned for the future. "How do you figure that?"

"I'm done losing to Derrick." Jeff shook his head. "All I need is some information. Not on every job, of course. That would look suspicious."

In other words, Jeff couldn't compete on a fair playing field. Good to know. "I work there. Screwing him screws me."

"You have a safety net in my office in the form of any managerial position you want. I'll make up a title for you."

Right, because that's how this worked. Once she broke the trust in one office, her reputation would be in shambles. No one would hire her, not even Jeff. But that didn't even matter because she wasn't tempted. Just because Jeff was that type didn't mean she was.

He'd made a similar offer at the lowest point in her business career. She'd been harassed and just lost Spence. Felt vulnerable and convinced she'd be fired. She guessed she'd given off a pathetic vibe. But still, she didn't bite then. She had no idea why Jeff thought she would now.

"You're asking the wrong person. I don't play like this." She had pride and integrity and didn't plan to forfeit either.

"You're going to regret this." Jeff stared at the untouched envelope then picked it up again. Slipped it in his jacket pocket.

"The lunch? I already do."

"We'll see how funny you think this is after..."

After what? She was dying to know. "Goodbye, Jeff."

She got up and forced her legs to move. Something about his tone and that last comment pulled at her as she walked away. The words could mean anything. But she'd learned early to expect the worst. Now she did.

Eleven

Spence followed her home that night. Abby left about fifteen minutes before he did because he got stuck on a phone call about a problem with a project at the University of Maryland. One of those calls he couldn't just jump off of because there were ten other bored people in on it who also wanted to get off the line.

The second after he hung up, he raced out of the office. Tried to act professional and nod and smile to everyone he passed in the office hallway but his insides churned. He'd heard the whispers about him dating Abby. Even spoke with Derrick about them. The conclusion was that Human Resources should talk to Abby to make sure she was okay. People dated. He and Abby knew the dangers because they'd already lived through them once. Mostly.

That left a clear line between him and Abby tonight. Except for the ongoing trust issues, his idiot father and the very real sense she was hiding something from him. All of those issues stayed stacked in a teetering tower between them, but Spence was ready to unpack.

He also ached to touch her again. Once had not been enough. The hurried sex in the pantry could only be described as explosive. He wanted to experience the joy of slowly getting to know her body. And that could happen tonight...unless he misread the cues, in which case dinner worked, too.

She'd slipped him a note with the security code for the garage and the number of the space to park in. Then, Abby being Abby, she re-sent the information by text. The numbers mixed with his memories of the pantry and clouded in his brain, but he managed to get inside the gate.

The elevator turned out to be tougher because it required the guy at the desk to call up and get permission from Abby to let him in. For one tense second, he worried she'd changed her mind and would say no, but the guy waved him up.

That was five minutes ago. Now he got off the elevator and shot Jackson's front door a quick look. Having him so close by rattled Spence but he pretended it wasn't a big thing.

He raised his hand to knock on Abby's door right as it opened. She stood there, hair falling over her shoulders and a welcoming smile on her face.

He almost lost it.

Somehow he managed to lean in for a quick kiss. Even the slight touch of their lips had his heart racing until the echo of it thumped in his ears. He stepped inside the condo and closed the door behind him. After turning the lock, he followed her inside the open space.

The condo was new, with top-end everything. Her

bedroom sat shadowed off to the right. He tried not to think about that room. Keeping his mind off the floor plan proved easy because he had something else—something much more interesting—to focus on right now.

Abby walked from the entryway through to the living room with those impressive hips swaying as she stepped. The drapes were drawn on the floor-to-ceiling windows behind her couch. Lamps lit the area in a soft glow. And she was wearing a dress. She'd been in a suit all day. He remembered because he'd thought about her skirt and the way it rode up her thighs, just a touch, as she walked.

The dress was solid red and bold. It wrapped around her with a same-color tie at her waist. He'd never seen it before but he was a fan.

As she stood there, her head tilted to the side and her hair cascaded over her shoulder. "Are you hungry?"

"Starving." He wasn't even sure if he could choke down food right now, but it seemed like a good answer. Logical in light of the time of night and the agreement they had to find food.

She made a humming sound. "That's a shame."

The list of take-out restaurants running through his brain slammed to a halt. "Excuse me?"

That smile, wide and inviting. Man, there was no way he was going to survive that. The seductive curve of her lips promised excitement. Or maybe he was still daydreaming. He honestly couldn't tell.

Reality blended with fantasy when he looked at her. Long legs and that face. Big eyes, full lips…yeah, he was lost. He had no defense against her.

She kept her hands at her side as she walked over to him. He would have moved but he was pretty sure his feet were welded to the floor. No part of him even flinched except the growing bulge in his pants. He really hoped that didn't make her twitchy. Another few minutes of her staring and she would notice. She couldn't *not* notice.

After a few yanks, she undid his tie and slipped it off his neck. Her fingers went to the buttons at the very top and opened two. When she slipped her hands inside the opening and placed her warm palm against his chest, he jumped. Couldn't help it.

"Are we eating?" The question sat out there. He sounded like he'd never had sex before, and he had. Plenty of times. But he didn't want to take a wrong turn here. He really wanted her to lead and take them down that hallway to her bedroom.

"You did say you were starving." She slipped her thumb up his throat to the bottom of his chin. Brushed it back and forth.

That touch fueled him. Spun him up and readied him for more.

"I can't remember what I said." He wasn't sure how he drove there without crashing the car.

"When?"

"Ever."

"That thing you do where you lose your speech when you touch me?" She leaned in and ran her tongue along the top of his ear then whispered, "Very sexy."

His cells caught on fire. He could smell her shampoo and feel her soft hair skim over his cheek. And that body. She leaned in, pressing her chest against his and his brain misfired.

"I don't want to misread…"

"I like when you're careful but you need to catch up

here." She bit down on his earlobe as she talked. Not hard but enough to get his attention.

The whisper of her voice echoed around him. He pulled back and looked at her. His gaze traveled over her face, looking for any sign of hesitancy. The blush on her cheeks and heat of her skin said yes. When her tongue peeked out, licked over his bottom lip, he may have said something. Who knew?

She shifted slightly and got a hand between them. With her fingers on that tie around her waist, she tugged. The belt came undone and the material keeping the dress closed slid open, revealing miles of perfect skin. She wore a pink bra that pushed her breasts up until they spilled over the tops of the cups and a tiny scrap that he guessed qualified as bikini bottoms.

It was a miracle his legs held him. Every thought about taking it slow left his head. Ran right out of there.

"I'm going to dream about this dress." He really wanted to buy her a thousand more like it. She could pick the colors. He did not care.

"About getting me out of it, I hope." With a shrug of her shoulders, she let the material slide off and fall to the floor with a swish. It pooled around her bare feet. Covered the soft purple polish covering her toes.

That choking sensation? He was pretty sure he swallowed his tongue. "Most definitely."

His words sounded garbled and a strange layer of fuzziness clogged his head. Whatever control he normally had he'd forfeited when he walked in the door.

A deep inhale didn't help. Neither did a silent count to ten. So, he gave in and touched her. Reached out and wrapped his arms around her. Lifted her off the floor and sighed in relief when her thighs clamped down against the outsides of his legs.

"It is unreal how sexy you are." Babble filled his brain, so he wasn't a hundred percent sure what he'd said, but she smiled.

Fingers slipped through his hair as her other hand skimmed down his back. "Still hungry?"

The light bulb clicked on in his mind. He finally figured out she wasn't talking about food. "I'll show you in the bedroom."

Somehow he got them there. Walked backward for part of it. Knocked his arm against the door frame and bit back a curse. Once he righted himself, he started moving again. His elbow slammed into the wall as he searched for the light switch. Then it was on and all he could see was her face above him and the bedroom right behind her.

He didn't waste any time. He stepped up to the edge of the mattress and lowered her. Let her slip down his legs. As soon as she sat down, her fingers went to work on his belt then his zipper. He tried to breathe in, rushed to get air in his lungs as she lowered her head and took him in her mouth.

One swipe of her tongue. One press of her hand against him, fingers around him, and his control snapped. As gently as possible, he pulled her away from him. His hands shook with the need to throw her back on the bed, but she did it for him. With excruciating slowness, she leaned back. Pressed her back on the mattress and flung her arms out to her sides.

She winked at him. "Why are you still dressed?"

Good question. He nearly ripped his shirt off then yanked his pants down. Probably set a speed record in getting naked. Then he crawled up her body, rubbing against her, over her. The resulting friction had him gasping.

"Condom." He couldn't forget this time. He'd never gone without protection before her. Before Abby and that pantry.

He didn't regret it, but he could do better. He owed her that along with so many other things.

He scrambled off the bed as she called out his name. Man, he loved the sound of his full name on her lips.

"Spencer, what are you…" She smiled when she saw the condom in his hand. "Yes."

"We'll be more careful this time." While she was sick, he'd texted her about birth control and their failure to use any. She assured him she was on the Pill, but they'd agreed a repeat of that move was not smart.

"Why are you still talking?" she asked as she reached up and pulled him back on top of her.

He kissed her then. Let out all the pent-up need and desire and plowed them both under. Kissed her until the blood ran from his head and his lower half pulsed with the need to strip her underwear off and throw it on the floor.

When he lifted his head, she looked dazed. Smiling with swollen lips and big watchful eyes.

"You are so beautiful." He meant it. Every word.

He'd never had any woman break through his defenses and reach inside him like she had. Through everything, all the pain and distrust, he could never wipe her from his mind. Now he knew he didn't have to.

His hand slipped behind her back to unclip her bra. Peeling it off her was like unwrapping the best present. His breath caught in his throat as his mouth dipped to kiss her. He ran his tongue over her, around her nipples, and felt her fingers clench in his hair.

Slow. She deserved all of his attention for as long as he could handle it. But then her hand snaked down his body. Those fingers wrapped around his length. He had to rest his forehead against hers as he gulped in air and wrestled for control.

"Spencer." She brought her knees up until the inside of her thighs pressed against his sides. "Go faster."

The words pummeled him and the urge to give in grabbed him. But this was for her. Tonight, and for as many nights as she would give him. "Soon."

He moved down her body, kissing a trail over her bare skin. Loving every inch of her softness, each curve. He reached her stomach and pressed a kiss on the slight bump he found so sexy. When she gasped, he did it again.

Turning his head to the side, he rubbed his cheek against her bare skin. "You are perfect."

"You…" Her back arched off the bed and those heels dug into the mattress.

There, sprawled out with her chest rising and falling on harsh breaths, she silently called out to him. Looked so inviting.

His mouth dipped lower. A finger slipped inside her as she shifted on the bed. He circled and caressed until her thighs clenched against his shoulders. He would never get a clearer sign of how ready she was, and he didn't wait for one.

Up on his knees, he rolled on the condom. Then his body slid over hers again. He pressed inside. Keeping his thrust slow and steady, he pushed until her body tightened around his. His brain, his muscles—every part of him—begged for release. But he held back. He needed to know she'd gotten there before he let go.

Her breaths came in pants now. Her exposed neck enticed him as her head pressed deep into the pillows. She grabbed the comforter, balling it in her fists. With every second, her control slipped further away and it was amazing to watch.

Her skin glowed as sweat gathered on his forehead. Pressure built inside him, clawing at him. Still, he didn't give in. He slipped his hand between their bodies. Touched her as he pumped in and out.

The trembling started in her legs. He could feel the muscles vibrate against him as the pulses started moving through her. Her hips lifted and her hands grabbed on to his shoulder. He waited until the last second, until she gasped and her body bucked, before he gave in to his own orgasm. It rolled through him, wiping everything else out.

For those few minutes, it was just him and her and the rhythm pounding in his head as he pushed into her. When the explosion came, all he could do was ride it out. Hold on to her, wrap his body around hers and give himself over to it.

It took a bit more time for his body to calm and the pulsing to stop. Reality came back to him in pieces. Her fingers brushing over his shoulder lured him in. He buried his face in her shoulder and inhaled. He'd get up, move—do something. Soon. But not yet…

He didn't know how long he rested with her on the bed with his eyes closed. It really didn't matter since she'd curled into his side with her hand on his chest. He slipped his palm up and down the soft skin of her arm, loving the feel of her.

This felt right. He'd ached for this, dreamed about it, got angry that he couldn't stop thinking about what this might feel like when he left. Being away from her and adrift, not having any real direction, was the answer then. He'd needed to clear his head. Yeah, he got the facts wrong and blamed her instead of dumping it all on his father where it belonged. After those few stunned seconds, he'd been so willing to believe the man who raised him and always disappointed him. Spence knew now that he needed to break the habit.

He was about to drift off to sleep when she started talking. She leaned up on her elbow and stared down at him. "May I ask you a question?"

And that destroyed any chance of him sleeping, possibly ever. He couldn't think of a time when that question ended well. "Why do I think I should say no? I mean, I can only mess up from here, right?"

She smiled as her fingertip traced his lips. "You're not going to mess up."

"I like how much faith you have in me." He folded the arm that wasn't holding her behind his head. "Go ahead."

"What are we?"

The wording was strange but he knew exactly what she meant. They'd spent every evening together since she got over being sick. He planned to repeat that pattern next week and for many after that. "You sure know how to lead with the big questions."

"There's gossip at work and—"

"Does that bother you?" Maybe he'd been too casual about the boss thing. He'd taken himself off all of her projects. He would be there if she needed to consult but they restored Derrick as her direct line of supervision. It was neater that way. A separation of work and private life. Better for her in case she did have an issue.

"Not if whatever is between us is real."

The words beat back the anxiety welling inside of him. He had an easy answer for this. "It's real."

"Are you just saying that?" Her eyes narrowed but amusement still lingered in her voice.

Despite her light tone, he took the question very seriously. "Because we're naked and in your bed and I'm hoping I get to stay here? No. I'm saying the words because they're true. Because they've been true and probably were even back when I messed up and pushed you away."

She blew out a long breath as her hand came to rest on his chest again. "I hate what happened to us back then."

Now was the right time for the apology. Nothing fancy. Just the truth.

"I'm sorry. Sorry I didn't listen or trust you." He brushed her hair off her cheek. "Sorry I didn't punch my dad in the face."

"I don't want to come between you."

Spence almost laughed at that. Might have if she didn't look so serious. "Not possible. There's no relationship to ruin. Not anything meaningful."

"Don't say that."

Spence refused to get into that argument now. She was decent and loving and probably thought Eldrick might have some good hidden down deep inside him. Spence knew better. Even with Beth's coaxing, Eldrick would never be a guy Spence trusted around Abby. Not again.

He needed her to understand Eldrick wasn't between them. "But this—us—it is worth saving."

Her eyes got all shiny. "So, we're in this."

A lump clogged his throat, but he swallowed it down. "We're in it."

Her mood switched again. This time to playful as she climbed on top of him. Straddled his hips.

"Good. Now we can have dinner." She poked him in the chest. "I seem to remember you owing me a burger."

"At your service, ma'am."

Twelve

The next week passed in a haze of happiness. A voice in Abby's head told her to be careful, not to let herself enjoy it too much because it could be snatched away so quickly.

She'd never gone for long stretches without something going wrong. Like, spectacularly wrong. A bad boyfriend, a huge problem at work. Having to move. A huge expense she hadn't prepared for. Running out of money. Until she'd found stability with her job at Jameson, the last two years had been a constant strain.

Just to be safe, the only thing she'd spent any money on since she started receiving the big paycheck was her condo. She figured she always could sell it if finances grew tight again. It was her rainy-day fund, in a way.

Looking around the dining room table now, she couldn't call up any of those bad memories or nagging worries. Probably had something to do with how loud the Jameson family was. Man, they could talk about *anything.* Carter, specifically, was a pro at talking.

They'd all gathered to celebrate the news from Ellie's doctor that she could move around a bit more. She came back from her appointment two days ago and declared a family dinner was in order. Verbally walked all over Derrick's objections and made it happen. To make her happy, and everyone seemed determined to do that, they gathered.

Even now they passed a roast, vegetables and potatoes around the long rectangle table in Derrick and Ellie's dining room. Dishes clanked as Carter and Jackson argued about the benefits of mashed potatoes over all other potato dishes. Jackson's sister and Ellie's best friend, Vanessa, couldn't make it on short notice, and Ellie's brother was away at some computer seminar, but everyone else was there.

"Are you okay?" Spence whispered the question in Abby's ear as he leaned in closer.

She reached out and slid her hand over his thigh. Gave it a little squeeze. It was tempting to drive him a little mad under the table, but really, she wanted to keep the connection. After their week together, she'd been spoiled. She hated any distance between them outside of work.

This sensation of falling and being caught was new to her. So foreign but not unwelcome. Her young life centered on her and her mom. They had been an inseparable pair. Then she widened her circle to include a few friends. Now, with Spence, she opened it again for this makeshift family that joked with her while enveloping her in its incredible warmth.

He kissed her temple. "I know you're not used to so many people."

Carter snapped his fingers. He sat directly across from Abby and pointed at the dish next to Spence. "Stop licking your girlfriend and pass the peas."

Spence made a groaning sound. "Are you sad because you don't have a girlfriend?"

"We should find him one," Derrick said as he forked the meat off the tray then kept passing.

From his seat at one end of the table, he looked like a king presiding over his lands. Abby thought that might have been a scarier idea and his dominance might have carried more weight if he didn't spend half of the meal making lovey eyes at Ellie at the other end of the long table. He'd protested sitting so far apart but Ellie assured him he'd have the best view that way.

Honestly, Abby found the two of them adorable-bordering-on-annoying. Spence once talked about the bumpy road they had to engagement. She'd been in the office, but Derrick wasn't really one to drag his home life in. He hadn't before Ellie, anyway.

Not wanting to fall behind on the verbal poking going around the table, Abby leaned across Spence and looked at the one person at the table who seemed to keep eating no matter what happened around him. "Jackson, what's your sister's dating status?"

Jackson didn't even look up from his plate. "Nope."

"Come on." Carter laughed. "But she already loves me."

Jackson glared at Carter before glancing over at Abby. "I work with this crowd. Do you think I want to be related to them?" He froze for a second, then held up the hand that just happened to be holding his knife. "No offense."

Derrick snorted. "How could we possibly be offended by that?"

"I like them." Abby leaned in closer to Spence, soaking in his body heat. "You've all grown on me."

Spence slipped his hand around her and gave her lower back a gentle massage. "Thanks, babe. And the feeling is mutual."

Abby didn't know how he planned to eat with one hand attached to her, but that was his problem. She savored the touching and the food. She was about to ask Ellie how she'd made the meal when she was still confined to bed or sitting down for most of the day, but then common sense kicked in. The two women in the kitchen when they all arrived at the house likely did all the work. Clearly there were some benefits of eating at a Jameson home.

The money—the stunning breadth of it—still didn't sit right with Abby. She wasn't used to all that wealth. The Virginia house looked like a school when she'd driven up for the party. Derrick's town house was nothing short of spectacular but still managed to feel homey, which she credited to Ellie's handiwork.

Abby had been raised with so little. She appreciated every last shoe in her closet and can in her pantry. She'd picked each item out and purchased them. The only thing that kept her from fidgeting when she thought about the reality of Jameson money was that Spence never showed any sign of being impressed with his bank account. If he had, she would have balked.

"You have pet names for each other. Cute." Carter sent Spence a bug-eyed look. "The peas, Spence."

Spence didn't move. "You have legs."

"If I have to get up, I'm punching you."

"You're both annoying." Jackson picked up the bowl and passed it across the table to Carter.

He dug right in. "About time."

Through the controlled chaos, Derrick let out a loud exhale. Abby never knew her dad but she assumed this was the ultimate dad move. Make a noise and get everyone at the table listening. *Smooth.*

"This nonsense is going to stop when the baby comes," he said.

"We'll be too busy fighting over who gets to hold him to argue about anything else," Spence said as he tried to steal the bowl of peas back.

Carter moved it out of reach.

Ellie eyed them all over the top of her water glass. "Or her."

"Speaking of which—" Carter cut into his roast "—are you still trying to sell that faulty birth control story to explain your current state?"

"My pregnancy doesn't need to be explained," Ellie said, emphasizing each word.

"Carter." Abby was pretty sure Spence kicked his brother as he said his name.

Ellie wasn't quite as subtle. She fixed Carter with a you're-right-on-the-edge glare even though she looked like she was fighting back a smile. "Don't make me burn your clothes in the fireplace."

He winced. "Hormones?"

She waved a knife at him. "Don't test me."

Abby felt a fog roll over her. The conversation picked at a memory she'd shoved to the back of her brain. A piece of information she didn't want to deal with that now came screaming back to her.

The Pill. Sex. Antibiotics. She'd started taking the meds that were in her bathroom the second she started feeling sick. That happened before she had sex with Spence. Before, during and after.

Antibiotics and birth control pills were a bad combination. Still a long shot for getting pregnant, but it could happen. Some medications played with the effectiveness of the pill. When she climbed out of her sickbed and remembered that, she'd rechecked on the internet. The news was not as negative on the possibility of getting pregnant as she'd hoped.

Good grief. It wasn't possible...was it?

Abby tried to remember Ellie's list of pregnancy symptoms, all that she had to fight off and go through.

"Faulty birth control?" Abby didn't mean to say the words out loud, but they were the only ones in her mind right now.

"Is this appropriate dinner conversation?" Derrick asked.

"It is in this house." Spence shrugged as he made another grab for the peas and reached them this time.

His look of triumph over something so simple made Abby smile. Or it would have if she wasn't busy counting days on the calendar in her head.

"The pregnancy is high-risk because my IUD failed," Ellie explained. "It's still in there."

Carter whistled. "Damn, Derrick."

"I didn't do it."

Spence glanced at Derrick. "Well, technically..."

"It kind of depends what the 'it' is in that sentence." Jackson froze in the middle of moving the roast closer to him. "Is that the doorbell?"

The bell chimed a second time.

"Isn't everyone here?" Derrick asked the question to the room in general. He clearly didn't expect an answer because he was up and out of his chair, on the way to the door.

A terrible thought ran through Abby's head. She

leaned in to whisper it to Spence. "If your father is back in town—"

Carter nearly dropped his water glass. "Don't even joke about that."

Footsteps echoed on the hardwood floor as Derrick walked back in. He held an envelope. He dropped it on the sideboard that ran half of the length of the impossibly long room. Never looked at it again.

"What was it?" Spence asked even though he didn't sound that interested in the answer.

"Delivery of work documents." Derrick's gaze flicked to Ellie as he sat back down. "Don't glare. I didn't tell anyone to send stuff here."

"Yet, someone did. Gee, I wonder why they thought it was an okay thing to do." She did not sound pleased.

Derrick winked at her. "You forget how important I am."

"That ego." Carter shook his head. "Unbelievable."

Jackson scooped up more potatoes. "Try working with him."

Carter glanced at her. She could feel the heat of his stare as the conversation bounced around her. She tried to keep up but the idea of a baby was stuck in her head now. She wanted to kick it out but it had grabbed hold.

"Abby? Do you have an opinion on that?" Carter asked.

She couldn't stop looking at Spence, imagining what their children might look like. If a kid would have his stubbornness.

When she realized the table had gone unusually quiet and everyone stared at her, she struggled to mentally rewind the conversation and come up with an answer. "Uh, no. I'm taking the Fifth."

The talking picked back up again. About food. About

work. About anything Carter could think of, or so it seemed.

Spence leaned in closer, brushing her hair back behind her ear. "You sure everything is okay?"

"Just thinking." And panicking and generally kicking her own butt for being so careless. She'd never done that before. With her luck, it would only take one time.

He smiled at her. "You can concentrate on anything with all this noise?"

"It's called conversation, Spence," Jackson mumbled under his breath.

Ellie groaned. "Enough talking. Eat."

"The pregnant woman has spoken." Derrick picked up his glass in a toast.

"You know, for that power to keep working, you're going to have to be pregnant all the time." Jackson flinched, which must have meant Ellie kicked him. She was right there, after all. "Hey!"

"I'm up to the challenge," Derrick said.

Some of the color drained from Ellie's face. "Let's start with one first."

Abby looked down at her plate. She really hoped she wasn't the one saying that a month from now.

It took another half hour to finish up and move the conversation into the living room. On Ellie's orders, the men cleared the table and argued during every second of their work as if they'd been sent into the mines to dig for coal.

Spence didn't mind helping out. He'd do dishes, but he refused to do them alone. In Derrick's house, that usually wasn't necessary because family dinners meant he hired people to handle most of the work. With Ellie being less mobile, Derrick was interviewing for a full-time cook, but he had to do it behind her back because she was not comfortable with the idea.

Spence glanced into the great room next to where they'd eaten dinner and saw them all gathered around, lounging on sofas. Arguing, like they always did. He was pretty sure that was part of the Jameson gene pool. Jackson probably picked up the habit by association.

The only person not having coffee and debating dessert options was Abby. She stood in the doorway between the dining room and the great room, watching. He'd picked up on her mood change earlier. His family could be overwhelming. He got that. But he sensed something else was bothering her.

They'd been growing closer, spending more time together. Talking about things other than work. He didn't want her to shut down now.

"You sure you're okay?" He slipped his arms around her waist and pulled her body back against his. "You got quiet."

She sighed. "That was a lot of activity."

"Yelling. A meal with this group is a lot of yelling."

When she leaned against him, he put his chin on her shoulder. Breathed, letting this moment settle inside him. The comfort of it made him think he misread her earlier. The slight tension running through her had vanished. Now she relaxed.

She rubbed her hand over his arm. "You love it."

He couldn't deny it. Today was the kind of event that drew him back to DC. Being able to unwind with them. Joke and have fun without fear of someone losing their temper or their dad storming in. "I kind of do."

"Was it like that growing up?"

"Hell, no." He thought about the right way to explain it. He wasn't asking for pity or suggesting he had it bad, not compared to other people. But it hadn't been good, either. "We weren't allowed to talk at the table."

She turned around in his arms to face him, never breaking contact. "Are you kidding?"

The concern was evident in her eyes. Healthy concern. He could handle that.

He brushed his fingers through her hair, loving the feel of it. "Does Eldrick strike you as a guy who wanted to hear what his kids had to say?"

She rolled her eyes. "My mom would come home exhausted and still listen to me babble."

She shared so little about her past and her life before. From the few bits she'd dropped, Spence had an image in his mind. She liked solitude and trusted very few. That probably was a smart way to live. At least it seemed safer.

But he did miss having someone who knew more about her and might be able to offer some advice to him now and then. Ellie only offered up so much. "I'm sorry I never got a chance to meet your mom."

"Me, too."

He hugged her then. Pulled her in close and wondered how he'd ever let go of her in the past. That had been a terrible mistake, maybe his worst. And that was saying something.

He spied the envelope that was delivered earlier. He'd forgotten about it. Since it lay there untouched, he guessed Derrick had, too. Spence almost reached for it now. He had no idea what could be so important for a home delivery. Then he saw the return address. "Jeff Berger."

Abby froze in his arms. "What?"

Not wanting to let go of her, Spence nodded in the

direction of the envelope. "The delivery was from him. The guy has this weird competition thing with Derrick."

Her expression stayed unreadable. "Why?"

"When Derrick saved the company, he did it by grabbing a bunch of small jobs, then expanding the business into new areas, both geographic and different types of projects." Everything had been a struggle back then. Spence was relieved they'd moved past those days. "He cut right into Berger's business and Jeff took it personally and has been looking for revenge ever since."

Abby's hands slid down Spence's arms. Her fingers slipped through his. "Wow."

"It's a stupid guy thing. Jeff gets spun up even higher because Derrick won't engage."

She frowned. "Then why was Jeff at the party?"

"Keep your enemies close." At least that's what Spence assumed. He hadn't bothered to ask because he didn't care that much about Jeff.

"I hate that saying." An edge moved back into her voice.

He decided to let it go. She'd tell him when she was ready. "But it's smart."

"Unfortunately, yes."

She was frowning again but Spence had the perfect temporary solution. "We need cake."

"My hero."

Thirteen

The sun streamed through her bedroom windows early the next morning. The sheers blocked most of the harsh light, leaving the room bathed in a hazy glow. Shadows moved across her beige walls. She tried to concentrate, to keep her eyes open and watch the play of shape, but they kept drifting shut.

Blame Spence. His expert mouth and those hands were at fault. His fingertips slipped over her as he placed a trail of kisses over her inner thigh. When his mouth reached the very heart of her, her hips angled forward, giving him greater access.

Heat pounded her as she shifted on the mattress. Her skin felt tingly, as if every nerve ending had snapped to life. The coolness of the room blew over her bare skin but she barely felt it. Not while Spence's warmth surrounded her.

Her hand dropped down and her fingers tangled in

Spence's hair. She lifted her head to get a better view. The sight of him there, snuggled between her legs, had a breath stuttering in her chest. He was naked and confident. That finger worked magic as it slipped inside her.

"Spence…" she said his name on a soft puff of air.

Without breaking contact with her body, he glanced up. She could see those eyes as his mouth worked on her. The tightening inside her kept ratcheting up, bringing her closer to the edge. The orgasm hovered just out of reach. She tried to clamp down on those tiny inner muscles. Bring his finger in deeper and hold it there. But Spence had other ideas. He flipped her over until she landed on her stomach.

"Yes. Please." Her body begged for his touch. Forget playing games, she wanted more and depended on him to give it to her.

His hand smoothed down her back. Started at the base of her neck and traveled the whole way to the dip in the very small of her back. The trail sparked life into her exhausted body. Energy surged through her one more time. She separated her legs, hoping he'd get the hint, but he just kissed her. Pressed his lips to the base of her spine.

The touch was sexy. So seductive.

But enough. She twisted until her lower body stayed pressed to the mattress where he straddled her. Her top half turned to face him. "You are playing a dangerous game."

"Just enjoying a lazy morning." But that smile suggested he knew exactly what he was doing to her.

"Oh, really?" She pulled her legs up, tucking them close to her chest, and sat up.

His eyebrow lifted. "I thought you wanted to be touched."

"On your back."

Fire flashed in his eyes. His body practically pulsed with excitement. She was pretty sure she saw his hands shake as he lowered his body down. He rested on his back with his knees in the air and his feet flat against the bed.

"Well?" The challenge was right there in his voice.

Silly man. "Maybe I should take my time."

She sat next to him and dragged her finger up his thigh to his hip bone. Avoided the place he most obviously wanted to be touched. When he lifted his hips, pushing his growing length closer to her hand, she continued on to his stomach. Skimmed her palm over the firm muscles there. The ridges were so pronounced. So sexy.

"Abby, I'm dying here." His voice sounded strained.

She loved that reaction.

Making sure to brush her body against his, she reached over him. Dipped down so her breasts pressed against him, but only for a second. He reached for her, but she'd grabbed the condom off the nightstand and sat back up.

Holding the packet, she hesitated. Memories of the dinner and the medication issue came rushing back at her. She thought about what could be and the decisions they'd have to make.

Then his thumb trailed over her thighs and slipped between her legs. "Hey, you okay?"

She heard the note of concern in his voice. Saw his eyes start to narrow. They would talk, but not now. She bent over him and pressed her mouth against his in a kiss that reassured him everything would be fine. In that moment, she believed it.

She opened the packet and unrolled the condom over him. Didn't waste another second thinking or debating. Not when he was right there and so ready.

She lifted one leg and straddled his hips. Pressed her palm against his chest. Her other hand went to his length. The slightest touch had his hips lifting, as if seeking out more. And she gave it to him.

She pushed up on her knees and fitted her body to his. Relaxing down, she let him slide into her. The connection, that friction had her heartbeat skipping again. Pressing on his chest, she lifted her body again. Slow and deliberate, she pulled up until they almost separated, and then she plunged down again.

The movement, the up and down, had her breath hitching in her chest. She squeezed her thighs together and heard him moan. With their bodies wrapped around each other, touching in so many places, every shift she made sent a vibration racing through him. She welcomed the surge of power that moved through her.

His hands slipped to the back of her thighs. His fingers clenched against her skin. "I need you to move."

It was so tempting to draw out the sweet torture. She tried for a few more seconds, but got caught in her own trap. Her heartbeat thundered in her ears and their joint breathing echoed around the room. The heated skin and slow thrust of his body into hers had that tension winding inside her again. Every muscle tightened as her head fell back.

She let her hair drop down her back. Dug her fingernails into his skin, imprinting marks on his chest. A wild need fueled her now. An almost primal need to get closer, to feel his body buck under hers.

His hands settled on her hips and he held her there. Kept her suspended on her knees as he lifted his hips up and down. That final move had her head spinning. The building inside her spilled over. The orgasm hit her before she was ready but right when she needed it. Raw and pulsing, her body let go.

She closed her eyes, enjoying the sensations riding her. Feeling him tense under her. She knew he was close and tightened her thighs on either side of his waist to make it happen. Then they both lost it. Their breaths mixed and their muscles shook. She came and he got there right after her.

There were words she needed to say. But her mind couldn't hold a thought. Whatever it was would have to wait until breakfast, or at least until her brain restarted. Until then she could close her eyes again.

She sank down, curling up on his chest. Loving the feel of his strong arms as they wrapped around her. Their bodies were joined and hot. They should head for the shower. That needed to happen...

She drifted off to sleep.

Two hours later, he walked around her kitchen, cursing her for not having milk in the house. She drank her coffee black and professed a general disdain for milk. She insisted adults didn't have a big glass of the stuff with any meal. She wasn't wrong about that part, but a guy needed certain things in his morning beverage.

Thanks to the sex, he was willing to let the oversight slide this time. Probably every time.

He turned around and leaned against the cabinet next to the stove. His gaze moved over the condo. From here, he could see the living area and catch a peek of the unmade bed they just crawled out of down the hall to the left. Another bathroom and bedroom sat on the right side of the condo. He barely ventured over there because he had no intention of sleeping separate from her.

The sectional caught his attention. The thing was not small. She mentioned something about wanting a couch that could function as a bed when she was too lazy to get up. A place she could curl up and watch movies. He wasn't entirely sure what that meant but from the pillows stacked on it and on the floor around it, and that blanket rolled up in a ball, he couldn't deny his love of relaxing on it with her.

"Good morning." She walked into the kitchen wearing a pair of shorts and a slim-fitting T-shirt. It had a tiny dog with big eyes on it.

He appreciated the outfit. It might be his second favorite, next to that red wrap dress. That thing went in his clothing Hall of Fame. He seriously considered wading into her walk-in closet to find it and move it to the front as a hint.

She was barefoot and those legs went on forever. Much more of this and they'd be back in that bedroom for round three.

She took his mug and grabbed a quick sip. "Have you finally come to your senses and started drinking your coffee black?"

"You're out of milk."

"I don't buy it."

"Which should be illegal."

She took another sip. "I have that stuff you don't need to refrigerate."

She had to be kidding with that. "Woman, no."

"Fine." She smiled as she poured her own cup and joined him in leaning against the cabinets.

They both surveyed the condo. It was a quiet, relaxing morning. Not the way he was used to getting up but he hoped it became a habit.

"I need to ask you a weird question."

And then she ruined the peace with that comment.

"You have got to stop beginning conversations with that sort of phrase." He pretended to wipe his forehead. "I'm already sweating."

"The topic won't help."

Yeah, he needed to put down the breakable mug. He set it on the counter and faced her, not sure what was about to hit him. "And?"

"We didn't use a condom the first time."

He let out some of the breath he'd been holding. They'd already been through this, but maybe she forgot because she was sick with a fever at the time. "I'm sorry. That was my fault."

She shook her head. "We were both there. We're both responsible for being…irresponsible."

That all sounded reasonable. "Okay. That's nice to hear but I admit I'm a bit lost because you're frowning and looking serious."

"What if I got pregnant?" The question rushed out of her.

He was happy he had a hold on the edge of the counter or he might have fallen to the floor. "Uh…is this hypothetical?"

"I'm serious."

He was terrified and his tongue might have gone numb. "I am, too."

"So?"

"Do you think you're pregnant?" He reached for her then. Put his hands on her waist and turned her until they stood only a few inches apart, facing each other head-on.

She put her mug down and rested her hands on his chest. "I don't know."

Not the answer he wanted…or maybe it was. He was new at this.

"Okay. Why do you think it's a possibility?" Because that had never entered his mind. They had sex without the condom and talked about it. About her being on the Pill and both of them always being careful until right then.

A new phase, a more responsible one, started. Now this.

"I was on antibiotics." She must have seen the confusion on his face because after a few beats of silence she continued talking. "The meds can mess with the Pill."

The comment triggered a memory. He'd known that. Somewhere in the back of his mind, he'd filed that information away, hoping never to need to use it.

He swallowed as he forced his voice to stay calm. Inside him was a wild frenzy. His brain skipped from question to question. His knees tried to fold. He wasn't completely sure he was still breathing. "Do you want to take a test?"

"We should."

She sounded so calm. How the hell was that possible?

"If you are…" He had no idea what to say next.

"Is that panic I hear in your voice?" A slight bit of anger vibrated in hers.

"No." Yes. Absolutely, yes. But they would get through it. "We'll handle it."

Her eyes narrowed and her body stiffened. "What does that mean?"

This was the one question he had the answer to. "We will do whatever you want us to do."

"Even if that means having the baby?"

His vision blinked out for a second. He looked at his life as it stretched out in front of him. He'd never seen an image that included kids. For Derrick, sure. The guy was a born father. He was even great with Ellie's grown brother. But Spence wasn't convinced he possessed the skills. Looked like he'd be taking every class available to try to get up to speed.

Somehow, he would manage. That's what he did. That's what she and a baby would deserve. No matter how limited he might be, she would be great. And he could learn to be better than his father ever was.

He nodded. "Even then. We'll have the baby."

She still hadn't moved. "Get married?"

He had no idea where that came from, but as he stood there, he realized he viewed that as a package. "Yes."

She touched a finger to the corner of his mouth. "You look a little green."

Of course he did. Anyone would. No one should waltz into parenthood without at least a little panic. "Didn't you when you first realized this was a possibility?"

For a few more seconds, she just stood there, staring at him in silence. Finally, a small smile broke out on her lips. Some of the tension strangling the kitchen evaporated as she nodded. "Fair enough."

Not the words he'd use, but okay. "Abby, you can count on me."

He hoped that was true. He wasn't the guy who stuck around, but he would. They may have stumbled through their relationship so far, and still kind of were, but they would resolve all of their issues and concerns. And fast. He'd make her happy and do what they needed to do. But they were dealing in ifs and not facts.

"We definitely should take the test." *We* being her,

and *test* meaning as many as he could find. There was no reason to believe one.

"Tomorrow."

He didn't understand the delay. "Why wait?"

"We're going to enjoy one more day of not knowing."

It hit him then. She really thought she was. She denied having symptoms…or had he asked that? The whole conversation was a blur. It would take days for him to unravel it and get his mind working again.

"If you want us to wait, we wait." It couldn't hurt anything. They would be so early. Not that he knew anything about babies or timing, because he didn't.

"You're a good man, Spencer Jameson."

He wasn't, but he was trying. For her. "Because of you."

"You give me too much credit." Her arms wound around his neck. The lightness in her voice suggested she'd dealt with the pregnancy information and had mentally moved on to the next topic.

He was not so lucky.

"You're the best thing that's ever happened to me." As he said the words, he realized he meant them. Without the pregnancy news, this is where he'd tell her he loved her. Because he did. He hadn't needed Jackson to tell him. Not really. The sensation that moved through him when he saw her, or even just heard her voice in the hallway, wasn't like anything he'd ever experienced. It filled him, made him feel whole.

But there was too much going on to say the words now. He didn't want one thing messed up with the other. When he said the words, he didn't want there to be any doubt why he did. That meant waiting, holding it inside for another few days, which was safer anyway. Once he said them, he wouldn't be able to call them back.

Her smile grew. "I am pretty great."

"And so modest."

She kissed him. Short and sweet. "And hungry."

"For food this time, right? I can fix that one right now." He pulled back, thinking to raid the refrigerator even though the idea of stepping outside for a few gulps of fresh air sounded good.

She caught his arm as he brushed past her. "Thank you."

Gratitude. He wasn't sure how he felt about that. Then again, he didn't feel much of anything at the moment. He was numb. "For?"

"Everything."

Fourteen

Abby didn't often get a summons to come to Derrick's office in the middle of the afternoon. He called her or sent a message. That worked best since she had a calendar full of meetings and phone calls, but she pushed everything for this meeting.

Now that the school renovation project was a go, she had about a hundred deadlines to set and people she needed to corral. Not that she minded. This was her favorite part, setting everything down and seeing the hard work turn into something real.

That's kind of how she thought of Spence. He'd stayed at her house for a string of nights. Settled in and looked right at home there on her couch. He'd even survived the baby talk this morning. She almost didn't. Her emotions had roller-coastered all over the place as she watched his facial expression change. Surprise to panic to should-I-run. The good news is that last one only came in a flash then was gone again.

But they needed to know the truth in case they had to make plans. No more guessing. She had two tests in her bag. Tonight they would have the answer.

Her stomach flipped at the thought. She'd held it together so far, but she was pretty sure she'd be bent over blowing into a paper bag no matter what the result was. The anxiety growing inside her guaranteed that.

Speaking of the possible future daddy...she looked up right as she turned the corner to the hallway leading to Derrick's office. Spence stood there. Tall and confident. The unexpected sight of him made her steps falter, but she quickly regained her balance.

"What are you doing?" She put her hand on his arm. Even thought about kissing him.

Despite the lack of traffic in this hall, she refrained from the public display of affection. It wasn't really her thing. They needed to keep a work–home life separation anyway. Human Resources had suggested a list of things they should do and not do. French kissing in the hallway had to be on there somewhere.

"Derrick asked to see me," Spence said.

Her hand tightened on Spence's arm. She didn't notice until his shirtsleeve bunched in her palm. "Me, too."

He frowned at that information. "Maybe Ellie?"

The thought tumbled in Abby's head. Her mind raced to the worst scenario. Just when she thought she'd stumbled on the worst, she came up with another. "Oh, no."

"It's okay." Spence put his hand over hers. The warmth on his skin seeped into hers. "He wouldn't be at work if something was wrong with her at home."

"Right." Derrick would burn marks in the carpet getting out of there and to Ellie. That's who he was.

But Abby got back to walking, just in case. Even picked up the pace a bit.

They passed by Jackson's office. His phone rang. The door was open but he wasn't at his desk. Not an unusual occurrence since he seemed to answer to everyone in the building. People called him for help and advice.

Derrick's door was open and she heard voices, both of them familiar. Carter mumbled something in an unusually serious tone. It was enough to get the worry churning inside her again.

Spence pushed open the door and they stepped inside. "What's going on?"

"We have a problem." Carter's gaze slipped to her as he spoke. "Close the door."

This couldn't be good. Closed-door meetings sometimes meant nothing, but the look on Carter's face—drawn and a bit pale—suggested this was big.

Spence shook his head. "What did Dad do now?"

Just the mention of him touched off a new bout of frustration inside her. Anger welled, ready to boil up and spill over. Eldrick had that effect on her and likely always would.

Carter continued to stare. A strange coldness washed over Abby. She was so used to his smile and joking. From the minute she met him, she'd been struck by his genuine warmth. Derrick had to work at it. Spence tried to hide his. Carter was open and out there…but right now, he held his jaw stiff enough to crack.

Derrick dropped a large envelope on his desk. It had been opened and there was a note on top and photos spilled out. "It's not Dad."

Now he looked at Abby, too. The joint force of Derrick and Carter's angry attention only upped her anxiety levels. She handled stress fine but this crashed over her.

She mentally raced through every project, trying to

think of what might have happened or gone wrong. It couldn't be the possibility of a new baby because she doubted Spence would have told them without knowing for sure or talking to her first. And she couldn't imagine either one of Spence's brothers having this reaction.

No, this was something else. Something fundamental that drove right to the heart of their loyalty to her and trust in her.

She looked at the familiar envelope. She couldn't place it, and then it hit her. The delivery at the family dinner. Jeff Berger, the big jerk.

"I don't understand what's going on," Spence said as he took a step toward Derrick's desk.

Carter kept his focus solely on her as he spoke. "Look at the photos."

Spence picked them up, filed through them, hesitating on the second before looking at them all again. With every movement, every shift, Abby felt her happiness drift away. Jeff had set her up. Somehow, he figured out how to get to Derrick. Worse, to Spence.

"What am I looking at?" Spence turned to her. "What are these?"

She couldn't avoid taking a turn now. She stepped up beside Spence and reached for the photos. Nothing in them proved to be much of a surprise. Her at the restaurant with Jeff. Jeff leaning in. His smile. It all looked intimate, so completely wrong and out of context to what really happened.

Never mind that she hadn't done anything wrong. That she'd turned Jeff down not once but twice. Several times, actually. She could feel the collective heat from the Jameson men's stares. It pounded down on her as she focused on the photos.

Jeff Berger was a piece of garbage. And he was determined to ruin her because she refused to dance at his command.

"There's a note." Derrick's voice sounded flat as he handed the sheet over to Spence then turned to her. "He says you approached him about working in his company. Offered proprietary information to him, saying he could expand and take us out of the market. He says he's warning me as a favor."

Her stomach dropped. She literally expected to see it hit the floor.

Her hands shook as she let the photos slip onto the desk. Denials and defenses crashed through her brain. She wrestled with the right thing to say, with how to explain what happened.

A warning as a favor. She wondered how long it took Jeff to come up with that gem. The man was a complete liar.

"Are you going to say anything?" Carter asked.

Derrick held up a hand. "Give her a second."

This time Carter snorted. "For what? She either has answers or she doesn't."

They were talking around her, over her. Derrick and Carter, but not Spence. All she cared about was his re-action. It took all of her strength to look at him.

She glanced over. Saw his wrinkled brow and eyes filled with confusion. Not hate or hurt, or anything like what seemed to simmer under the surface with Carter. No, Spence was struggling. She could see it on his face.

"It's not what you think." That wasn't the right thing to say but her brain refused to function. Her skin itched from being on display. Standing there in the middle of all of them having to defend herself...she hated Jeff for that. She would always hate him for that.

Spence hesitated for a second before he said anything. "Well, I think Jeff Berger is an ass."

Relief surged through her, but she tamped it down. She refused to get excited or believe that he wouldn't turn on her again. They had been through this sort of thing before. Denial mixed with disbelief.

"He insisted we meet." She left out the part about Rylan's role in all of this. He'd been complicit, but this part—all the trauma of this moment—was all on Jeff. This was about his vendetta against Derrick. The one she'd been dragged into the middle of and now had to fight her way back out of again.

"*He* did." Carter repeated.

She couldn't tell whether he believed her or not. Right now, the only thing that mattered was that they all listened. She needed Spence to step up and believe her. "Around the time you left, after the kiss and the mess with your father, Jeff contacted me. I was upset and frustrated and half convinced I was going to get fired…"

She stopped to catch her breath. She expected them to jump in and start firing questions at her, but they stayed quiet. They watched. Stood there taking it in with those matching blank expressions on their faces.

With no other choice, she pushed ahead. "I agreed thinking I might need to find another job."

Derrick frowned. "That was never a possibility. I begged you to stay."

"I know that now, but put yourself in my position. I'd fallen for a Jameson brother and now he hated me—"

Spence shook his head. "Abby, no. That was never true."

"Let her finish." Carter issued the order in a strangely soft voice as he sat on the edge of Derrick's big desk.

"It made sense that in a choice between me and Spence—worse, between me and Eldrick—that I would lose. So, I was looking at other options."

"I would have done the same." It was the first positive thing Carter had said.

That glimmer of support spurred her on. "Well, Jeff did offer but he wanted business secrets and information on Derrick. I said no. I stopped taking his calls. Made every contact from his office run through my assistant first to make sure it was legitimate and work-related. He kept at it, checking in now and then. I ignored it all."

"But not forever." Spence pointed at the photos. "You wore that suit to work not too long ago. That restaurant is new. This is a recent meeting."

The accusation hung right there. There was nothing subtle about what Spence was saying. But he wasn't wrong, either. Denying the reality would only make things worse. Plus, she wanted to be honest.

She never intended to hide and sneak around with Jeff. He made that happen and she got pulled in. She'd take responsibility for not going to Derrick about the contacts, but the rest of this was a battle that wasn't even about her.

"He recently sent me a note demanding that we meet again. It had been months, so the contact didn't make sense. I ignored him again, but he was persistent. A bit threatening."

Carter slipped off the desk to stand again. "What?"

She rushed to explain. "Not physically. I never felt that."

"He cornered you at the engagement party." Spence exhaled. "You two were on the balcony."

She wasn't sure what the extra fact added. Spence's voice, his expression…he didn't give anything away.

Doubts and concerns had to be spinning around inside him but he kept them all bottled up. Like the old Spence, he projected an outward calm while the storm raged.

That terrified her. Repressing could only mean bad things for them, for their future.

"He made it clear that our meeting would happen. Rather than fight it, I gave in." Her gaze traveled over them as she rubbed her hands together. Her skin was deathly cold. "Because I knew whatever he said wouldn't matter. I was never going to give him those secrets or work for him."

"What exactly did he want?" Derrick asked as he picked up his pen then put it down again.

"He didn't give specifics. He had an envelope for me but I refused to take it. I didn't even touch it because the whole meeting, the setup and nasty words, clearly were about wanting to get at Derrick and the company, and have an advantage in bidding. About winning contracts away from *us*." She added the emphasis to telegraph that they were in this together. Her loyalty stayed firmly with this company. Always. Even if she left, she'd never endanger what they'd built here.

"He's got a thing about Derrick." Carter shot his older brother an odd look. "You are going to have to confront him eventually."

Derrick nodded but didn't say anything.

"These photos." Spence fingered each one. "They look—"

"Staged." That was the right answer. She filled in the blank because if he suggested any other option she would lose it.

Her control hovered right on the edge. She wanted to open her mouth and yell at them. Surely they could see she'd been set up.

Spence nodded but his focus stayed on the photos. He paged through them one by one. Got to the last one then went back again. With every swipe of his hand, her fury built. It raced through her, fueling her.

"Clearly he had a photographer waiting." Anger vibrated in her voice.

Both Carter and Derrick watched her. Whatever they heard or saw had them both staring. Neither looked upset. It was more like they were analyzing her, testing her mood. Well, they didn't need to guess because she had every intention of unloading right now.

She slapped her hand over the photos, forcing Spence to look at her. "I have zero interest in Jeff and his bargains."

Spence nodded. "Okay."

Okay? "I said no because of you." She looked around at Carter and Derrick, too. "Because of all of you. Because I love this job, and I'm starting to love this family. And because being disloyal is not who I am. I can't believe I have to explain that to you."

Carter shook his head. "You don't."

For some reason that sent her temper flaring. "You believed the photos. When I walked in here, you thought I cheated on Spence or screwed over the company. Something."

"I read a note and saw some photos."

"And blamed me."

"Okay, hold it." Derrick held up both hands. "No one thinks you did anything. We wanted an explanation. It's clear this is Jeff being Jeff. I'm just sorry you got dragged into the middle of my garbage."

Her heartbeat still drummed in her ears. She wanted to believe that they saw the truth immediately. The rational part of her brain recognized that they had to go into this conversation wary and ask questions. But she was so tired of fighting. "I would never betray you."

Spence looked at her then. "Why didn't you tell me?"

The relief that had just started swirling through her petered out. "What?"

"We've been together nonstop. We've talked about other topics, very personal things. You never bothered to tell me about what Jeff did back then or what he was threatening you with now."

"So, this is my fault?"

The loudness of Spence's voice now matched hers. "I'm asking a simple question."

One that made her temper soar. He had a right to question. They did need to talk this through. She got all of that. But standing there, right then, in the middle of it all, she felt nothing but raw and hollowed out. Instead of leaping to her defense along with Derrick and Carter, Spence was still doubting her.

"He told me you wouldn't believe me."

"No, he's wrong." Spence shook his head. "I never said that."

He didn't have to. She heard the words so clearly in her head. "First your dad. Now Jeff. You never believe me."

Spence reached out and held her arm by the elbow. "Hey, that's not fair."

"When will I learn?" She pulled out of his grip. "You know when? Right now. I'm going to finally learn the lesson now."

The whole room vibrated from the force of her slamming Derrick's office door as she stormed out. Spence watched her go without saying a word. Speech failed him. He didn't understand what just happened. He'd been trying to reason it all out in his mind, every step. The idea that Jeff Berger was trying to push her around and she didn't tell him…it made Spence sick. What kind of trust was that?

He took a step, thinking to go after her. Carter blocked his path.

He loomed there. "You have a couple of choices about what you do next."

One. There was only one choice and Spence was about to do it. "I'm going to talk with her."

"Wrong one," Derrick said as he walked out from behind his desk to stand beside Carter.

They formed a wall in front of Spence. He would have to get around both of them to get out of there.

"What is this?" Spence looked back and forth between his two brothers. "You can't believe she's working with Jeff."

Derrick scoffed. "Of course not."

"She's not the type," Carter added as he shook his head.

Some of the indignation ran out of Spence then. He thought he was going to have to come to her defense, explain it to them. There was no way she would do what Jeff suggested. She'd had multiple chances to screw them all over and never took one. That's not how she operated. When she was ticked off, she fought the battle head-on. Spence knew because he'd gone more than a few rounds with her.

One of the things he loved about her was her refusal to back down. She fought for what she believed in and refused to be shoved around or forgotten. He found that drive, that will, so sexy.

"Then what's the problem with me going after her?" Spence asked because he really didn't get it.

Carter made a hissing sound. "See, you questioned her."

"No..."

Derrick nodded. "You did."

That didn't happen. "I never believed the note from Jeff."

"I wanted an explanation, which is fine. I'm not sleeping with her. But once she gave it, I was all in on her side." Carter winced. "But you questioned why she didn't let you rescue her."

"Women hate that sort of thing where you rush in and try to save the day without talking to them first." Derrick shrugged. "Or so I've been told by Ellie about a thousand times."

They had both lost it. Spence didn't understand what they didn't get about this situation. "We're dating."

Carter nodded. "Uh-huh."

"I'm in love with her."

Derrick clapped Spence on the back. "There it is."

Carter whistled. "Finally."

It was as if they had the code to some secret language he didn't have. "I hate you both right now."

"You and Abby need to learn how to communicate." Derrick made that pronouncement as he returned to his oversize desk chair and sat down.

"If you're ready to do that, you should go find her. If not..." Carter shook his head. "I'd wait until I had an epiphany."

"I don't know what either of you are talking about." Spence didn't. Advice swam around in his head. Competing feelings of frustration and desperation battled inside him. He didn't want the rift between them to grow. But he wasn't quite sure what he needed to do, either.

Then there was the baby. That issue never left his

mind. Bringing the possibility up now to Abby might get him punched. Even he was smart enough to know he needed to keep whatever was brewing between them separate from family talk.

He tried to come up with the right question to ask as Derrick picked up the phone. "Who are you calling?"

"It's time Jeff Berger and I meet."

"Do it in public and don't run him over with a car," Carter said. "If you do, make it look like an accident."

Through the haze of confusion one thought settled in Spence's mind. His brothers really did trust and believe Abby. She told her side and they fell into line.

Maybe now it was his turn.

Forget waiting. Now was the right time. He headed for the door.

Derrick hung up the phone again without dialing. "Where are you going?"

"To find Abby."

"I guess that means you've had that epiphany," Carter said, sounding pretty pleased with himself.

"No, but I'm hoping it will hit me on the way." Spence's fingers touched the door handle before he glanced back at Derrick. "I'll leave Jeff to you. If I confront him right now, I might kill him."

"Consider him handled."

One problem down. Now Spence had the bigger one to conquer.

Fifteen

Abby paced back and forth in her office. It felt as if hours had passed, but she knew that wasn't true. She couldn't see the clock or hear any noise. Her curt order to her assistant to hold all of her calls and visitors—something she'd apologize for later—probably said enough for the people outside her door to scurry away.

She wasn't one to close the door and demand peace. When she did, people knew it meant something. Since the gossip about her love life and dating Spence swirled around the office, some might even figure out the source of her frustration.

The chill refused to leave her bones. She had no idea how it was possible to feel hot and ice-cold at the same time, but there she was. The pain in her stomach and her head. Both thumped, demanding attention.

She didn't even hear the door open. She turned, thinking to go in search of something for the headache,

and ran right into Spence's broad chest. He reached for
her arms and held her, more to keep her from falling
than anything else. This wasn't a hug. There was nothing intimate about it. More of a safety-first sort of thing.

He steadied her then reached back to close the door.
There, that would stop the gossip. Abby almost rolled
hers eyes at the novice move.

"What are you doing here?" She thought for sure he'd
hide in Derrick's office all day. If he had a home, he
might go there but he didn't. And that bothered her, too.

All of her confusion and questions balled up together.
He'd left the last time. There was nothing stopping him
from going again. His reaction to the baby had been almost perfect. Sure, he wavered a bit at first but so did
she. But she sensed he was waiting to see if this whole
visit-home-to-Derrick thing worked out.

His hands dropped to his sides as he looked down at
her. "This time you ran."

She searched his face for any sign that they were
going to be okay. Not that she wanted a handwritten
agreement signed in blood. She didn't even require
some sort of long-term commitment, though her heart
begged for one. But everything about him, from the fact
he lived out of a bag to his office that still looked like
no one had been assigned there, showed that he lived
his life in a temporary fashion. She didn't know why the
Jeff Berger situation drove that point home, but it did.

Now what?

"I needed space," she said, knowing it sounded trite
and was only half-correct.

He nodded. "I get it."

That just made the confusion inside her spin faster.
"Do you?"

When he frowned at her, she decided to take hold of the conversation. That might be the only way to get through this. Then she could go home and curl up on the couch and forget everything about the last few weeks. Go back to building emotional walls and burying herself in projects in the office.

"Why haven't you started any new projects at work?" It was so simple that she wondered why she hadn't seen it before.

His eyes widened. "What?"

The response was fair. She hadn't exactly built up to it, but the topic was not going away. It had taken hold in her head and she had to ride it out now. "You're the head of new acquisitions. I think that's the fancy title, right? But I haven't seen you do one lick of work on anything but projects already in progress."

His hands went to his hips and a look of pure disbelief crossed his face. He looked ten seconds from exploding. "You're giving me a work evaluation?"

She couldn't tell if he was stalling while his mind came up with a snappy answer or if he really didn't understand how he came off to the world. "You're great at the job. I doubt you even realize how good you are. It's a natural skill for you. People listen to you. You're organized. You can get things moving and straightened out. You've been the perfect closer."

He shook his head. "What does any of this have to do with Jeff Berger?"

Nothing, everything. She wasn't sure how to explain how it all came together in her head, so she didn't even try.

She moved away from him, slipped behind her desk. Stood with her hands on the back of her chair. It provided a wall of sorts, a shield for what she feared was to come. "This issue is so much bigger than him."

He threw his hands up. "Fill me in because I'm lost."

But that tone. He wasn't engaged and listening, wanting to get it. That tone was defensive. It was the one he used as he prepared for verbal battle. She'd heard it before. He used it on business associates and on her.

It meant he was already closing a door. She could almost feel it slam shut on her.

"You're a good closer because what's required of that job is wrapping up and moving on. Your specialty area." It seemed so clear to her now. No wonder he volunteered to handle those tasks for Derrick while Ellie was on bed rest.

"We're back to talking about my dad and what happened back then?" Spence rested his palms against her desk. Leaned down and faced off with her right over her desk. "Are you kidding me? I thought we moved forward."

"When?"

"Isn't that what the sex was about?"

The walls shook from the force of his voice. She glanced at the door, happy that it was closed. But people walking by had to know a fight waged in her office.

Let them listen.

She struggled to keep her voice calm. Did not let him see that the sex comment slashed through her. "Have we ever dealt with the underlying issue?"

"That you're afraid of commitment."

Her mouth dropped open. She felt it go. "Me?"

He pushed off the desk and stood up straight again. "You are so sure people are going to leave you."

The comment hit its mark. She felt it right to the center of her chest. But he was missing a very important piece of this puzzle. "You did leave me."

"I messed up, Abby. I am sorry." He turned away from her for a second and wiped a hand through his hair. When he looked at her again, his eyes were wild. It was as if the warring inside him was tearing him apart. "I will say it to you however many times it takes to make it better for you. Just tell me."

It was so tempting to drop the subject. Go to him, hug it out. Pretend that this subject and the worry wouldn't haunt her nights...but it would.

"Promise me you won't do it again." It was an impossible request. So unfair of her, and she knew that. She just didn't know how else to say what she needed.

She'd spent a lifetime losing the people she loved. She closed the circle, only let a few in. But the point was she *had* let him in. Now she worried he was clawing against the walls to get out again.

"I...what are you talking about?" His voice came out as a ragged whisper.

"Jeff's stuff was another hole you could slip through. An excuse you could use to go."

Spence shook his head. His voice carried a pleading tone now. "I didn't. I stood in that office and defended you."

"You wanted to know why I didn't tell you about Jeff and his threats." The words stuck in her throat but she pushed them out. She'd only just figured out half of this herself, and it sucked to dump it on him. But it was about him. "In part, I wanted to handle it. Not give Derrick another burden. Back then, not give him a reason to doubt me because he was my boss and you were gone."

"Sure, that makes sense."

"This time, I kept it quiet so *you* wouldn't have a reason to doubt me."

His shoulders fell, as if the will had run right out of him. "You are confusing all of these things. They aren't related to each other."

"I can't wait around for you to leave me again." She almost sobbed when she said it, but there it was. The real fear. The one that spun around inside her, getting bigger, grabbing on to everything. It tainted the good times and made the idea of being pregnant almost impossible to bear.

His eyes looked empty now. The voice, the way he stood there, as if his muscles had stopped working. It all suggested that he was lost. She would do anything to lead him back to her, but he had to help her. He needed to recognize that this was an issue and fight with her.

"How about trusting me enough to know I'm going to stay."

The words pummeled her. "Trust is earned."

"You're saying I don't deserve it." It wasn't a question. He said it as a statement of fact.

That's not how she meant it. She did not see him as a lost cause. He was smart and funny, charming and sexy. He had a bone-deep loyalty, because that is why he came back to help Derrick. Not out of curiosity.

He was her everything and could be all she ever wanted. When she looked at him she knew she'd love him forever.

That realization had her pressing her hand against her chest. "I haven't seen many clues that you intend to put down roots. No house. No new work."

He made a strangled sound. "You and the baby. The *maybe* baby."

All the hope ran out of her then. She leaned harder

against the chair to keep from falling to the floor. "That's exactly the wrong answer."

"Why?"

"I need you to stay because you want to, not because you have to." It was just that simple. After a lifetime of settling for limited friendships and not going too deep, she wanted it all. "Until you make a decision about that, you need to stay away."

"Abby." He reached for her.

She was already moving. She held open the door, knowing he would go. He should. The things he needed to decide had to be done without her. All she could do was hope he'd come back. "The choice is yours."

Later that night, after ignoring a series of Jameson-related calls and Jackson's knock at the door, Abby sat on her couch. She'd put on her sweatpants and curled up in the corner. The move usually made her feel better, but not this time.

She wasn't alone, but she didn't blame the company. It was hard to get angry with a pregnant woman who refused to leave the hallway until Abby let her in. Stubbornness ran deep in Ellie.

"Are you supposed to be out of bed?" Abby asked for the third time.

Ellie didn't take the hint. She leaned into the cushions and rubbed her nonexistent belly. "This sounded like an emergency."

Not that Abby had thrown up the white flag. She'd purposely not bothered Ellie because she didn't want to upset her. She also didn't want Ellie getting together with another Jameson and ganging up on Spence. He needed to come to whatever conclusion he came to on his own.

Just thinking about that sent a new wave of sadness crashing through Abby. Spence was the type who did better with a little guidance. He was someone her grandmother would say *needed a good woman*. Abby really wanted to be that.

Since she didn't squeal, Abby knew that left a few suspects. "Derrick told you about what happened in the office."

Abby was pretty sure her fight with Spence had already made the rounds at the company. They hadn't been quiet. And the look on his face as he walked out of her office. She felt like she'd kicked a puppy.

"Derrick and Carter told Jackson, who called me. Then Derrick texted. Carter came by the house." Ellie cited the list in a singsongy voice. "Honestly, it was this weird chain of communication from Jameson men."

Abby noticed one name was missing. "Not all of them."

"No, Spence is likely afraid of me right now, which is not a bad thing."

Ellie's smile was almost chilling. Abby hated to think what that meant. "What did you do?"

"Told him to stop being a—" Ellie's voice cut off as she waved a hand in the air. "That's enough about him. How are you?"

Nice try. "A mess."

Ellie put a pillow in front of her and held on to it like a life jacket. "I can see that."

"Thanks." She owned a mirror. She knew.

"But the look is familiar. I had it when I thought Derrick and I were over."

Abby still couldn't believe that happened. "You two are so obviously perfect for each other."

Ellie snorted. "So, you can see it in others just not in your own life."

They'd circled right back to Spence. No surprise there. Abby was impressed with how quickly Ellie managed it. "You're lucky you're pregnant."

"Spill." Ellie threw the pillow to the side and shifted so that she sat sideways on the couch, facing Abby. "Now. I have a ticking clock here. Jackson brought me over. Once Derrick figures that out, he'll yell this building down."

Rather than debate about where she should be, Abby dove in. What was the harm in reliving this disaster one more time? "You heard about Jeff Berger."

Ellie nodded. "Yep, unfortunately. And if I never hear his name again, I'll be thrilled."

"Same here." Some of the energy ran out of Abby there. She'd been holding it together, but only by a thread. When she looked at Ellie's face now, she wanted to just get the rest out. "He's a runner, Ellie."

Ellie frowned. "This Berger guy?"

"You know who I'm talking about. He hasn't settled in. He's living out of your house and mine. His workload is a mix of odds and ends, other people's stuff." Abby cut off the list before it got so long that it strangled the last little bit of hope inside her. "You know he could pick up again."

"You're jumping around. First, this Berger guy. Now the running thing."

"It's all part of the same problem." At least it was in Abby's head. "He's looking for reasons to go. I tie him here. Other things tie him here. But does he really want to be here? I just feel like he's hiding things."

Ellie made a humming sound. "Like you did when you withheld the details of this Berger guy's threats."

Okay...well...that was an annoying comparison. "It's not the same thing."

"Sure it is. It's all about trust. Neither of you have moved past what happened before and forgiven each other."

Abby got stuck on the "neither" part. "What did I do?"

"Oh, most of the blame goes to Spence and his father. But how much of a fight did you put up?" Ellie's eyebrow lifted. "I'm betting you assumed Spence would leave, because your life is easier when you don't connect with people all that much. Then he confirmed your worst fears. Rather than yelling at him like he deserved, you retreated."

That was ridiculous...wasn't it? "I don't retreat."

Ellie let out an annoying snort. A pretty loud one, too. "Do you love him?"

Abby didn't stall or gloss over the question. She hit it head-on. "More than anything."

It felt weird to say the words. To hear them out there. She did love him. Like, couldn't-think-straight love him.

"Then let him in and insist he do the same with you." Ellie smiled as if she'd solved all the world's problems. "As an objective observer, neither of you is going anywhere."

"I'm not." Abby was hoping he wasn't. Which meant only one thing. Ellie was right. "You sort of make some sense. Kind of."

"That must have hurt to admit."

Abby made a face. "A little."

"Good." When Abby started to say something, Ellie held up her hand. "I mean it's good because the rest of the family is exhausted by the inability of both of you otherwise very smart people to figure this out."

This was the lecture Abby never expected to hear, but it made her feel better. She'd been blaming him and waiting for him to step up. Maybe she needed to make it clear that she could take a step, too. "Nice delivery."

Ellie's demeanor changed. She grew serious as she reached out and grabbed Abby's hand. "Trust him, Abby. Then maybe leave a little room to trust yourself."

Abby realized that for a person who didn't have many friends, she sure did pick the right ones. "Thanks."

Ellie gave Abby's hand another squeeze before she let go. "Before you do anything, do you think we can convince Jackson to get us some food?"

"It is one of his many skills."

"Good man."

Sixteen

Spence sat on the edge of his bed at Derrick's place, trying to reason out what Abby had said. He still thought she'd mixed up events and created a big thing that didn't exist. The running away issue…he had to own up to that. It was his go-to move and giving it up would take everything he had.

But he'd do it for her. He'd do almost anything for her.

"Why are you here?"

Spence looked up to find Derrick leaning in the doorway. He looked comfortable. Like a man who had finally found some peace At least until the screaming baby came.

"That's welcoming." Spence didn't bother to get up or move over. He knew Derrick would loom there, waiting for the right time to impart some wisdom. That was *his* go-to move.

Derrick let out a long and very loud exhale. "You

should be at Abby's, insisting you two can work things out."

"Can we?" That was the question that kept bouncing around in Spence's head. He'd never wanted anything this much.

"You know the answer. You're just feeling sorry for yourself."

As pep talks went, this was not one of Derrick's better ones. Spence was hoping for more. "Thanks, man."

"You have a right to. Your life is a mess." Derrick did step inside then. He walked over and sat next to Spence. "But she's the right one for you and you know that. Put away the fear and set down roots. You belong here. You belong with her."

He sounded like Abby. Their comments mirrored each other. Apparently, everyone else could see his fear. So much for the theory he did a good job of hiding it. "You make it sound easy."

Derrick laughed. "Oh, it's scary as hell. I know."

"And I have this." Spence reached beside him and picked up the unopened envelope from Eldrick. This was part of the requirements that would allow Derrick to take over the business. What needed to be done to make Eldrick slip away permanently, because Spence knew Derrick feared Dad would just walk into the office one day and try to run things again. The ownership percentages allowed him to do it.

"Open it." Derrick shrugged, acting as if his entire business future didn't ride on whatever was inside. "You may as well face everything at once. Let's see if you balk."

Spence ripped the top open. "And my list of requirements is...wait."

The air punched out of his lungs. Spence blinked

a few times, trying to bring the simple sentences into focus. This wasn't a legal document; it was…he didn't know what it was.

Derrick frowned as he grabbed the paper out of Spence's hands. "What?"

Go find Abigail. Beg her to take you back. She never betrayed you.

"Come on. Is our dad taking responsibility for something? That can't be right." It seemed impossible. Spence couldn't even get the words to register in his brain.

"Yes, but even weirder, I think he's matchmaking." Derrick turned the paper over then flipped it back again. "This can't be from Beth or her doing. The envelope was here long before the engagement party, and that's where she found out. That's all Dad."

"Our dad?" The one who harassed Abby and kissed her. The one who sent them down this awful road. "No way."

"Apparently people can change." Derrick handed the paper back to Spence. "Your turn."

An hour later, Spence stood at Abby's door. Without saying a word, she gestured for him to step inside. Didn't slam the door on his face.

That alone seemed like a step forward. "Thanks for letting me come in."

"You still have the key and the security codes."

Some of the hope inside him died. Her voice sounded flat and there was nothing welcoming about a conversation about security codes. "Is that why you agreed to see me?"

She stopped in the middle of her living room and faced him. She wore oversize sweatpants and a T-shirt with a rip along the shoulder seam. Her hair was half in and half out of a ponytail holder.

She had never looked more beautiful to him.

She sighed. "No, I agreed because I love you."

His mind went blank and his mouth went dry. He was pretty sure he made that up in his head. There was no way she said those words. "What?"

"There, I said it. I love you." She threw up her hands then let them drop to her sides again. "You ran out on me, and I am terrified you will do it again, but that's the truth. I love you, you big moron."

He was even fine with the last part. "Abby—"

"I believe in you even though you don't believe in yourself."

His brain finally signaled his legs to move. In a few steps, he was in front of her, had his hands on her waist and pulled her in closer to him. "Don't stop."

She frowned at him. "What?"

They *really* did need to work on their communication skills. He decided to start now. "I can't deny that there's this whirling sensation inside me. When things blow up and a fight that could shred everything looms, I go. It stops the arguing and I can catch my breath. I've been using that defense mechanism since I was a kid."

She started to pull away. "Right."

"Not with you." He hugged her even tighter. Pressed his lips against her eyebrow in a kiss that was meant mostly to soothe her but ended up calming him. When he pulled back, some of the wariness had left her eyes. "See, every other time, I walked away and the feelings, the churning, the reason I fled in the first place, disappeared. With you, the need only got stronger."

Her fingers clenched against his forearms. "You didn't come back to me. I waited for some sign. Any sign."

"I felt broken, Abby. I knew I had already fallen for you and then my dad…" Mentioning him could ruin everything. He wasn't the problem between them now. Not really. "Forget that. This was my fault. I left and I missed you every single day. I couldn't visit my brother because I worried I would see you."

She nibbled on her bottom lip. For a few seconds, she didn't say anything and he held his breath…waiting.

When nothing happened, he tried again. "It was a crappy thing to leave and then to make you wait. You suffered. I suffered. I don't want to do it anymore."

She brushed her fingertip over his bottom lip. "Can you break the cycle?"

She'd asked the question but he sensed she was starting to believe. To hope.

"Before you told me about the possible pregnancy, I wanted to tell you how I felt." He nodded toward the living room. "Sitting right there on that couch, I was going to tell you I loved you. That I'd figured out I would always love you. That you were worth sticking around and fighting through the mess."

Tears gathered in her eyes. "Spence."

He rushed to get the rest out. "I didn't tell you then because I didn't want you to think I did it because I had to, but I'll tell you now." He rested his forehead against hers and inhaled. "Baby or not, I want to build a life with you. That gnawing sense of wanting to bolt will likely always be with me, but I don't want to leave you. Ever."

She wrapped her arms around his neck. "Sounds like I'd have to go with you then."

The words were muffled in his neck, but he heard them. Also picked up on the happiness in her tone. How much lighter she sounded.

"That also works." He lifted her head and stared down into her eyes. "But really, I love my brothers. I've even gotten used to the office, which is nothing short of a miracle."

She smiled. "What are you saying?"

He recognized hope when he saw it. It soared through him, too. "Take a chance on me. I know I'm a risk, but—"

"Stop." She shrugged as she hugged him close. "It's too late. My life is already bound up with yours. I'm afraid you're stuck with me."

"I love the sound of that." He kissed her. Let his lips linger over hers, loving the feel of her body pressed against his.

"Good, because I plan on making it a requirement for the next fifty years or so."

He didn't try to fight the smile. "Then we should start now."

"I like your style."

It was well past two in the morning. They were in bed, lying side by side, recovering from what she might call the greatest make-up sex of all time. She'd mentioned that to him and he hadn't stopped smiling. Until right now.

She looked at his hands, those long fingers. Saw the white stick he held in a death grip. "You keep staring at it."

"It's so little and has the power to change everything with a plus sign."

He'd insisted on the pregnancy test after their last

round. She'd wanted cake, but he won the argument. Now, if only the panic screaming through her would stop.

"I could make a joke about how babies disrupt lives, but I'm not sure you're ready for that." She also wanted to point out that the Jameson men were pretty fertile and warn Carter, but the timing seemed wrong for that, too.

Spence shook the stick. "It should do something."

"Like?"

He shrugged. "Balloons should pop out of it. Maybe play music."

"It's not a magic stick."

He snorted as his head turned and he faced her. "It kind of is. We wave it and it changes everything about our lives together."

Skipping the cake might have been smart. Her stomach wouldn't stop dancing. "Well, that's true."

His eyes narrowed just a fraction. "You okay?"

"Scared." It would take her a while to figure out how to deal with this news. They'd have to make plans, but she knew they would do it together. He'd made that clear. "Not about us. Not about how much I love you."

He turned over and faced her. Wrapped an arm around her waist as he watched her. "But?"

"This is going to be hard. We're still trying to sort ourselves out as a couple and now we'll have this." A few hours ago, that would have terrified her, but not as much now. She just needed to make sure he agreed with her. "Spence, this is—"

"I'm going to get angry if you offer me an out."

"Six weeks ago, when you stepped back into my life, I knew you as the guy who bolted when everything got to be too much." She winced as she pointed that out. She didn't want to start another fight.

"Didn't we settle this?" But he didn't sound angry. Instead, he rolled her onto her back and balanced his body over hers.

She ran a hand up and down his bare arm, loving the feel of his sleek muscles under her fingertips. "I trust you to stay. The point is I want you to."

"Leaving you, losing you, ripped me apart." He pressed a quick kiss on the tip of her nose. "It was a wake-up call for me to get my act together."

She let the words settle in her head. Yeah, she liked the sound of that. A lot. "And I'm part of that act?"

He snorted. "You have the main role in it."

The last of her defenses crumbled. The walls came roaring down and took her doubts with them. In a few short hours, with a couple of words, he brought her peace. It would not be easy. Knowing the two of them, life would not be quiet or simple. It would be loud and loving and perfectly imperfect, and that sounded pretty great to her.

"I love you. You and your big messy family." Because when she claimed him, she decided she'd claim them, too. "Okay, not your dad."

"Remind me to show you something later." His smile was downright mysterious. "A letter."

She didn't want to know, yet part of her did. She guessed he did that on purpose. Reeled her in and made her care about Eldrick, which should have been an impossible feat.

"I hate letters right now." They reminded her of Jeff and no matter how tonight turned out, she still despised that guy.

Spence's smile only grew wider. "This one may surprise you."

"I'm intrigued." She was about to pepper him with

questions, but his hand slipped under the covers. Right down to her thigh. "Oh, yeah. There." Then those expert fingers traveled a big higher. "The letter can wait."

"Yes, it can."

"I'm going to let you show me how much you love me."

He rolled over her then. "Again?"

"I'm sure you can handle it."

He lowered his mouth until it hovered right above hers. "I can handle you."

"Show me."

* * * * *

COMING SOON!

We really hope you enjoyed reading this book. If you're looking for more romance, be sure to head to the shops when new books are available on

Thursday
14th June

LET'S TALK
Romance

For exclusive extracts, competitions
and special offers, find us online:

f facebook.com/millsandboon

⊙ @millsandboonuk

🐦 @millsandboon

Or get in touch on 0844 844 1351*

For all the latest titles coming soon, visit
millsandboon.co.uk/nextmonth